THOMAS F. MONTELEONE

This signed edition of

# FEARFUL SYMMETRIES

is limited to 750 copies

This is number __14__

Rick Hautala        Matt Eames

# FEARFUL SYMMETRIES

# BOOKS BY THE AUTHOR

## NOVELS
Seeds of Change [1975]
The Time Connection [1976]
The Time-Swept City [1977]
The Secret Sea [1979]
Guardian [1980]
Night Things [1980]
Ozymandias [1981]
Day of the Dragonstar (with David F. Bischoff) [1983]
Night Train [1984]
Night of the Dragonstar (with David F. Bischoff) [1985]
Terminal Road [1986]
Crooked House (with John DeChancie) [1987]
Lyrica [1987]
The Magnificent Gallery [1987]
Fantasma [1989]
Dragonstar Destiny (with David F. Bischoff) [1990]
The Blood of the Lamb [1992]
The Resurrectionist [1995]
Night of Broken Souls [1998]
The Reckoning [1999]
Benediction [2001]
Eyes of the Virgin [2002]
Submarine [forthcoming]

## SHORT STORY COLLECTIONS
Dark Stars and Other Illuminations [1981]
Rough Beasts and Other Mutations [2003]

## ANTHOLOGIES
The Arts and Beyond [1977]
Microworlds [1984]
Borderlands [1990]
Borderlands 2 [1991]
Borderlands 3 [1992]
Borderlands 4 (with Elizabeth E. Monteleone) [1994]
Borderlands 5 (with Elizabeth E. Monteleone) [2003]

## NON-FICTION & ESSAYS
The Mothers And Fathers Italian Association [2003]
The Complete Idiot's Guide to Writing a Novel [2004]

# FEARFUL SYMMETRIES

A SHORT STORY COLLECTION

BY

THOMAS F. MONTELEONE

CEMETERY DANCE PUBLICATIONS

*Baltimore*

2004

*This book is for*
ELIZABETH ESTELA,
*whose hand, and heart, and eye,*
*have not only*
*given it form,*
*but life.*

In what distant deeps or skies
Burnt the fire of thine eyes?
On what wings dare he aspire?
What the hand dare seize the fire?

What the hammer? what the chain?
In what furnace was thy brain?
What the anvil? what dread grasp
Dares its deadly terrors clasp?

Tyger! Tyger! burning bright
In the forests of the night,
What immortal hand or eye,
Dare frame thy fearful symmetry?

*—William Blake, 1793*

A project of this magnitude and stretch of time, when compared to the glaciations and warmings of the earth, is less than a geologic eyeblink, but for me, it represents the culmination of thousands of hours *not* spent watching ESPN. But more importantly, I know it would have never happened without the inspiration, support, belief, instruction, criticism, assistance, friendship, animus, and general ass-kicking of a legion of wonderful people, whose names will now be recorded in the annals of Literature, never to be forgotten. I list them in no particular order—especially alphabetical or chronological—and for any who believe I overlooked them, I sincerely apologize for not taking my selenium and my ginko biloba tablets this morning. And now, the people who are in some way responsible for what follows in this wondrous tome: my wife Elizabeth Estela, my daughter Olivia Francesca, my two sons Damon and Brandon, Mario Monteleone, Marie Monteleone, Frank Monteleone, Matt Eames, Ray Bradbury, Rod Serling, Theodore Sturgeon, Howie Lovecraft, Rick Hautala, Harlan Ellison, John DeChancie, Charles L. Grant, Pat Lobrutto, Sharon Jarvis, Al Sarrantonio, Roy Torgeson, Marty Greenberg, Roger Elwood, Gardner Dozois, Damon Knight, Eddie Poe, Mary and F. Paul Wilson, Gahan Wilson, Matt and Ann Costello, Peter Straub, Tamara Keurejian, Stephen King, Kirby McCauley, Doug and Lynne Winter, Howard Morhaim, Jules Verne, Rick McCammon, John and Joyce Maclay, Matt Bialer, Herbert George Wells, Steve Bissette, Peggy Nadramia, Ed Gorman, Richard Chizmar, Gary Raisor, Jim Morrison, Stan Wiater, Ray Manzarek, Bill Schafer, Jay Leshinsky, Michael Keating, Bob Schaller, A. E. Housman, Alan Clark, Dennis Etchison, Dave Bischoff, Karl Wagner, Rick Lieder, Johann Sebastian Bach, Pete Crowther, Ambrose Bierce, Arch Oboler, Chet Williamson, Richard Gid Powers, Ted White, Jill Bauman, Roger Zelazny, Frederick Brown, Bill Schafer, Steve Spruill, Bob McCoy, Scott Urban, Dave Hinchberger, Bob and Mary Booth, Dan Booth, Alan Ryan, Ray Harryhausen, Mike Bracken, Grant Carrington, Father Richard Colgan, S.J., Jeff Gelb, Ayn Rand, Kris Rusch, Craig Shaw Gardner, Carlos Batts, Richard Matheson, Phil and Anya Nutman, Andres Segovia, Octavio Paz, Poppy Z. Brite, William Blake, John Helfers, John Agar, Larry Seagriff, Robert Ludlum, Peter Enfantino, Jack London, Dave Silva, Paul Olson, Herman Melville, Walt Disney, Alex Toth, John Godey, Roy Chapman Andrews, Karen and Joe Lansdale, Jerry Williamson, Betsy Engstrom, Mark Ziesing, Mark Rainey, Edgar Allen Dog, a golden retriever, and Roxy, a chocolate lab.

ACKNOWLEDGMENTS

# CONTENTS

# F OREWORD

My first short fiction collection[1] covered my work from the Seventies and early Eighties, and the stories were primarily science fiction or fantasy—the genres where I broke in as a professional writer.

This one, my third, selects stories largely from the Eighties and Nineties, and reflects my shift into tales of horror, dark fantasy, and suspense. This book marks off an appropriate point, I think, where my sensibilities as a storyteller changed. There were plenty of stories to choose from over the last two decades (more than 50), but I tried to select pieces that reflected my range and my evolution as a writer. For that reason, they appear in the chronological order in which they were originally published.

The short story is supposedly no longer popular with readers, but I have a hard time believing it because I have always loved the form. And I think I know why. My appreciation comes from a very special moment in my life— an incident that still rings clear and true in my memory, which is a marker of its life-shaping importance.

----

[1]*entitled* Dark Stars and Other Illuminations, *Doubleday, New York, 1981. (with an introduction by Roger Zelazny)*

ASK THE NEXT QUESTION

I was 14 years old, just starting my freshman year at a Jesuit high school. It was a very traditional place, on a campus that rivalled the scope and beauty of lots of small colleges.

The main building housed a huge library defined by vaulted alcoves, polished mahogany wainscotting, 12ft. leaded windows, long reading tables with brass lamps and green-glass shades, and endless shelves of books. During the first week of class, they put all the freshman through "orientation," wherein they get you familiar with all the shticks at the school. One of the exercises was to spend a few hours wandering around the library, getting familiar with everything. It was an interesting way to get us freshman involved with the process of discovery and learning.

So, here I was, 14 years old, wearing my required sport coat and tie, meandering among the alcoves and stacks and carrels of the library, reading this title and that, pulling down ones that sounded interesting, learning the locations of various categories of reference materials. One of the orientation assignments included checking out a book to read for a report, and I was eager to find something that would be a kick to read.

And here's the weird part: I'm surrounded by thousands of old books, no dust jackets on most of them, no pictures or lurid covers to catch my adolescent eye—just a lot of cloth bindings and gold-stamped spines looking very classical—and I paused as my gaze settles, most randomly it seemed, upon a title called *Tales of Mystery and Imagination.* Yeah that one—by Edgar Allan Poe. Now, believe it or not, I'd never heard of him. He certainly hadn't been on the reading list of St. Charles Borromeo's Elementary School, and nobody'd ever recommended him to me. And other than my comics and stacks of SF and HDF paperbacks littering my room, we didn't have many books in our house. The name "Poe" meant nothing to the *tabula rasa* that was my puerile mind.

And yet, I reached out and pulled the book from its niche . . . as though drawn to it by some arcane force.

I can still remember the mental jolt I received as I read down the table of contents. You know what I'm talking about: "The Black Cat," "The Pit and the Pendulum," "The Murders in the Rue Morgue," "The Facts in the Case of M. Valdemar," "The Tell-Tale Heart," and on and on. The story titles seemed to glow like barbed, neon signs, leaping off the page to hook themselves in my imagination. I can remember thinking something like *this dude sounds pretty weird—my kind of stuff . . .* (well, maybe I didn't think of Poe as a *dude*, but then again, maybe I did . . .)

And so I checked out the book, and spent the next few nights reading into the middle of the night, lost in the dark fantasies of a brilliant, but tormented soul. It was a simple and pure joy I haven't experienced very often in life. I'd *discovered* Poe. In the same serendipitous way of all great discoveries, and it was like his work was *mine*, and nobody else knew about him. I can remember turning my friends, Bobby Schaller and Mike Keating, onto Poe, they dug him too. Such was my excitement and need to share it that I mentioned to my freshman English instructor how I happened onto this book of great short stories by a guy name Poe, and by the way, have you ever heard of him?

"Slightly," said my teacher with a smile.

So what's the point of this personal, although highly fascinating, aside? Simply this: it's hard for me to accept that I pulled down that book of Poe stories totally by *accident.* I mean, out of tens of thousands of books I could have stumbled upon, I just *happened* to have selected a collection of what may be the most seminal and influential group of tales in the history of literature, and surely in the history of darkly imaginative fiction . . . ?

Yeah, *sure.* Somehow, I just can't buy it. A preferable answer is I was *drawn* to it by means beyond my power to understand. Some of us *are* mutants, you see. We want to read the weird stuff, and a small percentage of our lot are compelled to actually *write* it. And as such, we beings who carry the gene for Darkness, we have an unconscious sensory power which helps us locate the good stuff and savor it the way one might sip a fine vintage in a cool cellar.

Yeah, I like that explanation, don't you?

And so, using Poe as an early model, I wrote short stories throughout adolescence. Even back then, I believed it was the toughest thing to write well. I've written books, stage plays, feature-length screenplays, articles, essays, and even some bad poetry, so I speak from experience. When I talk to aspiring writers, I always tell them: if you can write a *good* short story, you can write anything.

So, knowing that, you should surmise by now this book is very special to me. If you pressed me, I might admit to being more proud of it than any of my novels because it represents a span of time, and volume of energy spent, far eclipsing the amount expended on any other project I've ever created.

Okay, one more thing:

There's always a story behind every story. And throughout this book, I will introduce each story with something intrinsic to how the story came into being. If some of you aren't into etiological arcana, then just blow off these little italicized pieces, and go right into the stories.

But I should warn you—if you really are *that* much of a troglodyte, you're gonna miss an entire level of nuance, wit, and insight into the creative process. Because I plan to give you a look behind the curtain, a peek into the darker corners of a mind (mine, of course) always running at DEFCON 4, always alert, and always ready to do what my Jesuit high school instructors always urged me to do—*ask the next question.*

You see, that's the secret of not only being a competent human being, but also being a competent writer. I have always tried to look at things I encounter in life from every aspect, by turning it and twisting it and stretching it and squeezing it. Never being satisfied with just a single answer, I always bug and noodge my sources to give up everything they know.

Then you're ahead of the game. You know everything they know, *plus* everything you *already* knew.

I've tried to keep that philosophy in place whenever I sit down to write a new short story—and I've written and published over a hundred of them. The result, I hope, has been stories that weren't just tired re-treads of stuff you've read somewhere else. Chain-clanking ghosts; leering, seductive vampires; adulterous husbands and wives with schemes to eliminate their unsuspecting spouses; and let's not forget the shopworn voodoo curses; the sullen, methodical serial-killers; and all the re-inventions of Faust.

Now, I'm not going to tell you I've never used any of the familiar trappings of horror, dark fantasy, or suspense—especially since becoming one of the Usual Suspects in the anthology rackets[2]—but I will promise you my stories only use the standard genre props to *set-up* the tale. When I write a story, I think about the *easy* way to do it, the familiar route to follow, and then I summarily dismiss it. Time to take the theme or the idea and turn it inside-out, check out a new perspective, and of course—*ask the next question* about how I can make my story unique.

Okay, enough already.

Well, almost . . . .

I would be remiss if I didn't say a few words about the spectacular illustrations that accompany the text in this book. The artist is a young guy, Matt Eames, who was discovered working in a full-service copy-center shop by Elizabeth. When she saw a few samples of his work, she came home and told me she'd met a fellow-mutant, and she told me how good he was and how he needed to be working professionally. He showed us his sketchbooks and we could feel energy and enthusiasm and dedication leaping off the pages. He had that ineluctable *something*, that spark of original vision and talent that is somehow always recognizable, that separates the special from the mundane.

---

[2]*Even though the "serious critics," the New York Literati, and the ethereal ruminations of academe have all elegized the death of the short story for more than fifty years now, it's an unassailable fact the short story enjoys a very vigorous and exciting life in the groves of genre fiction. The stubborn popularity of original anthologies has been a major contributing factor. Elizabeth and I edited the* Borderlands *series, and there have been others over the years which have produced first-rate short fiction such as Harlan Ellison's* Dangerous Visions, *Kirby McCauley's* Frights *and* Dark Forces, *Charles Grant's* Shadows, *Dennis Etchison's* Cutting Edge, *Douglas Winter's* Prime Evil *and* Revelations, *and Al Sarrantonio's* 999. *There's also been an endless stream of theme-anthologies, which focus upon a particular idea or leit-motif and find writers who can create stories to fit the theme. They can be as familiar as* Great Stories About Haunted Castles *to something as esoteric as* Strange Tales of Suspense Involving Optometrists. *The part about finding writers to create stories for these theme anthologies is where it gets interesting. If you've been around long enough, you meet lots of writers (many of whom become good friends), editors, agents, and publishers. And if you're any good at what you do, you get noticed and you get asked to contribute stories to magazines and anthologies. You become one of the Usual Suspects who gets pulled in for a line-up every time a new anthology idea gets sold. Hence the reference footnoted above.*

So I asked Matt if he would be interested in taking a shot at illustrating some of my short stories for an upcoming book. I gave him my short course of Monteleone's Theory of Great Illustration[3], and he was cool, kept his composure, and tried to act like it was no big deal. *Sure, I can do that. No prob.* I e-mailed him a few stories and he came back with these dark images that knocked me out. Beautiful stuff full of drama and contrast. I contacted Rich Chizmar at CD Publications, told him I had discovered a new talent, and would like to have him be part of *Fearful Symmetries*. Rich trusted my instincts in these matters, and now you get to enjoy the work of Matt Eames too.

Okay. Time to get to work.

*Grantham, New Hampshire*
*May, 2004*

---

[3] *Which is basically this: I don't like story illustrations which merely depict a scene from a story. If I have done my job well, the reader already has a brainful of images based in my skillful use of language, and can very well* visualize *my narrative. What I infinitely prefer is to see illos which add a new dimension to the tale, which examine the theme and essence and mood of the story and create* new *images that you wouldn't already come up with while reading.*

# INTRODUCTION

Since this is an Introduction, let's start with how and when I first met Tom Monteleone. What happened is so indicative of Tom and his writing ("the person, the process, and the product") that it bears repeating. Truth is, it should be immortalized if only because it's so damned funny.

When I started out in my career as a "horror" writer, I had attended only a few science fiction or horror conventions. After *Nightstone* was published, Ginjer Buchannan (who recently edited a book for Berkley by A. J. Matthews, a good friend of mine) suggested that I go to a convention called NECon in Bristol, Rhode Island. (In my opinion, NECon is the only horror con worth going to annually. Check it out sometime.)

Not knowing what to expect, that summer I went. Not knowing anyone there (except Ginjer), I dutifully wore my name badge. ("Badges! We don't need no stinking badges!") Because I figured no one would know my name, I put the hologram from the *Nightstone* cover on my badge. After all, to most of the people there, I was my book.

During the traditional "Meet the Authors" party on Friday night, a guy who (let's be honest) might have had one or two drinks more than he should have came up to me, leaned

BURNING BRIGHT

close, peered at the hologram on my name badge, and in a burst of whiskey-tinged breath, said, "Hey! I read that fucking book. You the guy who wrote it?"

All I could do was smile and nod. I noted the name on his badge—Thomas F. Monteleone—and recognized it. I had read him. Better still, I had liked what I had read. As a neophyte at horror cons, I was instantly intimidated.

"Uhh—yeah, I am," was as witty a reply as I could muster.

"Man, I *loved* that book! Hey! You gotta have a drink with me!"

I smiled again, a little tighter, and nodded as he clapped my shoulder and held up the bottle of George Dickel Sour Mash (White Label), which he was currently consuming faster than I thought might be safe.

"You gotta have a Dickel with me."

Keep in mind, now, I'm Finnish. The definition of a Finnish extrovert is he's the one who will look at *your* shoes when he's talking to you. Tom is Italian and all that implies. Even if he doesn't know you, he'll clap you on the back and hug you. I don't need to tell you that I was a bit . . . perplexed as to how to respond. What I did was keep smiling while holding up the bottle of Sam Adams Beer I was nursing. Even at conventions, three or four beers in an evening is my limit.

"I'm all set, Tom, but thanks."

"No, no. You don't understand. (It sounded more like "unnerstan.") I loved your fucking book, and you gotta have some Dickel with me."

Tom pressed closer. I grew nervous. I didn't know him. I hadn't yet heard, much less witnessed, some of the antics which we later . . . .

Opps, sorry.

Under court order, I can't mention anything "pre-Elizabeth," (Tom's charming and talented wife), and I won't now other than to finish this short and relatively innocent anecdote.

"I appreciate your offer, Tom," I said, "but I only drink beer. I never drink distilled alcohol. I appreciate the offer but—"

"No, man. You gotta have some Dickel with me."

He hugged me even closer. We were almost touching noses. For a Finn, this kind of closeness can be very disconcerting unless you're . . . well, you know, unless you're *really* trying to get to know someone.

"Let me ask you something, Rick," Tom said after tilting his head back and taking another healthy gulp of Dickel. He leaned even closer, if that was possible. "Have you ever run your hand up the inner thigh of an eighteen year old girl?"

My mind went blank. Who *was* this guy was, and why was he asking such a personal question?

Swallowing dryly and wishing he would at least step back so the Dickel fumes wouldn't be quite so overwhelming, I'm sure I blushed as I said something to the effect of, "Uhh . . . Yeah, well . . . sure, but I—"

"Then I don't have to tell you how smo-o-o-oth this whis-key is."

I had my first drink of Dickel with Tom that night.

It wasn't the last.

Over the years, especially at NECon and a handful of HWA meetings and World Horror Conventions (which are fun, too, but nowhere near as much fun as NECon), Tom and I have become close friends. Tom isn't just a writer whose work I admire; he isn't even just a friend. He is as close to being my brother as we can get without actually mingling Italian and Finnish blood. More than that, we have collaborated on a few projects, and I have seen from the inside how Tom generates and develops ideas. I've seen him work.

You need read only a handful of his short stories or even just one of his novels (try *Blood of the Lamb* or *The Resurrectionist*) to know what kind of literary magic Tom can conjure. He is a craftsman who makes spinning a yarn look effortless when, in fact, I know that he puts a great deal of effort into every page that eventually comes out of his printer. Heart and soul and guts are the basis of any Monteleone story. That and a creativity and imagination that leaves many of us fellow writers choking in the dust. You'll see that as soon as you dip into this collection. I have never read a story by Tom in any anthology or magazine that wasn't one of if not clearly *the* best story. And now several of them are gathered here in *Fearful Symmetries*. If this career-spanning collection escapes winning an award or two, then it is simply because life isn't fair.

Well, life isn't fair, but winning an award or even a wheel-barrow full of awards isn't what Tom and his writing are about.

It's the words on the page.

The story.

The magic, and what it does to your mind and emotions.

I've seen this on the inside because I've read Tom, I've worked with him, and I've submitted stories to his ground-breaking anthology series *Borderlands*. My stories, by the way, were rejected because they weren't good enough. Friendship isn't going to cut it with Tom when it comes to writing. If the work isn't better than the best you can do, he won't accept it for his anthologies, and he won't shy away from telling you why. Tom has never shied away from telling you his mind. An old friend of mine from college used to say: "It's better to be honest than nice." Well, Tom lives by that. He has irritated and outright pissed off many people—writers, editors, and fans—but it has always been because what matters most is the writing!

Anything else is . . . well, simply not as important.

I'm feeling a little like I've had one or two more sips of Dickel than is advisable. I'm wandering all over the map here. It's partly because I can't tell you more stories about hanging out with Tom and some of the outrageous antics that ensued. And, frankly, I'm having a bit of trouble because, although I knew how to start, I have no idea how to finish this little introduction. I suppose I could discuss a handful of stories and tell you what I thought of them and why, and how I think you should appreciate them—(try not gasping while you read "The Wager," f'rinstance; tell me "The Night Is Freezing Fast" doesn't bring tears to your eyes)—but I won't. That would diminish the power of these stories. The stories speak for themselves, loud and clear, just like their author.

But if I've given you even some slight insight into Tom and his work, then I'll have done my job. I'm not sure I have or even can do that because—frankly—I don't know how he does it. I'm a writer and an avid reader. Like a practicing magician, whenever I read someone else, I try to see how they're performing their tricks so—maybe—it will help me make my own magic more convincing when I do it. Over the years, there have been many writers I've read and admired and learned from, but even collaborating with Tom hasn't given me any real insight into the process. If I may further mangle my metaphor, I invariably end up feeling like a ten year old who has done a few parlor tricks for friends and family, watching Houdini or Henning do their amazing thing and having no clue how they did it.

But we do have the stories, and we can read them. Why have you even read this introduction?

Go ahead.

Read Tom's stories. Be thrilled and amazed by a wide-ranging imagination that has peeled back every corner, light and dark, of the human mind and soul. These stories burn bright in the forest of the night. They are "fearful symmetries" that only Tom Monteleone could have delineated.

Enjoy!

*—Rick Hautala*
*Westbrook, Maine*

My oldest and one of my dearest friends in this business is Charlie Grant, also known over the years as C. L. Grant and Charles L. Grant. He was the creator and editor of the premiere original anthology series of the Eighties called Shadows, *and asked me to contribute to the very first volume. This was significant for me for several reasons—one, he thought I was good enough to help him launch a new series; and secondly, it would mark one of my earliest efforts to escape from the ghetto of science fiction.[1] Charlie had been lobbying for me to lean toward the direction of the* weird tale, *the stories of horror and suspense—a body of writing that was beginning to be called "dark fantasy."[2] And so I must credit him for quite literally changing the focus and direction of my writing career.*

*He is also responsible for the story, which follows—another of my earliest efforts in horror and dark fantasy. He was editing some other one-shot anthologies for Sharon Jarvis when she was at Playboy Press and they sported these great buzzword titles like* Fears and Terrors *(which are, by the way, the English translations for the names of the two moons of Mars). So Chaz calls me and says: give me something nasty and disturbing, but without being graphic. I came up with a simple, little tale of revenge that people tell me they simply cannot forget . . . even if they want to.*

---

[1] *Don't get me wrong, I loved science fiction as a kid and growing up. It was a literature of ideas which always made me think, and it gave me a lifelong dose of wide-eyed wonder about the world. It was the kind of writing that inspired me to dream about being a writer myself. The problem? After I started selling stories to the SF magazines and anthologies, I realized that I didn't think like most of the better writers in the genre, and that my future did not lie among the glassteel domes of the future cities and the trackless voids of space.*

[2]*The story was called "Where All the Songs Are Sad" and is reprinted in my first collection,* Dark Stars and Other Illuminations.

Elliot Binnder huddled in the corner of the dark supply room, caressing the business-end of a linoleum knife.

Outside, in the main corridor, the sounds of the hospital blended together: the paging system loudspeakers, the creaking wheels of gurney carts, offhanded laughter of passing student nurses, the occasional footsteps of someone passing close by the supply room door.

Dressed in hastily stolen hospital garb, Binnder appeared to be just another surgeon in the huge hospital. The pale green O.R. cap and matching pajama-like tunic and pants covered his street clothes; the surgeon's mask concealed his stoical features.

The shift change, he thought; I'll wait until the change of shift. Lots of confusion then. No one will notice me . . .

The blade felt keen and sharp as he edged it with his thumb, following its menacing curve down to the point. In the darkness, it reminded him of the talon of some horrible creature, and he smiled. He checked his liquid crystal watch, and smiled again. Not much longer now . . .

Balding, thin, and yet working on a double chin, Elliot Binnder did not normally appear very threatening. In fact, he was quite meek-looking, and had always thought himself the perfect stereotype of a timid bank clerk. In fact, he was a timid hardware store clerk.

Sitting in the dark, his mind drifted back over the chain of events that had brought him to his present state of mind and place in the cosmos. It *was the hardware store . . .*

. . . where he had worked for almost twenty years. *Twenty years*. The store had been owned by Leo J. Fordham, Sr., a kindly old gentleman who understood the faithful service and loyalty of good employees. Elliot had worked for the old man from the beginning, and gave the owner an honest day's work every day, year in and year out. Things went along pleasantly and after ten years' service, Elliot was made the manager of Fordham's Hardware—earning a good salary and making the payments on his bungalow. Mr. Fordham was very happy with his work, and had even loaned him the money for the down payment on the little house. Elliot Binnder was a happy, contented man.

That is, until the owner's son, Leo J. Fordham, Jr., started coming down to the store after school and on Saturdays to "learn the business." Still a teenager, the young Leo Fordham had already acquired a hard edge to his personality and an envious glow to his eyes. He looked like a vulture waiting to descend upon soon-to-be-carrion, and even back then, Elliot knew enough not to trust the owner's son.

As time passed, Leo Jr. spent his summers home from college in the hardware store, and he became an increasing source of annoyance and irritation to all the employees, especially Elliot Binnder. No matter how diplomatic, or "nice," Binnder attempted to be with Leo Jr., there was no getting around the young man's obnoxious nature and know-it-all attitude. Leo Jr. was contemptuous of Elliot's authority and took every opportunity to ignore his suggestions and disobey outright his requests in day-to-day business.

But Elliot had been a patient man, and he hoped that perhaps Leo Jr. was just another young man feeling his oats, as they used to say, and that time and maturity would change him into a more agreeable, reasonable person. Thus did Elliot avoid speaking with the father and owner of the store about the problems experienced with the son.

*Perhaps I should have said something . . .*

But he didn't say anything, and the situation became increasingly worse until, inevitably, Elliot and Leo Jr. hated each other. That was apparent to all the other employees, but unfortunately not to Mr. Fordham Sr., who was spending more time in his greenhouse and less and less time at his business. In fact, the only thing that kept Elliot sane and whole had been the casual mention by Leo Sr. that he intended to open another hardware store in the next town, and that he would be making Elliot a full *partner*—along with his son, of course. The papers, the old man told him, were being drawn up by his lawyers, and everything would be official as soon as his attorney came back from a trip to the Bahamas.

Time passed quickly it seemed, at that point, and Leo Jr.

graduated from college, married, and was often seen with his pregnant wife carrying about the next generation of the Fordham line. Elliot hoped that this coming responsibility, plus the inclusion of both into a business partnership would finally thaw out the relationship between he and the impetuous Leo Jr.

But it was even less than wishful thinking. On the same weekend that Elliot had told his wife of the elder Fordham's plans, he received a phone call from Mrs. Leo Fordham, Sr. The woman was on the brink of hysteria as she struggled to tell him that her husband had been killed in an auto accident only an hour previous. Elliot had been shocked—it was as though his own father had died and the sense of loss and sincerely felt grief was almost overwhelming. He could only think of never seeing the dear old man again, and was therefore not thinking of what further consequences might follow that unfortunate and very untimely demise.

Naturally, Elliot closed the store until after the funeral; and although he attempted to contact the son several times, he was unsuccessful. When he saw Leo Jr. at the funeral service, the young man ignored him completely.

But on the day business reopened, the young man was more than eager to speak with him. Elliot was not surprised to see the young new owner seated behind his desk that fateful morning. To tell the truth, Elliot had even expected it, and the demotion that would surely accompany the gesture. But he was surprised by Leo Jr. in a way he could not have expected.

"Good morning, Binnder, I've been waiting for you," the son had said.

"Have you?"

"Yes, and I'm afraid I have some bad news for you." Young Leo was almost grinning, unable to contain the obvious joy surging through him at that moment.

"What kind of bad news?" Elliot said.

"Oh . . . the worst, I can assure you. I'm afraid its 'pink-slip' time for you, old man. I want you to get all your shit out of here immediately. It's over and I never want to see your simple face around here again."

"What!" Elliot had said, his voice carrying all the shock and disbelief and pain that such cruelty could summon. "You're *firing* me? You're letting me go?"

"Oh yes. Absolutely." Leo Jr. had smiled at that point.

Perhaps it was the smile, the certain enjoyment the son had displayed then, or perhaps it was the years of resentment and hate finally bubbling to the surface . . . Elliot would never know for sure, but he did know he would extract his revenge on the young bastard who sat grinning before him. He *hated* him at that moment as he had never hated anything in his life.

And it was only the beginning of the ordeal.

Every place where Elliot applied for work, having cited his managerial experience at Fordham's Hardware, he was quickly denied employment. One prospective employer volunteered to Elliot that he had received a "less than glowing" reference from Leo Jr. It was apparent then, that it was not enough for the young son to simply dismiss Elliot in disgrace. No, Leo Jr. clearly intended to ruin him.

Elliot ended up working in a lumber mill, making half of his previous salary and sliding slowly under a wave of bills, loan notes, and other economic pressures. First he had to pull his son from private school, then he second-mortgaged the house, and had the car repossessed and the phone disconnected. His wife became disenchanted, then enraged at his inability to support her in her accustomed manner. The pressure continued to build until he thought he would go insane without some kind of release, some of kind of catharsis.

He was going to Hell in the old handbasket, and he decided that maybe he would take someone with him.

He would take his revenge. Leo Jr. would pay for his injustices, and he would suffer as no man had ever suffered. And so Elliot Binnder descended into the maelstrom that is the chaos of the broken spirit and the tortured mind, knowing that he would never return.

The only piece that remained to be fitted into the jigsaw picture of madness was the act itself, which came to him in a moment of pure inspiration—when his wife told him that Mrs. Leo J. Fordham, Jr., had given birth to a baby boy the day before.

Acting with quiet deliberation, Elliot went into his basement and carefully selected the proper instrument—a linoleum knife from Fordham's Hardware. Yes, he had thought with a smile.

This is perfectly ironic. It will do nicely.

He took a cab downtown to the hospital, took an elevator up to the Maternity Ward, walked the halls as though he might be an impatient expectant father, and waited for the moment when he was unobserved. When it came, he slipped into the supply room and quickly searched through the shelved stacks of linens and gowns until he found the proper disguise . . .

*. . . and now the time has come.*

There were the sounds of increased activity outside the small dark room, and Elliot arose quickly, concealing the linoleum knife beneath his surgeon's gown. Opening the door, he slipped out into the corridor unnoticed by the stream of white-uniformed nurses and orderlies.

*Yes, this was the perfect time.*

He walked down the hall, past the rooms of new mothers, to the glass-windowed nursery. His heart was pounding like a jackhammer in his chest and his spit tasted like paper paste, but it was not from fear, rather from the feeling of approaching triumph. *They can't catch me!* he thought and the certainty of that knowledge elated him with a rush of adrenalin. *They can't!*

Striding purposefully, confidently, he pushed through the door to the nursery, where a charge nurse sat at a small desk reading a copy of *People* magazine.

"Just a minute, Doctor," she said. "Can I help you?"

"Why, yes, you can . . . you can help me . . . by going *down,* bitch!"

He moved swiftly, striking her in the jaw with his fist. She dropped immediately without a sound, and he rushed past her, into the brightly illuminated, warm room where the tiny clear plastic cribs were arranged in two neat rows. There were at least twenty newborn children, and Elliot knew that he must act quickly

Each baby had a little bracelet, and it would be a small matter to search out the one with the Fordham name upon it. Or so he thought. Frantically as he held the tiny, pudgy little wrist of the nearest infant, he tried to make sense of the numbers and letters on the bracelet.

*Christ, it's some kind of code! No names!*

There was the sound of someone stirring beyond the door. *Not much time! I've got to do something!* He looked up to see his reflection in the glass window of the nursery, and beyond to the glared images of several of the staff watching him with growing horror. He realized that he was holding the linoleum knife in plain view. *Don't panic now! Think . . . think!*

Taking one step back, he looked over the collection of cribs and knew what he must do.

It's the only way to be sure, he thought, as he stooped over the first crib. And it won't take very long . . .

*This story represents a kind of victory for me. Pyrrhic, maybe, but still a mark of the triumph of true perseverance.*

*Let me explain. When I first started submitting stories for publication on a regular basis in 1970, one of my premier targets (other than the usual* Playboy, Penthouse, Atlantic Monthly, New Yorker, and Esquire) *was* The Magazine of Fantasy and Science Fiction, *which at the time was being edited by a dignified and courteous man named Edward L. Ferman. Whenever I pulled the last page of my latest story from my typewriter, along with the industry-standard SASE (self-addressed-stamped envelope), I would always send Ed a copy . . . and he would always attach one of his familiar rejection slips (printed on the backs of extra color pages from previous issues of the magazine) which had the usual "thank-you-for-submitting-your-manuscript-unfortunately,-it-does-not-suit-our-present-needs" stock reply.*

*I sent Ferman stories for* ten years—24 in all—*and he rejected every one of them. The 25th story, he bought. Now, by that time, I had been a professional writer for about eight years, so the sale was not the cause for momentous celebration it may have once been, but it still felt damned good. To finally get let into the clubhouse after banging on the door for so long. And the funny thing was, I don't think I ever bothered to send F&SF another story . . . not out of pique or anything like that, but the anthology markets were heating up in the early Eighties, and they were paying far better rates than the little digest-sized magazines could pay.*

*As for the story itself, which follows, I got some decent mileage out of it. I sold a teleplay script to a producer name Steve Yeager, who was pitching a* Twilight Zone *clone to Showtime called* Darksides. *My story was one of the pilot episodes,*

SPARE THE CHILD

*but the acting was so abysmal, Showtime thumbed the series down. At least I have a VHS tape of it to show the grandkids . . . ("Tape? What's that, Nono?") And, the late Karl Wagner also selected it for his* The Year's Best Horror Stories Vol. XI.

*People liked it. So will you.*

The nightmare began quite simply.

In fact, Russell Southers had not the slightest inkling that he was entering into a nightmare at the time. He was passing his Sunday as he always did in the fall: seated before the Zenith Chromacolor III, watching the Giants invent new ways to lose a football game, while his wife Mitzi read the *New York Times*.

"Jesus Christ!" yelled Russell, as the Giants' fullback bucked the middle of the Packer's goal-line defense for the fourth time without scoring.

"Oh, Russell, look at this picture . . ." said Mitzi, showing him a page from *The Times Magazine*.

'First down on the *two!* On the *two,* and they can't score! I can't believe it . . ."

"Russell?"

"What, honey?" He looked at his wife as the thought of how she could dare interrupt him during a football game (especially after thirteen years of marriage) crossed his mind.

"Look at this picture," she said again.

A razor blade commercial blared from the Zenith, and he turned to regard his wife. She was holding up a full-page advertisement from the *Times Magazine,* which featured a sad-eyed child in rags, framed by a desolate village background. It was a typical plea from one of those foster-parent programs, which sponsor foreign orphans in far-away countries stricken with war, famine, and disease. *SPARE THE CHILD* said the banner line atop the picture, while smaller print explained the terrible level of life, then informed the reader how much money to send, where, and how the money would help the poor, starving children.

"Yeah, so what?" asked Russell as he glanced at the page.

"*So what?* Russell, look at the little boy. Look at those big, dark eyes! Oh, Russell, how can we sit here—in the lap of luxury—while those little babies are starving all over the world?"

"Lap of luxury?" The commercial had ended and the Packers were driving upfield from their two-yard line with short passes and power sweeps.

"Well, you know what I mean, Russell . . . it says here

that we can be foster parents for a child for as little as fifteen dollars a month, and that we'll get a picture of our child and letters each month, and we can write to him, too."

"Uh-huh . . ." The Giants' middle linebacker had just slipped, allowing the Packers' tight end to snare a look-in pass over the middle. "Jesus!"

"So I was thinking that we should do something to help. I mean, we pay more than fifteen dollars a month for cable TV, right?"

"What? Oh, yes, Mitzi . . ." The Packers' quarterback had just been thrown for a loss, momentarily halting their surge.

"Well, can we do it?"

Another commercial, this time about the new Chrysler, hit the screen, and Russell looked at his wife absently. "Do what?"

"Why, become foster parents! Russell *look* at this picture!?"

"I looked at the picture, Mitzi! What do you want me to do with it . . . frame it and put it over the mantel, for Christ's sake!"

Unruffled, Mitzi remained calm. "I *said* I want to join the 'Spare the Child' program, Russell. Can we do it?"

"What? You want to send *money* overseas? How do we know the kids are even getting it? Look at that ad—do you know what it costs to run a full-page ad in the *Times!* They don't seem like they need our measly fifteen bucks."

"Russell, please . . ." She smiled and tilted her head the way she always did when she wanted something. The game was back on, and he was tired of being interrupted. *What the hell? What was another fifteen bucks?*

"All right, Mitzi . . . if you think we can do it." He exhaled slowly and returned to his game. The Giants lost anyway.

About twelve weeks after Russell and Mitzi filled out the Spare the Child application and had sent in their first monthly check (and their second and third), they received a letter and picture from their foster child. The envelope carried the return address of Kona-Pei—a small atoll in the Trobriand Islands group. Russell would not have known this piece of arcane geographical knowledge had he not received an official welcoming/confirming letter from the World Headquarters of Spare the Child several weeks previously. The letter also provided additional data.

Their foster child's name was Tnen-Ku. She was a twelve-year-old girl, whose parents had been killed in a fishing-canoe accident, and who now lived at the island's missionary post, under the guardianship of her kinship-uncle, Goka-Pon, the village shaman.

Tnen-Ku's picture was a small, cracked, 4x5 black-and-white Polaroid snap, featuring a gangly prepubescent girl. She had long, straight, dark hair; large, darker almond-eyes; cheekbones like cut-crystal; and a pouting mouth that gave the hint of a wry smile at the corners. She wore a waist-to-knee wrap-around skirt and nothing else. Her just-developing breasts were tiny, sun-tanned cones, and she looked oddly, and somewhat chillingly, seductive to Russell when he first looked at her photograph.

Somewhat fascinated, Russell scanned her first correspondence:

> _Dear Second-Papa Russell:_
> _This is to say many-thanks for becoming my Second-Papa. The U.S.A. money you send will let me not live at Mission all the time. You make my life happy._
> _Tnen-Ku_

Mitzi was not altogether pleased with the first correspondence because Russell was named and _she_ was not. And it was Mitzi's idea in the first place!

Russell Southers tried to placate his wife by saying that it was probably island custom to address only the male members of families, and that Mitzi could not expect the Trobriand Islanders to be as liberated as all the folks in northern suburban New Jersey. The tactic seemed to please Russell's wife, and soon her little foster child, Tnen-Ku was the prime subject of conversation and pride at Mitzi's bridge games and garden parties. In fact, she began carrying the picture of the young girl about in her purse, so that everyone would be able to see what her new child looked like.

Even though Russell found Mitzi's behavior effusive and a bit embarrassing, he said nothing. After thirteen years of marriage, if he had discovered anything, it was that as long as the indulgence was not harmful or detrimental, it was usually better to give in to make Mitzi happy. And it seemed as though it was the little things in life that gave his wife the most joy. So fine, thought Russell, what's fifteen bucks, if it makes my wife happy?

And so each month, he wrote a check to the Spare the Child Foundation, and about once every third month, he and Mitzi would receive a short, impersonal note from the young island girl with the hauntingly deep, impossibly dark eyes.

> *Dear Second-Papa Russell,*
> *This is to say many-thanks for more U.S.A. dollars. Maybe now I never go back to Mission. My life is happy.*
>
> *Tnen-Ku*

Perhaps the most exasperating part of the young girl's letters was the unvarying sameness of them, and although this did not bother Russell, it began to prey upon Mitzi.

"You know, Russell, I'm getting sick of this little game," said Mitzi, out of the blue, while she and Russell were sitting in bed reading together.

"What little game, honey?" asked Russell absently. He was right in the middle of *The Manheist Malefaction,* the latest neo-Nazi spy-thriller on *The Times* bestseller list, and was not surprised to be interrupted by Mitzi's *non sequitur,* since it had been one of her most enduring attributes.

"That foster child thing . . ." she said in some exasperation, as though Russell should have *known* what had been preying on her mind.

"You mean Tnen-Ku? Why? What's the matter?" Russell laid down the book (he was at a familiar part of the plot—where the confused, but competent, protagonist has just met the standard young and beautiful companion), and looked at his wife.

"Well," said Mitzi. "I mean, it's nice being a foster parent and all that, and I guess I should feel good about helping out a poor child, but . . ."

"But what?" asked Russell. "Is it getting to be old hat?"

"Well, something like that. I mean, those letters she writes, Russell. If you can even *call* them letters. They're so *boring,* and she never says anything interesting, or *nice* to us . . . I feel like we're just being *used."*

"Well, we *are* being used a little, but that's what it's all about, Mitzi."

"Maybe so, but I thought it would be more exciting, more gratifying to be a foster parent for a little foreign child . . ." Mitzi looked to the ceiling and sighed.

"But we're supposed to be doing it so that Tnen-Ku feels happier, not necessarily for our own betterment or happiness. Isn't *that* what's important?"

"Oh, I don't know, Russell. You've seen that picture they sent us . . . that little girl doesn't look like she's so bad off." Mitzi harrumphed lightly. "She looks like a little *tart,* if you ask me!"

Russell chuckled. "Well, you certainly have changed your tune lately."

"No, I haven't! It's just that being a foster parent isn't what I thought it would be . . ."

"Are you sure that you're not just getting tired of it, that the novelty's wearing off? Remember how you were at first about backgammon? The aerobic dancing? And when's the last time you went out jogging?"

"Russell, this is different . . ."

"Okay, honey. We can drop out of the program anytime you want. We didn't sign any contract, you know."

Mitzi sighed and looked up at the ceiling as though considering the suggestion. "Well if you really don't think she needs our help . . ."

"Wait a minute, this *is your* idea, remember?" Russell smiled, as it was always Mitzi's way—to twist things around so that it always seemed like Russell was the one who would bear responsibility for all decisions.

"Well, I know, but I wouldn't want to do anything behind your back. Besides, I was thinking that we could use some new drapes in the living room. The sun is starting to fade those gold ones, and we could use that fifteen dollars each month to pay for them . . ."

And so, having planted the seed, not another month went by before Mitzi announced to Russell that it was okay to drop out of the Spare the Child program, having already picked up a sample fabric book, trying to decide which new color would look best in her chrome-and-glass living room. Russell wrote a letter to the Spare the Child offices in New York City, politely explaining that financial pressure had forced them to withdraw from the program. He expressed the hope and good wishes that Tnen-Ku would continue to receive assistance from a new foster parent, and thanked them for the opportunity to be of some help, at least for a brief time.

Before the new drapes were delivered, he received a letter from the Trobriand Islands:

> *Dear Second-Papa Russell,*
> *The mission-peoples say that you will send no more U.S.A. dollars for me. I am very sad by this.*
> *That means I must live at Mission again, and I do not like that. Goka-Pon say a father cannot give up his child. Do you know it is forbidden? Please do not stop U.S.A. dollars. For you and me.*
>
> *Tnen-Ku*

"Now isn't that strange," said Russell, reading the young girl's letter over a Saturday breakfast. "Forbidden, she says . . . I wonder what that means? And what about this 'for you and me'?"

"Don't pay any attention to it dear. She's probably trying to make you feel guilty. You know what they say about people who get used to charity—they lose all incentive to do things for themselves, and all they learn is how to become professional beggars. By us stopping that money, we're probably doing the best thing in the world for her. Maybe she'll grow up now, and *be* somebody." Mitzi poked at the bacon which sizzled in the pan, turned over the more crispy piece.

Russell tossed away the letter and did not think about it for several weeks, until he received a plea from the Spare the Child Program to reconsider canceling his donation. It was similar to the form letters one gets from magazines when you have obviously intended to not renew a subscription. He was going to throw it out but decided that a final, short note to the offices would stop any further correspondence. He wrote telling them that he did not intend to contribute to the foster-parent plan ever again and wished that they would stop badgering him. That ended it, or so he thought.

Two months later, he received another hand-written note from the Trobriand Islands group:

*Dear Second-Papa Russell,*
*Mission-peoples say no more U. S. A. dollars from*
*you. This very bad. Goka-Pon say you must be pun-*
*ished.*

*Tnen-Ku*

Understandably, Russell was outraged and fired off another letter to the Spare The Child Program, enclosing a photocopy of what he termed an "ungrateful, arrogant, and threatening" letter. He informed the agency that if he received any
more correspondence from Tnen-Ku, he would initiate legal
actions against the agency.

A secretary from the Spare The Child offices wrote a
perfunctory apology which promised that Russell Southers
would not be troubled again, and this seemed to appease both
him and Mitzi, until three weeks later, when the cat died.

Actually, their cat, Mugsy, did not *die;* it had been killed—
strangled and then nailed to Russell's garage door above a
jerkily scrawled inscription which could have been in blood:
*Spare the Cat?*

It was as though the young girl had sent them more correspondence, although of a different nature. At first, Mitzi was
horrified and Russell infuriated. They called the police, who
did not seem terribly interested; the Spare the Child agency,
which denied any culpability; and Russell's lawyer, who said
that perhaps a flimsy case could be made against the agency
but suggested that one of Russell's friends was most likely
playing a very bad joke on him.

Russell was shocked to see the high levels of indifference
and lack of true concern for what was happening to him but felt
helpless to do much more than complain himself. He thought of
writing a long threatening letter to Tnen-Ku, but something held
him back. After all, it was impossible that the child had anything
to do with Mugsy's demise—the island of Kona-Pei was thousands of miles from New Jersey. But what the hell *was* going on?

*Second-Papa? Second-Papa . . . ?*

Russell was awakened from a deep sleep by the voice. In
the first moments of wakefulness, he found himself thinking

that her voice sounded very much like he would have imagined it to sound.

*Whose voice!?* Bolting straight up, Russell stared down to the foot of the bed and felt his breath rush out of him. His flesh drew up and pimpled and he felt immediately chilled. There was a figure, a young girl, bathed in a shimmering aura of spectral light, facing him. Her hair was long and dark, and her eyes seemed like empty holes in her face. Her thin, bronzed arms were reaching out to him . . .

"It can't be . . ." whispered Russell, his voice hoarse and full of uncontrollable fear, a fear he had never known.

*Second-Papa,* said Tnen-Ku. *I would have been happy. I would have been grateful to you forever. I would have come to you . . . like this . . . for make you happy . . . not sad.*

Russell blinked, looked over at Mitzi, who was still sleeping. For an instant, he wondered why she had not heard the child; then he realized that he was only hearing the words in his mind.

"Why?" he whispered. "What do you mean? Why are you doing this?"

*I would have given you this . . . .*

Russell stared at the young girl, watching her hands move slowly to her waist, to the simple knot which held the wraparound skirt about her body. With a deliberate slowness, Tnen-Ku worked at the knot.

*No!* thought Russell, feeling a conflicting rush of feelings jolt him. He wanted to look away from the vision, but something held him. The shining figure had taken on a strangely erotic, yet fearsome aspect, and he was transfixed.

As the knot loosened, Russell found himself entranced by the deep tan of her flesh, and as the cloth began to slowly fall away, he became fascinated by the suggestion of flaring hips, the roundness of her soon-to-be-a-woman's belly. He felt himself becoming sexually aroused as he had never in his life, and a fire seemed to be raging in his groin. Tnen-Ku held the fabric of the skirt by a small corner so that it hung limply in front of her, flanked by her naked hips and thighs.

Russell felt that he would explode from the throbbing pressure inside his trembling body, and watching her fingers release the skirt, he screamed involuntarily.

Instantly the vision of the girl disappeared, cloaking the

bedroom in darkness and the echo of his scream. Mitzi had jumped up, grabbing him.

"Russell, what's the matter with you? You're covered with sweat! What *happened?*"

Still trembling, Russell continued to stare at the foot of the bed. "Bad dream," he said weakly. "Bad dream . . . I'll be okay."

But he was *not* okay, and was never okay again.

For the first few days after the vision of Tnen-Ku, Russell Southers had convinced himself it had not actually happened, that he had witnessed nothing more than a singularly realistic dream of some of his darker subconscious desires. He found he could not rid his mind, however, of the disturbing image of the young girl untying her native skirt. He was thinking of her constantly as though becoming obsessed. While commuting to work, while at the office in Manhattan, and even at home with Mitzi watching TV, Russell was plagued by the vision of Tnen-Ku at the foot of his bed. When he concentrated on it, he could hear her voice calling out his name.

But that was only the beginning.

While watching the evening news after his daily martini, while Mitzi prepared dinner, Russell was shocked to see a bulletin teletype-overlay snake across the screen while the commentator spoke of a warehouse fire in Brooklyn:

## TNEN-KU IS WATCHING YOU
## SECOND-PAPA RUSSELL

"Jesus Christ!" yelled Russell, sitting straight up, staring at the TV screen, waiting for the message to roll across the bottom of the picture again. *Impossible! I didn't see it! But you* did *see it* . . . He felt a lump in his throat as he sat gripping the arms of his chair, waiting for a repeat of the words which did not come. He thought that he was starting to lose his sanity, and *that* scared him too. He was thinking about that little sexy brat too much, that was it. Got to stop thinking about it, that's all.

Shaken, he watched the news commentator drone on about more local happenings, but he heard little of it. He toyed with the idea of telling Mitzi what had been happening but thought that she would think he was losing his marbles. Mitzi had always depended on him to be strong and pragmatic and rational; he shuddered to think of how she would react to him showing such obvious signs of mental weakness. No, Mitzi should not know anything. Russell was going to have to handle this himself.

But it *did* bother him that Mitzi was not sharing in his . . . his what? His delusions? His guilt? She was blithely rolling along, having totally forgotten the Spare the Child Program in turn for some new, fleeting, but always enjoyable project. And it was *Mitzi* who had gotten him into the whole mess in the first place. It wasn't fair, thought Russell . . .

That night she returned to him and he sat up in bed, transfixed and captivated by her little brown body, wrapped in a shimmering cloak of light. She held something in her hands, which she slowly placed on the covers of his bed, then quickly disappeared.

Russell's throat was so tight that he could not swallow, could not have uttered a sound if he had wanted to. His hands were trembling badly, keeping pace with the thumping of his heart and his ragged breath. His mind was slipping away from him, and he sat in the darkness, resolved to see a psychiatrist the next day. Take the afternoon off and see one of his golf partners, Dr. Venatoulis.

Then he noticed something on the covers of the bed, something where the image of the girl had placed her hands, and he felt the fear grip him again. Pushing back the sheets, Russell groped about on the softness of the quilt and felt something hard and solid. *What the hell . . . ?*

It was a small, hand-carved box with a fitted top that slid open. Shaking it, something rattled inside, and he feared for a moment that the sound might awaken Mitzi. Quickly, Russell slipped out of bed and went into the bathroom, switching on the fluorescent lights around the mirror, and shutting the door. The box, when he opened it, contained scores of small white sticks, about half the size of kitchen matches, of uneven shapes. They seemed to be polished smooth and resembled ivory . . . or perhaps *bone.* The thought held him for an instant as Russell stared at the box, realizing fully and for the first time the presence of the box was physical proof he was *not* delusional, that he was not imagining things, and that, somehow, Tnen-Ku had actually been inside his bedroom, ten thousand miles away from her island home.

No! His mind screamed out the rejection of such a thought. And yet he stared at the evidence with eyes that were starting to water and sting from nervous tension.

The little white sticks were scattered across the top of the vanity Formica, and as Russell watched them, they began to move. Vibrating ever so slightly at first, tingling as if touched by a slight breeze, the bones—and Russell *knew* now that they were indeed bones—moved like iron filings over a magnet to form a caricature of a skull.

Screaming involuntarily, he swept the pieces off the counter scattering them across the bathroom tile. It was getting too crazy, too unbelievable!

"Russell, is that you . . . ?" Mitzi was knocking loudly at the bathroom door.

"No! . . . I mean, yes, it's me! Who the hell do you think it would be?"

"Russell, are you all right? What's the matter with you?" Mitzi tried the knob, but it was locked. "Russell?!"

"Oh Christ, *what?!* Yes, Mitzi, I'm all right. Go back to bed, will you please? I've got an upset stomach that's all . . ."

"I thought I heard you scream, Russell, are you okay? Why is the door locked? You *never* lock the bathroom door, Russell."

"I've got some bad gas pains, that's all. I—I didn't want to disturb you, honey. I'll be out in a minute."

He looked down to the floor and saw that the little bones had been moving while he spoke to his wife, gathering themselves together like a small herd of animals. They were arranging themselves into letters, like tiny runic symbols, which at first were indecipherable. But the more Russell stared at the configurations; he could read the message that was forming:

## PUNISH WITH DEATH

He wanted to scream again, and he held the sound in his throat only by the greatest force of will. He could taste bile at the back of his mouth as he bent down and scooped up all the little white pieces, throwing them into the toilet and flushing it repeatedly, until all the bones were sucked into the small porcelain maelstrom.

Luckily, when he returned to bed, Mitzi was already asleep.

He could not bring himself to tell his wife about the delusions he had been suffering, and he was ashamed to call up a psychiatrist, especially someone with whom he played golf on occasion. Since no real, hard evidence, no proof actually existed, Russell had convinced himself that what had been happening to him was the product of an overworked mind, a heavily wracked, guilty conscience, and too much displaced imagination. And so he tried to ignore the messages which Tnen-Ku sent him: the warning headline on the *New York Post* which disappeared when he picked up the paper from the subway newsstand; the skull-like configuration of the coffee grounds in his cup at Nedick's in Grand Central; the pair of dark eyes which seemed to be staring at him through the glass of the speedometer of his Monte Carlo; the familiar, half-whispering voice that he thought he could hear in the telephone in between the beeps of the touch-tone dial; the movie marquee he glanced at from the corner of his eye on 56th Street, which for a moment, until he had looked for a second time, had said: "Tnen-Ku Is Coming!"

Normally Russell Southers would have been greatly disturbed by the portents and omens jumping up unexpectedly from all parts of his everyday life. But he was becoming almost accustomed to the preternatural for one simple reason: he was losing his mind. Simply and totally. He just didn't care anymore.

*Let her come, goddamn it!* he thought as he rode the train home that night. *Let her come, cause I'm sure as shit ready for her . . .*

The conductor called out his stop, and he stood up in ritual-commuter fashion, single-filing out of the car and onto the platform with his fellow riders. Descending the staircase to the parking lot below, Russell scanned the amassed cars for his white Monte Carlo where Mitzi would be waiting to pick him up. It was wedged in between a big Ford station wagon and a TR-7, and as Russell approached the familiar vehicle he was shocked to see the dark eyes and long straight hair of Tnen-Ku watching him from behind the wheel. His first impulse was to stop in shock and surprise, but instead he forced himself to walk naturally, even waving and smiling as he approached the car. Better, he thought, to not let the little snit think she had rattled him. He would take the element of surprise and twist it back into her face. Surely the girl would not expect him to act so naturally.

He tried to keep thoughts of Mitzi from his mind, tried to not think about what that young brat might have done with his wife so that she could be replaced behind the wheel. No, it was better to concentrate on what must be done . . .

*"Hello, Second-Papa Russell . . ."* she said as he opened the passenger's side door and slid in beside her.

She was smiling and leaning forward as though she would like him to kiss her. *The little tramp!* Russell looked past her face to her slim neck, then reached out and wrapped his fingers around it. As he began to squeeze and he felt her struggle helplessly under his grip, he smiled slowly, feeling a wellspring of elation bubble through his mind.

"I've got you!" he screamed. "I've got you now, and you won't get away this time!"

Tnen-Ku opened her mouth, no longer a tart, sly curve to her young lips, but a silent circle of panic and pain. Russell tightened his grip on her neck and began to yank her back and forth. His hands and forearms were enveloped in a numbness, an absence of sensation, as though he were watching someone else's hands strangling the darkly tanned woman-child.

As her face seemed to become bloated and puffy, the color of her cheeks turning gray and her bottomless eyes bulging whitely, Russell's other senses seemed to desert him. The lights from the station parking lot grew dim, and he could barely discern the features of the dying face in front of him. He could hear nothing but the pounding of his own pulse behind his ears and was not aware of the excited shouts of people who were crowding around his Monte Carlo. Nor did he feel the strong, capable hands grabbing him, separating him from his dead wife, pulling him from the car.

Hitting the hard surface of the parking lot, Russell looked up at the ragged oval of faces peering down at him. Someone called for the police as he lay still, feeling the shadows of evening and fear crawl across his eyes. When the sound of the sirens pierced the night, Russell began to scream, spiraling down into the mind-darkness of defeat . . .

Somewhere in Manhattan, someone opened to a full-page ad in *The Times Magazine.*

*My ideas for stories come from all over the place, as we will discover, but very few are based on real-life models. An exception is the next story, which is based on a case study I remember reading in undergraduate school. It was called "Joey, the Mechanical Boy," and for some reason I never forgot it. Information affects in sometimes strange and wonderful ways and we all respond to it in different ways—sometimes emotionally, at others viscerally.*

*As far as this one goes, I have no idea why I carried the images of the little autistic kid around in my subconscious like a brown-bag snack, but I did. It was one of those items I figured I would work into a story sooner or later, and waited patiently for the structure to bubble up to the surface.*

*The impetus finally came when my old friend Roy Torgeson asked me for a story for a long-running anthology series he'd been editing called* Chrysalis. *Back in the Seventies I had sold him several stories for the series that had been decidedly science fiction; and Charlie Grant and I had sold him a dark fantasy called "When Dark Descends," but I didn't think he was really looking for the kind of horror and suspense I'd been writing in the early Eighties. So I told him maybe he wouldn't be all that interested in what I'd been writing lately . . .*

*Roy had this kind of dark chuckle that was very distinctive and he would let it out at just the right moments, and I can recall him doing it then. "Tom," he said. "You just write me a story . . . I know it will be good. I love your stuff."*

*That was all I needed to get me working. When I sat down to my Selectric (I think this was one of the last stories I wrote before getting my first computer . . . ), I wanted to give him something that*

THE MECHANICAL BOY

*would satisfy both his need for sf[1] and my own for something that investigated the inner, dark regions of the human spirit. You decide whether or not I succeeded.*

*Oh yeah, one final note: Roy Torgeson died about ten years ago, and I didn't hear about it for almost a year after the fact. Somehow it had slipped past me and it bugged me and saddened me. Roy was a brilliant guy, who had established himself as a shrewd book collector and a savvy entrepreneur. In the Seventies he single-handedly helmed a company called Alternate Worlds Recordings, in which he rounded up some of the greatest fantasists of his generation[2] and had them read their own works on LP records. He did such an outstanding job; he won a World Fantasy Award.*

*By now, many have forgotten him, and his thoughtful, intelligent contributions to the field, so this next one is dedicated to the memory of Roy Torgeson.*

⁕

---

[1] *standing for "speculative fiction," which is what science fiction used to call itself when it wanted to be taken seriously*

[2] *The list is kind of staggering: Robert Bloch, Fritz Lieber, Harlan Ellison, Theodore Sturgeon, and others I can't remember, but if you ever see any for sale, grab them up. They are what we mean when we use the word "classics."*

Billy was already awake when the nurse entered his room.

He was watching her as she approached his bed as morning light danced upon the windowpanes. It illuminated Billy's "Sleep Machine"—a fantastic array of strings, wires, vacuum tubes, burned-out light bulbs? and other scraps—which surrounded his bed like a cocoon.

"Good morning, Billy!" she said in a saccharine voice. "Time for breakfast . . . !"

As the nurse drew closer to his bedside, Billy stared in growing horror while she blundered into his "main current line"—a piece of thick twine which ran from his bedpost to an imaginary outlet taped to the wall. Her white-stockinged leg caught on the string, yanking it from its mooring, which caused Billy to explode in a frenzy of screams. Panic and outrage bubbled out of him like lava. His eyes bulged, his face flushed, as he writhed about the bed.

"Billy! Billy! It's all right! Billy!" The nurse reached down to touch him, to help calm him, knocking over a shoe box filled with old pieces of a radio, all taped together in a random fashion. Seeing this, Billy's explosive, terrified screams became intensified, and the nurse also became filled with panic.

There were urgent-sounding footsteps behind her, and she turned to see Dr. Martin Godell rushing into the room.

His white coat thrown open, Godell rushed past the nurse. "Goddammit," he muttered, as he reached for the end of the thick twine and retaped it to the wall. "There, Billy . . . it's all right now. I'm fixing it . . ." he said slowly, softly. The doctor picked up the shoe box, carefully rearranging the old radio parts, replaced it at the foot of the bed.

Billy stopped screaming instantly and fell back to his mattress, rigidly staring at the ceiling while he attempted to control his breathing.

"Doctor, I'm sorry," said the nurse quickly. "I—"

Martin Godell looked at her with dark, burning eyes. "You are new on this ward?"

"Yes, but I—"

"Were you not briefed on Billy's special condition?"

"Well, yes," said the nurse, looking down at her shoes. "But I didn't think it was as serious as—"

"Never mind," said Martin. He shook his head slowly, ran his fingers through his longish hair. "But in the future, I hope you pay more attention to the recommendations on the charts."

"I'm sorry, Dr. Godell. It won't happen again."

"I hope not," said Martin, looking down at Billy, who seemed to have recovered from his panic and was now lying on his back, hands by his sides, like a robot awaiting to be activated. "You may go now, Nurse. I'll take care of Billy this morning."

As the woman left the room, Dr. Godell regarded Billy, who seemed to be ignoring him totally. Nine years old, blond-white hair, Billy was at once fragile and formidable in appearance. His neon-blue eyes had a penetrating aspect which was unsettling to most who knew him, and yet his small, skinny body suggested all the images of the pathetic war orphan, the helpless street waif. As Billy lay before Martin Godell, he was humming to himself in a low pitch, like an engine set at idling speed.

It had been three years since Billy had been admitted to the Schaller Institute for Disturbed Children, and in that time, the boy had shown only a minimal response to treatment. His early diagnoses had been unanimous in proclaiming that Billy Hutton suffered from severe autism—but of a kind that was unique in the literature of child psychopathology.

In essence, Billy was a mechanical boy.

By the age of six, he had already evolved a complex, rational, and frightening array of characteristics which implied that he was a machine—a machine operated by remote control, and powered by other machines of his own delusional fantasy. Not only did Billy believe that he was a machine, but he had the uncanny ability to convey this feeling, to actually create the impression in others, that he was indeed a mechanical construct. He seemed to be a prisoner within his own body, or worse, a body without a soul—a child totally deprived of his own humanity.

His case history contained many of the classic elements which contribute to autism. Billy was born to very young parents who had clearly not wanted a child, and consequently was raised in an atmosphere of resentment, detachment, and ultimately, of loathing. He was never touched by his parents unless absolutely necessary, never cuddled or played with. He was left alone for many hours at a time, and was only attended when he was fed on a rigid schedule, or when his diapers needed changing. Later, his toilet training was carried out with a cold precision that left him confused and full of unfounded fears about human excrement. By the time he mastered speech, he spoke to no one other than himself, and then only in short, clipped passages which were colored by his own invented words and phrases. He showed a remarkable early interest in machines, and by the age of three was able to take apart and reassemble various household devices such as an electric fan, a radio, toaster, and a coffee grinder. From that point on, Billy Hutton began to perceive the world, including himself, in terms of machinery—probably because it was "safer" than trying to be human.

During the next three years, he had been placed in several special schools and institutes, but the host of teachers, therapists, and doctors who encountered him all eventually gave up in frustration. No one was able to break through the barriers which encapsulated Billy and his fantasies.

His elaborate "system" of wires, strings, boxes, and discarded electrical parts which surrounded his bed was called his "Sleep Machine," and was required while he slept to "live him" when he could not attend to this task himself. It was only one of myriad imaginary and sometimes artfully constructed devices which he needed to perform even the simplest daily tasks and functions. All his liquids were taken in with straws which were "connected" to Byzantine "Pumping Stations" made of boxes and hoses placed beside his mealtime trays. Solid food was eaten only after he had plugged himself to his "Energy Converter," another Goldbergian machine which Billy claimed allowed him to digest his food. He could not perform acts of elimination unless he held old vacuum tubes or portable radio circuit boards in both hands while he squatted over, but never touched, the commode.

It was only after the staff at Schaller Institute learned to play along with Billy's numerous machine-fantasies that he was able or willing to communicate with them. When the laws of his private, mechanistic universe were obeyed, he was cooperative and calm, although he seemed to regard all people with a cold disdain, which suggested that he felt sorry for the general lot of humanity who were not machines. He was a lonely, dissociated child, who did not appear to take joy in anything he did, or in any of the things which took place around him.

Despite his gradual acquiescence to the staff, he showed an almost uniform lack of improvement during his years of therapy. The only visible sign of difference in his behavior was an increased interest in drawing, which evolved from bizarre abstract circuit diagrams and wiring schematics into ingeniously designed blueprints for machines. Occasionally, when asked by Dr. Godell, Billy would make drawings of himself, which always resembled robots, or which depicted Billy locked deep inside a baroquely constructed machine.

Under Martin Godell's direction, Billy was administered every available psychological test—which indicated that he was of extremely high intelligence, facile, clever, and perceptive. Eventually, Godell ordered physiological tests as well, and the results were somewhat surprising. EKG and X-ray indicated that there was no organic brain damage, no neurological dysfunction or other physical irregularities. More intensive tests revealed, however, some interesting and quite baffling data. Although there is no correlation between brain-size and intelligence, it had been noted that Billy's cranial capacity, even at the age of nine, was more than 150 cubic centimeters larger than that of the average adult, and a CAT-Scan revealed unfamiliar convoluting of the brain surrounding the base of the hippocampus and also along the Fissure of Rolando. Billy also possessed an abnormally high concentration of Messenger RNA and Replinase. Gene density was also high, which indicated a higher chance for incidence of genetic mutation.

Everyone on the staff, except for Dr. Godell, was very surprised at the findings. The physiological tests suggested what he had already begun to believe—that Billy was not a typical autistic child, but something far more special, and possibly quite terrifying.

"The next case is Billy Hutton . . ." said Dr. Angeline Lorca, the Clinical Director at Schaller Institute. She was an austere, totally pragmatic woman who, as she approached the age of forty, had become an accomplished administrator in spite of her perceived political and sexist adversity. "Dr. Godell, the Hutton boy is one of your patients . . ."

Martin cleared his throat, glanced about the long conference table where he and the other psychiatrists sat with their monthly progress reports, then down to the end of the table to Dr. Lorca.

"Yes, that's correct," he said, waiting for a gesture from the darkhaired woman to continue. Martin disliked the monthly Clinical Staff meetings, mainly because Lorca conducted them as if each of the psychiatrists were on trial, rather than as participants in an open forum for discussion of treatment programs and individual patient problems.

"I've just finished your most recent reports on Billy Hutton," said Dr. Lorca. "Your 'treatment' program hardly merits the term, Doctor. No progress whatsoever. It seems as though the Hutton boy is merely wasting the staff's time. The latest incident with the new dayshift nurse was very upsetting to her, and I understand that you were quite harsh with her."

"I don't agree," said Martin. "Billy Hutton is the most challenging and most fascinating case I have ever encountered."

Angeline Lorca smiled sardonically. "That may be true, but we are not in the business of being fascinated, Dr. Godell. A lot of our private and public funding is predicated upon our record of successful treatment. Any more cases like Billy Hutton and we might be accused of logrolling just to get those fat foundation grants and government pork."

Martin shook his head slowly. "I have always believed that it was the duty of the therapist to be more concerned with his patients than his paychecks," he said, noticing that several of his colleagues had covered their faces to hide growing grins. He knew that few of them actually liked Lorca, but fewer still had the nerve to speak with her on her own acerbic terms.

Lorca smiled in a way which showed that she was not amused. "As Clinical Director, I must be concerned with all facets of operation at the Institute. The point I was trying to make, Dr. Godell, is that if we are unable to help Billy Hutton, then perhaps he should be transferred to another treatment center."

"What? You mean discharge Billy?" Martin did not try to hide his surprise and outrage. "To where? If we can't help him, then no one can!"

"Please don't raise your voice, Doctor."

"Please don't make me . . ." Martin was suddenly aware of the awkward silence at the table. Everyone was watching the two combatants, waiting to see who would strike the mortal blow.

Dr. Lorca steepled her hands and long, thin fingers in front of her face, stared at Martin with cool, green eyes. "Would you mind telling the staff why you object to discharging Billy Hutton?"

Martin cleared his throat. She was giving in a bit, giving him a chance, at least.

"It's in my last few progress reports," he began. "Perhaps more by implication than expressly stated, but I will try now to explain my current feelings about the boy. The last battery of physiological tests indicate that we are not dealing with a normal—if there is such a thing—autistic child. I cite the cranial irregularities and puzzling genetic data specifically. I feel that accepted treatment modalities are not sufficient in the Hutton case."

"And why not?"

"In order to help Billy," said Martin, "I must first understand the world in which he lives, the personal, cosmic laws which guide his behavior and his thinking. Until recently, I don't think I had the handle, the key."

"But now you *do?*" Lorca nodded her head patronizingly. "Would you care to share your ideas with the Staff?"

Martin paused, then shook his head slowly. "I think it is too early to do that, since I have only come upon them quite recently. I would like to wait until I can articulate my feelings a bit more lucidly."

"And what about a revised treatment program? Have you any thoughts along these lines?"

"Yes, I do. But again I would like to have more time to prepare myself."

Dr. Lorca closed the file folder before her, exhaled slowly, and glanced at the assembled Staff. "Very well, Dr. Godell . . . if no one has any objections, I will defer my professional opinion on this case until a later date. However, I would hope that some of your 'feelings' and your new 'treatment' procedures will be included in next month's progress report."

"I'll see what I can do," said Martin.

So staggering, so unsettling were his recent feelings about Billy Hutton that Martin was actually afraid to share them with the Clinical Staff. As though the word could make flesh his speculations, he avoided speaking his thoughts aloud. What he feared about Billy Hutton was too improbable, too bizarre; yet he believed, in his heart of hearts, that it was true.

Until recently, Billy's preoccupation with machines had been kept on the fantasy level, made real only through his own constructions of pseudo-devices from scraps of cardboard, string, and discarded light bulbs or parts from transistor radios. But now, Martin tried something new, and had been scheduling Billy's therapy sessions in different parts of the Schaller Institute, such as the Medical Lab, the Maintenance Shop, and the Computer Room.

The first time he had taken Billy to the Medical Lab, he noticed a slight change in the boy's usually placid expression— a brief surge of anticipation and wonder, which he had first noticed during the battery of physiological tests when Billy was exposed to a complex array of machines such as the CAT-Scanner and the EEG. As Billy stood in the center of the Lab, he clutched a cigar box tightly to his chest, from which several pieces of twine snaked into his shirt. He called this device his "Oxy-Forcer," which he claimed helped to "breathe me." There was a slight spark in Billy's neon-blue eyes as he walked to the Formica-topped counter to reach out and touch the centrifuge. His fingers almost lovingly caressed the polished metal surfaces of the small machine, and his grip upon his cigar box seemed less desperate, less urgent. He also examined the electronic, digitally registering scales, and an old IBM typewriter, which particularly fascinated him. Turning to Martin, he had an expectant expression that the doctor had not thought him capable of.

"Yes, Billy . . . what is it?"

"Current. Make current?"

"You want to turn it on?" For an instant, the corner of Billy's mouth twitched, and Martin thought that the forlorn street waif might actually smile. But as quickly as the expression suggested itself, so did it vanish.

Billy stared at him hypnotically. "Yes. Make current."

Martin nodded and flipped on the Selectric's switch. A low-level thrumming filled the room and Billy seemed transfixed by the sound. His face flushed as though he derived sustenance from the aura of the machine, and slowly he released his grip on his "Oxy-Forcer," placing it on the desk so that he could touch the typewriter with both hands and feel the vibration of its motor tingle along his broomstick-thin arms.

Martin allowed him to stand before the machine, like a worshipper, for the better part of the hour, then informed him that it was time to go. Reluctantly Billy let Martin turn off the machine, but before walking away from the desk, he picked up his cigar box and quickly thrust the pieces of twine back into his shirt, taking several deep and reassuring breaths.

The boy obviously preferred the surrogate machine to nothing at all and as Martin guided him from the room, he felt a twinge of uncertainty pass through his mind. It was a suggestion that he might be doing something terribly wrong.

For the next few weeks, Martin conducted his therapy sessions in the Lab and the Maintenance Shop, each time Billy becoming more actively involved in the functioning of the various machines at his disposal. But it was not until Billy visited the Institute's Data Processing Center did Martin notice definitive changes in the boy's demeanor.

Martin took Billy into the clean, bright room and let him discover the optical scanners, the TV display monitors, the line printers and the word processor, and even the insides of some of the cabinets. The effect on Billy was immediate and remarkable, and for the first time he seemed to resemble the bright, perceptive boy that his testing indicated. Martin observed in his notes that Billy seemed to sense the "greatness" of these computer-machines, and he wondered if his contact with them gave further proof to the boy's fantasy that machines were the superior entities in the world, and that it was indeed better to be a machine.

The next step in his treatment program was interaction, and therefore Martin taught Billy how to actually use the computers.

"This computer will play games with you," he told Billy, who was sitting reverently before a keyboard and a TV monitor. "Not like any games we have ever asked you to play before, Billy. Would you like to learn how to play?"

The small, blond-haired boy rocked back and forth in his chair, his blue eyes reflecting the bright colors of the display screen, his small hands holding the "Oxy-Forcer" close to his chest.

"Billy . . . do you want to play a game with the computer? Answer me, or we will go back to your room."

Slowly, Billy placed the cigar box on the desk top, next to the keyboard. "Play me," he said blankly.

"Watch the screen, Billy. In order to play, you must read the instructions, then spell out your answers with the letters on the keyboard, okay?"

"Play me," he said again with a touch of urgency. He began rocking more quickly.

"This game is called 'House Haunted,' and you must go through the house and find a treasure chest. But you must be very careful . . . there are booby traps, and ghosts and trolls along the way that can get you. You have to read the machine's instructions very carefully each time you take a turn, and you have to think before you answer each time. All right, if you're ready, I'll push this key, which will start the game . . ."

Billy nodded and the game began as Martin stepped back to watch the boy. After a few initial mistakes, he seemed to grasp the techniques of the game. Within the first hour, he had already "won" his first game—a fact which Martin found remarkable, and a feat which placed Billy's gaming skill far beyond the average beginner. But Martin was not surprised that Billy would perform well at the computer games. Despite what the skill indicated, the doctor felt compelled to continue the "therapy" sessions.

For the next week, Martin watched Billy become a total master of "House Haunted," and then successively more advanced games until, by the beginning of the next week, the boy was absorbed in a highly complex game called "Star Lords," which required abstract thinking in three dimensions, plus an understanding of time-distension effects in space flight at relativistic speeds. Billy demonstrated eidetic memory, imaginative strategy, and a keen perception of cause-and-effect relationships many "turns" in advance—much in the same manner that a chess master can anticipate forced moves by his opponent. Martin knew that only several of the Institute's most skilled programmers and analysts could cope with the complexities of "Star Lords," but little Billy Hutton absorbed the game with an almost supernatural ease.

During the times when he was playing with the computers, Billy now seemed like a normal nine-year-old boy. His eyes were bright and quick, his cheeks filled with a healthy color, and most importantly, he smiled. Martin observed that Billy almost seemed to be drawing some kind of energy from the machines he played, so great was his enjoyment and ability to emote naturally while at the consoles. It was equally difficult to accept how radically Billy would revert back to his usual, autistic persona when he was not in therapy with the machines and computer games. In fact, Martin was forced to admit that Billy's behavior, when away from the computers, was worse than before he had begun the new therapeutic techniques.

But that was only the beginning.

The following week, Martin Godell was visited by Nick Shepherd, the Institute's Data Processing Chief. He was a thin nervous man who had an almost continuous facial tic at the left corner of his mouth.

"Excuse me, Doctor, but we've run into a little problem over in the computer room, and I was wondering if I might talk to you for a minute."

Martin invited Shepherd to have a seat and made small talk about how he knew nothing about computers and could not imagine what he might be able to do to help.

Shepherd fidgeted nervously in his seat as he explained his problem: the computer-games programs had been tampered with.

"What do you mean, 'tampered with'?" asked Martin.

"Well, what I mean to say is that there are some new games added to the memory discs," said Shepherd. Tic. "And none of my people claim to know anything about it. In fact, they all swear they don't know anything and haven't been fooling with the programs."

"New games?" asked Martin, sitting up suddenly in his chair. "What kind of new games?"

Nick Shepherd laughed nervously as his mouth twitched.

"That's just it. None of us can figure them out. They're written in some kind of weird language—not normal computer language and not really English either. Every once in a while you can recognize some mathematical symbols and some physical relationships, but not much more. Carrington's been playing around with it and he thinks that some of it might have to do with relativity and time-space problems, but be says he's just taking a wild guess."

"And you think I may know something about it?" Martin sat back in his chair, using the voice he used to interview patients.

"Oh no," said Shepherd defensively, trying to chuckle but failing "It's just that I knew you had been bringing one of your kids over here to use the games programs, and I was wondering if you might have noticed anything funny."

Martin shook his head. "No, I'm sorry, Nick, but I haven't seen anything unusual." He felt the lie burning his tongue like a hot coal.

Shepherd stood up and shook his head. "And that's not the damnedest thing, Doc . . . the funniest part is that we don't even have a record of data input for these new games."

"What does that mean?"

"It's hard to explain," said Shepherd, his facial tic rapidly flashing, "and I know it's impossible but those new games seem like they just appeared inside the computer. Like the machine just thought them up itself! Isn't that crazy?"

"Yes," said Martin, "it does seem odd."

"Okay, well, thanks, Doc," said Shepherd as he stood in the doorway, preparing to leave. "I just wanted to check . . . you never can tell, and I thought you might have seen something funny, that's all. See you later. We'll figure this thing out, I guess."

As the nervous little man disappeared down the hall, Martin kept thinking of what he had just learned. Nothing funny at all. No, it was definitely not funny, thought Martin.

That evening, he took Billy to the Data Processing Center, and stood in the doorway, watching the boy approach the computer console. Sinking into the chair as if in a trance, Billy watched the display monitor as it blinked into life. Martin stared at the scene in disbelief, even though, by this time, he should have been expecting what he now witnessed. As soft humming sounds of the machines filled the room, Billy watched the screens, his arms folded calmly in his lap. Martin felt a lump growing in his throat, because he knew that Billy had not touched the consoles. He had not, physically, turned on the machines.

Forcing himself to watch what followed, Martin stared at the odd tableau of the boy and his machines. Yes, they were *his* machines, thought Martin . . . more than anyone else's in the world. He knew that now. The monitor flashed a series of symbols and letters, the lines skipping across the screen, filling it. At first, there was a slow precision, a measured rhythm to the information that flowed past the display, but as Martin watched, the process was accelerated, faster and faster, until he could not discern the letters and figures as they blurred across the monitor—flashes of color against contrasting backgrounds.

Martin watched Billy and the machines as they conversed, for that was surely what they were doing. It was an impossible pairing of boy and machine, yet it was happening, and Martin felt that he was violating some kind of taboo, as though he were witnessing some sacred rite. What was this boy? How would one describe him? A biological experiment, a prototype, the ultimate man-machine interface? Whatever words Martin might choose, he knew that the boy could somehow psychokinetically communicate with machines.

Even as he watched, he saw that an aura, a shimmering halo, was forming around Billy's body, around the machines. They were commingling, joining forces to become the single entity. Martin had a brief vision, a thought of the vast information network which bound the world together electronically and mechanistically, and he was forced to look away from the boy.

He felt he had been witness to some kind of new and very special creation. Billy was no longer a small, fragile boy, and Martin wondered what the world would try to do with him.

Or, perhaps it was the other way around . . .

*One of my earliest and most profound influences was Ray Bradbury. I will never forget discovering the Ballantine and Bantam Books reprints of* The October Country, The Illustrated Man, The Martian Chronicles, *and other magical books of stories by the man from Waukegan, Illinois.*

*The next story is definitely on the same evolutionary path as much of Ray's work. When I sat down to write it, I remember having several ideas in mind, which is usually how I get a story to take shape and finally a life of its own. Namely, I think of the kinds of people I will need to act it out; then I figure out what I want to say in terms of theme or motif; and then I start writing and see where the words take me. I rarely, if ever, know ahead of time how a story's going to end. I like to tell it to myself as I write it. I like to entertain myself. I like myself very much, you see . . .*

*Anyway, with this one, I kept thinking of that Bradbury tale in which an old man picks up a mysterious hitchhiker on a blistering hot, summer day. I was also thinking of the wonderfully close relationship my father and my first (and at that time, only) son, Damon had developed and enjoyed. Half-consciously, I decided I'd try to capture the essence of grandfather and grandson; as well as turning my memory of the Bradbury story inside out. The title is a line from my favorite source of titles: one of the poems in* A Shropshire Lad *by A. E. Housman.*[1]

---

[1] *Back in the Seventies, my old pal, Roger Zelazny, hipped me to Housman's poetry (which is some of the most lyrically brilliant stuff in the English language) as a great source of short story titles. Roger, who wrote the Introduction to my first story collection, died far too young from colon cancer, and I will always miss his mordant sense of humor, his effortlessly crafted prose, and his valued friendship.*

THE NIGHT IS FREEZING FAST

*The story has been reprinted numerous times but the most interesting and most recent has been in a British tome entitled* The Oxford Book of Christmas Stories. *I have to be honest here— as much as I like the story, I would have never picked it for a Christmas anthology . . .*

"Oh damn!" cried Grandma from the kitchen. "I've run right out of shortnin' for this cake!"

"Are you sure?" asked Grandpa. When his wife cussed, she usually was very sure. He eased the Dubuque newspaper down from his face and peeked at her through the kitchen door.

"'Course I'm sure! And if you want a nice dessert for after Christmas Dinner, you'll get into town and get me more shortnin'!"

"What's shortnin'?" asked Alan, ten years old and always asking serious questions at what always seemed like the wrong moment.

"But it's a blizzard goin' on out there!" said Grandpa.

"What's shortnin'?" asked Alan.

"Rolf, if you know what's good for you, you'll get into that town and get me my shortnin' . . ." Grandma used that tone of voice that Alan had learned meant no foolishness.

Grandpa must have noticed it too because he said "Oh, all right."

Alan watched him drop the newspaper and shuffle across the room to the foyer closet where he pulled out some snowboots, a beat-up corduroy hat, and a Mackinaw jacket of red and black plaid. He turned and looked wistfully at Alan, who was sitting on the rug watching the Chicago Bears play the Kansas City Chiefs on TV.

"Want to take a ride, Alan?"

"Into town?"

"Yep. 'Fraid so."

"In the blizzard?"

Grandpa sighed, stole a look toward the kitchen. "Yep."

"Okay. It sounds like fun . . . we don't get snowstorms like this in L.A.!"

"Fun?" said Grandpa, smiling. "Oh yes, it'll be great fun. Come on, get your outerwear on, and let's get a move on."

Alan ran to the closet and pulled on the heavy, rubber-coated boots, a knit watchcap, and scarf. Then he shook into the down parka his mom had ordered from the L. L. Bean mail order place. His first encounter with cold weather had been a great adventure, a great difference in his life.

"Forty-two years with that woman and I don't know how she—"

"What's shortnin', Grandpa?"

The gray-haired man had just closed the door to the mud porch behind them. He was muttering as he faced into the stinging slap of the December wind, the bite of the ice-hard snowflakes attacking his cheeks. There would be roof-high drifts by morning if it kept up like this.

"What? Oh . . . well, shortening is butter or oleo, or even cooking oil, I think. It's for making cakes." Grandpa stepped down to the path shoveled toward the garage. It was already starting to fill in and would need some new digging out pretty soon.

"Why do they call it that? Why don't they just call it butter, or margarine?" Alan had already lost interest in the question, even as he asked it. The hypnotic effect of the snow was captivating him. "Do you get storms like this all the time, Grandpa?"

"'Bout once a month this bad." Grandpa reached the garage door, threw it up along its spring-loaded tracks. He shook his head and shivered from the wind-chill. "And to think that your mom and dad are cruising the Caribbean! Hard to believe, isn't it . . . ?"

"I'd rather be here," said Alan, shaking his head. He smiled, obviously immune to the shrieking cold and the missile-like flakes. "This is going to be the first real Christmas I ever had!"

"Why? Because it's a white one?" Grandpa chuckled as he walked to the door of the 4-wheel drive Scout and slowly climbed in.

"Sure," said Alan. "Haven't you ever heard that song?"

Grandpa smiled. "Oh, I think I've heard it a time or two . . . "

"Well, that's what I mean. It never seems like Christmas in L.A.—even when it *is* Christmas!" Alan jumped into the Scout and slammed the door. "Boy, Grandpa, it's really coming down, now . . . "

As his grandfather backed the vehicle from the garage, swung it around and churned down the long driveway toward

Route 14A, Alan looked out across the flat landscape of the farm and the other farms in the distance. There was a gentle roll to the treeless land, but was lost in the wall of the storm.

In fact, Alan could not tell where the snowy land stopped and the white of the sky began. When the Scout lurched forward out onto the main road, it looked like they were constantly driving smack into a white sheet of paper, a white nothingness.

It was scary, thought Alan. Just as scary as driving into a pitch-black night.

"Oh, she picked a fine time to run out of something for that danged cake! Look at it, Alan. It's a regular white-out, is what it is."

Alan nodded. "Jeezoowhiz, how do you know where you're going, Grandpa?" The first twinges of fear were getting into his mind now.

Grandpa harrumphed. "Been on this road a million times, boy! Lived here all my life! I'm not about to get lost. But my God, it's cold out here! Hope this heater gets going pretty soon . . ."

They drove on in silence except for the skrunch of the tires on the packed snow and thunk-thunk of the wiper blades trying to move off the hard new flakes that filled the sky. The heater still pumped chilly air into the cab and Alan's breath was almost freezing as it came out of his mouth.

He imagined that they were explorers on a faraway planet—an alien world of ice and eternally freezing winds. It was an instantaneous, catapulting adventure of the type only possible in the minds of imaginative ten-year-olds. There were creatures out in the blizzard—great white hulking things. Pale, reptilian, evil-eyed things. Alan squinted through the windshield, ready in his gun turret if one turned on them. He would blast it with his laser cannons . . .

"What in heck?" muttered Grandpa.

Abruptly, Alan was out of his fantasy world as he stared past the flicking windshield wipers. There was a dark shape standing in the center of the white nothingness. As the Scout advanced along the invisible road, drawing closer to the contrasted object, it became clearer, more distinct.

It was a man. He was standing by what must be the roadside, waving a gloved hand at Grandpa.

Braking easily, Grandpa stopped the Scout and reached across to unlock the door. The blizzard rushed in ahead of the stranger, slicing through Alan's clothes like a cold knife. "Where you headed?!" cried Grandpa over the wind. "I'm going as far as town . . ."

"That'll do," said the stranger.

Alan caught a quick glimpse of him as he pushed into the back seat. He was wearing a thin coat that seemed to hang on him like a scarecrow's rags. He had a black scarf wrapped tight around his neck and a dark blue ski mask that covered his face under a floppy-brimmed old hat. Alan didn't like that— not being able to see the stranger's face.

"Cold as hell out there!" said the man as he smacked his gloved hands together. He laughed to himself, then: "Now there's a funny expression for you, ain't it? 'Cold as hell.' Don't make much sense does it? But people still say it, don't they?"

"I guess they do," said Grandpa as he slipped the Scout into gear and started off again. Alan looked at the old man, who looked like an older version of his father, and thought he saw an expression of concern, if not apprehension, forming on the lined face.

"It's not so funny, though . . ." said the stranger, his voice lowering a bit. "Everybody figures hell to be this hot place, but it don't have to be, you know?"

"Never really thought about it much," said Grandpa, jiggling with the heater controls. It was so cold, it just didn't seem to want to work.

Alan shivered, uncertain whether or not it was from the lack of heat, or the words, the voice of the stranger.

"Matter of fact, it makes more sense to think of hell as full of all kinds of different pain. I mean, fire is so unimaginative, don't you think? Now, cold . . . something as cold as that wind out there could be just as bad, right?" The man in the back seat chuckled softly beneath the cover of the ski mask.

Grandpa cleared his throat and faked a cough. "I don't think I've really thought much about that either," he said as he appeared to be concentrating on the snow-covered road ahead. Alan looked at his grandfather's face and could see the unsteadiness in the old man's eyes. It was the look of fear, slowly building.

"Maybe you should . . ." said the stranger.

"Why?" said Alan. "What do you mean?"

"It stands to reason that a demon would be comfortable in any kind of element—as long as it's harsh, as long as it's cruel."

Alan tried to clear his throat and failed. Something was stuck down there, even when he swallowed.

The stranger chuckled again. "'Course, I'm getting off the track . . . we were talking about figures of speech, weren't we?"

"You're the one doing all the talking, mister," said Grandpa.

The stranger nodded. "Actually, a more appropriate expression would be 'cold as the grave'. . ."

"It's not this cold under the ground," said Alan defensively.

"Now, how would you know?" asked the stranger slowly. "You've never been in the grave . . . not yet, anyway."

"That's enough of that silly talk, mister!" said Grandpa. His voice was hard-sounding, but there was a thin layer of fear beneath his words.

Alan looked from his grandfather to the stranger. As his eyes locked in with those behind the ski mask, Alan felt a burst of acid in his gut, an ice pick in his spine.

There was no staring at the stranger. There was something about his eyes, something dark which seemed to lurch violently behind them.

A dark chuckle came from the back seat.

"Silly talk? Silly?" asked the stranger. "Now what's silly and what's serious in the world today? Who can tell anymore?! Missiles and terrorists! Vampires and garlic! Famine and epidemics! Full moons and maniacs!"

The words rattled out of the dark man and chilled Alan more deeply than the cold blast of the heater fan. He looked away and tried to stop the shiver which raced up and down his backbone.

"Where'd you say you was going, Mister?" asked Grandpa as he slowly eased off the gas pedal.

"I didn't say."

"Well, how about saying—right now."

"Do I detect hostility in your voice, sir? Or is it something else?" Again came the deep-throated, whispery chuckle.

Alan kept his gaze upon the white-on-white panorama ahead. But he was listening to every word being exchanged between the dark stranger and his grandfather, who was suddenly assuming the proportions of a champion. He listened but he could not turn around, he could not look back. There was a fear gripping him now. It was a gnarled spindly claw reaching up for him, out of the darkness of his mind, closing in on him with a terrible certainty.

Grandpa hit the brakes a little too hard, and even the 4-wheel drive of the Scout couldn't keep it from sliding off to the right to gently slap a bank of plowed snow. Alan watched his grandfather as he turned and stared at the stranger.

"Listen, Mister, I don't know what your game is, but I don't find it very amusing like you seem to . . . and I don't appreciate the way you've dealt with our hospitality."

Grandpa glared at the man in the back seat and Alan could feel the courage burning behind the old man's eyes. Just the sight of it gave Alan the strength to turn and face the stranger.

"Just trying to make conversation," said the man in a velvety soft voice. It seemed to Alan that the stranger's voice could change any time he wanted it to, could sound any way at all. The man in the mask was like a ventriloquist or a magician, maybe . . .

"Well, to be truthful with you, Mister," Grandpa was saying, "I'm kinda tired of your 'conversation,' and I'd like you to climb out of here so my grandson and I can be on our way in peace."

The eyes behind the mask flitted between Grandpa and Alan once, twice. "I see . . ." said the voice. "No more silly stuff, eh?"

The stranger leaned forward, putting a gloved hand on the back of Alan's seat. The hand almost touched Alan's parka and he pulled away. He knew he didn't want the stranger touching him. More acid churned in his stomach.

"Very well," said the dark man. "I'll be leaving you for now . . . but one last thought, all right?"

"I'd rather not," said Grandpa as the man squeezed out the open passenger's door.

"But you will . . . " Another soft laugh as the stranger stood in the drifted snow alongside the road. The eyes behind the mask darted from Grandpa to Alan and back again. "You see, it's just a short ride we're all taking . . . and the night . . . well, the night is freezing fast."

Grandpa's eyes widened a bit as the words drifted slowly into the cab, cutting through the swirling, whipping cold wind. Then he gunned the gas pedal and the engine raced. "That's enough of that crazy talk, Mister. Have a nice day!"

The Scout suddenly leaped forward in the snow with such force that Alan didn't have to pull the door closed—it slammed shut from the force of the acceleration.

Looking back, Alan could see the stranger quickly dwindle to nothing more than a black speck on the white wall behind them.

"Of all the people to be helpful to, and I have to pick a danged nut!" Grandpa forced a smile to his face. He looked at Alan and tapped his arm playfully. "Nothing to worry about now, boy. He's behind us and gone."

Alan nodded. "He was creepy, wasn't he?"

Grandpa grunted, kept looking at the snowed-up road.

"Who you figure he was?"

"Oh, just a nut, son. A kook. When you get older, you'll realize that there's lots of 'funny' people in the world. Some funnier than others."

"You think he'll still be out on the road when we go back?"

Grandpa looked at Alan and tried to smile. It was an effort and it didn't look anything at all like a real smile.

"You were afraid of him, weren't you boy?"

Alan nodded. "Weren't you?"

Grandpa didn't answer for an instant. He certainly looked scared. Then: "Well, kinda, I guess. But I've known about his type . . . almost been expecting him, you might say."

"Really?" Alan didn't understand what the old man meant.

Grandpa looked ahead. "Well, here's the store . . ."

He eased the Scout into the half-plowed parking lot of Brampton, Iowa's only full-scale shopping center. He ran into the Food-A-Rama for a pound of butter while Alan remained in the cab with the engine running, the heater fan wailing, and the doors locked. Looking out into the swirling snow, Alan could barely pick out single flakes anymore. Everything was blending into a furiously thick, white mist. The windows of the Scout were blank sheets of paper, he could see nothing beyond the glass.

Suddenly there was a dark shape at the driver's side, and the latch rattled on the door handle. The lock flipped up and Grandpa appeared with a small brown paper bag in his hand. "Boy, it's blowin' up terrible out here! What a time that woman has to send us out!"

"It looks worse," said Alan.

"Well, maybe not," said Grandpa, slipping the vehicle into gear. "Night's coming on. When it gets darker, the white-out won't be as bad."

They drove home along Route 28 which would eventually curve down and cross 14A. Alan fidgeted with the heater fan and the cab was finally starting to warm up a little bit.

"Grandpa, what did that man mean about 'a short ride' we're all taking? And the night freezing fast?"

"I don't rightly know what he meant, Alan. He was a kook, remember? He probably don't know himself what he meant by it."

"But you said you were kind of expecting him . . . "

"Oh, I was just thinking out loud. Didn't mean a thing." Grandpa pretended to be concentrating on the road.

"Well, he sure did make it sound scary, didn't he?"

"Yes, I guess he did," said Grandpa as he turned the wheel onto a crossing road. "Here we go, here's 14A. Almost home, boy! I hope your grandmother's got that woodstove hot!"

The Scout trundled along the snowed-up road until they reached a bright orange mailbox that marked the entrance to Grandpa's farm. Alan exhaled slowly, and felt the relief spreading into his bones. He hadn't wanted to say anything, but the white-white of the storm and the seeping cold had been bothering him, making him get a terrible headache, probably from squinting so much.

"What in—?" Grandpa eased off the accelerator as he saw the tall, thin figure standing in the snow-filled rut of the driveway.

"It's *him*, Grandpa . . ." said Alan in whisper.

The dark man stepped aside as the Scout eased up to him. Angrily, Grandpa wound down the window and let the storm rush into the cab. He shouted past the wind at the stranger. "You've got a lot of nerve coming up to my house!"

The eyes behind the ski mask seemed to grow darker, unblinking. "Didn't have much choice," said the chameleon-voice.

Grandpa unlocked the door and stepped out to face the man. "What do you mean by that?"

Soft laughter cut through the howl of the wind. "Come now! You know who I am . . . and why I'm here."

Suddenly Grandpa's face turned pale, his eyes became vacant and empty. He nodded his head quickly. "Yeah, I guess I do, but I never knew it to be like this . . ."

"There are countless ways," said the stranger, who was no longer unknown to the old man. "Now excuse me, and step aside . . ."

"What?!" Grandpa sounded shocked.

Alan didn't know what was going on, but he could detect the terror in his grandfather's throat, the trembling fear in his voice. Without realizing it, he was backing away from the Scout. His head was pounding like a jackhammer.

"Is it the woman?!" Grandpa was asking in a whisper.

The dark man shook his head.

Grandpa moaned loudly, letting it turn into words. "No! Not him! No, you can't mean it!"

"Aneurysm . . ." said the terribly soft voice behind the mask.

Suddenly Grandpa grabbed the stranger by the shoulder and spun him around, facing him squarely. "No!" he shouted, his face twisted and ugly. "Me! Take me!"

"Can't do it," said the man.

"Grandpa, what's the matter?!" Alan started to feel dizzy. The pounding in his head had become a raging fire. It hurt so bad he wanted to scream.

"Yes you can!" yelled Grandpa. "I know you can!"

Alan watched as Grandpa reached out and grabbed at the tall thin man's ski mask. It seemed to come apart as he touched it, and fell away from beneath the droopy brimmed hat. For an instant, Alan could see—or at least he thought he saw—nothing beneath the mask. It was just an eye-blink of time, and then he saw, for another instant, the white angular lines, the dark hollows of the empty sockets.

But the snow was swirling and whipping, and Grandpa was suddenly wrestling with the man. Alan screamed as the man wrapped his long thin arms around his grandfather and they seemed to dance briefly around in the snow.

"Run, boy!" screamed Grandpa.

Alan turned toward the house, then looked back and he saw Grandpa collapsing into the snow. The tall, dark man was gone.

"Grandpa!" Alan ran to the old man's side as he lay face up, his glazed eyes staring into the storm. "What happened, Grandpa! Oh Jeez . . . !"

"Get your grandmother . . . quick," said the old man. "It's my heart."

"Don't die, Grandpa . . . not now!" Alan was frantic and didn't know what to do. He wanted to get help, but he didn't want to leave his grandfather in the storm like this.

"No choice in it," he said. "A deal's a deal."

Alan looked at his grandfather, suddenly puzzled. "What?"

Grandpa winced as a new pain lanced his chest. "Don't matter now . . ." The old man closed his eyes and wheezed out a final breath.

Snowflakes danced across his face, mixing with the first tears, and Alan noticed that his headache, like the dark man, had vanished.

I used to go to a lot of conventions, especially back when I still thought I was a science fiction writer. For any of you who've never been to one, I should tell you the ones devoted to genre literature (sf, fantasy, horror, mystery, or romance) are usually held at big hotels in mid to large cities on just about any week-end of the year, and are populated by large groups of fans, fair representations of writers and artists, and a scattering of agents, editors, and other publishing/media types. In recent decades, many conventions have become celebrations of excess, brimming over into tangential interests other than books—such as board games, video games, television shows, films, costumery, and even music.

I used to enjoy them because it gave me a great excuse to travel and sample other cities in practically every state in the country; plus I really liked catching up with writer-friends I only saw at gatherings such as " the cons." I also liked the opportunity to pitch new book ideas to any editor willing to listen and party hard at the same time.

But there's only been one convention I have attended for close to twenty consecutive years that really means anything  to me—a little one held every summer in Rhode Island called NECON. It has the highest percentage of professionals in attendance of any convention I've ever experienced, and it is also the most unassuming, laid-back gathering of ultra-bright, incredibly clever, funny people you'll ever find. Elizabeth and I have more fun at NECON than any other professional function we ever attend.

And it was at one such NECON, back in the early Eighties that I met a young, resourceful, and very bright editor from New York named Peggy Nadramia. She had started her own magazine called Grue, and was doggedly producing it from her Hell's Kitchen apartment.

YESTERDAY'S CHILD

*She asked me if I could do a story for her and I had one currently making the rounds that hadn't sold yet. I figured, hey, it may not be the most deathless prose I'll ever type (based on the rejection slips it had thus far garnered . . .), so maybe I should send it off to Peggy because she wouldn't* dare *reject it, and the story needs a home.*

*So I sent it; she didn't reject it; and here it is . . .*

Scott Fusina sat in his living room, thinking of the best way to kill himself.

It was Saturday afternoon and his television blathered on about a classic shoot-out between USC and Notre Dame. Scott was considering a classic shoot-out too; between the side of his head and the little .22 caliber he kept in the drawer of his nighttable . . .

His thoughts rushed about madly, connected only by tenuous causes and effects. Trish, his wife, hated him, and was sleeping with another man. Deanna, his ten year-old daughter, also hated him because she believed he deserted her. And to complete the feminine conspiracy, his mother was totally disgusted with him, claiming that he was the prime cause of her angina.

Considering everything else, it was no surprise that his once-envied position as the top salesman at Providential Mutual Life was fading like the color in a cheap T-shirt. The thought of going out and hustling life insurance made him want to vomit. He just didn't give a damn about his job or anything else in his life, not even his friends—who were lately treating him like he had leprosy.

He had heard that your married friends avoided you when you were going through a particularly nasty separation or divorce, and it was true. They did it because they unconsciously feared that what was happening to you might be infectious, that it might happen to *them*. And so they stayed away.

Nothing seemed to be important any longer. Nothing mattered, and he wondered whether pills might be easier than a gun. The thought of actually holding that cold metal up to his head and pulling the trigger . . . his thoughts were interrupted by a knock at the door, and for a silly instant he fantasized it being his wife and child coming to ask him to come home.

Such foolish dreaming was quelled as he opened the door to discover a more-than-middle-aged woman stationed outside the entrance to his second-floor apartment. He could not speak, and simply stared at her.

"Hello," said the woman gingerly. "I'm Emma Dodson from the Sudbrook Park Neighborhood Association, and we would like to know if you would be interested in volunteering for our Block Watch Program."

"Your *what?*" Scott was barely listening to her.

"Just temporarily, of course. We need some extra people to watch the streets tonight while the children go trick-or-treating in the Park." That was what all the residents of the neighborhood called the little suburban enclave—"The Park." Its tree-shaded streets were lined with 30-room mansions of a century past, many divided into fashionable apartments like the one he'd recently taken.

"Tonight?" Scott seemed stunned by the revelation. "Is tonight Halloween?"

Emma Dodson smiled. "Yes, it is, young man. Slipped your mind, did it? I'll bet you even forgot to buy some goodies for the kids . . ."

"Oh . . . yes, I *did* forget . . ."

She looked at him quizzically, then brightened. "Aren't you Marion's boy?"

"Uh, yes, I am . . . do you know my mother?"

Emma smiled. "Oh yes. I remember her walking you around the Park in a stroller probably close to forty years ago. Time goes by, doesn't it?"

"Yes, I guess it does . . ." Scott was barely aware of talking to her. His mind seemed filled with important thoughts.

There was a moment of awkward silence before Emma pressed him again. Would he be interested in taking up a station on a nearby street corner to help ensure that no harm came to the children of Sudbrook Park?

He heard himself saying yes, as though listening to a conversation in a distant room, and Emma handed him a photocopied map of the neighborhood, using a pencil to mark off the place where he would be expected to stand between 6:00 and 8:00 p.m. that evening.

"You do have a flashlight, don't you?" asked Emma.

"Yes, I think so . . . in my car, I think."

She smiled, thanked him, and eased herself down the stairs to the sidewalk. Possession of a flashlight and having a mother who'd lived in Sudbrook Park was apparently enough of a qualification Scott was not a pervert or child molester, and good material for Trick-or-Treat Block Watching.

After a simple, microwave cooking-pouch dinner from Stouffer's, Scott prepared for his evening's responsibility. Actually, he was grateful for the assignment. It was helping to get his mind off his great problems, and as long as he felt as though he had something to do, suicide seemed like only a possibility, rather than a certainty. Not the most encouraging prognosis, he knew, but at least it was something, right?

Wearing jeans, a flannel shirt, and a light jacket, he looked younger than his forty-one years as he exited the apartment. Down the outside staircase on the side of the old house, he noted that it was already growing quite dark. His landlord, who lived on the first floor, had already turned on his porch light— a sign that trick-or-treaters would be welcome.

Scott did not need Emma Dodson's map; he knew Sudbrook Park intimately. Walking to his assigned corner, memories of his youth in this neighborhood slowly crept back to stand like a waif at the doorway to his mind. It was a quiet residential area with streets vaulted by 100-year old poplar, oak, and chestnut trees. The gnarled giants towered over the Park's Victorian houses, cloaking everything in the earthy colors of Autumn.

Autumn. His favorite time of the year.

Scott had been living in such a terrible depression for the last eight weeks that he had almost been oblivious to everything. So much so, the passing of the seasons had been like the footsteps of strangers beneath his windows.

But Autumn was no stranger to Scott. From his earliest years, he had loved it as a special time. A time when the blistering heat-death of summer finally faded, when the evenings seemed to linger, and the woods blazed with spectral color. When you could rake enough leaves into piles taller than your head, and smell them burning in someone's back yard; when there was mist at morning and fog at twilight; when the moon seemed somehow fuller and bigger as it sailed against the blue aisle of the night.

Arriving at his "post," Scott peered up and down the tree-choked lane. Across the intersection, a street lamp defined a small cone of light sharply edged by the darkness beyond. A memory flashed into his mind: riding his big red Schwinn bike down to this corner to intercept the Good Humor Man every night at about this time. Unlike so many people he'd known, he had enjoyed a happy childhood.

So how the hell did he grow up to be so miserable?

He had moved back to his old neighborhood after Trish threw him out because he felt the need to be in the midst of comfortable, familiar surroundings during such a traumatic chapter in his life. Thomas Wolfe had instructed us, in a long, long book, that you can't go home again, and Scott wondered how axiomatic that notion might be.

Dusk crept through the streets like a predator, stealing the color and shape from everything it passed. Darkness filled in all the missing spaces as the moon began to rise. Jack-o-lanterns glowed and grinned from front porches and picture windows, and as though on cue, he heard the advancing vanguards of the kids, ready to launch their raiding parties for a few pieces of candy.

Flicking on his flashlight, Scott announced his presence to any who approached, identifying himself as a symbol of safety to the children of the Park. He watched them shamble past him in ragged little groups, up one walk, down another, cutting across lawns and almost crowding each other off some of the small front porches and landings. The cool night teemed with their unique sounds: rustling paper bags, rapid footsteps, and endless cries of "trick-or-treat!"

The pageantry of the evening made Scott think of his own childhood, and how Halloween had always been so grand to him. He remembered how he'd loved to create a new costume each year, and how he'd started planning it by the end of August, usually. A pirate, a space man (they didn't call them "astronauts" back then), a mummy, a cowboy, a robot . . . he had been a succession of cinematically-inspired images, but every one of them handmade with love and care.

Things were different now, he could see.

Almost all of the kids paraded past him in cheap ready-made costumes that you could find in any K-Mart and Woolworth during the month of October. Made from the flimsiest synthetic materials, they were usually just black coveralls with some Saturday morning cartoon character's picture appliqued across the chest. The accompanying mask was usually a one-dimensional, micron-thin shell of plastic with florescent paint hastily applied. Any connection between these "costumes" and something creative was purely accidental, and wholly unlikely.

But worst of all, the costumes weren't scary.

Scott smiled as two little kids passed him, one dressed as a woman named "Xena," the other a skeleton. The former, judging from the breast-plate-picture, was a shameless rip-off of Robert E. Howard, while the latter's chest resembled an illustration page from an anatomy text.

Whatever happened to those neat old skeleton suits with the bones painted down the arms and legs, front and back, and the rubber masks that covered your whole head so that you *really looked* like a skeleton? Whatever happened to wigs and greasepaint, and rags and old clothes?

These thoughts soughed through him like a breeze, long and warm and slow. He noticed the moon was high in the trees now. It still appeared to be a bloated sphere of pale harvest-orange, but it would be casting off the color as it continued its journey skyward. Memories reached out for him like opened window curtains touched by the nightwind. The smells and sounds of the evening seduced him, carrying him into the mist of a time long ago, but not forgotten. He found himself longing for the innocence and the industry of childhood, forgetting the fears and terrors that nightly accompany most kids to their beds. At this point in his life, for Scott Fusina, being twelve years old again seemed like a great idea.

He smiled at the notion as he detected movement in his peripheral vision. A flash of dull whiteness, kiting through the darkness like a windblown piece of paper. Turning quickly, he spun about to see . . . nothing.

Nothing there.

But I'd have *sworn* there was . . .

For some reason, the experience made him edgy, and more than slightly paranoid. He scanned the darkness beyond his post, beyond the pale zone of the street lamp, but saw nothing. He could hear the laughter of trick-or-treaters on the next street over, but his own territory was desolate and quiet.

Again, the night breeze reached out to him with a long, slow touch. There was a warmth in the air, like the breath of an unseen creature, and it smelled of crisping leaves and carved-out pumpkins. Turning his head, Scott looked up the street.

That's when he saw the figure step from the shadows. It moved with a dark grace, as though materializing from the essence of the night. Although the sudden appearance startled him, he could see by the small stature of the figure it was just a kid in a costume. Scott started to relax.

But he could see that this was no ordinary costume. A K-Mart special this was not. No, he thought as he watched the figure stride closer, there was a unique look to this costume . . . a *familiar* look.

The figure was dressed in the red and white regalia of a British Revolutionary War soldier, complete in most details from the brass buttons to the muslin-wrapped boots. He wore a full-flowing riding cape, which fell gracefully away from his broad shoulders.

But above the shoulders there was . . . nothing.

Scott smiled as he watched the Headless Horseman approach. True to Washington Irving's tale, the figure carried a brilliant jack-o-lantern under his arm—a surrogate head in search of his real one.

It was a beautiful costume—as good as the one Scott had created when he was ten years old . . . just like *this* one.

The Headless Horseman stopped perhaps ten feet distant, half-embraced by the shadows.

*Just like this one.* The thought echoed through his head as Scott studied the work of the costume. Wasn't that red jacket the same one he'd found in Aunt Maude's trunk? And wasn't that cape the one he'd made from one of his mother's tablecloths?

A chill passed through him like a point of cold steel. The Headless Horseman stood before him, silent and somehow defiant.

"Who *are* you?" asked Scott, his voice croaked.

A pause. Then, from within the depths of the costume: "You *know* who I am . . ."

"Do I?" Scott had a terrible urge for a cigarette, wishing for an instant that he'd never given them up.

The costumed figure placed the jack-o-lantern on the sidewalk, and with a few quick, practiced moves, unfastened the breast buttons of his jacket. The false chest and shoulders fell away to reveal the thin, angular face of a pre-adolescent boy. Dark hair fell across even darker eyes, which gazed at Scott with strength of the years which bound them together.

"This is impossible . . . " said Scott weakly.

"Perhaps," said the boy, shrugging artfully. "But that doesn't matter now, does it?"

"But *how* . . . ?" Scott still protested with shocked confusion.

The boy tilted his head. "Don't know. But look, here we are. Let's just accept it for what it is. . . it simply *is*."

"Oh man, this is crazy . . . I must be nuts!"

"Not yet, but you're on your way," said the boy.

"What're you doing here?" asked Scott. "How can this be?"

"This night always is, and I am always here . . ."

"What do you want with me?  Why are you doing this to me?"

"For starters, you're doing this to yourself. To *both* of us." The boy almost grinned. "You were missing me, calling out for me . . ."

"No I wasn't," said Scott. "This is crazy!"

"Maybe I should start with a few questions."

Scott laughed. "You sound like a cop!"

"What happened, Scott?  What happened to all the dreams we had?"

"I don't know . . . gone, I guess."

"Dreams are never really gone . . . they just change their names to things like 'crazy ideas' or maybe 'regrets'."

"Maybe you're right . . ."

Scott nodded as he remembered being ten years old and dreaming of being an architect, and how he built miniature houses out of balsa wood in his basement workshop. In that instant, he recalled so many things. They flashed through his memory like cards thumbed through a deck: the first guitar he bought for ten bucks, his collection of E.C. horror comics, his Gilbert chemistry set, the microscope, the motorbike he tried to make from the old lawnmower, and so many other projects conceived out of boundless energy . . .

"Do you remember when you made the mummy costume? How it started to unravel in the big parade, and how you wouldn't give up trying to 'fix it,' right up until it was too late?"

"Right up until I reached the judges stand with only a few strips left . . ."

Scott smiled at the memory. He hadn't thought about it in thirty years. "Yeah . . . and what about the tree house I built out in Smith's woods . . . ?"

The boy nodded solemnly. "Or the jungle riverboat, or the soapbox racer . . . it was all great stuff, always *will* be great stuff. We had something *special*, remember? And somewhere along the way, you've let it get away from you . . ."

"You wouldn't understand . . . it's different when you grow up. You have to have responsibility. . ."

"Yeah, sure . . . I know all about it: credit cards and mortgages and that kind of stuff." The boy paused, then stared deeply into him. "Listen, do you really like selling life insurance?"

"No, I hate it. I've *always* hated it."

"Then why do you do it?"

"It's a good way to make a lot of money, I guess."

The boy snorted. "*Nobody* grows up dreaming to be an insurance salesman."

Scott nodded. "I've always hated it."

"And maybe yourself too? For doing it?"

Looking up at the boy, Scott nodded. "Well, maybe . . ."

"Then I'd say it's time to quit, wouldn't you?"

"Yeah, maybe . . ."

"And what about this Trish? Do you really still love her? Did you ever?"

"I . . . I don't think so. It was all a mistake—a mistake I never wanted to admit." Scott looked down at his shoes, feeling very embarrassed.

"So admit it *now*. Really, is all this kind of stuff worth killing yourself for?"

Scott shook his head. "No, I guess not."

"Don't try to live for *any* of them," said the boy.

"What?"

"Haven't you learned yet—the world doesn't like dreamers?"

"What?" asked Scott.

"Most people don't want us seeing things differently than them. It's too uncomfortable, too scary."

"Man, you are right about that!" said Scott, starting to feel better.

"That's why you can *never* try to please them."

Scott nodded. "So young to be so wise . . ."

"I'm as old as you."

Scott smiled ironically. "Yes, I guess you are."

The boy hunched down and picked up his jack-o-lantern. "Listen, I gotta go now."

"So soon? We just got started."

"No, I think we're okay now."

The boy turned, began walking off into the shadows. Scott watched him move with an easy grace, a confident stride. It was an infectious kind of swagger.

"Hey!" called Scott, just as the figure reached the outer zone of the street lamp's glow. "Wait a second!"

Turning, the boy looked at him. "Yes?"

"I just wanted to tell you how much I liked your costume. Nice job. Really beautiful."

The boy smiled. "Thanks. But wait till you see the one I've got planned for next year . . ."

"You're right," said Scott. "I remember it . . . it was the best of them all!"

*Confession time: I sent Peggy Nadramia that last story before I actually read her magazine—yeah, I know, a real* faux pas. *And the sin was compounded when I realized I would have never sent her a quasi-sappy, still-got-that-Ray-Bradbury-jones kind of story you just read.[1]*

*No,* Grue *was not about pleasant nostalgia and inspirational messaging. It was grim and dark and relentless. And after spending some real time with the 'zine, I liked its . . .* starkness *. . . both style and artwork, and also its fiction. At a following NECON, I told Peggy I'd like to do another story for her, if she'd have me, and this time I'd try to make it harsh and weird and hard-edged so it would feel right at home in* Grue.

*So I checked this file I keep on the laptop (it used to be a little tin box of index cards, but Luddite I am not . . .) called "Ideas," which contained lots of lines or phrases that I key in whenever an idea or a scene or an image or character comes to mind that might someday make a good short story. When I was younger[2], I used to get these great ideas and they would stay with me till I actually wrote the story, but as I grew a little*

---

[1] *Actually, it turned out to be a decent enough theme, which was ripped off in a Bruce Willis movie many years later called* The Kid. *But now you know, friends, I was there first.*

[2] *There was something else that happened a few times when I was younger and would have a typically great idea for a story . . . I would get this cool idea and I would* tell *it to somebody (usually another writer or a friend) and then this totally weird thing would happen:* I would never write the story. *At first I wasn't sure what was going on, but I soon realized if I let the story out of its mind cage, it was simply* gone. *I didn't feel the drive, the* need *to actually write it down. It had been told in some fashion and that was, apparently, enough for my subconscious. So I knew from then on, I could never even* talk *about an idea for a story until after I'd written it.*

*longer in the tooth, I started to realize I was actually* forgetting *some of these brilliant ideas, and if I didn't start writing them down, I would be depriving the world of some of its greatest writings—mine.*

*So, moving right along, I look down my list of ideas and I see a line that says:* highway, guy just stays there . . .

*It's mental shorthand to myself, but I remember what I was talking about, and I start typing. Hours later, this is what printed out . . .*

Another one was coming up behind him—the one, he knew, to finally get him.

Looking in the rear-view mirror, John Sheridan watched the headlights of the car approach his position on the Interstate. There were no other cars in sight. Even though he was doing sixty-five—the most he dared in drizzling rain and ghost-tread tires which should have been replaced months ago—the lights were gaining on him. Homing in like a missile or a sparrow-hawk.

He white-knuckled the steering wheel with both hands as the dark, rain-flecked vehicle pulled abreast of him in the left lane. It seemed to hang motionless for a moment, keeping pace with John. Sensing its dark presence, he wanted to turn, to look at it, but could not. It was as though his neck had become paralyzed. He tensed for the killing blow . . .

Now!

But suddenly the other car was moving off, punching a hole in the misty rain, marking its path with a smear of red taillight.

John sagged behind the wheel, and was suddenly aware of his pulse thudding behind his ears, his breath rasping in and out, between clenched teeth. The whole fear-fantasy of someone creeping up on you on the highway and blowing you away was not an isolated nightmare. John had mentioned it to strangers in bars over lonely beers, and many had admitted to the same crazy fear. A couple of the weirder-looking guys had even said they imagined themselves, at different times, as both victim and predator. John knew what they meant—he'd imagined it too. Even though sometimes he thought he might be going goddamned crazy.

A lot of road-time could make you like that.

The wispy rain appeared to be easing off, and he angrily cut off the windshield wipers as he remembered the gun. The panic had throttled him, choked off all clear thinking, and he had forgotten he now carried something for the predatory sedan if it ever caught up with him—and he had a preternatural feeling that it would eventually catch up with him.

But there was no sense in punishing himself. He would simply be ready the next time. The highway ahead and behind him was empty and dark, like the flat and wetly shining hide of a giant eel. John found it comforting. He licked his lips, reached for a cigarette, lighted it.

Once again, death had slipped up beside him, but had passed him by. He felt the terror slip away from him as he accelerated and pushed towards Woodbridge and home. It was past four a.m. and he was glad the road was clear, even if just for the moment. He sometimes wondered how long he could hang on, being on the road so much. All this driving was making him more than a little crazy.

But like they said: if you want to make a lot of money, and you can't be a doctor or a dentist, then be a salesman.

And John was a hell of a salesman, that was for certain. At thirty-six, he was easily the best pipe-hawker Bendler & Krauch Plumbing Supply ever had. John's territory comprised of Delaware, Maryland, and Virginia, and he'd posted more plumbing fixture accounts with more clients in that territory than any other sales-route in the country.

His secret was simple: stay on the road. The more you traveled and talked to possible clients, the more you sold. Of course the guys in the office with families just couldn't stay out on the road for two, three weeks at a time the way John did. But what did he care if he didn't see his tacky little apartment in Suburban Virginia? He had nobody in his life, parents both dead, and not even a pet to worry about. Besides, if he kept it up at his present pace, by the end of the year he would have earned more than a hundred and fifty grand. Not bad for a guy with a degree in Cultural Anthropology.

The thought of the annual income made him smile, despite his nervousness. He took a final drag off the Marlboro and pushed it out the window into the slipstream. In doing so, he glimpsed a flash of light in the side-view mirror.

Even though the roads were still slick-lethal, he pushed down on the accelerator and his Chrysler New Yorker surged forward. Despite this, the headlights grew larger and more distinct, filling the rear-view mirror. The oncoming vehicle slipped out into the left lane of the Interstate, getting ready to pull alongside.

His hands grew moist, his heartbeat jumped up towards the fibrillation end of the scale. The glare of the other car's lights filled the rear-view mirror, a white, cool explosion of light reflected into John's face.

This was the one. The marrow in his bones sang out with conviction.

The other car's tires were keening in the rain, whirling at high-speed, sucking up the wet asphalt, almost hydro-planing. It became a roar, a scream in his left ear as he heard it, pulling abreast of him. His New Yorker was starting to drift back and forth across the right lane, losing traction, and still he pushed his speed higher.

But the other car continued to accelerate, gaining, overtaking him in the night, wanting only to keep pace for a single, final instant.

*No!*

The single word bounced around in an empty room in his mind.

The car was in the blind spot of his side-mirror. In another moment it would be next to him.

John Sheridan knew that he must turn his head to the left. Maybe then it would be all right . . . .

The idea that looking at the other car, actually looking into its dark glass, might end the craziness was appealing to him. For months now, he had been too terrified to even think of it, but suddenly, it seemed like the only solution.

To look over and see a normal human being would be all the proof, all the cure, he would require.

And so, as the dark shape pulled abreast of him, seeming to hang motionless for an instant, he recalled how all the craziness had started. John turned to regard the vehicle in the fast lane . . . .

. . . . he had been driving back from a 10-day selling spree through Western Maryland. The hour was late and the traffic on Interstate 270 heading south from Frederick was practically non-existent. He had purchased the New Yorker, and despite his endless smoking the *new* smell of the interior had not yet worn away. The in-dash stereo was blowing some electronic music by a Japanese guy named Kitaro, and John was leaning back, enjoying the powerful, gliding ride of the big Chrysler as he cruised the fast lane.

As he cleared a slight rise in the highway he was abruptly aware of a vehicle ahead on his right in the slower lane. Squinting out into the night, he could see a big, heavy car—a shapeless hulk, slicing through the darkness. John pushed down on the accelerator, moved to slip past the other vehicle. But as he pulled alongside, the other driver jammed on his brakes, slipped back in behind him in a crazy, erratic piece of driving. John thought nothing of this as he returned his gaze to the road ahead. And then the other car was pulling out on the left, jumping onto the shoulder and moving abreast of him.

As this happened, John felt the eyes of something staring at him. The skin on the back of his neck seemed to ripple as a coldness entered him. It was a very bad feeling—the empty bore of unknown eyes looking at you, through you.

The other car was still there, pacing him along the shoulder like a predatory beast. Without thinking, John looked over and saw that the other car's window was down, and that out of the darkness within, there came a black cylinder, pointed at him.

In that instant, he recognized it as the business-end of a gun barrel. It seemed to grow larger in his mind's eye—until it was like staring down the mouth of a bottomless well.

He may have screamed at that point, he could not remember, but suddenly the New Yorker was swerving sharply to the left. His tires definitely screamed and the heavy sedan lurched dangerously close to the car on the left, which had also swerved to avoid him. As John fought with the wheel to gain control, the other car accelerated and raced ahead into the darkness.

He was left breathless as his body thumped with the shock of adrenaline, which now ebbed out of his bloodstream. The crazy bastard had tried to *kill* him!

He couldn't believe it even as he watched the other car's taillights dwindle to tiny red specks on the horizon ahead. And yet it was true. John didn't know what to do first. Should he chase the guy down? Stop and call the police?

He realized that he hadn't caught a license number. In fact, had not even seen the guy's face—the end of the gun had seemed so big to obscure all else. The thought of pursuing the other car was not appealing. He didn't want to think about what he might do if he actually caught up with him. Better to just get it together, pull off at the next exit where there might be a phone, and report the incident to the State Police.

He drove on for another few minutes, gathering his thoughts and his composure. No other cars passed him. It was very late and few vehicles were still out on a weeknight. In the distance, on the shoulder of the Interstate, he could see the blood-red glow of taillights.

Cautiously, he eased off on the gas and approached the other car. As he drew closer, he could see from the configuration of the lights that this vehicle had not been the one which had attacked him. This car was sluiced off the road at a bad angle, had cleared the shoulder, and was tilted up onto a grassy bank.

An accident, maybe. He pulled in behind the other car and stopped, studying it for a moment in the wash of his headlights. He couldn't see anyone in the car, and he wondered if they had left the car to go for help. A crazy thing to do, especially if they had left all their lights on.

Leaving his own lights on, John left the car and walked slowly to the derelict. For some reason, he felt defenseless and naked in the cold play of his own headlights. With each step forward, he felt worse about the entire scene. Something was wrong here. The feeling hung over everything like a foul odor; you couldn't miss it. And as John approached the driver's side, he saw the bullet-hole in the side window, and the fear-thought not allowed now capered madly through his mind.

Through the fractured glass, he could see a body, a formless shape lying on the front seat. Fighting back the panic, he reached for the door handle and depressed the latch. He didn't want to see what awaited him, but he had no choice. As the door swung open, he heard a woman's voice moaning in pain, trying to speak.

When he leaned in to pull her up into his arms, he saw that she was a young woman in her twenties. He could also see the blood on her cheeks, and the hole in her skull where her eye had been. (He would later learn from the doctors that the bullet had entered her left eye, and in one of those crazy, life-saving quirks of fate, had exited through the sinus cavity under her right eye without damaging the brain.) The visual effect was so unnerving, so unreal; she looked like she wore a cheap mask.

He carried the victim to his car, and drove her to the nearest hospital where they saved her life, but not her eye. Her description of her attacker was as vague and yet as similar as John's, and he knew that the bastard would not be found, would not be caught.

And that meant that he was still out there somewhere, running the highways, ready to try again. As time passed, the incident did not grow less vivid in his mind, but more so. When he could sleep, his dreams were filled with visions of the dark his sedan. When awake, he could not get the single obsessive thought from mind—that the driver would eventually find him, and complete the job unfinished . . .

. . . John Sheridan peered through the dark glass of the other car, and for an instant saw his own reflection, which masked the face of the driver. But that no longer mattered.

It was *him*. He could feel a reptilian chill in his certainty of this.

93

And this time, there would be no panic. This time John was prepared, and in a long-planned maneuver, he jammed on his brakes for an instant. The effect was startling, as the car on the left seemed to hurtle forward.

Cutting the wheel hard, John slipped in behind the predator, tail-gating him crazily. The driver of the other car seemed confused with the sudden turn of events. John kept his New Yorker close behind the sedan as it weaved from side to side in the fast lane. Reaching beneath the driver's seat, John pulled out the .38 caliber special he had purchased in the sporting goods store in Springfield.

Now the sonofabitch would know what it felt like . . .

He cut the wheel to the left and slipped his heavy car onto the shoulder, to the left of the fast lane. His worn tires whistled and scritched as they purchased on the loose gravel, but he accelerated anyway. A touch of his finger lowered his right window and the howling dampness of the night leaped in.

Lurching crazily, the New Yorker raced along the shoulder, gaining on the dark sedan, pulling alongside with an inexorable movement. The other car could not escape now. Looking over, John picked up the gun and sighted along its short length. The car in the fast lane was drifting into view through the open passenger's window.

The night rushed by, the windstream ripping and tearing at him. His forward speed was close to ninety as he kept the pace, and suddenly he was abreast of the predator. Forgetting about the road ahead, he looked to the right, aimed the gun.

Through the dark glass, he could see the vague shape of a face in profile, looking straight ahead. As the two cars plunged into the night, side by side, he waited and watched until the face turned to look at him. He wanted the bastard to stare down the bottomless well of the gun barrel. And then, as if on cue, the other driver turned—

—and John Sheridan faced *himself.*

It was a single slice of time, a solitary instant that exploded like a photographic flash in his mind. Impossibly, John stared at his other self, his *doppelganger* in the other car. And in that strobe light of recognition, he felt the acid burn of *deja vu* as the other car swerved dangerously close to him.

Things happened quickly then. He grabbed the wheel tightly, crushed down the accelerator, and jumped back into the fast lane as he tore quickly away from the other car. He was confused now, but he kept thinking about how easy it would have been to have pulled the trigger.

He continued at high speed until he advanced upon another car in the right lane. It was a woman, alone, looking straight ahead. Slowing, he pulled alongside, raised the gun, and waited for her to turn her face . . . so he could look her in the eye.

*As with most of the tales in this volume, the origin of the next one has an interesting history. It started the same way many do: an editor called me who was doing an anthology of original stories and asked me—being one of most Usual of Suspects—to contribute a story. This time, the editor was Kristine Kathryn Rusch, and the book was to be called the singularly unbeguiling name of* Pulphouse, *and would not be a "theme" anthology, which meant I could write my story about anything I wanted.*

*Okay, cool, I thought . . . so ah,* what *am I going to write about?*

*So I check my list of ideas, and I see a note that says:* Mike's strange date. *More mental shorthand, this one intended to jolt my memory of a real-life event that happened to an old pal of mine named Mike M. The true incident was one of those things so . . . odd that I had never been able to get it out of my mind. It was one of those things I'd always felt had the makings of a truly bizarre tale and that's exactly what I eventually wrote.*

*But wait, there's more!*

*We must climb into my Time Machine and jump ahead about 8 months—after I'd sent the story to Kris Rusch and she accepted it, and it finally appeared in print. It was the first volume of the* Pulphouse *anthology series, and as I looked over the book and read the stories therein, several thoughts arose primary. One, it got my vote as the Most Ugly Tome I'd ever seen. The print was so muddy, it looked like photocopy from a Xerox machine knock-off from Azerbaijan; the pages were bound in the cheesiest line of what they call "pleather;" and the overall effect was the quality of those Gideon bibles we've all found in our hotel nightstands. But Secondly, as I read the stories I noticed a disproportionate number of them were written for, or at least played to, a* very *specific theme: the usual and now-very-familiar feminist credo:* I am woman, hear me roar.

NOBODY'S PERFECT

*I groaned loudly and resisted a sudden urge to throw the book across the room.*

*Not because the stories were badly written (most of them were quite well crafted, actually), but for a far more personal, ego-driven (and therefore* more important*) reason. You see, my story, "Nobody's Perfect," just* happened *to have a female protagonist, and with a little psycho-socio-shoehorning, some readers could force it into the feminist-mold.*

*And why is that so bad? you might ask . . . ?*

*Because I have spent almost thirty years of writing in strict avoidance-mode of any fiction that smacked of sucking-up to whatever was the latest trend, social conformity, or politically correct bullshit. Because I don't think I have ever couched a social diatribe or supra-moral tract in the guise of fiction. If I have a socio-political statement to make, I prefer to just toss it into a column[1] and as they say in my family:* fuggheddabouddit. *I guess I didn't like the idea that people would read my story in* Pulphouse Volume 1 *and think I was pandering to what was obviously (to me, anyway) an editorial bias, hot-button, hobby-horse, or whatever you want to call it, because I basically HATE that kind of bullshit in fiction.*

*Yeah, that's it. "Nobody's Perfect" was not written with any political ax a-grinding in the background. I'd rather have my fingernails yanked off with a pair of needle-nosed Craftsman pliers than have to cop to* that *nonsense. It was basically a fictional exploration and jump-off point based on what happened to my friend when his date opened the door to greet him. And need I add: he was nothing like the character named Salazar, okay?*

---

[1] *I've been writing it for more than 25 years and its called* The Mothers And Fathers Italian Association, *and it contains some of my most brilliant, outrageous, and downright funny non-fiction I've ever done. It has been running in* Cemetery Dance *magazine for around ten years now, and if you've never read it, go grab a copy of the magazine and do yourself a big favor. As they say in the commercials: you'll be glad you did!*

Lydia thought she might be able to like this guy. He seemed different from all the others. There was something mysterious about him, something exotic, and her intuition told her to expect an interesting evening.

❖

Salazar noticed her . . . aberration as he sat in her living room, watching her. She stood in the kitchen struggling to open the twist-off cap of a Michelob bottle.

He smiled just slightly. Odd he had not observed the deficiency previously . . .

Not that it mattered much, if at all. If anything, it somewhat intrigued him. He would still dispose of Lydia like all the others, and he was confident that her meat would steam with exquisite flavor.

Salazar allowed himself a small, anticipatory smile. He was not certain what excited him the most, what provided him with the most pleasure—the initial search for suitable prey, the stalking-time when one had been selected, or the final act of consummation? There was a grandness about it all which inspired him, drove him with a fervor that religious zealots would envy.

The ritual was so wonderful, and the meat always so utterly tasty . . .

. . . It had been a Saturday two weeks earlier when Salazar fixed upon *The City Paper's* classifieds ad for volunteers. He had been scanning the "Personals," which had proved to be a good place to find prey—although he had been careful not to establish any patterns which the police might notice—when his eye drifted down to the "Help Wanteds" and read:

VOLUNTEERS needed to read and record literature.
Books For The Blind. For details call 344-8899

For some reason, he re-read the listing, and a familiar wave of heat rippled his body, exciting him in an almost sexual way. In that single instant he knew the Fates were reaching out to him, directing him to his next mission.

This would be perfect, he thought with a thoughtful nod of the head. Visions of young, single women—most of them probably single, unattached, and bookish—burned in him. Young women with time on their hands. Soulful and naive do-gooders. Yes. This set-up would be perfect.

He called the number and was given an address downtown near the bohemian section of the city. It was a waterfront neighborhood which had recently enjoyed a renaissance in the form of countless new bars with catchy off-beat names, art galleries, little theatres, antique shops, and several alfresco restaurants. Yes, Books For The Blind was open on Saturdays, and yes, they would be glad to have him come down for an audition.

It was not unusual for Lydia to spend her Saturday doing volunteer work. She found it a pleasant change of pace from her week-day position as a Systems Analyst for Westinghouse, and since she liked to read anyway, the Books For The Blind situation seemed ideal. The day had turned out to be bright and crisp, suggesting better weather still ahead.

As Lydia walked through the quaint, neighborhood of Fells Point, she did not, as she often did, let herself dwell upon all the pain in the world, all the discomfort and sadness, the injustice and the plainly cruel. Sometimes, when she reflected upon the daily horror in the world, it affected her physically as well as mentally—tiny needles of pain would tingle up the right side of her body, as if a precursor to a special kind of heart failure. Throughout her young life, she had probably absorbed more than her share of the world's pain, but it had left her undaunted, making her even stronger and more positive in the long run.

"You'll do just fine," said Mr. Hawthorne, a reed-thin nobly-balding gentleman, who looked to be in his late fifties. He sat opposite a folding table, wearing headphones which were connected to an ancient, boxy, reel-to-reel recorder.

"That is wonderful," said Salazar. "When do I start?"

Hawthorne looked at his watch. "If you can wait until four or so this afternoon, we're going to have an orientation class for all the volunteers we've selected today."

"That would be fine."

"Very good. You'll be getting a schedule for when you can come in at night and read into one of our recorders. We want to make sure everyone knows how to operate them properly." Mr. Hawthorne smiled primly. "Plus, you'll need to know a few basics about how to handle mistakes—so that when the tapes are edited, they will sound as smooth as possible."

"So it will not be necessary to take the machines home with us?" said Salazar.

"No, they're a bit too bulky to be very portable, I'm afraid. If we could get a larger budget, we would like to buy some new equipment, but . . ."

"I see." Salazar did not want his evenings tied up with such obligations. The thought touched him that perhaps this had been a bad idea after all.

"Is there something wrong?" asked Hawthorne. "Didn't I tell you the hours?"

"No."

"Sorry about that. Does your work schedule conflict? Do you work in the evenings?"

"No, not really," said Salazar. "It is just that I am often very busy at night."

"Well, perhaps you'd like to try it for a while and see how it's working out." Hawthorne smiled a weak, thin-lipped smile. "If it sounds like I'm cajoling you, I am. You see, we don't get that many men to volunteer for this kind of work."

"Really?" His waning interest in the project sparked and crackled.

"That's right," said Hawthorne with a smile that tried to be sly. "Lots of young women, though."

Lots of young women.

"It will be no problem. I will return at four."

Passing the audition proved easy for Lydia. She'd always enjoyed theater, and had also done a little singing. Everyone told her she had a pleasant voice, a good voice. She entered the orientation room and took a seat in front of one of the old tape recorders which had been carefully arranged on long tables. Other volunteers were already seated and others slowly drifted in. There was nothing to do but wait for things to get started.

He passed some time by walking around the neighborhood, in and out of some of the art and photography galleries, which he loathed. To see the garbage which passed for true art these days ignited within him a burning anger of righteousness. He wallowed in the ferocity of his outrage, drawing strength and resolve from it. The decadence of art was only one of many signs pointing to the coming Apocalypse. Such signs, and he saw them everywhere, beautifully reinforced his own special preparations for survival. For March, the weather was surprisingly mild and many people herded along the sidewalks, pretending to be enjoying themselves. He looked closely at many of the couples, immediately despising the males and thinking his usual thoughts about the females.

Despite the intoxicating surges of rage which powered him as he walked the streets, he did not actually prefer being out among the mortals for long periods of time. He felt far more comfortable, more secure in the relative solitude of the Post Office, where he operated his mail sorting machines with mind-numbing efficiency, where he need not speak to anyone other than himself, where he could concentrate on his special thoughts without distraction or interruption. And of course, nothing matched the solitude of his fortress-like rowhouse in one of the city's forgotten neighborhoods. Like a great womb, the old house encapsulated and protected him. It was the place where he'd been born, had lived his entire life, even after his mother died. It was the place where he believed he would achieve his immortality.

Growing tired of the sidewalks and the galleries and still having almost an hour to kill, he drifted into one of the trendy bars where they served sushi and many foreign ales and beers.

The dark interior was more suitable to his mood, even though he found it somewhat crowded as he straddled a stool. He did not like crowded places.

Sipping upon a seltzer and lime, he glanced around the bar to see several young women, and some who were not-so-young, studying him as well. This did not surprise or excite him, however. His Mediterranean face was softly featured, naturally handsome. His liquid, puppy-dog eyes and warm, resonant voice attracted women. His delicate manner of speaking, the way he carefully pronounced all his words without contractions, charmed most females.

But Salazar ignored them because he knew better than to be seen associating with any of them in public. It was too easy to be seen, to be witnessed and thereby connected.

No. He had his own methods. Methods proved successful over many years.

He arrived at the volunteer center a few minutes late and the receptionist ushered him into a large room filled with long tables and many people sitting at them. Mr. Hawthorne was already droning on about how to operate the recorders as Salazar moved quickly to the closest open chair. Taking a seat in the second row, he looked with great disinterest at the old Webcor which squatted in front of him.

A growing excitement smoldered in him like early bursts of heat from a pile of oily rags. He loved the overall somatic control he conjured up at such times. All his senses operated at the brink of overload; he never felt so incredibly alive as when he plunged into a new hunt. Salazar absorbed the scent of the woman to his right—a faint blend of Halston perfume and natural perspiration. It was a natural pheromone to him. His peripheral vision recorded a splash of blonde hair, small movements of her left arm. Stealing a quick glance to his right, he was rewarded with a stunning vision.

Instantly he knew that it was not mere chance which had placed him next to a very special prey. Truly the Fates did conspire to help him, a belief he often pondered. The young woman to his right possessed not the glitz of a Cosmo cover-girl nor the sexual artifice of a Playmate . . . just a natural grace, an innocence which seemed to radiate from her soul like a beacon. In an instant, he had mentally photographed her.

Sea-green eyes, long lashes. High cheekbones, and sculpted facial planes. Pert nose and streamlined lips with just the hint of fullness. Strawberry blonde hair, long and full. It was rare indeed that he found one so perfect.

She wore a loose, baggy lavender sweater with macrame laces up the front. It was not something designed to be sexy or revealing. But the way she leaned forward over the table, enabling her to inspect some facet of the recorder's controls, gave him a perfect view of her breasts.

More perfection. Full and upthrusting, but not actually large or pendulous. Delightfully pink aureoles, fully defined, as though swollen, protruding from the rest of the breast. The nipples themselves, while semi-erect, were not thick or obtrusive.

Hawthorne's voice had deteriorated to something less than the idiot-hum between radio stations. Salazar flirted with the state of total rapture.

"Hi!"

The utter cheeriness of the soft voice was like a slap in his face. Stunned, Salazar looked up to the beautiful woman smiling at him. Her age could have been anywhere between eighteen and thirty.

"Hello . . ." he said, trying to keep his voice from cracking. He was not accustomed to be caught staring. "I just wanted to see if we all had the same kinds of machines . . ."

"I think so," she whispered.

Salazar noticed that Hawthorne had stopped talking and everyone was fiddling with their tape machines, obviously testing out some procedure.

"I'm . . . Tony . . . Tony Vespa," he said in a half-whisper. He used the phony name he'd given Hawthorne. "Nice to meet you."

"Lydia McCarthy," she said, still smiling. "Likewise."

"What category did you sign up for?" He didn't really care, but a desperate urge burned within to preserve their contact. Even though he had not availed himself of any of the other prey available, he knew she was the one.

"Oh, I picked the Classics . . ." said Lydia, a seasoning of regret in her voice.

He smiled at her. Most women found his smile disarming and ingenuous. She reciprocated, and his pulse jumped. Salazar was certain she had no idea how she affected men. No teasing. No flirting. Everything was very natural with her. She would be perfect.

"What're you going to be reading?"

"What?"

"The tapes." she said. "What category did you pick?"

"Oh . . . I'm doing some spy thrillers and some mysteries." He could care less about the goddamned blind . . .

"All right, now, I think you've all got the basics," said Hawthorne, his voice intrusive and alien. "Don't forget—it's okay to make mistakes . . ."

Lydia's attention returned to the front of the room. Salazar stared at her, invading the front of her sweater with his hungry eyes. She would be so sweet . . .

"I'm going to call you out by the category you selected," said Hawthorne. "When you hear your group called, please come up and get your assignments and schedules. If you have any conflicts, you can work them out with our receptionist. Are we ready? All right . . . let's take the Classics first."

"That's me," said Lydia, gathering up her purse and down jacket. "It was nice meeting you . . ."

Salazar was stunned by her sudden movement. His gaze left the front of her sweater and searched out her green-flecked eyes. But before he could say anything, she had turned away, slipped into the stream of other readers moving quickly past Hawthorne's table. A surge of panic choked through him. He should change his category! He should follow her.

But he could do no such thing. He could not draw attention to himself, or worse, connect himself with her in any way. Occupied with precautionary thoughts, he was barely aware of her receiving her book-assignment and exiting the room.

Hawthorne, meanwhile, had moved down his list, calling on Biography, General Non-Fiction, Contemporary Fiction, Romance & Gothics, and Science Fiction, before finally hitting Spy & Mystery. Salazar played out the charade, accepted his schedule with feigned interest, then exited as quickly as possible without appearing to be in a hurry.

The hallway was empty and so was the lobby, other than the receptionist's desk. Lydia McCarthy was gone and if her phone number was unlisted it was possible he'd lost her forever. But he didn't give up that easily, retreating back down the hall to Mr. Hawthorne's vacant office. Moving quickly, Salazar rifled through a folder full of applications on the pristine blotter.

More quickly than he expected, he found Lydia's form, instantly committing her phone number to memory. Right away, the familiar, explosive sensation of great warmth suffused him. Intimate. Comforting. He felt full of power and confidence as he strode triumphantly out into the hall, through the lobby, and out into the cold, late afternoon.

It had been so easy after all. The digits of her phone number blazed in the center of his skull.

The temptation to rush home to call was seductive, almost overpowering, but he told himself he would wait until Tuesday.

✧

Tony Vespa.

At first the caller's name meant nothing to her, but he ignored her initial confusion and re-introduced himself. The handsome, dark-eyed guy at the volunteer center—she suddenly connected the name and the face. He had seemed so very nice. So polite and charming. And as he spoke, he continued to reinforce that first impression.

She was pleased that he'd called, and she was not really all that surprised that, after some small-talk, he asked her out—some drinks and maybe some dancing at Edgar's. Saturday night, around eight?

"Yeah, that would be great," she heard herself say, perhaps a little too enthusiastically. "I've never been there, but people at work say it's real nice."

He confirmed her address, then prepared to end the conversation.

"Gee, do you have to go so quick?" asked Lydia, hoping she didn't sound too forward.

"What do you mean?"

"I thought maybe we could talk for a while. Maybe get to know each other a little better . . ."

He chuckled softly. A soft, seductive sound, even through the receiver. "Plenty of time for that, Lydia. Good night."

✧

Saturday night, eight o'clock. She had opened her apartment door to him wearing a dark blue jacket-and-pants ensemble over an ivory satin blouse. The silky material conformed to her flesh in such a way it was obvious she was bra-less.

And then she'd asked him if he wanted a beer while he waited for her to finish getting ready . . .

. . . and Salazar now watched her working hard to twist off the cap with her left hand while she held the Michelob bottle awkwardly in the crook of her flipper-like right arm.

How had he not noticed it?

He could not keep his gaze from the deformity. Foreshortened, stick-thin, slightly twisted. Just beyond the permanently half-bent elbow protruded three stiff, semi-formed and useless fingers. A withered arm.

The thought lit up his mind like a cheap neon sign. He looked away from the kitchen, trying to seem interested in the contemporary decor of her living room. A withered arm.

So taken had Salazar been with the perfection of the rest of her, he had somehow failed to notice. He had not actually seen her . . . all of her. He wondered if this sudden knowledge would make any real difference, and his first inclination was probably not. His image of perfection was of course destroyed, but he could still feel his hot blood pounding in his head. No, it would still be all right.

"Here we go," said Lydia brightly as she exited the kitchen and extended the bottle to him with her left hand.

Looking up, he tried to smile, tried to keep his gaze from drifting down to that hideous thing sticking out of her sleeve. "Thanks . . ." He accepted the bottle and took a careful sip. It was not a good thing to drink alcohol, but the charade must be played out. He knew that one bottle would not foul his plans.

"I'm almost ready," she said, turning down the hall towards her bedroom. "Just a few minutes, really."

"We have all the time in the world," he said.

✧

A single, unsettling thought that something was not quite right touched her mind as soon as she climbed into his beat-up Chevrolet. The interior was rimed with a furry patina of grime and dust, the windows so fogged with dirt she could barely see the streetlights in the distance. An aroma of Lysol spray trying to mask a deeper, more hideous odor assailed her as he closed the door. There was something familiar about the smell— a slightly rancid, yet somehow metallic redolence, but she couldn't place it. She had never been in such a filthy car.

In addition, he never spoke to her after slipping into his seat and keying the ignition. Watching him, Lydia noticed how he gripped the wheel with both hands, knuckles white, arms rigid. He stared straight ahead, eyes not even blinking. There was something chilling about him, a sudden coldness that was reptilian. She could almost see it lurking beneath the surface of his handsomeness like the creature in the black lagoon. How could she have not noticed it before?

The Chevrolet accelerated quickly under his unflinching control, changing lanes in the heavy city traffic like a checker zig-zagging across its board. Landmarks blinked past her window and she realized they weren't headed for the hotel district where Edgar's was located. With a shudder, Lydia knew she wanted out of the car—as soon as possible.

She tried to make a few jokes, to get him talking, but he ignored her completely. His coldness radiated outward, touched her, and the inside of the car felt like the bottom of a well.

"Where are we going?" she asked sternly.

He turned a corner roughly, leaving a wide thoroughfare for a narrow, neighborhood street. Poorly lit, the street assumed a mantle of foreboding shadows.

"I said where are we going? Why won't you answer me?"

This time, he turned and smiled at her.

"We're almost home," he said in a reverent whisper. He sounded stagey, but also frightening.

She knew she didn't want to be anywhere near this creep's home. As the car slowed for a red traffic light, she whirled awkwardly in her seat so her left arm could reach the door handle.

Yanking it upward, she gasped when nothing happened. Almost without effort he lashed out with the back of his hand.

The force of impact almost unhinged her jaw. Stinging flashes of pain lit up the inside of her skull; nausea and dizziness welled up like a black geyser behind her eyes. She collapsed into the corner of the seat and the door, fighting the urge to pass out, to give in to him. No. She would never do that. She kept repeating the thought as though it would give her strength.

Her mind raced with half-panicky thoughts. How could she have let this happen? He'd seemed so normal, so nice . . . and she had so few dates, so few chances to get out and be like everybody else.

But even her earliest memories confirmed she'd never been treated like everybody else. Just because her pregnant mother had been prescribed a drug called Thalidomide, Lydia had survived as an Outsider. She learned as a small child how to live with the special pain of rejection, of words like freak and monster. She knew intimately the simple cruelties, and countless, unseen injuries. Like a grey, mottled tumor, her pain clung to the depths of her soul. But rather than allowing it to become a malignant destroyer, she had used her pain as a source of power, of soul-energy. She had learned to accept the pain, break it down into its molecular parts, and re-build it into a driving engine of confidence and inner strength. Lydia had always faced the torment with a special dignity, always growing more formidable in the process.

But now, she faced something far darker . . .

Salazar was feeling very strong since slapping her across the face. The contact with her flesh had exhilarated him. Electricity danced upon the tips of his fingers, singing to him in a chorus of power. Whipping the steering wheel to the left, he jockeyed the car down another side street, then left again into the alley behind his house. As he braked to a halt, his passenger lunged for the door latch. He smacked her again—this time hard enough to break the skin across her cheekbone and to stun her into semi-consciousness. Moving quickly, he grabbed a roll of duct tape from the glove compartment, tearing off a strip to seal her mouth. Then before she regained her senses, he pulled her from the car and fireman-carried her towards the house. Draped limply over his shoulder, she felt almost weightless to him. His entire body hummed with infinite vitality; the sensation was intoxicating, sensuous, almost divine. He moved with stealth and silence even though high fences shielded him from the eyes of any curious neighbors. The light of a half-moon cut a pale blue path through his trash-littered backyard. Salazar followed it to the outside cellar steps and descended with his prey into the familiar darkness.

Tiny flames wickered in the distance. With a great effort, Lydia lifted her head to stare at the candles casting orange light and long shadows across the cellar. She forced herself to sharper awareness. Something was restricting her good left arm, holding it almost straight up, and she gradually realized he'd manacled her against a damp, chilly wall of stone. A second bracelet and chain hung past her right shoulder, rendered useless by her withered arm. But cold metal looped both ankles; short chains tethered her spread-legged to the wall.

The bastard . . . !

Her anger threatened to banish the numbing chill of the cellar. The first tendrils of rage were reaching into the core of her being, seeking the energy which seethed there. She would—

The tape was ripped savagely from her mouth, twisting her neck to the side. Stinging pain ate into her face as she detected movement in the shadows. He appeared out of the darkness, his eyes wide with pleasure. He appraised her with a grin and chuckled to himself. The taut muscles of his chest and arms strained against a plain white T-shirt, over which he wore a thick leather apron. Slowly he raised a barber's straight razor until it was level with her eyes. The blade looked insanely sharp.

Lydia recoiled from the shining weapon, thrashed against the chains, but no sound could escape her throat.

"It's okay if you want to scream," he said in a whisper. "Nobody can hear you down here. They never heard any of the others."

Behind him, next to a work bench full of tools, an old gas

stove heated two large stewing pots. Adjacent to the stove at the end of a large, darkly stained, wooden table sat an electric rotisserie. Its interior glowed a deep orange from the glow of its heating elements.

An alarm was going off in her head. It was the klaxon of sheer panic. Naked fear capered like a demon across her mind. She was going to die. She was going to be sliced and gutted like a sacrificial pig. For an instant the alarm screeched so loud, so insistently, she felt she was plummeting into the abyss of madness.

"Going to cut you up," said the monster in the leather apron. His face moved to within inches of her own. His breath smelled of decay, his eyes as flat and dead as a shark's. "And then, I'm going to eat you . . ."

No.

The single word took substance in the very core of her being. It rose up in her, gathering up the stuff of anguish and suffering and plating itself with it like newly-forged armor. A vortex of anger whirled into life, kicking out sparks of defiance. A silent cry of pure, sweet outrage streaked out of her like an explosion of radio waves from a star going nova.

In that single instant, she hated him. Completely. With a cosmic finality.

Her anger and her hate fused into something new, becoming a tap-line which drove down into the deepest core of her soul.

"Here we go," said the monster as he slipped the razor's edge into her blouse, bringing it down with slow precision. The blade separated her clothing effortlessly, slicing it away like rice paper. He continued down until he had opened her garments as if they'd been zippered. With a technique smoothed by years of practice, he began removing the tatters of her clothes. As the last of her blouse fell off her right shoulder, revealing her deformity, he paused as if to study the withered append- age. His gaze seemed to traverse the short length of her slightly twisted humerus. Twig-thin, punctuated by the suggestion of an elbow and a stump of misshapen flesh, it looked unfin- ished. Three proto-fingers jutted stiffly from the stump.

He reached out and touched her right arm, slowly running his fingers down to the useless travesty of a hand. She wanted to recoil from his touch—for most of her life she had avoided touching her right arm as much as possible—but she refused to give him even the slightest satisfaction that he offended her. The limb had always been numb, essentially dead, but as his fingers played along its length, she felt a slight warmth beneath the shriveled skin.

"Never seen anything like this," he said as though to himself. "Maybe I'll save it as a souvenir . . ."

He looked up from her twisted arm, smiled widely.

"Why don't you scream?" he asked softly. "It's okay if you want to scream . . ."

More expert snicks of the blade, and everything fell away except her panties. Her pale skin goose-fleshed from the chilly dampness, then flushed as a wave of humiliation passed over her.

But she would not let the indignity deter her from the climax of her rage. The maelstrom of hate for him continued to expand inside her, faster and more deadly than a metastasizing growth. Like a hungry cancer it fed upon the storehouse of her pain and humiliation—a lifetime's worth. In a frenzy of building pressure, her loathing sought an outlet . . .

"This will be nice," he said, slipping the edge of the razor inside the elastic band of her panties. Slowly he moved it down, paring away the last boundary to her nakedness. Lydia stared straight ahead into the distant shadowed corners of the room as her underpants fell away in ribbons. He placed the cold steel of the blade flat against her lower abdomen, moved the blade downward over her mons, scything her blonde pubic hair like wheat, until he reached the beginning of her labia. Slowly he rotated the blade so that its cutting edge faced upward and perpendicular to her body.

"This seems like a good place to start," he said in a half-whisper.

No!

The rage from the core of her being, engorged from the surfeit of her pain, sought form. She blinked her eyes, flinching away from the blade, and sensed that things were somehow slowing down. The warmth in her withered arm surged, bursting forth with white heat in all the places where he'd touched her.

All the years of her suffering, the humiliation and exquisitely distilled anguish, were taking substance now. Time almost stopped for her. The catalytic moment had arrived. Something shifted in the cosmos, and the great wheel of being sought a new balance-point. When he touched her dead flesh, he'd unwittingly switched on the radiant energy of her soul.

He moved the blade upward; the cold edge of steel touched her. It was only an instant, but she could feel the heat expanding, suffusing her arm with a life it had never known. Time slowed, spiraling down into a dark well. A total spectator, Lydia watched as her withered arm moved—moved for the first time in her life. Its pale flesh almost incandescent with vengeful energy, her limb lengthened, swung forward.

Things were happening so fast, and yet she could see it all unfolding with exacting detail. Time fugued around her like a storm.

He looked up as her arm moved, for the moment forgetting his intended upward thrust of the razor. His eyes widened as the stump of flesh flattened out and the stick-like projections swelled and grew into taloned, grasping fingers. Like a spade-claw, it raked his face, and she could hear him scream slowly through the underwater-like murk of distended time.

The sound of his own pained voice, his scream of pain and terror, stunned him as much as the transformation he was witnessing. As his own blood warmed his ruined cheek, he found himself marvelling at the exquisite tang of his own coppery fear, his own pain-fire burning. So different . . . so ironically reversed . . . fascinating as much as horrific. The girl's face had become twisted into an unrecognizable mask. The gaze of her sunken eyes stared through him, past him, and into a timeless place. Her transformation was a gift from the Gods, he realized in the final moment. It was a miracle, and only he had been chosen to witness the event. Salazar smiled through his pain and his fear, and awaited her special anointing . . .

In an instant the hand reached into his face, index and middle fingers puncturing his eyes, the newly-formed thumb hooking the roof of his mouth. Gristle and bone collapsed from the unrelenting pressure; the razor fell away from his hand. Then the arm shot out, straightening, as the hand held his head like a ten-pin bowling ball. For a moment, he hung there, suspended, a grim marionette, legs and arms flailing through a final choreography of nerve-shock and death.

Finally, like a crane jettisoning its cargo, the hand released his stilled body. Then, powered by the last sparks of her rage and her pain, the hand yanked free the manacles from her wrist and ankles. Lydia blinked her eyes in the candlelight as her time-sense telescoped back to normal. The right side of her body seemed aflame and her heart raged in her chest as if it might explode. The monster lay at her feet and she'd killed him. Her stomach lurched, sending a hot column of bile half-way up her throat.

The horror of knowing she'd actually killed someone was tempered by her realization of how it had been done. Looking down at her new right arm, her new hand, it seemed impossible that it could really be there.

She kept waiting for it to fade away, to shrink back into the desiccated parody she'd always known.

But it never did.

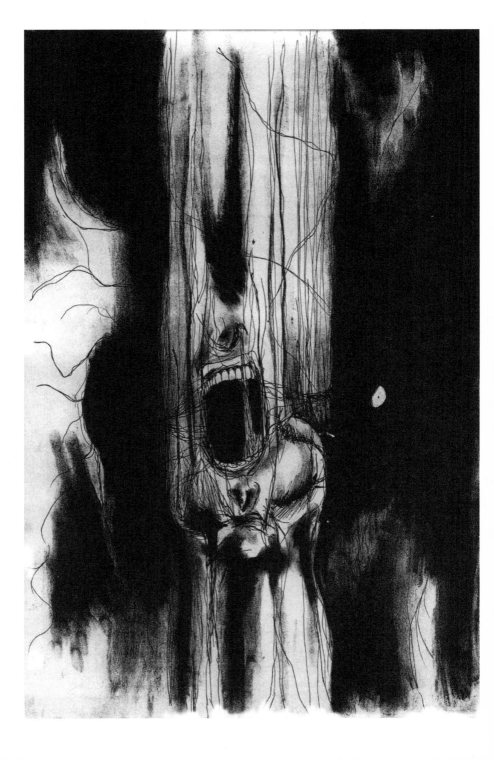

*When you've known somebody in this business as long as I've known Charlie Grant, you're probably going to have to make reference to him more than once. Case in point, the next story. In the late Eighties, the genre of straight-up Horror was more than just healthy in the publishing world; it was a freaking juggernaut. One of its dominant high-priests was none other than my pal, Chaz, and he had a string of successful anthologies on his* curriculum vitae, *which had garnered him respect and a handful of awards. One series he was doing with the flagship publisher of quality dark fantasy, Tom Doherty's Tor Books, was called* Greystone Bay—*a fictional town, in which each volume would feature stories that illuminated a particular (and weird) aspect of this eerie, fog-shrouded, coastal New England village.*

*Insert by-now-deadingly-familiar scene here: editor (this time it's Charlie) calls me and asks for a story. He wants it for Volume 3 of the Greystone Bay series, which is subtitled* The Seaharp Hotel. *Which, you can figure, means all the stories required the town's strange, old, hotel prominently featured in some way.*

*Okay, I can do that, I tell my buddy. And I sit down to write. The subtext of this one includes various nods to another of my early addictions and influences—none other than Howard Phillips Lovecraft, himself.[1] Although I tried to avoid mimicking HP's verbal avoirdupois and epistolary surfeit, I did want to pay my* homage *and carry on the tradition even if only in a small way.*

*I also wanted to come up with something truly horrific, and here's what I ended up telling myself . . . .*

---

[1] *Maybe I'll tell you later on about how I discovered Lovecraft . . .*

"**E**xcuse me, sir, but aren't you forgetting something?" asked Roger Easton, chief bell-boy at the Seaharp.

"What's that?" said the thin, disheveled guest who was walking toward the door with two arm-loads of baggage.

"That other box," said Roger, pointing to a fairly large container in the corner of the room. It looked like one of those thin-slatted crates they shipped bottled water in.

The guest stopped at the door, eased his bags to the carpet, and looked back over a bony shoulder at Roger. "Oh, that . . ."

"Yeah," said Roger. "Want me to get it for you? I can carry it out on the dolly."

The guest looked at Roger for a moment, then tried to enact a small smile. "Actually, no, I don't."

Roger was taken aback. What the heck was going on here? From the minute he first saw this guy, he figured he was a weirdo—what with the trimmed goatee and the thick horned-rim glasses and the baggy suit. The guest looked like one of those jazz musicians or French painters you always saw in cartoons. Of course Roger made it his business to know as much as possible about all of the Seaharp's guests, and he already knew this guy was a professor from Miskatonic University, and he'd been in Greystone Bay to give one of those weekend self-help seminars to all the yuppies.

"Is everything all right?" asked the guest. Roger had apparently been staring at him mutely. He did that sometimes without even realizing it. He'd start having some interesting thought, and bang, there he'd be—staring off with his mouth hanging open like he was trying to catch flies with it. He closed his mouth and gathered in his thoughts like a pile of crumpled-up laundry.

"Oh, it's just that we don't usually allow people to leave stuff behind," said Roger. "If you lose somethin' or forget somethin', that's one thing. But people don't usually leave stuff on purpose."

"I am," said the professor.

The abruptness of the man's answer surprised him, but Roger could only say: "And why's that?"

The tall man paused and looked at Roger. "What's your name, son?"

Roger told him.

"Do you make good tips here?"

"It's okay, I guess . . . why?"

The professor reached into his pocket, pulled out a roll of bills. "I make out pretty good with my seminars," he muttered. "Here, take this and do me a favor, all right?"

Roger accepted the bill, not wanting to steal a glance at the number on its corner, but when you were getting a big tip, bell-hops had this sort of sixth-sense about it. Roger just knew it was a good one and he had to check it out. Once a guy from Texas had given him ten bucks, then there was that woman from New York who promised him a twenty if he'd—he looked down into his hand—My God! A hundred!

"Something wrong?" asked the professor, still looming over him.

"Jeez, no, but, well, I . . . I never got a tip like this before!"

"Nor will you probably ever again. No matter, you have one now. I want you to do me a favor, all right?"

"Yeah! Just name it!" Roger stuffed the bill into his pants pocket. It seemed to glow with its own heat, radiating wealth up and down his leg. A freakin' C-note!

"As I said before, I intend to leave that small crate behind. It isn't necessary for it to remain in this room, however." The professor cleared his throat, stared at Roger intently.

"Yeah, okay. So?"

"So I want you to do this for me: put the crate somewhere safe and secure within this hotel. Hide it, if you think it necessary, but remember, it must remain within the walls of this building. Is that clear?"

Boy, this guy was sounding pretty weird, thought Roger. 'Course, there was nothing weird about the hundred-dollar bill warming up his pants pocket.

"Is that clear, Roger?"

"Huh? Oh yeah, sure. I can find a place to keep it. No problem."

The professor nodded. "Very good. Now, here, take my card. There's my phone number on it. I want you to call me at the University if you have any problems. I will be stopping back once a week to check on the crate. Understood?"

Roger accepted the card. "Yeah, but why?"

"Well, it's quite simple really—I want to know what things look like in a month or so."

Jeez, that reminded him. "Hey, I meant to ask you. Just what is it you got in that crate, anyway?"

"It is none of your concern." The professor's voice was flat and stern, reminding Roger of his dead father's.

"Jeez, I don't know . . . I don't want to do anything that's gonna get me in trouble."

A large, bony hand suddenly vised down on his shoulder. "If you don't want to help me out, I'm sure I can find someone else who can . . . especially for a hundred-dollar tip."

The thought of losing his tip sent a blue bolt of current through Roger like he'd stuck his finger in a light socket. Jeez, this guy was serious.

"Oh, no sir! You don't have to worry about that! Listen, I was just tryin' to make conversation. I don't really care what's in the crate, honest. And I'll hide it for you, no problem."

The man stared at him, as though evaluating the proposition, then nodded slowly. "Very well. Keep my card. You shall call me if anything untoward occurs between my visits. Now, let's go. I have a long drive ahead of me."

"Yes sir!" said Roger, grabbing the handle of the dolly. As he walked down the hall toward the elevator bay, he could almost hear the crackle of that crisp bill against his right thigh, and he began thinking of ways he could spend so much extra cash.

"I can't believe you wanted to stay in this goddamned place," said Angela in her whining, yet still acidic tone of voice. It was a voice Daniel Rosenthal had grown to despise in a surprisingly short amount of time.

"Christ, honey, we just got here," he said softly, trying to keep from sounding shitty. He really wanted to make a sincere effort. "What's wrong with it? Let's give it a chance, okay?"

Angela preened in the mirror, fingering this curl or that one. Daniel wondered why she just didn't get her hair exactly right, get it encased in lucite, and forget about it.

"The Seaharp Hotel!" she muttered. "Didn't this town ever hear of a Holiday Inn?"

"They're all the same. This place has character." Daniel opened his parachute luggage, started hanging up his shirts and pants.

"But there's nothing to do here, Danny-Boy. No sauna, no pool. They don't even have a night-club."

He walked over to her, put his arms around her while she continued looking at herself in the mirror. She was not the most beautiful woman he'd ever been with, and her body was just average, but there had always been something about her that attracted him.

"If you recall, honey, we're supposed to be 'doing' each other. Isn't that what this little vacation is all about?"

He'd felt her tense up as soon as he touched her. Six years of marriage and there was about as much warmth between them as ice cubes in a tray. He'd truly loved her, but she did not love him. It was that simple, and he was having a hell of a time accepting it. They'd read countless books, been to counselors and therapists, and nothing had essentially changed. Angela resented him. She was intimidated by him, threatened intellectually by him. His list of accomplishments (Daniel Rosenthal was a nationally renowned orthodontic specialist, the author of several definitive textbooks, a wildly successful public speaker, and the holder of sixteen dental patents) made her feel inadequate, stupid, and hopelessly inferior. Since marrying him, Angela had learned to loathe Trivial Pursuit. She felt powerless and inept in his presence in all things but one—and it was from this single thing that she had fashioned a most terrible weapon.

Daniel had always been a naturally affectionate man. He gave his love freely and he craved it in return. And when Angela finally learned this, she lunged for her newfound power with a vengeance. Her rejection ate him up like the cruelest of cancers. When he would tell her he loved her, and only a cold, black silence welled up out of her in reply, the bottomless pain and naked fear in his heart ranged outward like a beacon of loneliness.

Only Angela had the power to hurt him so exquisitely and she wielded her special weapon with the skill of a neurosurgeon. If he made no overtures, she could let them live like brother and sister for months at a time, and then almost whimsically deign to open her legs for him when she felt like it. Like a dumb mutt, he would sit up and get ready for her, waiting for her to toss him a doggie-treat.

She turned and slipped out of his embrace, walked to the window, stared out at the manicured hedges and lawns of the grand old hotel. Keeping her back to him, she spoke to the leaded glass panes. "Oh yes, I keep forgetting. This is our 'second honeymoon,' isn't it?"

Daniel couldn't ignore the sarcasm in her voice. "Well, we didn't have much of a first one now, did we?"

He was referring to her wrenching a disc in her back as she picked up a heavy suitcase from the airport's luggage carousel. He was referring to ten days at Lake Tahoe with her complaining of increasingly intolerable lumbar pain and avoiding even a comforting touch from him the whole time. He was referring to her answer when he suggested they substitute with mutual oral sex until her back healed:  I guess I should tell you now, Dan— I've always hated doing that to you, and honestly I don't think I could ever do it again.

He remembered wondering back then what her definition of love might be (since it obviously didn't include giving to your lover because it made him feel good. Or deriving pleasure from simply knowing that you made him feel good).

Angela whirled angrily from the window, her face twisted with a special loathing. "You prick! You always bring that up when you have nothing else to say!"

"Well I guess it's a measure of my pain, Angela. The memory won't go away."

"You bastard! You act like it was my fault!  Like I hurt my back on purpose . . . !"

"You mean if you hurt it at all." The words came out of him without a forethought. He knew immediately how much they would hurt her. He didn't really want that, did he?

She rushed him, raising her long fingernails at him like talons, going for his face. "You bastard!" she cried out, again and again.

This was not going well at all, thought Daniel, as he fended her off.

✧

Roger ended up stashing the crate on the fourth floor, at the end of the wainscotted hall in Room 434. The smaller rooms up there were practically never used, especially in the off-season. And now that November was only a couple of weeks away, nobody would be checking that room very often, if at all.

After he'd carefully hidden the container behind the valanced draperies, and turned to leave, Roger had decided that, damn it, he *did* need to know what was in that crate. Its size and weight indicated something substantial, and if it was something like a safe, then maybe he should know about it. A fantasy of the professor being a secret embezzler or bank-robber made him smile. Roger could confront him with his hidden cache of loot, and make him split the money. Yeah . . .

But his get-rich-easy dreams faded quickly when he pried back one of the thin, wood slats of the crate to discover one of those big bottled-water bottles in there. Just like he'd first imagined. Now what the hell was going on here? Looking closer, Roger noted that the water was not clear like bottled water. Rather, it had a murky, greenish cast. Peering in through the single open slat, he could see nothing in the water, but his instincts told him the bottle could not be empty. After prying the top of the crate loose, he carefully eased the thick-walled glass container from the crate. It was bulky and probably more than three feet high. He carried the bottle closer to the window and even then, at first glance, he couldn't see a damn thing. Now why the hell was he hiding a bottle of creek-water for?

It wasn't until he started to roll it back under the draperies that he saw it.

Just for an instant, then it was gone. A flash of color and reflected light, like a polished fish-lure spinning through the water. Roger stopped moving the big bottle, again peered into the aquarium depths.

There it was. The little bastard. Jeez, it was small, but it was there.

The light had to hit it just right or he couldn't even see it, but once he knew what he was looking for, he kept relocating it every time it would disappear. It reminded him of that tropical fish they called a neon—not because of its shape, just its colors, which kept changing like an electric rainbow. It's shape was hard to figure. Definitely not a fish-shape, though. It was more like a blob. No shape at all, really. Roger wondered if he could see arms or legs or eyes in that tiny shapeless mass, and decided that he couldn't really see much of anything.

But that had been more than a week ago . . .

True to his word, the professor came by to check on things. Roger was very courteous to the man and persuaded him to let him tag along for the inspection.

"All right," said the professor. "Let's have a look."

Roger nodded and uncovered the bottle, then jumped back away from it instinctively when he saw the shape within its brackish depths.

"Damn . . . !" he said automatically, his breath hitching up in his throat. He hadn't been prepared for what he now saw behind the glass.

The tiny sliver of colored tissue had been replaced by something a little larger than a softball. No, that wasn't right. It hadn't been replaced . . . whatever it was in there had grown. The little bastard was growing, Jeez . . . .

The professor calmly went about observing the thing and making notes on a little pad he'd pulled from his coat. Roger peered down at the pulpy mass and winced. It was uglier than anything he'd ever seen. Essentially shapeless, it reminded him of a freshly excised organ like maybe a spleen or a brain or something. There were convolutions and folds of tissue; there were tendrils and other streamers of meat hanging off it; there were objects that might have been the beginnings of eyes and tiny clawed appendages. Roger remembered once as a kid his mother cracked open an egg and it had a half-developed chicken in it, and this thing in the bottle almost reminded him of that. It was the weirdest thing he'd ever seen, no doubt.

But calling it weird didn't cover all the bases. No way.

As Roger stared into the dark green liquid, the creature moved toward him, flattening somewhat against the glass. He sensed the thing would have liked to have grabbed onto him, and he didn't like that feeling even a little bit.

He also sensed something else about the creature: that maybe it was evil.

The professor continued to write something hastily in his notebook, not standing until he was finished. "All right, son, you can cover it up again."

As Roger followed his instruction, a question occurred to him—if that thing had grown so much, just what the hell was it eating? He decided he'd ask the professor.

"A good question," said the man. "But I'm afraid it's a bit too early to tell. Let's wait another week or so."

Melanie Cantrell checked the lock on the door to her hotel room. She'd already put the *Do Not Disturb* sign on the knob, but goodness knew she didn't want any maids coming in while she was in the middle of . . . of what she was here to do.

The last phrase stuck in her mind like a line of lyrics on a scratched record. Here she was ready to do it, and she couldn't even bring herself to mention the word. She turned away from the door, passed a small mirror on the wall—something to afford a guest a last-second check of one's hair or clothing before leaving the room—and stole a look at her own face.

Bloodshot and raw-rimmed from all the tears, her eyes looked like some zombie's from a bad movie. The muscles in her jaw, taut and corded, had contorted her normally pretty features into a mask of tense pain. Oh God, what was she doing here? She turned away from the mirror and began to unpack her suitcase. She carried several changes of clothes, extra towels and dressings, a few books, and her diary. After she emptied her bag, her gaze fell upon the telephone, squatting like some kind of dark creature by the side of the bed.

She still had a chance to call Teddy and tell him where she'd gone . . . and why.

But no, she wasn't going to involve him in any of it. She'd already decided that she would go through it alone. Besides Teddy would've went crazy if he ever found out she'd let herself get pregnant. He was like that when she did something he didn't like, screaming and yelling, and even hitting her once in a while. She looked away from the phone, wishing just for a moment that Teddy was the kind of guy who could be gentle sometimes. She'd never known a man who could be gentle, and her mother had always told her there was no such thing. She figured it must be true.

Well, she told herself bravely, it was time.

Melanie opened her little travel-bag and dug through till she found the vial of pills her friend, Cathy, had given her. Cathy was the only person in the world who knew she was spending the weekend at the Seaharp. Melanie didn't want anyone to know, but Cathy had been the one who got her the drugs that would make her miscarry (it was easy with Cathy's older sister going to pharmacy school!). And besides, if anything happened to her, she wanted somebody to know where to look for her.

Melanie walked into the bathroom and shook out three of the pinkish pills, washed them down with water just the way Cathy said she should. It would take a few hours before her body would begin to rebel against the intruder in her womb; it would be best if she went to sleep for awhile. Walking from the bathroom, she passed an open closet harboring several coat-hangers.

Pausing, Melanie looked into the darkness at the triangles of wire, and the memory of old horror stories rose up in her mind. She wondered what she would do if the pills didn't work.

Oh Teddy, she thought, as tears stained her cheeks. I love you.

When Roger and the professor checked the bottle the following week, he hesitated in pulling back the draperies.

"Go on, son" said the professor, notepad already in hand.

Roger did it and looked into the water. What he saw made his stomach churn. The professor started writing like crazy.

What was going on here? thought Roger. The damned thing was disgusting. A fuckin' monster—that's what they were growing in there.

Jeez, it looked worse than ever. The image of the undeveloped egg-embryo needed to be revised; it had changed, warped into something really alien, something bad. And it had been doing some serious growing—the bulk of it barely fit within the confines of the bottle. The thing had grown not only larger, but darker. Its dissected-organ appearance glistened with pulsating life. There was a sac-like thing which almost glowed with orange movement. There was something that could have been an eye. A tendril-like arm. Was that a claw? Seaweed-like stuff flowed and wavered in self-contained currents. The amorphous body constantly in ebbing motion, Roger was unable to recognize what was really growing in there. But whatever it was, he knew two things for sure: it was a nasty motherfucker and it couldn't get a whole hell of a lot bigger without busting the glass bottle.

"You didn't tell me it was gonna get so big," he said.

"I didn't know what it was going to do. This was an experiment, remember?" The professor's voice was calm, even. In control.

"Yeah, I guess you're right," said Roger. "But, man, it looks bad, doesn't it? It's getting crowded in there."

"No, I still think there's plenty of room."

"What is it? You never told me?"

The professor rubbed his chin pensively. "I'm not sure."

"Well, listen, is it dangerous?" Roger figured it was—no matter what the professor said.

"Probably. I don't know yet."

Roger swallowed hard. Now there was an honest answer if he ever heard one.

"Where'd you get it anyway? Are you a biology-guy?"

The man smiled thinly. "No, I'm an archeologist—I found the, ah, spores of this thing in a stoppered vial thousands of years old."

"Really? Where?"

The professor shrugged. "The ruins of a building dating back to early Mycenaean times. I brought it back from my last dig."

"Yeah, I got you." Roger didn't know from mice an' eons, but he figured the professor was onto something pretty weird, so he figured he oughta just play along.

"There were writings, too," said the professor. "They spoke of this as a deimophage. Fascinating, don't you think? I tried controlled experiments at the university with laboratory animals, but I didn't have much heart for the torturing necessary, you see."

Roger frankly didn't see at all, but he nodded his head solemnly as the professor rambled on.

"Besides, it wasn't working. None of the spores did anything. I decided they required spontaneously generated human emotion, so I thought of the most suitable test environment—hence the Seaharp!"

"Yeah . . . right," said Roger, having lost the thread way back there somewhere. "Hey, is it okay to cover it up now?"

The professor nodded. "Till next week."

"You sure it's gonna be okay. If it grows as much this week as it did last—"

The professor waved off his protest. "Everything will be just fine, Roger. Let's be off."

"Yeah?" said Bobby Kaminski, grabbing the receiver from its cradle. He'd been pacing about the hotel room, waiting for the call for what seemed like an eternity.

"Okay, man, we're in the lobby. What room you in?"

"Two-O-Five," said Bobby. "You got the money?"

"Hey, man . . . sure we do. You got the shit?"

Bobby nodded, rubbed his nose. "Yeah, I got it." He was getting bad feelings about all this, but there was no turning back now.

"Okay, keep it stiff, man. We'll be right up."

Bobby hung up the phone and began pacing the hotel room again. How did he ever get involved in this crazy bullshit? If he wasn't such a goddamned cokehead . . .

He didn't much like himself, but he didn't like dealing with this guy, Andy, a lot worse. Sherry'd hooked him up, but Bobby didn't like the looks of Andy, didn't like his scent. The Good Fathers of Greystone Bay didn't have much compassion for dealers and Bobby was feeling pretty paranoid. Either this guy Andy was a narc, or he was just bad news. Either way, Bobby didn't dig the set-up—that's why he kept his jacket on; that's why he kept his snub-nose .38 in his shoulder holster.

Hard knocks at the door broke up his thoughts. He opened the door after checking the peep-hole.

"Hey, dude, how's it hangin'?"

Andy was standing there in his leather gear, punctuated now and then by chrome studding and chains. He smelled of grease and road-grime. Behind him were two other bikers who looked like they could have been tag-team members from a World Federation Wrestling bout. One of them carried a small nylon Nike sportsbag.

"I thought I told you to come alone," said Bobby.

"Hey, I don't go nowhere without my stick-men," said Andy, who remained standing in the hallway. "So, are we comin' in, or what?"

Bobby stood aside and the trio entered—the two goons immediately casing things out like good goons should. He didn't like this situation at all. His nose was itching and burning. He'd love to take a toot right about now, but he needed to be clear, to be ready for anything.

"Okay, where is it?" asked Andy.

Bobby opened the top dresser drawer and pulled out the kilo, nicely wrapped and sanitized for their protection. "You got the money?" he asked. His voice sound weak, reedy. Scared.

Andy smiled and nodded to the goon with the Nike bag, who threw it on the bed. Unzipping it, Bobby wasn't really surprised to see it was filled with cut-up newspapers. So it was going down like this . . .

Swinging around, he reached for his gun. Better to take out Andy, then maybe reason with the other two.

But before he could complete the turn, something stunned him, creating a stinging halo around the back of his head. His knees jellied up on him and huge arms caught him as he started to go down. Bobby was dazed as they frisked him.

"You were right, Andy—he was hot," said the goon, stripping out his piece.

"So you were going to shoot me?" asked Andy.

Bobby was too numb to respond. He knew it wouldn't do any good anyway. One of them ripped open his shirt. Then somebody was fumbling with his belt and zipper.

"Just for that" said Andy. "I'm gonna let my boys have a little fun before they ex you out, man."

The pain in the back of his head bloomed like a miniature nova, but it proved to be only a sweet prelude . . .

✧

Roger was getting very freaked out when the professor didn't show up for his weekly visit. It had been a bad week at the Seaharp anyway—Mr. Montgomery had been highly upset by the murdered drug dealer they found in 205's bathtub. Roger was just glad he hadn't been the one to find the poor bastard.

He waited all day on Saturday, and still no professor. Roger called at the University on Sunday, but nobody was answering any of the phones. On Monday, he spoke to a woman who gave him the bad news: the professor had slipped in the shower and fractured his skull. He was now at the Miskatonic University Hospital, comatose.

Great. Just great.

That night Roger decided he'd better check on the thing in the bottle, but he didn't know what the hell he'd do if he got himself up to the fourth floor and it had already broken loose.

When he pulled back the heavy draperies and saw the bottle still intact, Roger exhaled—only then realizing he'd been holding his breath. His luck was holding, but just barely, it seemed.

The creature had grown horribly. It didn't look like there was any water left in the bottle at all. Just this bloated, sickly-green, tumorous thing. Its amorphous shape pulsed with life like a giant, beating heart. Jeez, it looked like it was growing larger as he watched it, like it would break the glass any second.

He had to get it out of there. Like right away. No way it was going to make it through another night. Just get it out. Dump it somewhere.

Roger told himself he'd worry about the details later as he hefted the bottle into his arms and slipped into the deserted hallway. It had to be at least three times as heavy as it had been before and he wondered how that could even be possible. Roger kept wondering what he would say if he saw any of the Montgomerys coming down from their apartments on the fifth floor. All he needed was to get caught by them before he reached the service elevator.

The old service elevator creaked and groaned its way to the musty basement, where Roger eased the bottle past the doors and across the cluttered floor. Lawn furniture, croquet sets, umbrellas, and other seasonal equipment littered the path to the exit doors. The bottle seemed to be getting heavier with each step and Roger prayed that he didn't stumble on something or lose his grip.

It wasn't until he'd carried it out to his four-year-old Camaro that he'd thought of what to do with it. Placing it carefully in the back seat, Roger tried to avoid looking into the dark center of its mass. There was something very much like an eye looking back at him. Its whole body, now pressed against the glass, heaved like a beating heart. He couldn't wait to get rid of the ugly son-of-a-bitch.

Turning off Harbor Road onto Port Boulevard, Roger drove carefully through the center of Greystone Bay. It was getting late in the evening and things were quiet. Lightning flashed in the Northern skies and he wondered if a storm might be descending on the coast.

With the bottle wedged into the floor-well behind the shotgun seat, he headed straight out of town on Western Road, past the industrial parks and the other new development in some of the farmlands. There was a place up in the hills off Western Road where the government had operated a toxic waste dump. Public outcry had it closed down about fifteen years ago and since then it had become a favorite spot for adventurous kids who wanted to do some make-believe exploring and teen-agers who wanted to do some real exploring in the back-seats of their cars.

As Roger drove up the abandoned road with his headlights off, past the battered chain-link fence and gate, memories of evenings spent up here with Diana wafted back to him like a subtle perfume. He wished they'd been able to work things out. He still missed her sometimes. The thought wistfully distracted him as he pulled up and killed the engine.

Carefully, Roger slipped from behind the wheel, went around and pulled the bottle out from behind the passenger seat. When he reached down to pick it up, the thing inside lurched and churned, like it had tried to get at him through the glass. God, he hated it! He couldn't wait to dump it into the well and be done with the whole mess.

He'd found the well years ago when he'd been kicking around the site. The wooden well-cover had half-rotted away and somebody had tried to batten it down with a piece of corrugated steel. It was a half-assed job, and Roger had pulled back the metal and peered down into the shaft in the earth. He couldn't see any bottom and a stone dropped into the darkness fell for what seemed like a very long time before splooshing into the water.

The perfect place to dump this thing, thought Roger as he carried the bottle the remaining few feet to the lip of the well. The circumference of the opening looked narrow, but it wasn't—certainly wide enough to swallow up the water-fountain bottle. Sucking in his breath, he wrapped his arms around it and prepared to lift it over the opening.

The timing was flawless.

The thing must have sensed its fate because as soon as he embraced the glass, the creature inside heaved upward. With a smart little snick! the neck of the bottle just snapped off, pushed out and up by a thick tendril-like arm. It happened so fast, Roger didn't have time to react. All of a sudden this fleshy tuber shot up past his face.

Instantly he was stunned by the overpowering stench of it. The inside of his nose stung, actually burned from the acid-stink of decay, of swamps. It was a batrachian smell, a hideous smell, of something impossibly old. He staggered backwards, then spun around, still holding the bottle. And then the glass was cracking, fracturing in all directions. The thing, once free seemed to be expanding like a balloon being filled with air. Roger was awash in the foul bath of its prison, smelling like the grave. More tendrils shot out embracing him like clinging sea-weed. He screamed and a long tuberous finger leaped into his mouth, forcing its way down his throat. He gagged, heaving and puking, but still the appendage wormed its way into the depths of his stomach. He could feel it wriggling about, and he puked again.

Reeling now, locked in a death-dance with the thing, he staggered forward and tripped over the lip of the well. Head-first, he pitched downward into the shaft. The opening was just large enough to accept the width of his shoulders, pinning his arms to his sides. He plummeted into the darkness, picking up speed. His mind threatened to blank out from the sheer panic, and then suddenly he was jerked to a jolting stop. Reaching a more narrow spot in the well, his body was wedged vise-like in the shaft.

And still the creature clung to him, wriggling and sliding about, appearing to assume a more comfortable position, probing him obscenely.

His thoughts were short-circuiting as he realized there was no getting out, that he was going to die suspended upside down and being slowly eaten from the inside out by the monster from the bottle. He wanted to scream, to cry out, but the tendril stuffed into his mouth wouldn't allow it.

Slowly the creature kept adjusting its position, re-arranging itself, moving and exploring his body with its many arms, leaving a viscous trail of slime everywhere it touched his flesh. He was almost numb from shock and exposure as it moved against him, sending lancets and pincers and thorns into him.

Under his fingernails, in his ears and up his nose, through his armpits and groin, and even up his ass. The thing shot him through with a raging inferno of pain. All his nerve endings sang with torment. His brain threatened to buzz away into the idiot hum of white noise, of absolute pain.

And the thing swelled with pleasure and satiety.

Time lost all meaning in the dank confines of the well. The constant symphony of pain precluded any serious thinking, and all he wanted to do was die.

But Roger Easton didn't die.

Days. Weeks. Time became an ugly smear across the back wall of his mind.

He had no idea how long he lay wedged in the well, but he knew it was longer than he should have lived without food or water. But gradually, in the short, dark spaces of thought between the rhythmic beats of agony, he grasped what must be happening: the thing was keeping him alive in the white-pain darkness. Somehow, the creature was feeding him parts of itself, as Roger in turn fed *it*.

It was the perfect relationship, and he knew it would last for a very long time . . . .

*One of the oldest (and often the dumbest) pieces of advice that gets tossed at young writers is "write what you know." Yeah, right. Young writers, by dint of their very youth, usually do not know jack about much of anything. So what's up with that old shopworn saw? Not much, usually. I always tell writers to write about what intrigues them, scares them, infuriates them, or makes them feel good, or* whatever *motivates them to write in the first place. Just keep writing—that's the most important thing. I tell them sooner or later you* will *know more than jack, and you'll be an even* better *writer, but be patient. And once in a while, you will have something to write about that you* actually do know *from a personal experience.*

*Now the reason I slipped into lecture-mode for a moment is to prepare you for the background to the next story. Because it is based on a real guy named Kenny (not Denny), and his real story. It was one of those things I experienced and never forgot. I never knew I would ever turn it into a story until the day Dave Silva called me to invite me to contribute to an anthology he and Paul Olson were doing called* Post Mortem—*but it had to be a ghost story. I said yes, because I love Dave and his work, and because I love the challenge of taking the traditional ghost story and trying to do something different with it. I had no idea what I would do until I started to write, and then I remembered a night when I was back in college, and this guy was hanging at our apartment and he told us something that never left me . . . .*

THE RING OF TRUTH

"**I** even shot a pregnant woman, once," Reitmann said. His voice was hard and crisp and totally without emotion, but there was a scary smile forming at the edges of his mouth.

I sat on the floor, listening to his story while rock music filled in the dead spots. My three room-mates and I were all half-drunk, but the wine did nothing to dispel the palpable sense of dread, the stench of a triumphant evil which pervaded the room.

The lights from our Christmas tree colored each of our faces in various hues of horror and revulsion, but nobody told Reitmann to stop—especially after he told us about the "Ring of Truth."

Denny Reitmann was one of those guys you meet in college and you just *know* he isn't going to be around for the commencement exercises. At least *I* knew it.

Ex-high school jock—but not the quarterback or shortstop type—Denny was your basic offensive guard, or maybe a catcher. In high school, he was the guy who could never get the experiments to come out right in chem lab, who was always clowning that he'd cut off his fingers in metal shop. He was the one who could eat fifteen hot dogs at the Spring Fever Fair, and cut the loudest farts during P.E.

And when a guy like Denny Reitmann went to college, it was only because there was nothing better to do at the time.

Then, it seemed like all of a sudden there was a shitty little "military action" going on in Central America, but most people didn't care about places like El Salvador or Honduras or Nicaragua. The stock market was fluctuating as usual, interest rates were rising, and the import-wars were getting pretty fierce. A lot of the second-level nations like Mexico and Brazil had stopped paying even the interest on their billions-plus loans to the U.S., and a nasty recession was getting ready to take a bite out of the country's hind-parts. As a result the poor minorities were being ground up in society's gears pretty good.

But if you were twenty years old, white, and going to a monstrous diploma-factory like the University of Maryland, everything seemed to be just fine.

Denny Reitmann roomed in my dormitory on the College Park campus, and although you couldn't say that he was my friend, or that I hung around with the guy, I guess I knew him as well as anybody did. He didn't seem to have any real close buddies. Oh sure, everybody laughed at his crude jokes, and we all shook our heads when he would proudly announce his abysmal grades, but none of us was really "tight" with him.

It was like all the guys could sense Denny's true "essence"— kind of bleakness. A void where his feelings should have been, is probably the best way to describe it. I mean, you could look into Reitmann's eyes, and not be completely sure there was anything behind them.

It was right after Christmas vacation in my sophomore year, and everybody was piling back into their rooms to start boning up for the end-of-the-semester grind—Finals.

Everybody, that is, except for Reitmann. He came back with the rest of us, but only to clean out his dresser drawers, desk, and closet. "I'm packin' it in, you guys," he told anyone who would listen. "I figured it out, and even if I ace all my finals, I'm still gonna flunk out, so what the fuck, huh?"

I guess a few of us tried to talk him out of it in a half-assed kind of way, and some of the other guys took him down to the Rendezvous for a farewell drink, but the overall reaction to Denny Reitmann's departure from academe's fair grove was a big ho-hum. Besides, there wasn't really much time to mourn the dead; those Finals were always a bitch, right?

I made out all right with all of them, even Organic Chemistry—the only one that really had me sweating. I knew that without decent numbers in Organic, not even that semi-bogus med school in Grenada would let me through the door. Thus triumphant, when Semester Break finally arrived, I went off with my room-mate, Bob, to ski in western Massachusetts at this great slope called Brody Mountain.

When we came back to the dorm to begin the Spring Semester, there was the usual joking and back-slapping and glad-handing. Everybody seemed keyed-up for the start of the long haul into Summer. So it wasn't until a bunch of us were getting ready to take the hike to the dining hall that somebody noticed the postcard tacked to the bulletin board by the door to the lounge.

Postmarked at Fort Benning, Georgia, the card bore a short, hand-scrawled note which read:

Hey Guys,

I was getting board, so I joined the Marines. They shore do make things rough on us down here, but I think its going to be O.K. I like the rough stuff. Study hard and (smile) don't be like me.

Denny Reitmann

"Jeez," someone said. "The asshole joined the Marines, can you believe it?"

"With Reitmann, I'd believe anything . . ." I said.

"I guess that's what happens when you get B-O-A-R-D," said my room-mate, pulling the card off the corkboard and tossing it in the trash can.

Everybody had a quick laugh, and we piled out the door, on our way to get some over-cooked vegetables and the day's Mystery-Meat Special. By the time we entered the dining hall, the conversation had become fixated upon the perfectly shaped ass of a blonde girl standing several places ahead of us in the line. I don't think anybody gave Denny Reitmann another thought until he came back from a place everybody started calling "the 'Dor" . . .

. . . right before Christmas a year later. I was almost mid-way through my junior year. Bob and I had taken an apartment with two other guys from the dorm, and we were having a great time playing the sophisticated-young-man game.

A lot can happen in a year. I had discovered Mahler and Beethoven, French wines like Poulligny and Cabernet, the irrefutable logic of Bertrand Russell, the lyrical essays of Loren Eiseley, and—well, I think you've gotten the point. I was becoming enlightened and enriched and all that shit.

I was also becoming terrified of the El Salvador war.

They say that everything that goes around, comes around, and goddamn if this wasn't the whole Vietnam mess all over again. The radio was daily talking about Sandinista body counts versus GI casualties—as if we were talking about sporting events instead of people killing each other. The network and cable evening news looked like an old Sam Peckinpah film, and I kept thinking about how close we all were to being part of the horror show.

The horror show crept a little closer the day the apartment phone rang five or six times before anybody bothered to answer it.

"Hello . . ." I said.

"Jack, is that you?"

"Yeah, who's this?"

"It's Reitmann! It's me, Jack. How ya doin', man?"

I did a mental double-take, realizing at last with whom I was speaking.

*Reitmann,* for God's sake! Talk about the last guy I'd expect to hear from . . .

"Yeah, right . . . well, how are you, Denny? Where are you? What've you been doing?" I found myself saying the semi-automatic greetings, asking questions I didn't really care to have answered.

"I'm back on leave . . . from the 'Dor, man. They were lettin' us finish up our hitch a little early 'cause-a Christmas—you know how that goes . . ."

"Yeah, right," I said, at a total loss as to what to say next. What the hell did he want, calling me? How did he find the number? And most importantly, why *me?*

"Listen, I'm at my mom's place, and it's gettin' kinda beat around here, and I was wonderin' if I could stop over for little while, huh?"

"Jeez, Denny, I don't know . . . we're all getting ready to study for some exams."

"Your mom gave me the address," he said as though not hearing me. "And guess what? Your apartment's pretty close to my mom's, so it's no hassle, man. I'll see you around eight, okay?"

Before I could say anything, he'd hung up. I told Bob and Mike and Jay we were going to have company, and received a mixture of reactions. Of which, Mike's was the best: "Well, at least he can tell us some war stories . . ."

And he certainly did.

✧

"A *pregnant* woman . . ." said Jay. "Christ, Denny . . . why?"

"Because she was a fuckin' 'beaner,' that's why!" Reitmann's eyes were like tiny steel balls, like a rat's or maybe a raven's. "They all carry grenades and shit, man . . . they all want to kill themselves an American. And besides, it was my job . . . I was a Sniper."

"What do you mean?" I asked. Mike passed me the chianti bottle and I poured another glass. I was already blitzed pretty good, and this last one was just icing. I had been amazed at how the Marines had changed Reitmann in such a short time. His playful, kind of dumb, but almost likable, mannerisms had been sawed-off along all the edges, filed down until there was only a crude undercarriage left. And on that raw frame, the jarheads had constructed their killing machine—a guy full of hate and poison and a belief that everybody in the world was ultimately out to get you. Reitmann looked at me as I exhaled.

"A sniper, man! Don't you know what a sniper is?" His voice had turned suddenly acidic, condescending.

"Yeah, I guess, but maybe you should clarify any misconceptions we might have."

Reitmann explained that Snipers were specially trained "gyrenes" who spent upwards of thirty days at a clip out in the jungle, alone, playing a crazy survivalist game, eating whatever they could find, and shooting whatever moved. After a month or so like that, they would report back to their Base for a few days R & R, and then back into the "bush" for more grub-eating and beaner-popping.

Denny smiled that half-crazy smile as he nodded. "Yeah. You see, we were special, my squad. You had to be special to be picked for the 'Black Aces' platoon . . . that's what they called the Snipers—the Black Aces."

"Why?" asked Bob.

Reitmann shrugged. "Don't know. They just did. My sergeant had these special decks of cards. Don't know where he got 'em, but it was a deck of nothin' but aces of spades, you know? And when we first got to Usulutan, he passed out a deck to each of us Snipers."

"What for?" asked Jay.

Reitmann smiled, chuckled a bit. "That was the neat part, man. See, each time we zapped a beaner, we were supposed to leave one of them Aces on 'em. It was like a sign that all the Sandies knew about—they all knew the snipers were real bad-asses, you know?"

"Kind of like a calling card," said Jay.

"Yeah, I guess." Reitmann was looking far off, as though reliving moments in the past. Again, that weird smile was starting to form at the corners of his mouth. "I used to use their own knives or bayonets, and stick my Aces to their chests—ain't no way they'd miss it that way."

"I guess not," I said.

"Hey, they were scared shitless of the guys in my squad! Especially after my sergeant started the 'Ring of Truth'."

Denny Reitmann smiled and nodded to himself. There was a cold shine in his eyes that gave me a chill.

"The 'ring of truth'?" asked Jay. "What was that?"

"Check this out," said Denny, as he jumped limberly to his feet. His hand lifted his bulky sweater above his waist to reveal a brass ring attached to a leather harness. The harness slipped over his wide belt.

"Here it is," said Reitmann. The ring was perhaps four inches in diameter. It looked awkward and uncomfortable.

"I don't get it," I said. "What're you talking about?"

"We used 'em to carry our ears, man," said Denny. "That's how we earned early leave on our hitches."

"Your *ears?*" Bob started giggling. He was pretty drunk.

Reitmann looked at him with cold, black eyes. "Yeah, man. You see, every time we sniped somebody, we'd cut off their right ear and put it on our ring. When we'd come back to Base every thirty days or so, we'd turn in our ears and get credits towards an early 'out'."

"Kinda like savings-coupons," said Mike. "Or green stamps . . ." He looked as repulsed as the rest of us, and had not been trying to be funny.

Reitmann grinned, then chuckled. "Yeah! Yeah, I never thought of it like that! Coupons . . . I like that." He paused, his ball-bearing eyes turreting about the room. "You see, with them ears, there wasn't any bullshit about how many beaners you plinked. Great system, huh?"

"Yeah, just great," I said, perhaps a little too sarcastically. Some things never changed, and I wasn't really surprised to hear the Marines were still using such incentive programs.

Reitmann's expression shifted as he glared at me. Teeth bared like fangs, jaw muscles taut, the flesh about his eyes all pinched inward.

"You don't like that, Jack?" He said tauntingly. "A little too strong for you, huh?"

Jay cleared his throat. "Let's face it, Denny . . . it's a little strong for anybody, don't you think?"

"Christ," said Mike. "How'd you keep them from rotting? Didn't they start to stink after a while?"

"Yeah, they stunk a little, but it wasn't as bad you might think. After you been out in the bush for a couple weeks, everything smells like its dead." Denny chuckled at this small jest.

"But most of us used to carry a mess-canister of formaldehyde. I'd stick 'em in there for a couple days, then dry 'em out on a flat rock in the sun. After that, they'd usually hold up till you got back to Base anyway."

The conversation deteriorated from that point onward, and as the effects of the wine wore off, everybody had about enough of Denny Reitmann. I think it was right after he told us he planned to carry a .45 caliber automatic on his person for the rest of his life (so that he could "waste anybody who fucked with him"), that I announced I had to get up for an eight o'clock class.

Everybody else picked up the suggestion and suddenly Reitmann was being escorted to the door. He paused and looked at us for a moment, then he smiled.

"You buncha pussies think you got it good, don't you? Well, I'm tellin' you . . . your turn's gonna come. You'll see what it's like to finally be be a man."

Mike grinned. "I don't think so, Denny. I told the Board I was a fag."

We all laughed, and Denny appeared insulted, perhaps a bit angered. I didn't think it was a good idea to intimidate this poor asshole.

"You can laugh all you want, but just remember that it's men like me that's protectin' all the wimpies like you guys. That's why I'm goin' back . . ."

"What?" I said. I couldn't help myself. "Why?"

Denny's grapeshot eyes gleamed. "Cuz I got a score to settle with a couple more wet-backs . . . for the guys in my squad that didn't make it?"

"Jeez, Denny, that's nuts," said Bob.

"Do you know what the Sandies did when they catch a Sniper?"

Before any of us could answer, he continued: "They always cut his dick off and stuff it in his mouth."

Reitmann grinned crazily. "Yeah. That's the way I found two of my buddies . . ."

Nobody spoke for a moment, and the silence grew quickly awkward, painful.

"Good night, Denny," I said. "Be careful. When you go back . . ."

He grinned that crazy grin for the last time that night and slapped my arm extremely hard. "You too, Jack . . . all of you. And who knows, when you guys get down there, I might be the guy waitin' to greet you when you get outta the chopper!"

"I wouldn't be surprised," said Jay.

And then we shut him out into the night, into the void where our thoughts never ventured. I can remember a great sense of relief passing over me, as though I'd been told a great plague had finally ended.

"That sucker's stone crazy," said Mike.

"I feel sorry for him," said Jay. "They've turned him into a monster."

"He's a fucking psychopath," I said. "I don't ever want to see the son-of-a-bitch again. He gives me the creeps. Did you ever try looking into his eyes?"

"Can you believe he's going back?" asked Bob.

"I hope he stays there," I said. "Him and his 'Ring of Truth' . . ."

Five years later people were still dying in Central America, and the newest President (God, how I loathed the man!) was trying to get the country out of the whole mess "honorably." It was a joke, but nobody was laughing.

Especially me.

The year I finished medical school, the Draft Lottery pulled my birthday up as Number Nine. Very, very bad. But I had already started my first year of Residency at Johns Hopkins, specializing in laser micro-surgery on the nerves and capillaries. Since this was a fairly new field, the Army decided that I could be very useful in saving severed, or partially severed, limbs.

And so even though I was drafted, they gave me a commission, and after boot camp, shipped me off to a V.A. hospital in Philadelphia for some experience before getting a free ticket to the San Salvador Base Hospital and a chance to save a few GI's extremities.

We had a ward in Philly for 'Dor vets who came back in such bad shape, they'd never been able to leave. Para- and quadriplegics; the Johnny-Got-His-Gun basket cases; men with half their skulls and brains and faces blown away; guys with so many organs missing, they had to stay forever hooked up to a series of artificial support machines; and the Section Eights, the Funny Farmers.

Of course, that's where I saw Denny Reitmann again.

It's funny, but I had almost been expecting it on an unconscious level. I had tried to forget about the night he showed us the brass ring on his belt, but I knew it would shamble through the back-corridors of my memory forever.

Denny Reitmann and his Ring of Truth.

I knew, even back then, that both of them would be part of that psychic baggage I would always carry with me. And when I first entered the part of the hospital known as the "Permanent" Ward, walking down the rows of beds which contained every horror and abomination committed to human bodies you could ever imagine, I had an odd feeling pass through me. It was like those times when you can sense someone watching you, usually in a crowded, public place, and you turn around and bang, there he or she is—caught, staring right at you. I experienced a kind of psychic, pre-emptive strike as I accompanied Dr. Barahmi on his rounds. In an instant, I *knew* that I would see Reitmann in one of the beds up ahead. It was an unshakable certainty, an absolute knowledge, and it caused my knees to go weak for just a moment.

Catching myself on the rail of the nearest bed, I paused and shook my head, as if to clear it. Please, I thought. Not Reitmann. Anybody but him.

But I found myself walking past the beds, scanning the faces of the doomed souls within them, actually searching for the familiar features I knew I was going to see.

"Jack!" Reitmann's voice was raspy. "Jack Marchetti!"

Turning to the right, I saw him waving his arms frantically. His complexion was pallid under the fluorescent light, his eyes like single spheres of birdshot, were sunk into his skull. There was no impish grin about to appear in the corners of his mouth, there was no pinched sneer. His face was a design for panic and fear and despair. Reitmann looked hideous to me—a specter from a past I wanted to forget.

"Hello, Denny," I said softly, my voice shattering.

I reached out and shook his hand.

"You know this man?" asked Dr. Barahmi.

I nodded, fighting a lump in my throat. I thought I might actually faint, or maybe heave my guts out. Denny appeared anxious, as if there was a terrible fear inside, just waiting to break free. He wouldn't let go of my hand. "You a doctor now, Jack? You come to get me out of here?"

I could only nod, then shake my head, confused.

Denny burst into tears as he tried to speak. "All you guys tried to forget about me . . . everybody wanted to forget about me . . . everybody but you, Jack. I knew you were different from the rest of them . . ."

I swallowed with difficulty. "I'm . . . I'm no different, Denny." I'm probably worse, I thought.

Dr. Barahmi patted my shoulder, and backed away to give us a private moment. It was at that point that I noticed the absence under Denny's sheets. Picking up the covers, I could see that he had lost both limbs just below the knee. Denny suddenly stopped his crying.

"Mine," he said in a terrible, raspy whisper. "Got me on my third day back, the motherfucker . . ."

"You shouldn't have gone back. You'd made it, you were safe." He shook his head. "None of us are ever safe, Marchetti. Not even guys like you."

There was something about the way Reitmann intoned that last sentence which made me recall his calling us "pussies" for dodging the draft any way we could. Ducking the pain and the horror had been a double-edged sword. A part of me was of course glad I hadn't been maimed or crippled, but there was another part of me which carried a shapeless guilt for not taking my chances like all the poor bastards in the ward which surrounded me. This was not a subject I liked to dwell upon, or even think about, but there was something about Reitmann which was bringing it to the surface.

"You've been here since the last time I saw you?" I covered up the stumps of his legs, tried to look into his spooky eyes.

"That's the ticket, man. Right after New Year's my legs bought the farm, and they skied me outta there. Been here ever since."

"Why? You look like you could have prosthetics with no problems. A little therapy and you could be walking all over the place."

He chuckled inappropriately. "Even with new legs, I couldn't get away from them . . ."

"What? Away from who?"

"So I figure: why bother?"

"Denny, what're you talking about?"

He looked up at me and started laughing. "Didn't they tell you, Jack?" His throat filled with a hyena-like cackling and he threw his head back against his pillow. "I'm as crazy as a shithouse rat!"

Dr. Barahmi appeared soundlessly by my side and tapped my shoulder. "I am sorry. You could not have possibly known. Come. Perhaps we should leave now."

Numb, I must have nodded my head, and allowed the Chief Surgeon to guide me to the exit from the ward, and out into the antiseptic nothingness of the central corridor. But even out there, I could hear the lunatic laughter of Denny Reitmann. As we entered the elevators, the cackling seemed to change into a wind-swept wailing, a preternatural banshee's scream. The sound echoed in my skull even as the doors closed and we began our descent. It was at that moment that I knew I must try to help Denny Reitmann.

Spending a few hours in the Medical Records Library told me all there was to know about him. After stepping on the mine, he lost a lot of blood before the medics could get to him. After suffering from severe shock, he lapsed into a coma for almost a month. When he woke up on the hospital ship to find his legs gone, whatever was left of his mind—whatever part the Marine Corps had not already ravaged—caved in. For the better part of the next three years, Denny exhibited all the symptoms of catatonia. Gradually he began to respond mimetically to the most routine stimuli, and, after a visit from a member of his Sniper squad, he finally started showing signs of a possible recovery.

He made an effort to locate the others in his squad, and this desire for contact was very helpful in Denny regaining his verbal abilities. For the next two years, the entries in his file were the expected kinds of progress-notes on a recovering schizophrenic. His chemo-therapy, originally high doses of Prolyxin, had been tempered over time to include the usual spectrum of anti-hallucinogenics like Haldol, Mellaril, and finally settling on the old stand-by: Thorazine. He responded well in both group and individual therapy, and the notes on that period of his treatment were encouraging. Denny's prognosis changed from "guarded" to outright optimistic until . . .

. . . until he learned that the other members of his squad were dying off, one at a time, but quickly and inexorably.

When Denny learned that the last cohort from his "Black Aces" squad had died, his condition deteriorated rapidly. His file noted increases in chlorpromazine-therapy, his repeated mentions of "visions, voices, and sounds in the night." His hallucinations increased, and he became extremely paranoid and fearful of each coming night.

It all sounded rather typical to me, but not having had any psychiatric work since the survey-stuff at med school, I figured the best thing to do would be to check with Denny's therapist, Dr. Michelle Jordan.

Her face was vaguely familiar to me when we met in her office. I guess I'd seen her walking in the halls or in the elevators but, prior to finding Reitmann, I wouldn't have had much reason to talk to her. Dr. Jordan looked very good for a woman in her early forties, and she seemed pleased to see me take an interest in her patient. Which was fine with me. I mean some of the more insecure types feel very threatened when another doc tries to study one of their guinea pigs.

"To be honest with you," I said softly, "in my thoroughly unprofessional opinion, Denny didn't seem very crazy to me."

Jordan fired up a Winston. On her desk lay a huge ceramic ash tray from the Occupational Therapy Shop (I recognized the mold) overflowing with butts. "No, he doesn't show any symptoms unless you get him on the subject of his squad."

"Are they all dead but him?"

She nodded, took a deep drag.

"How the hell did he find out?"

"Denny became a prolific letter-hack. He had managed to keep in touch with each one—there were only eight of them, actually."

"And they're all dead. Seems pretty weird, don't you think?"

Jordan shrugged, dragged.

"You know how they all died?"

She nodded. "A variety of things. A couple from diseases. The rest were accidental."

That struck me as very weird, very strange. "Foul play suspected in any of them?"

Dr. Jordan smiled. "'Foul play,' Doctor? Do you read a lot of English mystery novels?"

I smiled, maybe blushed a little. "What I meant was: do you think any of them might have been killed? You know—murder?"

"You know, I've never really given it any thought. Why do you ask?"

I shrugged. "I don't know, really. What's he afraid of at night?"

"He won't tell me," said Dr. Jordan. "If I could find out, I could maybe help him work past it."

"Maybe he'll tell me," I said, getting up. The room was so rank from the cigarette smoke, I had to make tracks.

"They want this," said Denny as he reached into the drawer of his bed-stand, fumbling around for something.

I had visited him just before nightfall, and had closed off the bed's privacy curtains to suggest that we were more alone than we were. I hoped he might open up to me.

"Who's 'they,' Denny?"

Ignoring my question, he kept rooting around in the drawerful of junk until he found the object he was looking for. He held it up for me to see.

"This is it. You remember what it is, don't you, Jack?"

Even in the dim light, the brass ring seemed to glow with an eerie warmth, a power. It was a talisman of evil, a magnet which could draw the darkness to it. I felt a tightening in my throat as I looked at the ring. My eyes felt as if they might start watering.

"Yes," I croaked. "I remember it."

Denny laughed, his eyes beading down like Timken bearings and staring off into space. "It ain't really the ring they want, Jack . . . it's these . . ."

Denny gestured along the ring, and I knew immediately that he was seeing things I could not see. And I knew now who "they" must certainly be . . .

It was funny, but it was right at that moment that I realized how wrong I had been about poor Reitmann. I thought back over how I had consigned him to humanity's trash heap, how I'd condemned him for being such a soul-less bastard, for letting the jar-heads turn him into a fucking monster. But now, as I sat there watching him twitch and leer and squirm in his bed, I knew that the guilt was writhing and twisting through him like a swarm of maggots feasting on a fresh kill. It was eating him alive like a cancer, a leprosy of the soul.

Looking at Denny was like looking into a mirror. That's the way it is whenever we really take the time to look at anybody else, I guess.

"I'm the only one left," said Denny. "They got everybody but me."

"Why would they leave you till last?" I said almost in a whisper.

He chuckled, pointed at the flat sheets below his knees. "Because I'm the easiest . . . I'm not going anywhere."

It seemed as good an answer as any, and I nodded, but said nothing. I couldn't think of anything to say. How do you tell a guy with grooves of terror etched permanently into his face there's no such thing as the boogeyman? How do you explain that the embodiment of guilt can assume many shapes and guises? That we all create prisons of our own devise?

No. That's all bullshit to somebody who's been standing on the edge of the Pit, who's been hearing the demon-cries, and the flap of the leathery wings of madness.

"Help me, Jack . . ."

"What can I do?" I looked at him and, for an instant, he appeared to be a little boy, propped up on a fluffy pillow, waiting for a bed-time story. There was a simple pleading in his features, and for the first time, a sadness in his eyes.

"Stay with me . . . when they come, if you're here, maybe it will help."

I looked out beyond the privacy curtain to the nearest window—a black rectangle where night tapped upon its pane. A tomb-like quiet pervaded the ward, as though it waited collectively, expectant like a crowd at a public execution.

"Will you, Jack?"

"What?" I looked back and the little boy was gone. Denny was again the steel-eyed, twisted wretch. He was just a piece of litter tossed out the window while we all careened down hell's highway. My mind was wandering. I hoped I didn't appear to be ignoring him.

"I said will you stay with me, Jack?"

The thought of sitting by his bedside until he fell asleep should not have freaked me the way it did. My gut reaction was to say no, and simply slip away into the night. Denny Reitmann was waiting for something, and I didn't want to hang around to find out what it was.

But I tapped his shoulder reassuringly and forced a smile to my face. "Sure, Denny. I'll stay."

Some of the anxiety seemed to go out of him after that. He smiled, closed his eyes, and nodded his head. I thought about giving him a shot to put him out for the night, and getting me off the hook, but I just couldn't do it to the guy.

In addition, there was a part of me that wanted to know what he was so damned afraid of. If he thought his victims were coming back to reclaim their ears, I wanted to be there to help him get through the trauma.

I owed him that, at least.

Crazy or twisted or whatever—Denny Reitmann had sacrificed his legs. I'd never even given up anything for Lent.

And so I sat there in the darkness watching him lay on his back, eyes closed, chest rising and falling. Starlight and the albedo of a half-moon spilled through the nearby window, giving everything a whitish-blue cast. The air was tinged with medicinal smells such as ether and iodine, punctuated by the night-rattles of labored breathing, of troubled sleepers coughing and rasping through their dreams.

I don't know how long I sat there, listening to night-sounds, but at some point I must have slipped into a half-sleep, because my neck jerked up, snapping back to reluctant consciousness. For a moment, I didn't remember where I was, and the disorientation startled me. Responding to some atavistic stimulus, my heart began hammering and I was instantly awake. I looked at my patient, who slept calmly.

Then, suddenly, he opened his eyes, wide awake. It was weird the way he just came awake like that.

"What is it, Jack?" Reitmann's voice reached out in the darkness.

I looked at him, just as a draft of cold air passed over us.

"What do you mean, Denny?"

"Did you feel it, just then?"

I couldn't bullshit him. "The cold . . . ? Yeah, I felt it."

"They're comin', man. It's tonight. I can feel it."

His face had become drawn and pale, his eyes jittering around, blinking furiously.

"Take it easy, Denny. Why would they wait until now, after all this time? Why would they . . . do it . . . when I'm here? Don't you think that would be too much of a coincidence?" I tried to smile casually.

"Maybe they've been waitin' for you too, Jack . . . maybe you owe them too?"

Reitmann's voice had a fragile edge on it, but his words still cut me. What the hell was he talking about?

"Listen . . . !" Reitmann half-whispered.

"I'm sorry, Denny, but I don't—"

I stopped in mid-sentence. I *did* hear something: footsteps, bare feet, slapping on the cold tile of the outer corridor, growing louder, getting closer. There was no rhythm, no pattern to the sounds. A cacophony of uneven slaps and drags and shuffles.

"Aw, jeeziz . . . ! It's *them*, Jack! I know it is!" Denny screamed and his voice seemed to resonate through the ward, as though we were inside a vast cavern.

The sounds of advancing feet grew louder, thicker. Whoever it was shambling up the hall, they made up quite a crowd.

Standing up, I started away from the bed, and Reitmann

reached out to grab my arm. His palm was cool, but slippery with sweat. "No, don't go!"

"Denny, I just—"

Looking out into the ward, I blinked my eyes, lost my voice. The ward was gone.

A low, living, ground fog was boiling up like dry-ice on a stage. All around us, the fog rolled in like waves on a beach. The double row of beds had vanished. The walls, windows, bedtables, everything . . . was *gone*.

"What the hell—?" There was a piece of me that desperately wanted to believe that this was one hell of a nightmare, that I'd better make myself wake up now because things were getting out of hand.

But there was no waking up from this one.

Denny must have seen them before I did because he started screaming, pulling himself out of the bed with his hands.

There was movement in the fog. Shapes coalesced slowly, like the ghosted images on a snowy television screen. The uneven cadence of their approach grew more distinct, and I could see the point men, the van, homing in on us.

Some of them were stick-figures, bone and tendon animated by the whirling, karmic forces which turn the gears of Eternity. Others, lean and brown-skinned, were more whole, but on the right sides of their heads, *none* of them had any ears . . .

Reitmann had pulled himself up against the headboard of his bed, teetering on his stumps. The drawer to the bed table rattled open and he thrashed around the contents frantically.

"I got it! I got it right here! I got it!" He repeated the words over and over like a litany, and without turning around, I knew what Reitmann was looking for.

There was no way to tell how many of them were there, but I saw women and children among the ranks of soldiers. Some of them were so far gone, you couldn't tell male from female, though . . .

Oddly enough, the initial jolt of panic left me when I realized that I couldn't run, that there was no place to hide. I accepted this and waited for whatever was to come.

The first wave of them reached the end of the bed, splitting their formation and swarming around both sides of it. I could smell their foulness, the corruption which steamed off them in acrid sheets. The air was thick with the sting of their hate, and I began suffocating. They surged all around me, pressing me into the soft decay of their flesh.

Reitmann had descended into babbling madness. A pitiful wailing escaped him as they surrounded him, absorbing him into their mass like a cancer would devour a healthy cell. He threw the ring at them, and it disappeared in their midst. Reitmann continued to scream but I could no longer see him. I was overcome by a paralysis which also had a calming effect on my mind. I watched everything with the detachment of an only mildly interested spectator.

Abruptly, the screaming stopped, as though choked off. There was a finality about the silence which enveloped me as totally as the crush of putrid bodies. I could see their heads all turning, heads with new, right ears. Slowly, silently, they turreted about until the eyed and eyeless alike were all looking at me . . .

. . . Orderlies found me the next morning, sagged in my bedside chair. Reitmann had died during the night, leaving us with a bug-eyed, lip-peeled expression engraved into his waxy face. One of the orderlies said Denny looked like he'd opened the cellar-door to Hell, and I wanted to tell him how close to the truth he might have been.

But I remained silent, waiting for them to gurney his legless corpse off the ward. My memories of what had happened were painfully crisp, having none of the ragged edges of a nightmare. But I also had the feeling there was a segment of the whole experience still missing. Something else had taken place last night, I was certain, but I didn't remember until much later in the day, when evening crept up to windowsills on stalking-cat feet.

I was in the hospital cafeteria standing in line. Ahead of me were several medics—part of a class receiving emergency field surgical training—and as I stared at their uniforms, a vision passed through me like a wide, cold blade.

Like an epiphany, I had a flash of memory which filled in the dead space. I suddenly knew what I had so obviously repressed.

"Are you all right, Doctor?" asked a nurse who had been standing behind me. Looking down, I saw the contents of my tray littering the floor. I felt as though emerging from a time-fugue.

"I don't know . . ." I said, and staggered from the line feeling the stares of others in the room as I turned in slow circles. I wanted to escape, but there was no place to run.

Then, remembering:

They had taken me to their battlefield. A vast, featureless plain where time melted and ran like lava, where light and shadow danced eternally at the limits of your peripheral vision. The ground was thick with their bodies. Stacked and jammed like endless cords of kindling wood, the arrangement of battle-corpses stretched off to the dim horizon in all directions. But there lay some who still lived, who still twitched and shook in the depths of the charne-field, and it was for them that I had been brought. Down all the hours of the tunneled night, I pushed back entrails into ruptured bellies; pulled shrapnel from slivered torsos; sutured severed legs and arms . . . and ears. I washed myself in the equitable blood of revenge. There was no end to the carnage, no end to the tuneless song of their pain.

But it was not this knowledge which had so stunned me, as much as the certainty they would be coming back for me— *tonight* and every other night.

For as long as the hate burned like the heart of a star . . .
*Forever.*

*Back in the late Seventies and early Eighties, there was a talented writer by the name of Alan Ryan, who broke in writing under the editorial eye of Roy Torgeson. He lived in New York, started attending the usual circuit of conventions, and that's where I met him. He came up with this idea for an anthology called* Halloween Horrors, *which he sold to my old goombah, Pat Lobrutto, when he was the editor at Doubleday, and the book appeared to good reviews. Flushed with success, Alan talked Pat into a* Halloween Horrors II, *and asked me to do a story.*

*I grabbed one of my favorite reference books when I am doing a story which requires a grounding in myth, ancient history, folklore, and all that other old magick stuff*—The Golden Bough: A Study in Magic and Religion *by Sir James George Frazier (1922)[1], and found some arcane references to Halloween, or as some call it "All Hallow's Eve'n." I used a kid as my protagonist because Halloween and kids are a natural combination, and wrote a story that has proved to have remarkable legs.[2] Alan accepted it, paid me for it, and I waited for it to appear in print . . . for about ten years. For some reason or another,* Halloween Horrors II *was never published, and I had the story in the file waiting patiently. After the statute of limitations expired, I figured I could sell it somewhere else, and Rich Chizmar bought it for* Cemetery Dance. *I guess the lesson learned here is patience—if your story is any good at all, it will eventually force its way into print and the minds of your audience.*

---

[1] *I'm giving away trade secrets here, but hey, I do it in the hope that at least one of you out there will go on to be a great writer because I inspired you and influenced you. So let me say* The Golden Bough *is one of those great treasure chests of Cool Stuff. I guarantee someone of imagination could find more story-ideas in its dusty pages that he or she would ever have time to write . . . So if you don't have a copy on your shelves, go get one, and . . . do-it-today!*

[2] *The story has been reprinted in several languages, included in a "best of" anthology, adapted as a comic, and produced by George Romero for his* Tales from the Darkside *TV series. Hey,* all *my short fiction should do so well . . .*

THE CUTTY BLACK SOW

T welve-year-old Jamie stood with his parents and his little sister, Gloria, around Great-Grandmother McEvan's bed while a cold autumn wind rumbled the shutters and whistled through the seams of their old house. Rain tapped on the windowpanes like tiny fingers, slapped against the shingles like sheets on a clothesline.

Great-Grandma was a tiny bird of a woman at the age of 103. She had always looked the same to Jamie: silver-blue hair in a bun, thin pointy face, dark sparrow eyes, and long, spider-leg fingers. But she had always been a strong old woman. She had never been to a doctor in her life, and she had birthed eight children. Lost five, and raised the rest as best she could.

Now she lay in the warmly lit bedroom, her eyes closed, mouth half-open, breath wheezing in and out of her like a cold wind.

"She's not going to make it, is she, Dad?" asked Jamie with the matter-of-factness of a twelve-year-old.

"Jamie! Stop that!" said his mother.

His father sighed, touched her arm. "No, he's right, Hon. He's just saying out loud what we've all been thinking . . ."

"Is she going to die?" asked nine-year-old Gloria with a touch of awe in her voice. "Is she really going to *die* right here in our house?"

"We don't know that for sure, sweetheart," said Mother. She looked at her husband. "Should we call Dr. Linton?"

"I don't think there's much use in it. You remember what he said . . ."

Jamie noted that no one was actually crying, but everybody was fighting their feelings. They were all witnessing something they had known was coming for awhile now. He was thinking about the idea of death and dying, and how it changed people into such bad imitations of themselves. His great-grandmother had always been so lively and active. She had entertained him and Gloria with stories of her native Scotland and the Highlands she loved so dearly.

Now there would be no more stories.

The sheets rustled as the old woman stirred. Jamie saw her eyelids flutter as she gathered the strength to look at him and the others around her bed. "What day is it?" she asked.

"Thursday," said Jamie's father, without thinking.

A pause, then: "No . . ." Great-Gran's voice was hoarse and low. "What date?"

"Oh . . ." said his mother. "It's the thirtieth."

Another pause, a wheezing of breath, then: "Of October?"

"Yes, Great-Gran," said Jamie, keeping his own voice low and soft.

"All Hallow's Even," said the old woman. There was a different tone in her voice, an inflection that could have been awe or respect, or even fear.

"What? What did she say?" asked Jamie's mother.

"I'm not sure," said his father. "Grandma, what was that you said?"

"All Hallow's Even. I'm going to die. On All Hallow's Even."

"Jim, what's she talking about?"

"Halloween," said Jamie's father. "Tomorrow's Halloween. That's what they called it in Scotland."

"But why . . . I mean, what does she mean?" Jamie's mother held his father's arm tightly.

"I don't know . . ." his father looked at his watch.

Outside a gust of wind whispered against the house. "Eleven-thirty. It'll be the thirty-first soon . . ."

Jamie's mother leaned over the bed, tried to talk to Great-Gran, but the old woman's eyes had closed and her breathing had returned to its former shallowness. Turning back to her husband, Jamie's mother looked distressed.

"I think we'd better call Dr. Linton."

His father nodded, sighed. "All right, I'll call him. You kids, it's time to get off to bed."

Hours later, Jamie lay in his bed in the darkness. The storm still buffeted the house and the trees around it. He could not fall asleep, was not even feeling tired. He'd been awake when Dr. Linton arrived, wet and blustery in the downstairs foyer. The tall, white-haired doctor had looked in on Great-Gran, then returned downstairs to confer with Jamie's parents. He listened to Dr. Linton's words: " . . . and I'd say there's nothing much more you can do to make her any more comfortable. She's lapsed into a coma. Might hang on for weeks—or, she might not make it till morning."

The words stung Jamie as he lay in his dark bed. Great-Gran dying was one of those terribly impossible things to imagine. She'd *always* been a part of his life. Rocked him as a baby, fed him his bottles, bathed him, and always the stories about Scotland. To think of her as *gone* was like knowing when you woke up in the morning your right arm would be missing. Unthinkable.

And yet, true. She might not last the night.

He didn't know how long he lay in his bed without sleeping. Long enough for the storm to quiet and his parents to finally retire to their bedroom. Long enough for the heavy clouds to part and let the moonlight creep through his window. Jamie wanted to fall asleep, but he could not.

More time passed. In the silent house, he could hear every creak and groan of old wood, every tic of cooling radiator pipes. And then a new sound: Great-Grandmother was talking. She sounded so bright and clear that he imagined she must have arisen from her coma. A spark of hope was ignited in him, and he slipped noiselessly from the bed to creep into her room at the end of the hall. The door was open and the room was stalked by tall shadows of old furniture, cast by the feeble glow of a night-light.

Silently, Jamie approached the bed. If anything, the old woman looked worse than before and she spoke as though in a trance.

But her words were soft and clear: " . . . and down we would go to Balquhidder with the other children to gather for the fires. A-beggin' from the folk, and we would say 'Give us a peat t'barn the witches, good missus!' Pile it high, we would! With straw, furze and peat . . . what a beautiful Samhnagan it would be!"

Jamie felt a chill race down his back. He thought of calling his parents, but they would only make him go back to bed. Yet he sensed an urgency in the old woman's voice, and he knew he'd never remember what she was trying to say—especially the funny words. Then he thought of his tape recorder, and moving quickly, silently, he retrieved it from his room. Turning it on, he captured the trance-like ramblings of the old woman.

" . . . and the fire would burn through the night on All Hallow's Even, and we would dance about it, we would! The fire that kept away the Cutty Black Sow! Kept it away from any soul who died on that witches' night! Till the heap had turned to bright red coals. And we would gather up the coals and ash in the form of a circle. Then into that circle we would put stones—one marked for each member of our families. The stones were our *souls,* don't ya see! And as long as they stayed inside the circle of Samhnagan, ole Cutty Black could not harm us! And in the mornin' everyone would run to the cool ashen circle—to make sure that not a stone was disturbed or missin'. For if it was, the soul that stood for that missin' stone would be *took* by the *Cutty Black Sow!*"

Jamie listened as the old woman rambled. It was some memory, a bit of remembered childhood. He tried to speak to her, to ask her what she meant, but she continued on to the end, the last words only a whisper.

He waited for her to continue, but there was nothing more. Great-Gran's breathing became ragged, catching in her hollow chest, then wheezing out as if released by a cruel fist. Suddenly her body became rigid, and then a tremor passed once through her bones. Jamie watched as her drawn little body rose under the bed-covers for an instant, then fell slack, her head lolling to the far side of the pillow.

He could not see her face, yet he knew she was gone. There was a coolness in the room that had been absent before. He felt utterly alone in a vast darkness despite the pale glow of the night-light.

Slowly, Jamie thumbed off the Sony recorder as his gaze drifted to an old Westclock on Great-Gran's bureau. 4:35 in the morning. She'd been right: she did die on Halloween.

He padded silently back to his room, replaced his cassette recorder on a shelf by his bed, then woke up his parents. He told them he had heard Great-Gran making strange noises, and that he was afraid to go see her. His father moved quickly from the bed and down the hall. A few minutes later he returned to announce quietly that she was gone.

The time had come when they could cry. Jamie's mother held him while they both sobbed, and she whispered that everything would be all right.

But he was thinking about the recording he'd made—and he was unsure if what his mother said was altogether true.

Halloween came early that year because nobody went back to sleep. They sat in the kitchen having a very early breakfast while the sunrise burned through the autumn trees in the backyard. Then, while Jamie dressed for school, his father made lots of phone calls, and his mother cried openly a few more times. Gloria was still asleep as Jamie sat in his room and replayed the tape he'd made. To hear Great-Gran's voice, knowing she was gone, gave him a strange feeling. It struck him that he was listening to those "last words" everybody talks about.

Listening to her words for the second time, he realized the old woman was fearful of dying on Halloween. She was telling him something—something important. Her people had always protected anybody who dies on that day. Protected them from the Cutty Black Sow—whatever *that* was . . .

Jamie stuffed the Sony into his backpack, along with his schoolbooks, and returned to the kitchen. His mother poured him another glass of orange juice.

"Your father's not going to work today," she said. "He can drive you and Gloria to school."

She paused as though suddenly remembering something important. "Oh God—she's still asleep. I've got to wake her up, and tell her . . ."

His mother left the kitchen, leaving Jamie alone again with his thoughts. He could hear his father's muffled voice as he spoke on the phone. Other than that, it was quiet. He thought about Great-Gran, wondering if she'd *known* he was listening to her last night, if she'd been talking about that stuff with the stones for a reason.

Jamie couldn't get the story out of his mind as he and Gloria rode into town with their father. The bonfire and the stones and the Cutty Black Sow. At school he waited until study hall just after lunch, then transcribed the recording into his math notebook. When it was written out, he was able to study the words more carefully, and he became even more convinced that Great-Gran had been giving him a message.

Jamie asked Miss Hall, the school librarian, for books about Scotland and Scottish folklore. Usually quiet and dour, Miss

Hall volunteered that she was Scottish on her mother's side, and it was good to see young people interested in their heritage.

With her help, Jamie figured out a lot of what Great-Gran had been talking about. Samhnagan was a ritual bonfire, burned on Halloween night to protect the people from the forces of Evil, and to save the souls of any who died on the Witches' Day. There was nothing about the "Cutty Black Sow," but Miss Hall told him that she would be happy to look it up when she went home that evening. Jamie thanked her and gave her his phone number, making the librarian promise to call if she discovered anything.

On his way home on the bus, Jamie planned his evening. He knew what he had to do for his great-grandmother. Gloria kept interrupting his thoughts and, finally, he knew he'd have to talk to her.

"Do you think we'll still be able to trick-or-treat tonight?" she asked solemnly.

"Gee, I don't know, Gloria. I wasn't really thinking about it. I guess I figured we'd go, but I might have to do something else"

"Oh yeah?  Like what?"

He considered telling her what he intended. Sometimes Gloria could be trusted with secrets, but oftentimes not.

"You wouldn't understand," he said after a pause. "Something Great-Gran wanted me to do. For her."

Gloria's eyes flashed. He had her hooked now. "But she's dead now . . ."

"She asked me last night—right before she died. It was like a . . . a last request."

"Really?" Gloria's voice flirted with true awe.

"Yeah, but this is *secret*, you understand?"

"Sure I do!  I can keep a secret."

"Now listen, if I tell you about this, you have to *swear* you won't tell anybody—not even Mom or Dad, okay?"

"Gee, what're you going to *do,* anyway?

"You swear?"

She nodded with great seriousness. "I swear."

"All right," said Jamie. "Last night . . ."

✧

When the bus dropped them off at the house, Jamie's mother informed them that The Undertaker had picked up Great-Gran. Jamie went into the backyard and sat on a swing. To his right was a barbecue pit and outdoor fireplace. If he was going to build a fort, that was the place. The yard was enclosed by tall oak and poplar trees, and a cool wind sifted through the brown and orange and yellow leaves, shaking them loose and bringing them down all around him. It was pretty, but he found it also very sad.

The back door slammed and Gloria ran down to the swing-set. "I just talked to Mommy, and she said we can still go trick-or-treating!"

"Okay."

"They're going to be at the funeral home, but she said I can go out as long as *you* stay with me. Then we gotta go to Mrs. Stamrick's house when we're done. They'll pick us up there when they get home, okay?"

"Yeah," he said absently. "That'll be fine. But we'll have to make that bonfire first."

"What?"

"C'mon, Gloria. Get real. I just *told* you about that."

"That didn't make much sense to me." She grimaced.

"Well, it did to me. And I gotta make that fire for Great-Gran. She wanted me to."

After dinner that night, Jamie's parents left for the funeral home. He went out to the backyard, down toward the woods which bordered the property, and began gathering up sticks and branches from a big deadfall left from last winter's storms. He also gathered up five stones about the size of baseballs. As he began arranging the wood in his father's barbecue pit, he heard Gloria coming down the back steps. She was dressed in her trick-or-treat costume—a skeleton in a hooded robe.

"Getting it ready?" Gloria asked as she watched.

"What do you think, stupid?"

"I'm not stupid. I was just asking."

With matches he lit the wood; it took several attempts to get the heavier branches burning, but soon the fire licked and cracked with a small, contained fury. It warmed their faces and cast a hot orange glow on the surrounding trees. Jamie piled on more wood from the deadfall, and the blaze became a small inferno, roaring as it sucked up the cool autumn air.

"It's going good now," said Gloria, entranced by the ever-changing shapes and glowing coals.

Jamie finally pulled an El Marko from his jacket pocket and an old rag he'd taken from his father's workroom in the basement. He wiped the stones as clean as possible, then marked each one with an initial.

"What're you doing now?" asked Gloria.

"I have to fix the stones. One for each of us in the family. See that G? That's for you. And these are for Mom and Dad, me and Great-Gran. Now, we have to throw them into the middle, like this." Jamie tossed Great-Gran's stone into the center of the coals. Then he tossed all the others in, one by one, with a small amount of ceremony. "There, it's done."

"Why'd you have to do that, Jamie?"

"Because. That's the way they always did it. To protect us all . . ."

"Protect us?" Gloria giggled beneath her skull-mask. "From what?"

"I'm not sure . . . from the Cutty Black Sow, I guess."

"What's *that*?"

"I don't know," said Jamie. "I couldn't find out."

The only sound was the wind in the treetops and an occasional pop of a coal cooling down.

"Hey," said his sister. "Are we gonna go trick-or-treating or what?"

"Oh yeah, I guess we can go now," he said.

"Finally!" Gloria turned toward the house. "I'll be right back out—gotta get my shopping bag!"

Then they went trick-or-treating and when they returned from a tour of the neighborhood streets, it was almost totally dark. Jamie guided her back to their house and Gloria reminded him that they were to go to Mrs. Stamrick's place.

"In a minute. I want to go check on the fire."

"Aw, Jamie, I'm tired . . ."

"Look, it'll only take a minute. Come on, you got what you wanted, didn't you?"

"Oh, all right." she followed him as Jamie took a flashlight from the garage and moved close to the barbecue pit. Only a few orange embers belied the location of the small bonfire. He played the light over the ashes, searching for the five stones in the debris.

"What're you doing?"

"Just checking to see that everything's OK." He counted the stones as the beam of light touched them: three . . . four . . . where was the last one?  From the looks of the ashes and embers, the wood had collapsed, then spilled toward the edge of the firebrick. He directed the beam down to the patio and found the fifth stone, amidst a scattering of ash. It had fallen from the fire, and he remembered his Great-Gran's words: *"no stone should be missing or disturbed . . ."*

Jamie bent low and saw in the flashlight beam that it was the stone with a just-legible "J" on its face.

*His* stone. His *soul?*

It would be best if he left it as it lay—undisturbed.

"Hey, look," said Gloria. "One of 'em fell out!"

Before he could say anything, his sister, costumed as a miniature Grim Reaper, swooped down beside him and grabbed for the stone.

"No, Gloria!  Don't touch it!"

But her fingers had already encircled it, had begun to pick it up. In that instant, Jamie felt a jolt of energy spike through him. His heart accelerated from a burst of adrenaline, and suddenly Gloria screamed.

Pulling her hand back, she let go of the stone in the same motion. It was flung into the darkness and Jamie could hear it thump upon the lawn somewhere to his right.

"It burned my hand!" sobbed Gloria. "It was still hot!"

"I told you not to touch it!  Oh, Jeez, Gloria, you really shouldn't have touched it!  I've got to find it!"

"Let's go to Mrs. Stamrick's. Come on!"

"No, wait!  I've got to find that stone . . ."

"What for?  It's just an old rock. You can get it in the morning."

"No, it might be too late then." It *might* be too late already, he thought.

Despite Gloria's protests, she helped scan the lawn for the missing stone. She must have heard the urgency and fear in

Jamie's voice because she even got down on her hands and knees to grope about in the grass.

When they found the stone, it was still hot, but cool enough to pick up. Jamie carefully returned it to the spot where she had first disturbed it, and hoped that nothing would be wrong. After all, Gloria hadn't meant to touch it. Perhaps it would be all right since it was not yet morning.

He and Gloria went to Mrs. Stamrick's house two blocks away, and she welcomed them with affectionate hugs and kisses and mugs of hot chocolate. She spoke in saccharine tones and made a fuss over them.

Outside the clapboard house, the wind began gusting. Jamie listened to it whistle through the gutters and downspouts as he sat in Mrs. Stamrick's parlor watching a situation comedy on TV.

Gloria was busy pouring her loot into a large mixing bowl on the floor; Mrs. Stamrick oohed and aahed appropriately as his sister scooped up especially fine prizes from the night's haul.

Jamie sipped his cocoa and watched TV without actually paying attention. At one point he thought he heard something tapping on a windowpane, even though the others did not seem to notice. When he took his empty mug into the kitchen to place it in the sink, he heard another sound.

A thumping. Outside.

Something was padding across the wood floor of Mrs. Stamrick's back porch. It was rapid and relentless, as though some heavy-footed dog, a large dog, was pacing back and forth beyond the kitchen door.

Slowly Jamie moved to the door, but could not bring himself to draw up the shade and peer out. The thumping footsteps continued and at one point he thought he heard another sound— a rough exhalation, a combination of a growl and a snort.

Moving quickly out of the kitchen, he told Mrs. Stamrick that it sounded like there was a big dog on her back porch. She walked past him into the kitchen, raised the shade and looked out. Seeing nothing, she opened the door, admitting a cool blast of face-slapping wind—the only thing that was out there.

"It must have wandered off," she said. "Nothing's out there now."

Jamie nodded and forced a silly grin, then let her lead him back into the parlor.

While Gloria was dozing off on the couch, Jamie tried to get absorbed in a cop-show drama. But he couldn't concentrate on anything except the sounds of the wind outside the house. And the sounds of other things he couldn't always identify.

When his father arrived to pick them up, Jamie could not recall ever being so glad to see him. He picked up his sister's treat-bag as his father carried the sleeping Gloria out to the car where their mother waited. As Jamie walked down the driveway toward the safety of the big station wagon, he listened for the sounds, searched the shadows and the shrubbery that lurked beyond the splash of Mrs. Stamrick's porch light.

He sensed there was something out there, could almost feel the burning gaze of unseen eyes, the hot stinging breath of an unknown thing so very close to him.

In the car, he exchanged small-talk with his parents. It was best if he tried to act as normal as possible. But his mother turned to look at him at one point, and he wondered if she sensed—as mothers often can—that something was not right with him.

As soon as the car stopped in the driveway, he jumped out and moved quickly to the back door, waiting for his father with the keys. A single yellow bug-light cast a sickening pall over everything, but it also sparked off feelings of safety and warmth.

Finally, they were all inside the house, which afforded him a feeling of warmth and safety. While his father carried Gloria off to bed, his mother checked the Code-A-Phone; its greenlight signaled calls waiting. Jamie hung up his coat in the closet. In the other room he could hear his mother as she played back the tape from the phone answering machine—mostly messages of condolence from friends and relatives. He was about to go down the hall to the stairs when he heard a loud thumping noise outside the kitchen window.

He fought down the urge to run blindly to his mother and wrap his arms around her. The sound of her voice breaking the silence almost made him cry out.

"Jamie," his mother called. "There's a message for you here."

As casually as possible, he moved to the table where his mother rewound the tape and replayed it.

" . . . Hello, Jamie. This is Miss Hall. I found what you were looking for in some of my books at home. I guess you're out trick-or-treating, so you can call me back till 11:00, if you want. Bye now . . ."

His mother glanced at the kitchen clock as she stopped the tape. "It's only ten o'clock. Are you going to call her?"

"Nah, it's getting late. I'll just see her on Monday, I guess."

His mother smiled as she returned to the rest of the messages, and Jamie moved quickly up the stairs to his room. He said goodnight to his father, undressed, and slipped under his sheet and quilt.

It was at least a half-hour after his parents had also gone to bed when Jamie heard more of the strange sounds, the thumping footfalls of something in the yard beneath his window. His room faced the rear of the house, his window overlooking the roof of the back porch. Broken moonlight splintered the darkness as he slipped from the covers and forced himself to look out.

The jutting slant of the roof obscured his line of sight, and for a moment, he saw nothing unfamiliar. Then, for an instant, one of the shadows moved, seemed to step back into the deeper darkness of the yard.

Looking beyond it, Jamie was surprised to see the still-glowing embers of his bonfire at the end of the yard. From this distance, they were nothing more than points of deep orange, but he would have thought they'd be dead by now. The rising wind must have stirred up the last coals.

Again came the faint sounds of something moving with a heavy-footed gait. And the distant, snorting breath he had heard once before.

Jamie was trembling as he moved away from the window, and it became suddenly important that he speak with Miss Hall. He moved quietly downstairs to the kitchen phone, and looked up her number in the phone book.

Miss Hall answered on the fifth ring.

"Miss Hall, it's Jamie . . . I'm not sure what time it is, I hope I'm not calling too late . . ." his voice sounded unsteady.

Miss Hall chuckled. "Well, almost, but not quite . . . uh, Jamie, what did you need this information for? It struck me as somewhat odd that—"

"Oh, just for a project I was doing. About Halloween and all." There was a pause, and when the librarian did not reply he rushed on: "You said you found it for me . . ."

"Yes, I did." There was a sound of papers being shifted about. "Yes, here we are . . . let's see, in Scotland and Wales, there was a belief that bonfires protected people from demons and witches."

"Yeah, I already found that stuff," he forced himself to speak in hushed tones. "What about the . . . the . . ."

"Oh yes, the 'Cutty Black Sow' . . ." Miss Hall cleared her throat. "You see, it was a common belief back then that demons could assume the shape of animals. And it was believed that on Halloween these demons took the shape of a pig—a large black-haired creature that walked on its hind legs. Its hair was supposed to be bristly and closely cut. The 'Cropped Black Sow,' or the 'Cutty Black Sow,' was what they called him."

Jamie felt stunned for a moment, and he tried to speak but no words would come out.

"Jamie, are you there?"

"Yes! Oh . . . oh, well, thank you, Miss Hall. Thanks a lot. That's just what I needed to . . . to finish my project."

"Well, I'm glad I could be of help, Jamie. It must be pretty important for you to be working on it this late."

There came the sound of footfalls again. This time, they seemed so loud in Jamie's ears that he almost felt the house move from the impact.

"Yeah, it's pretty important . . . I guess. Listen, I'd better go, Miss Hall, thanks a lot."

He hung up the phone before she could reply, and moved quickly back to his room. He didn't want to wake up his parents, or tell them he was scared, but he didn't know *what* to do. The thumping grew louder and it was now intermixed with snuffling, snorting sounds.

The kind of sounds a pig would make.

Jamie looked out his window. The yard seemed darker than before, but the embers of the fire in the distance seemed brighter . . .

. . . until he realized that the embers were not brighter, but *closer*. And that the two fiercely glowing orbs were not coals at all . . .

They were *eyes*.

Backing away, he heard scraping sounds. Rough, abrasive, crunching sounds, as though something was scrambling for purchase on the side of the porch, something trying to climb up, towards his window.

The sounds were very loud now. The old wood of the house groaned and scraped as it was splintered. It was so *loud!* Why didn't his parents hear it too! Jamie jumped into his bed, grasping at the covers the way he had as a child when he had been afraid of some terrible night-thing.

Something scraped across the windowpane as ember-eyes appeared beyond the glass . . .

He must have cried out, although he didn't realize it, because he heard his father's voice calling his name. Relief flooded through him as he heard his father's hand on the doorknob.

"Jamie, are you all right?"

The door swung open, and he could see a tall silhouette against the bright light of the hall beyond. Quickly he glanced back to the window, and the burning eyes were gone. He felt silly as he tried to speak.

"Dad! Yeah, it's OK . . . just a bad dream, I guess."

His father said nothing as he walked into the room, drawing close to the bed. In the darkness, he sat on the bed and drew his son close to him. Jamie relaxed in the comforting embrace, and put his arms around his father.

He was about to tell his Dad how scared he had been, when his hands touched the back of the neck of the thing which held him, when he felt the close-cut, bristly hair . . .

*Okay, being raised in the richest of Catholic heritages[1] and all that, I guess a little confession is good for me once in a while. So: back in Ancient Times, when I was single and crazy and before I met Elizabeth, I used to read the* Penthouse *letter columns. The only problem was all those dumb pictures used to get in the way . . .*

*Yeah, sleazy, I know, but I did it for the entertainment value and the occasional inspiration.*

*Inspiration for what?*

*Well, a story, of course. And I can remember one month, there was this letter from a guy[2] living on his folks' farm and he sounded like a very lonely guy. A very sad guy. A very weird guy. His letter was long, rambling, replete with enough misspellings, malapropisms, and skewed perceptions to even make the Bowery Boys howl. If you read between the lines, as I in my wisdom could do, you would have seen a seething cauldron of pathology, a mind stewing in its own fermented juices. I read the letter over a few times because I simply couldn't get over the author's plaintive cry for help and his obvious signal he was going down for the count in short order.*

*And so, with that in mind, I will leave it to your judgment and fervid imaginations to decide which parts of the story which follows are fictive and which have been appropriated in all their factual frightfulness from one very scary letter.*

---

[1] *My father was even a Knight of Columbus.*

[2] *Yes, I know a lot of the letters in those mags are fakes. I didn't just roll off the tailgate of the zucchini wagon; hell, I even have some friends who make a decent buck knocking out a batch of perversion every month. The point taken,* Penthouse *does get some legitimate letters and I would swear this was one of them. It had that singular* texture *that was too real in a stark, and quite dreadful, manner. Trust me on this one.*

LOVE LETTERS

June 19
LetterBoxes
P.O. Box 69
Intercourse PA 17534

Dear LetterBoxes Ladies:

Okay, I'm sending you my money order for $19.95. You can write me
at the address on the envelope. I'm already excited.

Yours Truly,
Wayne Gundersen

_____

Wayne Gundersen
July 8
RFD 12 - Route 43
Ingram WI 54535

My Dearest Wayne:

   I was so glad to get your letter. I've
been waiting to find a pen-pal for so long
now, and now that I know you'll be writing to
me, it just makes my whole body tingle, especially my pussy (if you know what I mean!). I
thought you might want to see what I'm talking about, so I sent you a picture. (smile)
   I didn't think you'd mind . . .
   Well, I'd better be getting back to work
at the shoe store. I'm the Assistant Manager. Write soon!

Yours,
Candy

Candy
July, 8
c/o LetterBoxes
P.O. Box 69
Intercourse PA 17534

My Dearest Candy:

I was real glad to get your letter but I thought it would be maybe a little longer. Good to know you got a job though. Assistant Manager sounds good to me. I never had a job. Just work on this farm with my Dad now that my stepmother left us (okay with me cause I kind of hated her). I got 2 sisters (I kind of hate them too, but at least I can peek at them when they are in the bath room). I'm going to be a senior in high school this Fall, but I can't wait to get out of that place. Bunch of rich snots and grits and uppity girls (not like you). I've never had a girlfriend, and only once I had sex with somebody else (do you have sex?), but I can't ever tell about that. But I might tell you someday, if we stay real close like I think we will. Why don't you write and tell me more about yourself, and I'll tell you more about me and my dog Bowser. Oh yeah and thanks loads for the great picture! I keep it in my socks drawer and I'm putting a Polaroid of me and Bowser in the envelope. He likes to take showers with me.

Yours Truly,
Wayne

Wayne  Gundersen
August  23
RFD  12  -  Route  43
Ingram  WI  54535

Wonderful  Wayne:

   The  weather  is  so  hot  this  time  of  year  I
just  hate  to  wear  clothes—know  what  I  mean?
In  my  apartment,  after  work,  I  just  walk
around  naked  all  the  time,  only  it  can  be
such  a  bother  to  remember  to  keep  my  shades
down.  Sometimes  I  forget,  and  I  guess  I  give
my  neighbors  a  thrill.  I'm  sending  you  a
picture  of  what  you  might  see  if  you  were
standing  outside  my  window.
   I  love  to  get  your  letters,  so  write
soon!

Your  Girlfriend,
Candy

August 23
c/o LetterBoxes
P.O. Box 69
Intercourse PA 17534

Sweet Candy:

   Your last letter was great even though it was short. I was
wondering though how you got that picture of yourself through
your bedroom window? And speaking of pictures, how come you
didn't say nothing about the picture I sent you? It must be nice
to have a typewriter to write your letters on. I'm thinking of

buying one at the Sears in town so my letters will look as good as yours. School starts soon and I can't wait to show the kids my letters from you. Maybe now they'll understand how important I am to have a great girlfriend like you. My stepmother always told me I'm a loser just like my father, but she never really knew me like you do. I feel like I could tell you anything Candy. And maybe I will someday. Well I got to go to work for Dad. Write soon.

Lots of Love,
Wayne

————————————

Wayne Gundersen
October 10
RFD 12 - Route 43
Ingram WI 54535

Big-Wad Wayne:

I have decided to take up camping this Fall. There's something about being outside, close to nature, that makes me hot (if you know what I mean)—no matter what the temperature! The last time I camped in my tent, I crawled into my sleeping bag without a stitch on, and I felt so lonely without you and your big piece of manhood to keep me company.
Just to show you what it was like, I'm sending you a picture of me just before I zipped up my bag. Please write soon, I think I'd just <u>die</u> if I didn't get your letters!

Love Forever,
Candy
P.S. I'm supposed to remind you—this is your

third letter from me and the people here who
run LetterBoxes wanted me to remind you to
send in another $19.95 for three new ones!
We've started such a great relationship, I
know you won't forget. Thanks, Sweetie!

Candy
October 10
c/o LetterBoxes
P.O. Box 69
Intercourse PA 17534

Sexy Candy:

   Okay, here's another money order. I sure do like your letters and
the picture of you in your sleeping bag. I like to camp too, but
mostly I like walking in the woods north of our farm. I found an old
well there and the wood cover had rotted through. The kids
always said that a bum had fell in the well a long time ago and
when he started to rot, he poisoned the water. I used a boat
anchor to fish up some pieces, and I'm not sure it was a bum and I
heard the voice of the thing that lives down there and feeds
off the parts. It wanted me to bring it food so I started catching little animals and throwing them down there, and the thing
really liked that. It really liked the kittens and the baby pigs. I
still go there sometimes, but not as often since you and me fell in
love. I'm planning a surprise for you soon!

I Love You,
Wayne

181

Thomas F. Monteleone ⎯⎯⎯⎯⎯⎯⎯⎯⎯⎯⎯⎯⎯⎯⎯⎯

Wayne Gundersen
November 24
RFD 12 - Route 43
Ingram WI 54535

Wild-Man Wayne:

   Thanks for sending in another $19.95.
I'll make sure your next three letters are
worth every penny!  Old Man Winter is here
and that means it's time for me to curl up
on my bearskin rug by the fireplace. I love
to feel all that heat on my naked skin! (I
hope you like the picture of me in front of
the fire . . . ). I get lonely, and I wish
you were here during these long winter
nights.

Your Hot Woman,
Candy

⎯⎯⎯⎯⎯⎯⎯⎯⎯⎯⎯⎯⎯⎯

Candy
December 15
c/o LetterBotes
P.O. Box 69
Intercourse PA 17534

Hey Listen Candy:

    Sorry it took me so long to write back but I had this surprise
for you. When I got you last letter and picture I told my father I
needed some money to buy a table saw for the shop in the
garage and I used the money to take a Greyhound bus to

Intercourse Pennsylvania. But the lady at the post office counter there had never heard of you. She didn't want to tell me anything but I waited in the parking lot till she got off work that night and I told her about the well and the animals and then she told me that all the mail to LetterBoxes got forwarded to Denver Colorado. How come you never told me you lived in Denver? I love you and I can't keep living like this. We need to be together Candy. So don't worry. I'll find a way to get out to Denver so we can be together.

I Love You,
Wayne

---

**UNITED STATES POSTAL SERVICE**
**Official Business**

Hiram Gundersen
December 18
RFD 12 - Route 43
Ingram WI 54535

Mr. Gundersen:

I would like to speak to you in person at your earliest convenience. Please call me at (717)555-2300 so that we may arrange an appointment.

Thank you very much.

Sincerely,

Albert Moler
Postal Inspector
Mid-Atlantic District 4

### U.S. POSTAL SERVICE INTER-OFFICE MEMO

**To:**    District Supervisor
**From:**  A. Moler

January 10

Here's something else on Case #66782-4. I thought it might be a good idea to have some on file ahead of time just in case there's any funny business later.

When I received no response from Wayne Gundersen's father, and had no luck in reaching him by telephone, I had the investigation transferred to Mid-West District 3. Inspector Hans Juernburgh conducted a personal interview with Hiram Gundersen.

Just to make sure nothing's out of order on this one, I thought it might be a good idea to attach a xerox of Inspector Juernburgh's report.

enc. Inspector's Report, Mid-West District 3

### U.S. POSTAL SERVICE INTER-OFFICE MEMO

**TO:** District Supervisor
**FROM:** H. Juernburgh

January 26
Case #66782-4.

I visited the farm of Hiram Gundersen on January 25. It is a run-down operation. If I had to describe the place in one word, "grim" would be my first choice. "Scary" my second. Mr Gundersen is a small acreage farmer near Ingram, Wisconsin. He denies allegations that his son, Wayne, had ever been to the Intercourse Post Office, and stated that he would swear in a court of law that the boy was working on the farm on the day in question  (November 27). He would not allow me to speak to his son, and when I asked for permission to look around the property, he threatened me with a post-hole digger. Mr. Gundersen's exact words were "Get out of here before I open you up for a piece of snow-fence."

I left the property immediately. FYI: unofficially and off the record, it's my personal opinion Hiram Gundersen is only half-wrapped. There's no doubt in my mind the son scared the pee out of our District 4 employee, but we would have a difficult time proving it. I don't see any choice but to drop the matter, but I think we should alert the local authorities to the situation out at the Gundersen farm. If the son's anything like the father, I'd say we have a couple of weirdos on our hands.

------------------------------

Candy
February 3
c/o LetterBotes
P.O. Box 69
Intercourse PA 17534

My Candy:

It's been a long time I've been waiting to get another letter from you. I figured something must be wrong when I got a check from LetterBotes. I couldn't understand it because I never asked for a refund. Please write me Candy. I will die if I don't get some kind of proof that our love is still the best. I got a visit from a postal inspector awhile back, but my Dad talked to the guy. You didn't tell anybody I was looking for you did you? Lately I been spending more time with Bowser. He likes the showers more and more. I don't want to sound like I'm getting angry or making any threats, but if I don't get a letter from you soon, I might have to start writing to some of the other women who really like me and would love to be my girlfriends. Like maybe Madonna and Paula Abdul (even though I think she might be a nigger) and Tiffany. When I go out to the woods, the voice in the well tells me things about you that maybe you don't love me anymore and maybe I'll just start listening. Think about it.

Still Yours,
Wayne

---

Paula Abdul
February 5
Apet Records
Box 13788
Northridge CA 91324

Dear Paula,

I had to tell Candy it was over. You are the only woman in my life now, and I promise to make you happy forever. When I see you at your concert, I'll show you my love meat. I'd do anything for you. Even kill or die for you. I like to watch you dance and can imagine you doing with no clothes definitely not for MTV. Bowser likes you too even though he's only a dog and won't be allowed in the shower with us. Write soon.

Love Always,
Big-Wad Wayne Gundersen

April 21
Darin McDowell
Los Angeles Security Services
23444 Melrose Ave
Suite 655
Los Angeles CA 90069

Mr. McDowell:

Enclosed please find this month's batch of letters. Things are getting pretty hectic as we prepare for Ms. Abdul's first concert tour of the year. As usual, thank you very much.

Sincerely,

Jamie Lerner
Personal Secretary to Ms. Abdul

---

MEMORANDUM

**From:** Darin McDowell, Director
**Date:** May 3
**To:** Joseph D'Agostino
**Re:** Priority Ones

Enclosed please find NA's of all the Priority One letters. We have a Red Flag on Subject #1 (Wayne Gundersen). Be aware that Subject #1's letters rang up the highest scores ever recorded on all three Test Indices. Subject #1 is considered to be extremely unstable and dangerous. I want you on location in Wisconsin for a complete dossier work-up. The Abdul tour starts next week—with a stop in Madison, so we will want to be ready for anything.

**MEMORANDUM**
**CONFIDENTIAL**

**From:** J. D'Agostino
**Date:** May 19
**To:** Mr. McDowell
**Re:** Wayne Gundersen

Everything I've been able to uncover about the subject indicates we have a real doughnut on our hands.

No known friends, bad relationships with his teachers, parents, and the local authorities. School records show below-average Stanford-Binet intelligence scores, unsubstantiated claims of sexual abuse while still in elementary grades, poor classroom attendance, and non-existent parental involvement with the education process. A series of misdemeanors on the county docket ranging from Malicious Destruction of Property to Animal Cruelty to Voyeurism.

I've been able to observe the subject at fairly close range. He spends most of his time just meandering around the family farm or in the nearby woods. Once in the woods, he either stands over the opening of an abandoned well talking to himself, or committing acts of sodomy with his dog. We are talking about a very sick boy out here in cheese country.

———————————————

Paula Abdul
June 12
Apet Records
Box 13788
Northridge CA 91324

My Paula,

I don't understand what is going on here. Why did you let

those men jump on me at your concert? I tried to tell them you said it was okay to come up and sing and dance with you. They took me to a trailer and used Bruce Lee stuff on me. The police were just as bad, and I kept waiting for you to come and save me and you never did. Don't you still love me? And when are you going to buy my Dad's farm so we can get rid of him and my two (brat) sisters? The thing in the well told me I should be mad about all this, but I love you so much I just can't. But write soon or I will be upset.

Your
Wayne Gundersen

---

**MEMORANDUM**

**From:** Darin McDowell
**Date:** July 15
**To:** Joseph D'Agostino
**Re:** W. Gundersen

Sorry to keep you twisting in the wind so long, but it looks like you're going to have to stay on this one. We've faxed copies of all our documentation to the Portage County D.A. The ball's in their court now. Till then, I want you so close to Gundersen he'll have to goose you to get into his pajamas at night. Talking to the kid's father is a waste of time. Talk about chips off the old block. Continue to fax me a weekly report memo. I want our documentation to be air-tight in case we run into trouble down the line. And Joe—thanks for going the extra mile on this one.

Paula Abdul
July 31
Apet Records
Box 13788
Northridge CA 91324

My Naked Dancer, Paula:

Okay, everything is ready for you out here. You can buy every-thing and nobody will say anything about it. Bowser says he will like you too. I'll teach him to lick you in the shower like he licks me. The only problem we're going to have is keep the thing in the well happy. The more I give it to eat the more it wants and it says it will make me do what it wants. You have to come out here and help me.

I Love You Paula,
Wayne The G-Man

---

FROM THE DESK OF
HUGHES STURDEVANT, ESQ.
PORTAGE COUNTY DISTRICT ATTORNEY'S OFFICE

August 15

Judge Hartkey:

After reviewing the material on the case against Wayne Gundersen (case #33467), I've decided not to pursue charges. The State's evidence is mostly based on what even a public defender is going to have thrown out as hearsay or innuendo. Admittedly, we have a kid who appears to be potentially dangerous, but, at least up until now, hasn't actually committed any crimes.

Give me a call if you have any comments, suggestions, etc. By the way, I saw Leo in the cafeteria yesterday, and he is itching for a rematch on the links this Sunday. Interested?

Hugh

—PRIVATE INVESTIGATOR MISSING—

**Ingram, Wisconsin** – The Portage County Sheriff Stanley G. Houseman today confirmed claims made by the Los Angeles Security Services that Mr. Joseph D'Agostino, a long-time employee of LASS, has been missing without a trace for twenty-one days. Mr. D'Agostino works for a private agency which provides maximum security for public figures such as singers and actors. When President of LASS, Darin McDowell, was questioned about the presence of Mr. D'Agostino in Portage County, Mr. McDowell freely admitted his employee was working on a confidential company assignment. Sheriff Houseman also confirmed the search for Mr. D'Agostino has already commenced.

**CONFIDENTIAL**
MEMORANDUM

**From:** M. Lonnigan
**Date:** August 22
**To:** Darin McDowell
**Re:** Ingram WI

Hard to believe it took that asshole Sheriff this long to listen to us. They just dragged the abandoned well at the Gundersen farm and found what we figured—plus a lot more. Looks like Joe's been in there at least two weeks. The rest of the family's been there maybe a week longer. They also found some bones of another body—probably the stepmother. But here's the weird part: they found the Gundersen kid in there too. There were parts of his fingernails on the edge of the well, like he was trying to hold on and something was trying to pull him in. The local John Laws were so glad to wrap this up, they just glossed over that little oddity. I might go back tonight and check out the scene after the County ME pulls out. I'll call you later.

---

—SECOND INVESTIGATOR MISSING—

**Ingram, Wisconsin**—Sheriff Stanley Houseman refused to confirm or deny claims that a second investigator from the Los Angeles Security Services, a Mr. Mickey Lonnigan, may be missing in Ingram, Wisconsin. The President of the California-based company, Darin McDowell has announced plans to personally investigate the matter.

*This one was for a theme anthology entitled* Obsessions *edited by a talented writer, Gary Raisor, who doesn't write enough. From the title, it was obvious what kind of stories he was looking for, and I figured I would use the opportunity to expand my range a bit and try to come up with something from one of the outer orbital paths of human oddity. Weeks went by and I kept ticking off items from the list of obsessive subjects and only two held my interest—one was about those compulsive hand-washers, Kleenex-wipers, and door-lockers (you know the types whose stories show up on the* Discovery Channel *every once in a while), but I couldn't get a handle on the actual direction of the plot, couldn't get the thing moving with enough internal momentum that would eventually propel me to a resolution, an ending[1]; and the second one was—well, I can't tell you that.*

---

[1] *and if you been paying attention, you know that's the way I like to write short fiction—i.e. by the seat of my pants. I love to see where the words and complications will eventually take me. I can't think of anybody better I would want to tell me a story than* myself.

THE PLEASURE OF HER COMPANY

Are you sure it's really *hers?*" asked Stanley Devereaux.

The man named Harkey smiled, displaying uneven, yellow teeth. He was seated across the table from Stanley Devereaux, scraping dirt from under his fingernails with a Swiss army knife. Harkey directed his gaze down at the velvet sack, which rested between them, flanked by an ashtray and two bottles of Beck's dark.

"C'mon, Stan-boy, would I shit ya?" he said. "Of *course* it's hers!"

"Where did you get this fancy bag?"

Harkey shrugged. "I got a friend. Deals in jewelry and you know—crystal and shit like that. He's got plenty of 'em layin' around. Thought it would be a nice touch—puttin' it in somethin' velvet, you know?"

Stanley Devereaux was suddenly aware of his breathing, of his tongue lolling dryly in his mouth, of his pulse pounding behind his ears. Speed-metal music seared the smoky atmosphere of the club and a double-bass rhythm synched-up with his heartbeat. Women in glitzy colors rainbowed past his table, but he ignored them as he continued to stare at the velvet bag.

"But *how?* How did you do it?"

Harkey shrugged, reached into his scuffed leather jacket to scrounge out a pack of Camels. Nobody smoked Camels anymore, but this shabby little guy did. "How'dja think I did it?! I went in and I *took* it!"

Stanley reached out, tentatively fingered the satin cord which held the opening to the sack fast. His blood swelled in his veins. An erection hardened in his boxers. Jesus, he couldn't believe this!

"Hey! Not so fast . . ." Harkey barked out a mouthful of smoke with his words. "There's my fee, remember?"

"You'll get it. You always do." Stanley nervously rubbed his lips with the back of his hand. "I just want to see it, if you don't mind."

"Not in here, man. Are ya fuckin' nuts?" Harkey pushed the velvet sack closer to Stanley Devereaux.

"Here—touch it. Feel it through the bag, man. It's the *goods*, man, I guarantee it."

Stanley's breath hitched up in his throat, which felt as though it had tightened down to the diameter of a straw. He couldn't believe this, still! Slowly, he let his soft, somewhat plump, accountant's fingers probe and touch the object concealed by the velvet bag. The expected contours and surfaces passed beneath his touch and he felt himself smiling. His erection was like the handle of a hatchet and his breathing had jagged edges.

Have to get control of things. Take it easy. Don't let this creep see how it was affecting him.

Plus, there was one more thing . . .

"Okay, it feels okay, but how do I know it was *hers*—I mean *really* hers? You got any proof?"

Harkey reached for his Beck's, sucked down a mouthful with enough lack of style to let some of it dribble down his stubbled chin. "You'll get all the proof ya need when ya watch the news tonight."

Checking his watch, Stanley frowned. "It's already after 11:00. Too late. You could be bullshitting me."

Harkey grinned again. Stanley had always thought he looked like that character actor Harry Dean Stanton—only more depraved, more dissipated.

"I ain't bullshittin' ya, Stan. When you go home, catch the Cable News. They got it goin' around the clock."

He was right about that. "Okay," said Stanley. "I want to take this with me and check the news. When I get my proof, you get your money."

"My ass . . ."

"Come on, Harkey. You know where to find me. I'm not going anywhere, and you know I'm good for it."

Harkey giggled. "Yeah, yer right—I know where ya live, Stan—baby. So if ya don't come through with the cash after tonight, I'm gonna hafta come lookin' for ya."

Stanley was already getting up, pulling his trenchcoat over his Perry Ellis jacket. He picked up the velvet bag and tucked it under the folds of the coat. "I'm going home, Harkey. I want to see this for myself."

"Yeah, I bet ya do . . ."

Stanley stepped back and let the music and the insect swarm

of the crowd flow over him. Harkey dissolved into the smear of color and sound, and suddenly the air seemed cleaner. Falling into the leather womb of his BMW's front seat, Stanley placed the velvet sack on the passenger's side. Pale sodium light filtered down from the parking lot's overhead lamps, casting everything in sick yellows.

Open the bag. See it. Touch it. Hold it close!

Hand on the ignition key, he grappled with his own impulses.

Despite the damp chill in the night air, his hands were sweaty-slick. He looked at the bag and its contents seemed to be throbbing like a dark heart.

See it! Touch it!

No. Somebody might discover him. Better to just get the hell home. To a safe haven. To the Shrine.

Summoning up his will, he keyed the ignition and pressed down on the accelerator. His 832i, a typical L. A. Jungle predator, turboed silkily from the lot and onto Sunset. He headed west, exceeding the posted limit, ducked onto Laurel Canyon, then west again on Mullholland. The whole time he wrestled the car through the endless turns and hitchbacks, Stanley expected to see the colored lights in his rear-view mirror, to have some meddling cop shine his flashlight into the car and pin the velvet bag under its beam. He swallowed hard as he pulled into his driveway on Beverly Glen. He killed the engine, and gulped several breaths. His pulse had been jumping and he needed to just calm down. Another minute and he'd be safely inside, and no one would ever know. In his peripheral vision the bag again seemed to pulse and throb like a shining, black organ. Quickly he snapped his head to the right, stared at the object and exhaled only after convinced it was not really moving.

Maybe it was wrong what he'd done? Perhaps this was carrying things too far . . . ?

No, of course not, screamed his next thought. It was the *only* thing to do. The ultimate acquisition. He smiled. Yes, it was certainly that. Stanley Devereaux nodded to himself, felt himself growing hard again.

Carefully, he picked up the bag to cradle it close to his chest. When he had locked himself in and left his London Fog crumpled on the foyer tile, he began to feel secure for the first time that evening. He reached quickly for the remote control, which infra-redded his Sony out of that dead zone where TVs waited for human attention. Punching through the numbers until he found the Headline News Channel, Stanley didn't take another breath until he heard the familiar voices of the cable news anchors.

Like a statuette Buddha, he sat cross-legged in the floor watching the flickering images, letting the voice-overs bathe in their waters of forgetfulness. He held his prize in his lap in a sort of trance, not really registering any of the information or advertisements. He remained inert, a cold vessel, empty of thought, waiting for the news segment which would either justify or abrogate his vigilance.

And then suddenly it appeared.

Video tape footage from Westwood Memorial Park. The smooth skin of the pink marble crypt violated as thoroughly as a schoolgirl's virginity. As the on-the-scene commentator monotoned the horror and depravity of such a desecration, the camera zoomed in on the bronze faceplate, the dates and the name which had never lost its magic.

It was true! The bastard had done what he said . . .

Reality seeped into Stanley like a subtle acid. What had been total fantasy, now consummate fact, initially stunned him.

He'd done it. Actually done it . . . ! Slowly, he rose to his feet, fighting a sudden disequilibrium, an unsteadiness in his legs. He remoted off the television and stood in the darkness cradling his prize with a new care, a new passion.

It was time.

As he walked through the house, each room he passed was like the shedding of another false skin, another faked aspect of his life. His den, his office, his bedroom—where he paused only long enough to strip naked and pull on a silk kimono he purchased on his last vacation in Tokyo.

He descended the basement stairs, crossed the tile of a sterile, banal "rec" room replete with *de rigueur* bar and pool table, and touched a concealed button in a cabinet of bowling trophies. The cabinet swung inward on hidden hinges to reveal a sub-basement room. Stanley had explained to the contractors who'd built it to his specs he wanted a place to hide from the Charlie Mansons of the world. The builder, a grungy Italian, had grunted a conciliatory agreement and finished the job without further comment or opinion.

Of course the room had really been built for her Shrine.

Soft, corniced and baffled lighting kept harsh shadows away from everything, and discreet spots and high-hats accented and highlighted the prize pieces in his collection. He paused in the center of the room, as he always did, and allowed himself the small ritual of surveying everything, of absorbing the warm glow of the artifacts, the memorabilia, the *kitsch*. He could feel its radiation penetrating him like gamma particles and it was truly good. Everywhere her image and her presence assaulted the eye.

Movie posters from every celluloid appearance; blow-ups of all the famous photographs; original paintings, sculptures and collages; rare record albums; and shelves of books. Then the rarer items like shoes and dresses from various films, autographed napkins, and even a man's handkerchief with the imprint of her blotted lipstick. There were tapestries, souvenir glasses, ashtrays, even lamps in her image. If her spirit had inspired the creation of the object, Stanley had tracked it down and made it his own, had brought its energy into the reservoir that was the Shrine.

Indeed, her Shrine was unique. It was a psychosexual power plant, a place where mythic lines of force converged and matrixed into something greater than the sum of its parts. He could just stand there and *feel* the energy of her spirit humming through the room's atmosphere. Like high-voltage wires vibrating in the nightwinds, the place sang to him. Stanley knew it was unique in the world. No place like his Shrine. He'd created it for her as much as for himself. As long as the Shrine existed, she would never really be dead.

Stanley didn't merely believe that. He *knew* it as surely as he breathed. You couldn't enter this hallowed place and *not* feel it, not know it instantly.

In his hands, the velvet bag grew warm, began to breathe like the bellows on a respirator.

No. That's crazy.

He stared at the bag and it was still. It was dead.

Standing before the altar, he loosened the drawstrings. The first thing revealed: her hair. Even in the dim light, he was shocked to see the platinum brightness of it, undulled by time. His erection began anew, his breath hitched.

Her hair. My God, I'm actually touching her hair . . .

With trembling fingers, he peeled back the rest of the velvet. No!

Even as he touched the side of her head, the skin cracked, flaking away like old plaster. Stanley dropped the velvet bag to the carpet as he stared at the skull—for that's really what it was. Despite the blonde hair still clinging to the partially preserved scalp, exposure to the air had quickly attacked the rest of her head. Lidless and eyeless, her dark sockets stared into that place where everyone will eventually look. Once pink flesh now ash-gray and crumbling even as he watched, like a delicate French pastry. His stomach lurched, his tumescence faded, as he watched the rest of her lips fracture and fall away to reveal a smile never caught by eye or camera.

It couldn't be *her* . . .

The thought flared and died like a damp match. She was going to dust in his hands! Quickly he moved her to the place he'd reserved at the center of the altar, gently facing her outward before any more of her classic beauty disintegrated in his hands.

Tears pooled in the corner of his eyes as he stared at the grim parody of what she'd once been. In that instant, he felt the entropic weight of an unfeeling universe, sensed the pointlessness of all that crawled and struggled for a few brief years of life. Everything was nothing, he thought. Nothing but a cruel joke if even a goddess eventually comes to this.

He rubbed away the tears, his moisture mixing with the dust of her flesh to make an exotic mud upon his fingertips. The thought both chilled and excited him. What a way to finally join with her . . .

Looking up from the grim cement between thumb and index, his gaze fell again upon her skull. Perhaps it was the indirect light, or the shadows cast by the high-hats, he wasn't sure. But her face, what was left of it, had reassumed some of the glow it once held in life. Maybe it was just his imagination, but since reaching the altar, her skull seemed more acceptable, more beautiful.

And finally Stanley could smile. It was the magic of this

place, he knew now. The collective force of all her myriad totems. As long as there were memories of her, as long as there were places like his Shrine, she would never really die.

Her skull stared at him, smiling most beguilingly, and it seemed to radiate a warmth, a perceptible glow. She was pleased with what he'd done for her, for bringing her back to life . . . and she wanted him.

Stanley stepped forward, feeling his erection rise once again.

*There have been times in my checkered and storied career when I was a member of several different writers' organizations.[1] In every instance, in the fullness of time, I learned the error of my ways and quit each and every one of them. But before I did, I gave of my time and my abilities to each group in the hope it would do some good both for them and for me. One of the things the HWA had inaugurated was a series of theme anthologies for its members, with each volume being edited by a well-known writer who would select a theme that would resonate well with his or her own corpus of work. Robert R. (Rick) McCammon edited one called* Under the Fang; *my buddy F. Paul Wilson created an interconnected masterpiece called* Freak Show, *and another of my pals, Peter Straub, edited one called* Ghosts. [2]

---

[1] *One of the worst was the National Writers Alliance, which eventually coalesced into a mouthpiece for all the usual leftist, socialist, anti-free enterprise bullshit that I just absolutely* hate. *When I attended a meeting in which the New York City Chairman showed up saying we had to start working harder for "writers of color," I stood up and announced I was quitting. I told her nobody needs to know the shade of a writer's skin; they only need know his/her thoughts; and the only colors any writers need to worry about was black print on white pages. End of* that *tune. Another more entertaining group was the SFWA, and perhaps the most sadly earnest bunch, the HWA.*

[2] *These earliest HWA anthologies received quite a bit of critical acclaim, produced some award-winning material, and in the case of* Freak Show, *became something of a genre classic. However, some of the later offerings were far less successful in both conception and execution. One of the most embarrassingly bad was* Beneath the Tarmac, *which examined a really sparkling original concept—a haunted airport built on the always-reliable Indian burial ground, and I* still *refuse to believe Ramsey Campbell was the progenitor of such a numbingly stupid idea. Others in the series included Whitley Strieber's* Aliens *and Robert Bloch's* Psychos, *about which I will have some words later.*

*McCammon's concept was a "shared world" book in which all the stories must take place in a world in which the "vampires do the math"—that is the eventual geometric progression that would logically occur if mortals continued to be bitten and infected and turned into vampires. In a surprisingly brief amount of time, practically the entire population of the planet would be vampires. At first reading, this sounded challenging, but you see, I have a problem with writing "traditional" stories about the more traditional horror and dark fantasy themes[3] and writing the 118th variation of the whole vampire shtick[4] just didn't interest me at all. But the anthologies were paying something on the order of 15 cents/word, which translated into some serious jing, and I wanted to cop some for my own pockets. So what to do? The answer was write a vampire story that was in some way* not *a vampire story. Why don't you check out this next one to see if I pulled it off.*

---

[3] *A philosophy which became the primary editorial beacon for our Bor*derlands *anthologies—no ghosts, serial killers, vampires, serial killers, werewolves, serial killers, mummies, or serial killers need apply. They didn't, and the stories we published were groundbreaking and generally excellent. But that's material for another time.*

[4] *Hey, I got it! I'm gonna write a novel about a vampire who's a detective! . . . a day care mother! . . . . a soldier! . . . an astronaut! . . . an archeologist! . . . a movie star! . . . a hemotologist! and well, you get the picture, right?*

Vandemeer had tasted its heat, felt its light ripple, his flesh like boiling oil. Its memories burned in him, a phantom-fire that whipsawed across the ragged prairie of his mind. Doomed to remember pain so exquisite, he discovered a strange and asymmetrical beauty in it.

He suspected his suffering had altered him, but in what way, he didn't yet know. Darkness capered on the other side of the hospital room window like some strange beast. He longed to run along the nearby beach and drink in the coolness of the night. Even more than a draught of human blood, he needed the freedom, which lay beyond evening's gate.

"You're looking better tonight," said a familiar voice.

Looking away from the half-slatted blinds, Vandemeer assayed his visitor, a man named Cordescu, who had been part of the First Generation, and who had been in charge of Project Lux since its inception. The man moved to his bedside, pretended to be checking the fittings of an IV tube, through which coursed the intimate, dark river.

"Thanks," said Vandemeer. "But I don't really feel better."

"But the physicians say you *are*. So do I."

"What do you want, Professor?"

"Would you rather I left you alone?"

Vandemeer nodded, looked between the lines of the window blinds. "Soon enough." Cordescu smiled thinly. He was tall and silvery gray, his bearing aristocratic. "Some news first."

Vandemeer sighed. "If you're here to tell me they're letting me out of bed tonight, I already know that."

The professor waved off his words with a casual turn of the wrist. "This is more important. You're popular among the masses, Vandemeer. You're the first of our kind who's gone to Hell and come back to tell about it. You're their hero."

He snorted, shook his head. "I'm a curiosity, maybe. Maybe even a freak, but no hero. What do they want with me?"

"They want you in the Senate."

"Take that shit out of here, would you please . . ." Vandemeer wouldn't look at him.

"I'm serious."

"So am I," he said. "I'm a scientist, not a politician."

"You're a public figure now." Cordescu smirked as he paced with careful measure about the white room. "The first of our kind to survive a complete sun-cycle. You are a *fait accompli* celebrity."

"I didn't do it for fame."

Cordescu shrugged. "Nevertheless, you're famous. You're their hero."

Vandemeer shook his head, chuckled bitterly. "Some hero! For a week I was half-blind, half-crazy, and so weak I couldn't walk! Has my adoring public been getting all the clinical details?"

The professor, looked at him with well-dark eyes framed by his proto-typical Slavic face. "The public, as always, remains on a need-to-know basis."

Vandemeer looked away, letting his mind race with the moon for a moment. Although he looked no older than thirty-five, he approached his one-hundred-twentieth birthday. There was a rugged handsomeness about him—not movie-star material, but women liked him well enough. In life, in a time which now lay in the pre-Cambrian epoch of his days, he'd been an immunologist on the come, building a rep as one of the smart guys, one of Stanford's best bets for a Nobel. But that was a long time ago. They don't give out prizes anymore.

"I need an answer," said Cordescu.

"I need lots of them."

The Professor's unflappable exterior started to slip. "Is this new arrogance part of your malaise?"

It was Vandemeer's turn to shrug. "You're the doctor. You tell me."

Cordescu's refined edge crumbled. "Listen to me, you bastard . . . ! I don't care if the sun almost made you a basket-case. If you want to remain on this project, you'll stop talking to me like that!"

"Then how am I going to continue my research if I have to be in the Senate? Make sense, and *I'll* try to do the same."

Cordescu scowled at him. "You idiot! Don't you realize it's just a figurehead position? You're a hero to our kind. We're entering the second century of war with the human scum, and you represent the Final Solution. Don't you understand that?"

206

Vandemeer smiled. "Perfectly . . ."

"Then you will accept?"

"Why do I have this feeling I never had a choice."

Cordescu smiled. "Vandemeer, please. There're *always* choices . . ."

He turned in his bed. His flesh still tingled, but movement was no longer the painful exercise it had been. "Get me out of this bed, and I don't care what else you have planned for me."

"We're almost ready to duplicate your experiment. Hastur has volunteered. I imagined you'd want to be there when we commenced the dosage."

"So thoughtful of you . . . especially since it *is* my experiment." Vandemeer sat up straighter. For the first time since being hospitalized, he found himself regarding his work with his old fervor.

"We'll be running a final batch of tests nightmorrow, then Hastur will be ready."

"I'll want to see the numbers before you expose him."

Vandemeer did not particularly care for Hastur, but he saw no need to make him suffer prematurely.

"And so you shall." Cordescu nodded, turned and walked to the door before looking back. "Take a walk, Van. Get your legs and your appetite back. We have history to be made."

Vandemeer said nothing as his Project Chief vanished beyond the threshold. As if on cue, a nurse appeared in the door. Leggy, with very strong thighs and a generous ass, she was the kind of woman he would normally desire. Oddly, he felt nothing as she performed her scheduled maintenances. Something might be wrong with him. An after-shock from the exposure? There was always the risk of some delayed reaction. The undead suddenly dead. He smiled at the ultimate cosmic prank.

"Something funny?" she asked.

"No, not really . . . ."

She shrugged as she punched some new numbers into his diagnostic console. "Are you ready to get out of that bed?"

"What do you think?"

"Are you going to need some help?"

He'd needed no help. Indeed, after an hour of attentive workouts in the physical therapy ward, he was cleared for whatever he wanted to try. First he wanted to visit his lab, and then perhaps, a walk on the beach. The soft sand would be both a challenge and comfort. His laboratory was deserted. His equipment and instruments appeared to be untouched in his absence. Only the centralized, and therefore shared, laminar-flow cabinets and cryo-chambers where all the recombinant work was done showed signs of others' presence. Vandemeer stood in the center of the room and stared into the glass-walled case where his vaccine awaited further tests. He approached the case and stared in at the vials of precious liquid. He smiled ironically. Less than two hundred milliliters represented almost twenty years of research. Would it work for anyone else, or was he merely a freak? He reached out to touch the security cabinet.

His palm-print accessed the digital scanning lock and the glass barrier slid into a recess in the case. Picking up one of the two hundred-milliliter vials, he stared into its depths as though answers might be suspended within its colorless solution.

What have you done to me?

The thought rattled within him as he recalled the agony of the sun. But he'd survived, and that had been the point of it all, wasn't it?

The glass vial felt slippery in his cool grasp. Had to be careful. Replacing it would require years of lab-time. Slowly, he returned the container to its special shelf and palmed the lock shut. There was nothing for him to do down here for now; the laboratory no longer felt like his special and private place.

He left the lab and exited the building, walking slowly and carefully down to the edge of the continent. Even in summer, the nights on this part of California's coast were bracingly cool. Vandemeer stood on the beach listening to the endless symphony of the sea. Breakers on the rock jetties, gulls screaming out their hunger, the whisper of receding tides. Behind him, the Point Lobos Installation loomed above the cliffs like a gathering of featureless tombstones in pale moonlight. Against the blue-black music of the spheres and the sea, the buildings seemed obscene to him. As a signature of humankind's arrogance, the Installation had been ugly enough, but the presence of his own breed had perhaps further corrupted the beauty of the place.

Turning his back on the cliffs, he regarded the ocean and its magic as if seeing it for the first time. He walked without measuring time or distance, or even his thoughts. As he walked along the water's edge, entering a small cove, he noticed an oddity about the place. Perhaps it was the underwater configuration of the shoreline, or maybe a lack of the under-tow, he could not know for certain. But as the tide retreated, the wet sand became littered with the casual debris of life.

Creatures, once cast out, that could not return whose presence created a narrow band of sand where death scurried boldly. Even as he approached the place, gulls swooped down to feast among the dead and dying organisms of the sea. The screams of the birds were a final alarm, a final solution.

It made Vandemeer think of the unpredictability of the sea and of all living things. And from such thoughts, he thought of his own non-life. The sea, wellspring of life, brought him to that grim awareness. Even though he was undead, but not living, he remembered what it had been like.

To be *alive*.

It burst out of him in an instant of soul-pain, exploding as the primordial galaxies had done, expanding into endless night.

It was a sensation, a memory, an emotion not felt in an achingly long time. Vandemeer wasn't sure he'd like it, but he'd recognized it for what it was, and could at least accept it as genuine.

He walked further into the midst of the sea-strewn carcasses and the birds scattered, screeching and cawing out their anger.

A cool breeze invaded his unzipped jacket, making cold flesh even colder. But it felt good, it felt right. Taking longer strides, he increased his pace until he was almost jogging across the sands. He remained parallel with the beach and continued away from the Installation until it was obscured beyond a point of land. The region had remained remote and he expected to see nothing but bare beach and ragged sea. Slowing his pace, Vandemeer, finally came to rest.

The vault of the sky bled toward the coming dawn. Perhaps an hour away. Surely no more. He wondered if he would be much affected by the coming light, and decided he would not push things just yet. He'd proven the vaccine worked, but there was still more testing to be done. Let them do it. Turning, he headed back the way he'd come, back toward the Installation. As he walked and approached the cove, he felt invigorated, renewed. The beach was so desolate, so peaceful, a palliative for his tortured psyche. He relished the isolation, the removal from the hard-edged realities of the world. He even smiled as he basked in the dark glow of his solitude.

And so he was surprised when he saw the human.

A woman. Long hair, straightened by the wind; baggy clothes which failed to conceal her lithe, almost thin frame. She walked down the beach, away from him and towards the cove, with an athletic stride, a dancer's grace. As he watched her, a thought touched him: *They move differently than us.*

He slowed and kept pace with her—just far enough behind to keep her barely in view. She did not sense his presence and her night-vision could not be sharp enough to actually see him.

A space of time expired as he matched her gait. His following her had been an instinctive reaction, done without conscious assent. He had no idea how long he followed her like that, but it suddenly struck him that he felt no hunger. The intimate thirst was simply . . . *not there.*

The realization stunned him for an instant, like a slap unexpected. Perhaps it was the intravenous treatments, his weakened condition, any one of a hundred factors intruding. Whatever, it unsettled him to not be regarding the human female as something akin to cattle.

Watching the woman, he saw her approach the cove, bend down and pick up one of the creatures on the drying sand. Slowly, she stood, her silhouette dark against the coming amethyst dawn, and tossed the object out to sea. She repeated this maneuver several times as he began walking again closing the distance between them.

As he drew closer, he could see she was most likely in her late twenties or early thirties. Although no classic beauty she was certainly not unattractive. Moonlight clarified her angular features, accented the blonde strands of her hair. There was something sensual about her, but in an aesthetic, rather than erotic way. He must have been moving very quietly, because she didn't notice his presence until he was almost close enough to touch her.

And still, within him, there was no thirst . . . Turning, a little too quickly to not reveal the sudden fear in her, she regarded him with animal wariness.

"It's a beautiful night, isn't it?" he asked, his voice almost cracking.

"Yes, it is," she said almost whispering the words. "But it's almost dawn."

He nodded, knowing what she meant.

"Who *are* you?" she asked, looking out to sea. "No one ever comes out here."

"I'm on a journey," he said, trying not to lie.

"And you're not one of *them*? You're not afraid of them?"

Vandemeer cleared his throat. "I won't harm you. Believe me. If I was one of them, you'd be dead by now. You know that."

She exhaled as though with great effort. Some of the fear slipped away then and she looked into his eyes as though searching for that spark of true life all humans possess. Then, abruptly, the suggestion of a smile began to appear at the corners of her mouth. Turning, she began walking down the beach.

He followed at a respectful distance, watching her crouch down to examine the body of a starfish quivering on the sand. She took the sea-thing into her hands.

"Do you . . . collect them?" he asked.

"In a way, I guess. But only the living."

He didn't understand what she meant, but remained silent as she stood and waited for a new wave to break on the beach. Drawing back her arm, she hurled the starfish into the deep water. It disappeared behind the breakers.

"Maybe it'll live now," she said, wiping her hands on her pant legs.

"Do you walk here very often?" He didn't really care, but he wanted to hear the music of her voice again. "Oh yes," she said. "Whenever I can. Every night if I could. But not always here. There are so many coves along this coast. So many nights . . ."

He nodded as though he understood and followed in silence until she came upon another beached creature, which still glistened with the faint glow of life. Most would be repulsed by its shape—a blistered crab-thing with long, sagging antennae.

211

She picked it up in delicate, pianist's fingers and again threw it far into the dark waters. It made a brief splash in the moonlight and was gone.

She said nothing, didn't even look at him, and continued to walk along the water's edge. He thought about how silly, how futile her actions were. No matter how many she saved from oblivion each night, it could not matter. Death raced across the beaches at a greater pace than hers.

"Do you live nearby?" he tried to sound as non-threatening as possible.

"Sometimes. Not always."

She looked into his eyes again, as though searching again. He could smell the apprehension on her, but it never coalesced into fear. He found that he was attracted to her—not physically but emotionally. There was a vital force in her, which touched him in ways he'd believed long-dead. He was suddenly rocked by a sensation of being utterly *alone* and he wanted her to know this.

But he couldn't find the words.

She smiled a small smile this time, turned, and resumed her patrol. He followed her, watched her rescue another air-choked thing.

"The sun returns," she said, looking up at the orange and purple smears to the east.

He nodded, trying to conceal the shock which braced him.

There came a roaring in his ears, and it grew until it was a scream that echoed down the corridors of space and time. The moon fell and the stars bled across the sky, filling his mouth with the sting of their salt.

Faltering, he staggered away from her.

"Are you all right?" She looked at him with renewed fear.

He turned away for a moment. "No. It's okay. I'll be all right."

Memories and sensations raged though him like acid in his veins. He didn't want her to see him like this. The sun had crested the eastern horizon and its warmth played across his flesh. But it did not burn him.

She watched him stand with his hands at his temples, but there was relief in her gaze. The sun had brought her that.

"I've . . . I've got to go . . ." he said, spinning off into the blaze of the dawn as though under a spell. If she replied, he didn't hear, didn't remember. He was walking toward the slabs of stone on the faraway cliffside. He was lost, yet he was not. He feared something, but had no way to articulate that fear. But it tasted bitter like arsenic, and spoke of death. He inhaled deeply of the sea-choked air. The salty breath of the ocean, which once had carried the earliest seeds of life, rushed into him like an invading virus. The whitening sky spun and sparkled across his vision and he remembered nothing more.

Until he awoke to a montage of white and green. Staff moved about him in his hospital bed. More tests: wires, screens, charts, tubes, broken pieces of sentences. The vaccine was valid, they told him. New tests with Hastur would begin tomorrow, and truly a new age would *dawn* among his kind.

Late into the next evening, Vandemeer left the Installation, letting the indigo arms of night embrace him once again. Without pausing to consider why, he knew he was being drawn back to the beach and its receding tides. He walked with a long stride to the cove beyond the point. The wine-dark sea was smooth tonight, but the retreating tide had already speckled the sand with new dead and the dying. But tonight, Vandemeer knew he was seeing things differently. As his footprints marked the sand, he searched for traces of *hers*.

The moon grew high and small as clouds raced to clutch it far above his head. The wind grew stronger, cooler. He stood in the center of the cove, feeling lost, disconnected, abandoned.

There was no sign of her and he began to wonder if she really existed. *So many beaches. So many nights.* Who was she, anyway? Maybe all was simple madness . . . No. There was something magic about this place. He couldn't give up so easily. Where he now walked had been a solitary human being who nightly paused to battle death. And now he was learning that even for his own kind, perhaps there were different kinds of death.

Looking up, he saw movement on a jutting point of land. Someone approached the cove with an easy, distant grace, and he knew it was her. He wanted to break into a run, to race to her side, but something held him back. Once, as she grew closer, she paused to pick up something from the wet sand and return it to the sea. Again, she paused when she saw him

213

standing amidst the shadows of the shoreline. He stood waiting as a wave broke and the ebb tide fell away from him.

Looking down, into the swirling muck and sand that slid past his boots, he saw something shining. In the swirling foam, there was a small and slimy thing. Its pores glutted with sand, it slowly suffocated in the night breeze. Vandemeer stooped down and picked it up, feeling tiny spicules tickle his palm. The creature beat feebly with the rhythm of the living, and he resonated to the sensation.

She drew closer and he took steps toward her. She looked at him and almost smiled. Her gaze dropped to the thing he held in his hands.

"I'm sorry . . . about last night," he said. "I really don't remember—"

She silenced him with a simple gesture—an outward glance of her eyes and a slight tilt of her head.

"I'm sorry if I scared you. I'm sorry," he continued. Then, after a pause: "I've come to . . . to join you."

This time she did smile, moonlight burning in the amber of her irises. Vandemeer looked at her, feeling a smile forming on his own lips—the first in a long, long time. "Please do . . ." she said and looked out to the star-filled sea.

Pulling back his arm, Vandemeer flung the creature out into the night. Time seemed to slow as he watched the thing's path describe a graceful arc across the sky. Masked by the whisper of the surf, it penetrated the surface.

He felt an atavistic surge within himself, like a starburst in his thoughts. He felt strangely renewed and paused to wonder what was happening to him.

"It's beautiful, isn't it?" she whispered.

He kept looking out to sea as he nodded in response. The urge to touch her hand, to share the moment more deeply, broke in him.

"Your name," he said as he turned to face her. "What is it?"

But she was gone.

Stunned, Vandemeer whirled about, but there was no one with him. The echo of her words still drifted across the surface of his mind. Trying to reject the shock, the utter impossibility of her disappearance, Vandemeer sought for answers when he knew none would be found.

He felt a momentary disorientation as he ordered his thoughts. Starlight skittered across the ocean's surface; thoughts of the sea and its secrets entered and retreated like the tides. He had no idea how long he stood on the edge of the water-world, as the coming dawn stretched out before him. It didn't matter now.

Turning away from the wet sand, he leaned into the wind, in the direction of the Installation. It was a long, slow, and lonely walk. Interrupted several times when he found something which needed him on the sand, his trek gave him the time he needed to absorb what he'd learned, to re-dedicate himself. Ahead, in the distance, the monolith of the Installation soared above the cliffs. He thought of its corridors, almost deserted during the diurnal cycle, and how he could move unimpeded into his lab. Where he would access his records and his vaccine. He had worked so hard and so long.

But there was one last thing to do.

*Okay, this story was written for another of the HWA anthologies, the aforementioned* Freak Show *edited by F. Paul Wilson. But to say that Paul merely "edited" the book does him a great disservice because he went beyond that duty to create an intricate overlay, a back-story, which not only connected[1] all the stories in the anthology, but allowed each tale to move a larger story along to a satisfying conclusion. Paul wrote short pieces that wove everything together and the result was a literary* gestalt *that was not short of brilliant—in which the final resolution was far greater than the mere sum of its parts.*

*As far as my story goes, I think it stands on its own as a fine study in character and emotion, but when you see the reference to a "piece" for Oz's device, you will understand why it is there. I very much loved the challenge of helping Paulie create* Freak Show, *and I stand by my claim that it is a truly wonderful piece of work. If you don't have the book, try to find it in either its unbelievably cheesy paperback edition from Pocket Books, or the lavishly beautiful Borderlands Press limited edition with illustrations by Phil Parks.*

---

[1] *The shtick used to connect the stories is a quest, which all the main characters of all the tales must eventually join. The man who runs the Freak Show, Ozymandias, is building a machine called "the Device," and he has asked all his companion-freaks to help find the parts for this machine, which had been scattered and/or hidden all across the country during one of the traveling show's previous circuits. This story was originally titled "Oyster Bay, New York," which was the town where Oz's Freak Show had stopped for a run.*

CARMELLA AND THE MISSING PIECE

"**I** had the dream again," said Carmella Cerami.

She looked across the breakfast table at George Swenson. "About the guy in the hat?"

She nodded, pushed a strand of long dark hair from her cheek. "It's more than a dream, George. I *know* it is."

He sipped from his coffee mug, his gaze alternating between her dark eyes and the red-and-white checks of the tablecloth. "One of your 'visions,' huh?"

"For what they're worth," she said, half-grinning. "Sometimes they mean something, and sometimes, you know, nothing . . . But *this* one—this one's so real! He's so handsome and well-dressed, but I can't see his face because of the hat being kind of slanted down. And he comes to see me, but not when I'm in the sideshow, and he doesn't see me as a Freak. But . . ."

"But what?" asked George.

"But there's something different about him, something almost . . . dangerous."

"Does he try to hurt you?"

Carmella smiled wistfully. "Oh no, nothing like that. He's kind of mysterious—like those men in the old black and white movies, like Garfield or Bogart."

"I don't get to see many movies . . ." George rippled a tentacle, fidgeted with his coffee mug. He seemed to have something on his mind.

"The old movies are the best," said Carmella, feeling her mood begin to brighten. It was always like that—the more she distanced herself from her dreams and her sometimes prescient visions, the happier she would feel.

She drew a breath slowly; autumn was in the air. A woodsy sachet which always comforted her. It was her favorite time of year—the end of the hot, dusty weather of summer and the change of season's colors. Time to switch from iced lemonade to hot cider and a cinnamon stick; time to end the roadshow for another year. They were on the home run now. No more gawking faces, no more—

"Hey, Carmella, you okay?"

She looked up at her friend as though he were a stranger. What had he been saying?

"I'm sorry," she said softly. "I was just thinking . . . and drifting away . . . 'woolgathering,' my mother used to call it."

George nodded, tried to smile, doing an awkward job of it. She knew he wasn't trying to court her; he had a girl—a Straight. Just like Carmella wanted. She'd always had a wish-fantasy that someday she would leave the Show and end up with a normal man—a Straight of her own. Despite her reputation as a flirt with a great body, she liked to think of herself as a dreamer. Blowing the show was a fantasy she'd sheltered and protected like a baby bird with a broken wing.

More importantly, it was one of the things she'd promised her mother when she died two season's back—

Like a cruel hand, a black memory slapped her. Blinking her eyes against the vision, she fought against re-seeing the grim tableau: the dark interior of their trailer near the end-days. Dying oh-so-slowly, her mother had curled herself into the depths of her bed where the light could not reveal her sagging flesh. As the cancer continued to feed, speech became almost impossible, but Carmella's mother had forced the words to come. It had been a time of last things—last words and last chances—and both mother and daughter knew the importance of such things. Her mother had been re-hashing a familiar wish—that she find a man who would be good to her, who would stay with her, ". . . and not run off like your father did you."

The words had become like a well-known litany, but this time her mother added something new.

"Carmella, listen to me . . ."

"Not now, Momma. Rest."

Her mother had smiled weakly. "Plenty of time for that. Listen."

Carmella nodded.

"I want you to blow the show."

The words had shocked her so. "What? Momma, *why?*"

"'Mellow, this is no life for a young woman. You deserve better, you deserve a *life.*"

"The Show's the only life I've ever known . . . It's okay."

Her mother winced. "That's my fault," she said. "I should've given you a better chance . . ."

"Momma, don't talk like that. You've been good to me."

Her mother looked directly into her eyes, her gaze dark, piercing. "Just promise me, Carmella."

"All right, I promise."

"There's one other thing—" A cough savaged her sagging chest before she could continue. "You won't be able to leave until you . . . you do something for Oz."

"Mr. Prather? Do what? Momma, what're you talking about?"

—and that's how Carmella had learned about the Device. Her mother had tried to hide and protect her from the knowledge. She hadn't wanted Mr. Prather harassing Carmella about finding something so alien and unknown. But death would shift the mantle of responsibility to her daughter's shoulders.

She'd never forgotten her mother's final warning: Find the Piece, Carmella; Oz won't let you leave until you do. Don't be trapped like I was. Trapped. Carmella had never let the word fade from her—

"Oz has you hunting for the last Piece, doesn't he?" George said abruptly.

"Uh . . . yes, he does." She looked at George's face—his expression seemed odd, unreadable.

"Maybe it'd be better for everybody, Carmella, if maybe you didn't find it."

"What? How can you say that, George? What do you—"

"Shit," said George, getting up quickly from the table. "I better get to work. See ya."

Carmella had been staring absently toward the woods at the opposite end of the field when she suddenly focused on George's exit. Beyond him, she saw the reason for it. One of the bull-necked Beagle Boys lurched through his rounds among the trailers, making sure everybody was heading out to their stalls in the sideshow tent.

And immediately behind him, walking in long purposeful strides, came Ozymandias Prather. He seemed to be looking at her in his oddly indirect way as he drew closer.

"Hello, Carmella," he said in his deep, resonant voice.

"Good morning, Mr. Prather." She stood up, started gathering her breakfast things to a tray. "I was just getting ready to—"

"I know you were. Just one moment, my dear."

There was something commanding about Ozymandias Prather. Whether it was the way he looked at you, or the inflection in his voice, or perhaps something altogether indefinable, one thing was certain—people paid attention to him. Carmella stopped in mid-step. "What is it?" she asked, already knowing what he would be saying.

"Oyster Bay is our last chance this season," he said. "Almost everyone has come through for me—except *you.*"

"Mr. Prather I don't even know what I'm looking for. Even *you* can't tell me what it looks like."

"You'll know when you've come near it," he said. "You'll *feel* it and you'll simply *know.*"

"I hope so," she said. "I hope you're not upset with me."

Prather smiled and it was a clumsy gesture. "Of course not. It's only that I grow impatient. To be so close and yet so far is most frustrating. I'm sure you can understand that. Although I can't explain it yet, you must believe me when I promise a better life for *all* of us when the Device is complete."

Carmella nodded. Prather's words had become a familiar refrain and she almost could recite them by heart.

He turned and moved away from her, long legs scissoring him along the path between the trailers. One of the Beagles pulled in beside him like an ugly tugboat eager to service a cruiser, and the pair headed back toward the midway.

Cleaning up quickly, she retreated to her trailer where she applied overly dramatic make-up—false eyelashes, pencil-arched brows, Chinese-red lipstick and rouge—and slipped into her costume. When she emerged she had transformed herself into "Madame Cerami, Seeress of the Mediterranean Isles." Her garishly painted billboards portrayed her to the public seated behind a crystal ball, holding it so that the sixth finger on each hand was clearly and obviously visible. The same for her jewelled, satin head-dress, which had been designed to accent the third eye in the center of her forehead.

Growing up among the Freaks, Carmella had never been overly sensitive or neurotic about her mutations. Indeed, her mother had always seemed far more disturbed about her differences than Carmella ever had. And yet, when she traveled among the Straight people she styled her hair in ways which concealed her extra eye, or wore hats which performed the same function.

All those "normal" people—most of them would get very bothered by her extra eye even though, if they took the time to really look at it, they would realize it was as beautiful an eye a woman could have. The shape a perfect Sicilian almond, long lashed, an iris of gold-flecked chestnut, clear, and radiant.

But it was a false perfection; the eye was blind. Had it been blue-frosted by a hideous cataract, it could see no less.

No, Carmella's special eye, the source of her special sight, actually lay within the dark folds of her mind, in the place where dreams and fears and hope break free. Her visions were full of mist and mystery, brooding views of things dark and personal, often fraught with symbols of sex and romance. So full of shadow and smoke—these visions—that she'd long ago learned not to trust them, even if she *could* understand them clearly.

The boards called her a "Seeress," and she had to smile at that. The stories she made up for the rubes who paid for a quick look at the future were inspired by the horoscopes in the morning papers. Cheap prophecies for crippled spirits. Carmella believed it was a fair exchange and nobody ever came back to complain anyway.

As she entered her tent through the back entrance, she could feel the pent-up expectations of the crowd about to be loosed upon the Freaks; could smell their anxiety coming off their pack like the sour-musk scent of bad sex.

Her stall was set up as a space-within-a-space so that she was visible to everyone who passed by, close enough so that no one could not notice the fingers and the eye. The crowd could press against the wire mesh and peer into her inner sanctum where she sat under dramatic purple-gelled light, fondling a cheap glass ball. For an extra few dollars, one of the Beagle Boys dressed in mufti would let one of them into her tacky salon for a quick reading from the crystal globe. And as always, she could hear the sting of their voices.

As diverse as the Freaks might be, there was one experience they all shared: listening to the Straights talk about them as if they weren't there. As if they were dumb circus beasts; as if they were insensate lumps who couldn't be touched by human speech; as if they had no feelings and could not be hurt.

"Jeez, check out *this* one!"

"Oh-my-God . . . what a shame. . . !"

"It is real? Did you see it blink!"

"How can she *stand* that?"

"And she would've been such a *pretty* girl . . ."

"Nice set-a jugs on her, though."

*"These people make me sick . . . "*

Carmella had heard them for so long, it was no longer surprising how unoriginal their responses had become, how numbingly similar. And yet, their words had never lost their power to deal out the pain.

She looked into their faces as they filed past. They seemed better dressed, better groomed than most. Oyster Bay was near a few colleges and some high-tax real estate. It had been a traditional spot on the tour for a long, long time, before the area had become a place of wealth and influence, but the people still came each year to get funky with Peabody's Traveling Circus. Maybe they needed a break from their VCRs and their BMWs and their CPAs; maybe they wanted a taste of the way it used to be.

Maybe they needed something to laugh at . . . ?

Most filed past, with Labor Day indolence, pleased enough to gawk and stare and mouth an insult, but some paid their dues to the cerberus named Beagle. Carmella gave them her inscrutable smile as she coaxed visions from her crystal with six-digit strokes.

There is money in your future.

Watch out for friendly strangers.

Your love life will take a fortuitous turn.

Next month is a good month for starting new projects.

A life-long dream will soon come true.

*Your family is concealing shocking news.*

The usual litany of hollow hopes and fears flowed from her full lips like the promises of a virgin. Everyone loved it whether they believed it or not. The night slouched past her and finally a bull-horned voice dispatched the hanger-ons, the deadbeats, and the late-comers. As one of the Beagles closed up her stall, she pulled off the head-dress, ran fingers through her long, auburn hair. It felt good to be free of it.

Leaving through a back-entrance, she could smell the blended scents of the midway—cotton candy, fried food oil, and crowd-sweat. Even though the tension of the night's performance was easing out of her, she still felt anxious, as though she sensed something frustratingly unclear. Just knowing this was the last weekend of the tour was making her what momma used to call "antsy."

By the time she reached her trailer, she decided she would go into Glen Cove, a neighboring town with a strip of friendly late-night restaurants and bars. She needed a change of scenery. After shedding her costume, and a quick and rare shower courtesy of the Nassau County Recreation and Parks Department, Carmella prepared herself for a late evening among the Straights.

When the cab picked her up, she looked like any other young woman who cultivated a casually fashionable look. Wearing a baggy silk blouse, a sleekly-cut skirt, and a pair of white cotton-lace gloves, she could have easily passed as a C. W. Post student wearing the latest rock-music styles. Thick bangs covered her forehead, and the gloves concealed her extra fingers. The costume was perfect and no one would ever suspect she wasn't One of Them. She smiled wanly as she considered her life as a series of changes from one costume to another. Maybe it was time to change all that.

"Where to, Madam-Lady?" The cabbie checked her out in his rear-view mirror as he punched in his meter. He sat on a seat cover of woven wooden beads and spoke with a Middle Eastern accent. He didn't seem to notice anything strange about her. Good. She'd assumed her "disguise" was flawless.

"Glen Cove. The Gold Coast."

He nodded. "Gold Coast. No problem. You have been visiting the bazaar?"

Carmella smiled. "You mean Peabody's—the road show?"

"Yes, yes. The 'road show.' I am thinking the wrong word. It is not 'bazaar,' no?"

She smiled again. "Well, I don't know about that. Most people think it's pretty bizarre . . . ."

The cabbie nodded and grinned, obviously not catching her play on words. He turned his attention to the road, abandoning Carmella to her thoughts.

The darkness and the sense of impending adventure made her think of her mother's wish for her to blow the Show. She squinted against headlights of oncoming traffic and wondered what it would be like to own her own car, to learn how to drive it. Traveling with the mud show all her life had left her oddly unprepared for life in the Straight world. Even a simple thing like climbing into the family wagon and driving off to the food market was totally alien to her.

She wondered what other complexities awaited her, and how fearful, how difficult it might prove to be. But despite such thoughts, she still clung to vague dreams of romance and money and plastic surgery. Her tickets to the land of Straight living.

The cab burrowed into the darkness between the North Shore towns as she settled back into the vinyl-covered seat. A familiar tingling across her forehead signaled the onset of another vision and she recoiled from it with an equally familiar tightening in her stomach. Her third eye began to tear, and she closed all her eyes tightly. The movie screen in her head, the place where they ran the twenty-four hour skull-cinema, was misting up, getting foggy. She could see the now-familiar man in the slouch hat standing in a pool of street-lamp light like a guy in an old movie. She tried to make out his features, but his face remained in shadows. He reached out to her; the gesture could have been menacing, but maybe not.

Blinking her eyes, Carmella realized she'd been clenching her teeth. Her jaw muscles ached, and she concentrated on the pain as the vision faded. She was left with the unfounded notion that tonight was the night she would finally meet him.

The thought charged her with comfort and fear . . . and a surge of sexual excitement.

It had been a good summer for John LoMedico. His sports book had never been better—what with neither the American or the National League showing any really great teams, none of his bettors had a chance of doing much damage; and of course, *nobody* picked horse races! That, plus all the *finocchios* playing daily numbers, and a little loan-sharking here and there, and you were talking some serious profit-taking. Pretty good, when you figured that the NFL hadn't really cranked it up yet. That's when you really raked in some dimes.

At forty six, "Johnny-Doc" LoMedico had never done an honest, hard day's work in his life. And it showed. His hands were smooth and soft and accented by several tastefully extravagant rings. His hair was still dark and full, and not a wrinkle in his stress-free, dago-handsome face. Not a day older than thirty-five, he looked. Not a day. And all because he never bought that whole ramadoola about working hard and being honest.

His Uncle Paulie'd told him, back when he was just a kid hanging out at the family candy store in Flatbush, that working stiffs were the biggest suckers in the world, that nobody should even get outta bed in the morning for what most dummies brought home in a *month*. Johnny remembered all the neighborhood dads; how the poor bastards used to drag themselves home from shit-paying, shit-jobs every day.

He was fourteen years old when he swore he'd never let that happen to *him*.

That's when he started running numbers out of the candy store for Uncle Paulie. That's when he was making more in a *night* as a high school punk than a lot of his friend's fathers took home all week. Eventually, when he got a little older, he started keeping a sports book, getting his own stable of customers together, kicking back some *trib* to the Manzaras, and generally just lovin' life. He made excellent money and he never got greedy. That was the secret—never get greedy and everybody left you alone. Nobody fucked with you. The years rolled by and Johnny Doc never tried to horn in on somebody else's action, never tried to chisel or jam anybody, and he got a rep among the wiseguys as a very straight player. This helped in a couple of very important ways—everybody trusted him, plus the Manzaras protected him fiercely because he contributed so much to the Family's honorable image.

John smiled as he drove his Q45 down Jericho Turnpike. He'd just picked up a big pay-off from an Oyster Bay dentist who'd liked the Buccaneers plus the points. There wasn't a better feeling in the world than riding around with a chunk of tax-free, folded Green in your pocket. Nothing like it—not even great sex, and he'd had enough of both to know, thank you.

Entering the town of Glen Cove, he headed for Manny's Place and parked in the side lot. The evening was grinding down, but there were plenty of cars still huddled in the spaces. He could hear music leaking into the night as he adjusted his hat and straightened his tie. His reflection in the car's dark glass pleased him—Johnny Doc looked good.

Despite the lingering humidity outside, the bar's interior was comfortable. Some couples were draped over each other on a postage stamp dance-floor; others traded *bon mots* as they solidified earlier pick-ups and connections. The witching hour approached when the lucky ones would start draining off into the night for a few hours of sweat and passion. It was getting late, but it wasn't *too* late. As the door closed behind him, all the heads at the bar turned to measure his entrance. Some of the women allowed themselves glances which lingered and John clocked each and every one of the interested parties.

Plenty of time for that later. Business always came first.

Scanning the tables and booths, he found Jimmy back in the corner with two older guys who figured to be horse-players.

"Mister John!" said Jimmy. He looked to be about thirty-seven or so, dressed like he was always getting ready to play golf, and had a habit of smiling even when there was nothing funny going down. He stood up and shook John's hand vigorously, then introduced him to his companions. "This is Augie— my father-in-law, and this is Marv, he's a buddy."

Handshakes all around. Normally, when there were new faces unexpectedly in attendance—like Augie and Marv—John was a very suspicious man. But after all the years in the business, you got to know who's a cop and who's a *cetriole*, and John could lay heavy odds that Augie and Marv couldn't find their own behinds with a coupla funnels. If they were cops, he *deserved* to get busted.

So John took the end seat of the corner booth, and calmly waited. Jimmy handed him an envelope discreetly. No need to check it. Jimmy sold commercial real estate and his paper-count was always jake. Music and cigarette smoke swirled and eddied around them like fog in a cheap mystery movie as Jimmy continued to smile. "Can I get you a drink, John?"

"No, thanks," he said. "I think I'm going to do a little trolling at the bar . . . see who bites, huh, Augie?"

Jimmy and the old man chuckled. They *all* bite," said Marv. "Watch it, son."

"Yeah," said John. "Everybody's got a set of choppers when it comes to love, don't they?

They all had a good laugh at this and John used the natural pause to make good his exit lines. The last thing he wanted to do was sit around with a bunch of losers and talk sports. Truth to tell, Johnny Doc was sick of the whole sports thing. He couldn't give a shit who had the best quarterback, or the worst bullpen, or the loudest home fans. He didn't understand how *anybody* could care about the outcome of something so trivial as a *game* unless they had some money on it. A friend of his who taught Philosophy at Hofstra told John he'd become jaded, that he'd lost the appreciation of sport as a pure expression of desire and performance. Yeah, sure. That too.

Turning away from Jimmy's table, John adjusted the rake of his hat and focused-in on the row of females sitting at the bar. That was one of the good things about Manny's—it had become a great place to meet people who just wanted to meet people. No Great Expectations, and no searches for your soul-mate, and no questions asked.

He wedged in next to two housewives zeroing-in on the gray horizon of fortysomething and got Frankie's attention. "George Dickel—rock it, with a chase of coke on the side."

"George's what!" asked the frizzie-haired blonde closest to him. She punctuated her wit with a witless chuckle. "I'd be afraid to ask for a drink with a name like that."

"It's sour mash," said John, mildly interested as he scanned the topography of her face. The lines beneath the makeup spoke of kids off to college and a husband lost within the circles of corporate-hell.

"Sour mash?  Why would anybody want to drink something that sounds like it should be mopped up off the floor?"

"Because it tastes good?"  Frankie dropped the two glasses in front of him and he sipped at the Tennessee ambrosia.

"Can I try it?" asked the blonde. At least she seemed adventurous.

He looked at her tutie-fruitie cocktail, grimaced, and did a little Bogie on her. "This ain't gonna taste like that neon light you're drinking, shweetheart . . ."

She giggled and sipped cautiously from his glass. Coughed. Rolled her eyes.

"Whew! Why would *anybody* want to do that to themself?"

"It makes me horny as a hoot-owl," said John. He took back the glass, turning it to avoid a rim-smear of dark lipstick, and knocked back half of it. A tiny sip of Coke and he was in business.

"I never did it with a hoot-owl," said the Frizzy Blonde.

John laughed politely and glanced across the bar where a dark-haired woman of maybe thirty was nursing a daiquiri. He'd seen her when he'd first walked in, and she'd been watching him then, as she was now. He smiled and touched the low-slanted rim of his hat. She nodded and proffered a small smile in response. She wasn't just attractive or pretty; she was centerfold material. Her hair was an explosion of auburn hair, framing a face that spoke of classic Mediterranean statuary. Eyes as dark as the windows in a stretch limo and as full of the secrets behind its glass. Lips that had been designed to do nothing but the best finished off a face that could only be Italian. A woman like her was used to things like the utter impracticality of linen napkins, the joys of Paganini, the cool rush of satin sheets, the necessity of *paté de foie,* the comfort of silk kimonos and leather upholstery.

And even if she wasn't, she should be.

He finished his Dickel, signaled Frankie for another. Still plenty of time to make some kind of significant contact. She'd sent the guy next to her crashing and burning a couple of times, but he was too stupid or too wasted to realize he might as well be a leper.

"So what's your name? And how come you still got your hat on? Do you keep it on in bed too?"

He looked back to the Frizzy Blonde and made a point of not smiling. "You ask a lot of questions."

"I like a lot of answers," she said with a giggle which wouldn't've sounded right even on a teenager.

John looked at her and smiled, touched her shoulder softly. "Listen, could you excuse me for a minute? I think I see my sister over there."

"Your sister?"

"Yeah, and I've got a message from Mom I gotta make sure she gets."

Before the woman could say anything, he was up and moving around the horseshoe of the bar. Gliding to a stop next to the wild mane of auburn, he cleared his throat softly. ""For a second there I thought you might be my sister, but now that I get up close, I can see I made a mistake."

"Maybe you didn't" she said.

"Really?" Inside he was grinning widely. Yeah, the old radar was still in working order—just like all the other equipment.

"I know this is going to sound funny," she said. "But I had a . . . a funny feeling, almost like a dream, that I was going to meet you."

He smiled. "You mean I'm the Man of Your Dreams?"

"Not exactly," she said. "I'm not sure what you are."

"What's that supposed to mean?"

She brushed her long fingers across the wave of hair on her forehead. It was an automatic gesture, born of long-habit. She started to speak, paused, seemed to think better of it. Finally: "I don't why I told you that . . . I'm sorry."

"Hey, no problem. You want to sit at one of the booths?"

She smiled, obviously grateful to be let off the hook so easily. "That would be fine."

An hour later, they had managed to divulge enough information about each other to make things interesting. But John still wasn't taking any bets on how the night might end.

He wasn't surprised when she admitted she was Italian, and that she'd always dreamed of being a dancer or an artist or maybe even an actress. But when she hit him with the carnival road show, he kind of did a double-take. She wasn't the type you'd expect to be part of a bunch social rejects like that. Something funny about it, but he wasn't in a mood to play Detective.

Doctor, maybe.

If he could find the right nurse. And maybe he had.

She didn't ask him to further define his work when he told her he was a "short-term investment broker," and that was just as well. Despite her work in the "mud show," as she called it, she sounded like the type who wouldn't be impressed with a bookmaker. Funny, but the longer they talked the more he was getting the impression she was overly fascinated with him.

But why? He hadn't said anything all that dazzling, and had in fact let her do a lot of the talking. So what was going on here?

Carmella felt like she was falling down the rabbit-hole—like Alice in the old cartoon movie. The longer she talked to John, the more convinced she'd become that he was the one she'd already dreamed about. He'd taken off the stylishly-raked hat, fully revealing the rugged good looks the dreams had always kept obscure. She found herself attracted to his down-to-earth mannerisms and his lack of a need to try to impress her. From the moment he spoke to her, there was something *different* about him, something that was reaching her on some lower-psychic level. It was like the low-frequency signal from the reptile part of our brains, that thumping, blood-beating rhythm that spoke of sex and danger. Excitement and dread flowed into her, commingling like oil and water, to produce a hybrid emotion that she could not identify.

There was something about him. Something that kept her on edge, expectant—but of what she was not sure.

She'd talked a lot to mask her anxiety, to find out more about this man named John. She needed time to sort out her feelings and yet she knew there was no time. There was a sense of the storm just beginning to gather power to itself, of the impending maelstrom, the white-heat star ready to nova.

She was suddenly reminded of a memory from childhood. It was cold and snowy and Christmastime; she and Momma were visiting with people up north, relatives, maybe. It was an old house, and Carmella had found the steps leading to the basement where a great coal furnace squatted and glowed in blue-edged darkness. She could remember standing in front of its heavy, slatted door from which a terrible heat radiated with red teeth. Like a torpid beast, the furnace slouched and whispered its coal-fire voice at her. There was something horrible behind that slatted door, something which danced in unimaginable heat and anger, something which beckoned to young Carmella.

Come here, child. Touch my hot metal. Open me. Look into my burning heart, if you dare.

The memory seared her and for an instant John's words went away and she was a little girl again, standing in the pit of the cellar, before the glowing, grinning beast. The door of red teeth like a giant jack o'lantern was speaking again. Carmella had reached up and sprung the latch on the grate and fell back screaming as the dragon-breath roared.

Sitting before John was like that. She wanted to reach out, to throw open the door to his soul and let whatever would come screaming out consume her. More than lust. More than dread. Whatever it was, she knew she could not leave him until she understood why the fates had forced them together.

And so she did not hesitate when he suggested they take a ride down by the coast. The moon was rising above the Sound, he said, and the dark water was speckled with the mooring lights of pleasure craft—it was pretty, romantic even, if that's what she was looking for. He spoke straightforward, didn't play around with his words, and she liked that. She wanted him and he wanted her—they just had to work out the final logistics.

His black Infiniti crouched by the coastline like a predator waiting to pounce. She sat in the soft leather of its passenger seat looking out at the moon-freckled water, feeling the effects of the liquor spin through her head. Neither of them spoke for several minutes, but the silence had not become awkward. Rather, it drew them closer, bonding them in some yet to be understood way.

Finally, he touched her shoulder. Gently. With *rispetto.* Respect. "Hey, it's getting late. You want to come to my place, or do I take you home?"

Turning, she paused to let heart stop racing. "Yes," she said without letting herself think about it. "Your place. Hurry."

He nodded, and keyed the ignition. As the car glided away from the shoulder of the coastal road, she kept herself from thinking about what was happening. The risks didn't matter this time. There was something urgent, something important, in their meeting. She hated to use such a clichéd word, but she knew it was something *fated.* She had no choice now but to play it out.

The house was more ordinary than she expected. It re-sided in an older neighborhood of Oyster Bay—the kind of place that usually included the wife, the kids, and the station wagon. The usual suburban tableau. John LoMedico didn't seem to fit in that picture, but she didn't care.

Once he guided her inside, they moved through the maze of rooms and hallways in semi-darkness, both of them aware of an animal urgency, of that familiar, unquenchable and searing *need*. It was like a third presence, pushing them together, pulling them through the shadowed house.

Half-closed vertical blinds painted the king-sized bed in thick stripes of shadow and pale light from a moon as high and full as her breasts. He kissed her gently with a hint of more passion to come, teasing, promising. She slipped off his jacket, unbuttoned his shirt; he fumbled with the catches and zippers of her ensemble. There was something wonderfully erotic to be slowly undressed by your lover and she tried to control the pace, to savor each moment.

As their clothes began to fall away, some with effort and others with a clumsy tug, they began to lose themselves in the dark pool of each other's desire. A mutual abandonment, a magic chemical bonding that spoke of a closeness neither could have anticipated. Exhilarating and fearful at once, Carmella had never felt anything like it. No man had ever made her feel like this . . .

"Do you feel it?" she whispered as he kissed her swollen nipples. "What's happening to us?"

"I don't know . . . I've been trying to ignore it . . ." There was a sincerity in his voice. He wasn't humoring her, he sounded wary, cautious. "You feel it too, huh . . . ?"

She nodded, arched her back in response. Whatever it was, she had fallen prey to the aura of danger which had enveloped him. Intoxicating, alluring, teetering on the edge of control. He was kissing her, tonguing and licking her and nothing mattered beyond that single moment. Moving up to kiss her cheek and blow warmly in her ear, he stopped suddenly.

"Oh Jesus . . ." he whispered hoarsely.

"What's the matter?" she asked, sitting up as he backed away from her. Even in the slatted light, she could see the revulsion, the abject fear in his eyes, and she knew what had happened. Automatically, her hand moved to her forehead, to protect, to conceal.

"Jesus Running Christ!" John LoMedico didn't so much as move away from her as he *leaped* backward into the shadows of the room. He slammed into a closet door and sagged down to the carpet where he buried his face against drawn-up knees.

His breath came in ragged sobs.

"I'm sorry . . ." she offered, trying to maintain control of her voice. This had never happened before. She didn't know what to say, how to handle it. She had no idea he would react so . . . negatively. Was she *that* repulsive? "I . . . I don't know . . . maybe I should have told you . . ."

He looked up, his eyes catching just enough moonlight so she knew he was staring at her. "Oh, God . . . you don't understand, honey . . . you don't understand . . . Oh, Christ! Is this crazy or *what?*"

"From the show . . ." she started to talk without thinking, rambling. "We're all like this . . . well, not exactly like *this*, but—"

He gestured for her to stop, forced himself to stare at her. "You don't get it . . . you don't get it, Carmella." John LoMedico crawled over to the bed, touched her knee as he struggled to stifle his sobs and his jagged breathing.

"Tell me," she whispered, feeling comfort in his touch.

"Hey, don't think it's you, honey. You're beautiful," he said, letting the words leak out of him like water from a cracked vase. "You've always been beautiful . . . you were a beautiful baby . . ."

He stopped, letting his words echo in her mind. And just that quickly she *knew* what he meant.

"Oh no . . ." she managed the two words before a stringent pulse of pure pain/joy spiked through her.

John LoMedico forced himself to stand, gathering his clothes about him, turning his back and awkwardly stepping into his pants. The task seemed to calm him, give him strength. The words rambled out of him. "I met your mother almost thirty years ago—Jesus, at a fucking carnival!—I should've thought something was funny right away when you called it 'mud show.' And you kinda looked familiar to me . . . Your mother, she was older than me. I was just a kid . . ."

"You don't have to—"

"No, lemme get this out. Christ, I've been carrying this around for a long time, honey."

"I never knew anything about you . . ."

"That's because your mother didn't either, I guess. When the carnival came back the next summer—right here on The

Island—she surprised me with the baby . . . *our* baby. It was you . . . and you were . . . you were different, and I guess I went kinda whacko. Hey, I was sixteen years old—what did I know about being a man?"

"So you split?"

He hung his head, shook it slowly, then nodded. "Oh yeah," he whispered. "I told her I never wanted to see her again . . . and I didn't . . ."

He moved to the wall, leaned against it as though he wanted to melt into it, and he started to cry. Softly, in a dignified way, but she could feel the pain coming off in hot sheets like the furnace of her childhood. "I'm . . . sorry . . . Carmella . . ."

"Please, don't be," she said, pulling her clothes together, dressing quickly. She felt like there was so much they could say to each other, but she knew it wasn't necessary. Her half-toned dreams made sense now, in their usual muddy way, and with such understanding, she felt a sense of peace, of release.

"I'd better go," she said softly.

"Yeah . . ." He continued trying to fade into the wall. "Give me a minute or two and I'll drive you. Wherever you want to go."

She sighed, shook her head. "You can't take me *there*, but you've got me started in the right direction."

"Huh?"

"Never mind. Too hard to explain."

"You mean you don't want a ride?" He looked at her for an instant, then toward the window.

"I think I need to be alone. I need to sort things out."

Her father moved to the bedstand table and picked up the phone. "Let me at least get you a cab."

She considered the option of walking the deserted streets, but not for long. "All right . . . thanks. I'll wait out by the door."

As he called for directory assistance, Carmella slipped down the shadowed hallway, into the living room. Even the absence of light could not diminish the gaudy accessories and furnishings. Lots of draperies, fake roman columns and statuary. As her gaze traversed the fireplace mantle, the silhouettes of framed photos and knick-knacks failed to catch her attention . . . until she noticed a patch of moonlight caught on something round and smooth.

A crystal ball. Smaller than a real one, like hers. But there was beauty in its petite symmetry. Its glass held pale power of the moon. Fascinated, she moved to touch it but stopped halfway . . . Rather than merely looking at the object, she seemed to be listening to it. A subsonic hum. Soft, gentle. Like a ballad in a minor key.

*The Piece.*

No, it couldn't be. And yet the feeling and the knowledge engulfed her. The words of Oz haunted her: *when you've come near it . . . you'll simply **know** .*

Her pulse jacked behind her ear, the tips of her fingers tingled. Reaching out, she picked up the crystal sphere, and felt its coldness.

No. Something was wrong.

It was dead. Its promise a lie. Carmella felt dizzy. Anxiety catching up with her. The emotional floodgates had been opened and she was going to get caught in the backwash. It was too much. Too much at once.

"The cab will be here in a minute or two," said her father. His voice had been not more than a whisper, but she started, almost dropping the crystal.

"Hey, something the matter?" He walked closer, but not too close.

"I . . . I don't know. I thought I recognized this glass."

He almost smiled. "You *should*—you're mother gave it to me. That first summer."

*Wait!* Oz was right. Too many coincidences. It had to be The Piece. And yet . . .

"Maybe you should take it," he said. "Maybe if you gave it back to . . . to your mother . . . maybe it would make things a little better."

She could not tell him her mother was dead. For a lot of reasons.

"I don't know," she said slowly replacing the sphere to the mantle and the silvery ringstand which held it. As her hand drew closer to the polished mahogany ledge, her fingertips grew warmer.

The stand . . .

"Did she give you this part too?" she asked, already knowing the answer.

"Sure," he said. "Take it, go ahead. Give it to your Mom, I want you to."

Carmella picked up the stand—three graduated rings given form by external braces that looked like the flying buttresses of a gothic cathedral. The metal was almost pearlescent, like platinum. There was a *density*, a sense of great mass about the metal object; it spoke to her. Tonight she had found both her past and her future.

The Piece.

"My mother would be very grateful . . . if you would give it to me."

"Take it. It was never mine. You mother said it would bring me luck, and I gotta tell you—I think it always did."

"Thank you," she said, carefully placing the worthless glass and its magical stand in her purse.

The man named John, her father, almost smiled this time. He was about to speak when an auto horn beeped briefly, respectful of the hour and the neighborhood.

"Go on," he said, kissing her forehead, almost brushing the lid of her third eye. "My daughter . . ."

Carmella looked at him and he looked sadder than any man should ever be. "Thank you," she said. "I'll come back someday, and maybe then I can call you 'father'."

"Yeah, okay . . . I can settle for that."

The cabbie beeped once again, and she opened the screen door, looked back and smiled. "Goodbye," she said.

Oz was waiting for her in her trailer.

"How could you know?" she asked, clutching her handbag to her breasts.

The tall, gangly man shrugged. It was a disconcerting gesture, almost mechanical. "Sometimes we just know things, don't we, Carmella?"

"Sometimes . . ."

"I'll be needing it, my dear," he said as he stared at her purse.

Opening the clasp, she reached in past the crystal globe, to touch the light-heavy metal. It reacted to the warmth of her hand as though alive and she could almost swear it had begun to glow. She handed it to Oz, who held it up to the dangling light above her tiny kitchen table.

"Yes," he said. His hand trembled. "I knew this one, this

final one, must be circular. I would have never imagined the struts like this, but yes, very ingenious, actually . . ."

Carmella watched him become absorbed in the warm glow of the Piece, which seemed to have acquired a soft incandescence under his touch. She suddenly felt his presence in her trailer intrusive, and something not at all desired. She cleared her throat and he looked at her as one might regard a slight irritation.

"So you're done with me?"

"Yes, you've done well. All of you have done very well. We head south in the morning."

"I won't be coming back," she said.

He nodded. "Yes, I remember your mother always wanting you to be free of us."

"I promised her."

Oz smiled. It was an awkward gesture. "Yes, well, I suppose you did . . . but you must know you're not going anywhere."

"What? What did you say?" Her stomach began to twist as she glared at him.

"No one blows the show unless I say. And especially not now. The Device will be ready soon."

"I don't care about your device!" The words exploded from her like lava. She had never raised her voice to him before, and a bleak point of fear touched her mind.

But Oz just smiled. "Oh, but it cares very much about *you*, my dear."

"I can't believe this . . ." Tears came, despite her wanting to retain control. "Oh, Momma . . ."

He pocketed the series of concentric platinum rings, turned toward the door, then wheeled back upon her. "Carmella, someday you will thank me for this. Someday very soon."

He closed the door and it sealed shut with the sound of a final breath. She fell against it, biting her lower lip against the pain of frustration. What good was it to find the truth if it could never set you free?

Carmella felt herself sagging to the floor, where she drew up her knees to huddle within the prison of the night. At dawn, the wheels would turn; a new hope clanking south to be born.

*I wrote a column once about the Three Stupid Questions people always ask you when you tell them you're a writer. Number Three is "Wow . . . well, where do you get all those weird ideas?"[1] My answer, depending on my mood and the hipnicity of my audience, varies, but a partial truth lies in simply* paying attention *to what is going on in the Real World. And that is the problem with most people—they walk around in a practically impenetrable intellectual force-field, through which curiosity, wonder, and plain old knowledge are unable to pass. In either direction. Most of us (you and me* not *included), in some weird, post-modern version of Bartleby the Scrivener,* prefer not *to know much of anything.*

*Well, I guess that's why they're not writers. I have learned to do the opposite and it's served me well. Never stop noticing what's going on around you; because that's where you will find some of the most chilling material for stories. Many years ago, maybe even as many as twenty, I can remember listening to the news while I was driving, and there was this clip about a guy being prosecuted in one of the southern states for what sounded like a very odd offense. The identity of the state will remain anonymous because I can't remember which one it was, and because they may have, by this time, passed a law to protect people from the kind of predicament in which my protagonist finds himself.*

*Of course, there is no problem without a solution, and that's what the following story is all about.*

---

[1] *Number One is "Oh . . . okay, well, have you ever had anything published?" and Number Two is "Hmmm, Do you use your real name?" For an elaboration of this whole phenomena, please check my collection of essays,* The Mothers And Fathers Italian Association.

The bastard's house looked just about the way Doctor Frederick Wilhelm had figured it would: a squat little cape cod with tiny little rooms and unit air conditioners sticking out of every window. The lawn needed cutting and nasty-looking weeds choked what was left of the flower beds. A beat-up, boxy-looking Ford hulked in the driveway like the dinosaur it was. No way Raczkowski would replace his wreck with anything new—he was a used-car kind of guy.

Wilhelm smiled at his small joke, and moved stealthily from the neighboring house's shrubbery, across the unkempt crabgrass and clover, to crouch next to a rusting Sears Roebuck utility shed. Moonlight blued everything in pastel half-glows. Frederick wondered how visible he would be to anyone idly glancing in his general direction.

Probably not very. People usually weren't looking out their windows at 3:00 AM. But if they were, they most likely were sitting in the bathroom trying to purge a raging gastro-intestinal system—and not look for a Midnight Skulker.

A Skulker.

Is that what he was?  No, not exactly.

He allowed himself a little smile, then inched around the shed to the rear of the house carrying a classic Gladstone bag by his side. He had little trouble negotiating a cellarway and steps leading down to a basement door. Silent. Like a snake in the woods. Actually, he was surprising himself a little. I'm pretty damn good at this.

When the basement door turned in his hand, he nodded as though expecting it. An article he'd read in Newsweek reported more than 40% of all homes in America were left unlocked on a regular basis. And besides, Raczkowski had seemed like the type who wouldn't be real careful.

With a gentle surge forward against the wooden door, Frederick let himself into the dark clutter of the basement. An assortment of smells greeted him: sawdust, soap detergent, paint thinner, WD-40, all overlayed by a general mustiness. He used a penlight to carve a narrow path through the shadowed junk—

cardboard boxes, Hefty bags of old clothes, garden tools, patio furniture, abandoned appliances, broken toys. It was like many of our basements and attics, he observed casually. One of those places where we stash the pieces of our lives we can't live with anymore, but somehow cannot consign to the oblivion of the trash-man.

He moved to the stairs. Old. Wooden. No railing, which was again typical. Frederick moved up to the plywood door, turned the cheap brass knob. Again, there was no resistance and he was suddenly in a cramped hall, illuminated only by seeping moonlight through venetian blinds in the living room. It was a space punctuated by empty Bud cans, the carcass-boxes of home-delivered pizzas, empty cheese doodle bags, and overflowing ashtrays. The coffee table in front of a red velvet mediterranean couch was the removable hard-top from a Chinese red 55 T-Bird. Cute. Real cute.

Is this what Raczkowski was doing with his money? What an asshole . . .

Unable to resist his curiosity, Frederick checked out the kitchen, and was pleased to find it as filthy and disarrayed as he'd hoped. Butter melting in its wrapper on the counter-top, Dunkin' Donuts moldering in their boxes, a sinkful of dishes crusted with hard fragments and probably crawling with bacteria. Anyone who lived in such squalor deserved whatever misfortune might come their way.

Frederick smiled. And tonight, that misfortune is *me*.

Turning from the kitchen, he crossed the living room and ascended the shag-carpeted stairs. His Reeboks carried him up in total silence. So quietly, in fact, he could hear the sinusoidal breathing of Donald Raczkowski before reaching the second-floor landing. The sound was a medium-pitched fluting, symptomatic of a deviated septum, and like a beacon, it directed Frederick to the left, to stand in the doorway of a bedroom which reeked of un-emptied ashtrays, un-laundered bedclothes, and a particularly foul blend of semen and cheap after-shave.

Just enough ambient light filtered through the chintz curtains to detail the body sprawled stomach-down on the bed. Being the overweight, unsightly mess he was, Raczkowski had no bed-partner—just as Frederick had expected.

Moving quickly, just as he'd practiced it hundreds of times, he knelt by the bed, reaching into his bag for the prepared syringe. Smoothly, with the soft, expert touch of many years of practice, Frederick injected 40 cc's of Xylothal into the blubber of Raczkowski's bicep. The large man grunted awake from the puncture-prick, started to raise up his sour bulk on one elbow, but his eyes rolled back as the drug reached his cortical area.

Another grunt and he fell into the fouled bedsheets on his back. Just barely conscious, he looked glassily at Frederick, who waited for recognition to flicker like a dime-store flashlight behind Raczkowski's eyes.

"Good evening, Donald. It's Doctor Wilhelm."

The large man grunted weakly. Ah. Recognition at last.

A slight dilation of the pupils. Fear? One could only hope.

"I've come to get something that's rightfully mine," said Frederick. "—your left arm . . . ."

Ah, yes. The eyes definitely widened on that last phrase. He knows. He remembers. Good.

Xylothal was an interesting drug. It had the ability to keep a patient on the edge of consciousness, with no loss of sensory input, for many hours at a time, while simultaneously damping down all entire voluntary motor centers. In other words, Raczkowski would retain full awareness of his surroundings without being able to move a muscle, and still feel pain.

That was the important part. The man would need to feel pain all along the spectrum, from mild discomfort to mind-ripping agony. The man needed to be paid back for all the anguish and torture he'd inflicted upon Doctor Frederick Wilhelm.

As he reached into the Gladstone for his scalpel case, Frederick's mind rewound some choice memories, replayed them faster than real-time . . .

. . . and once again the rain-black skin of the Interstate was slithering beneath his Cadillac Seville. He'd been driving back from a much deserved golf-vacation in Myrtle Beach, South Carolina. Frederick was tapping out a rhythm on the steering wheel as his Alpine car-stereo played a CD called  Digital Duke, and Ellington had never sounded sweeter. Frederick Wilhelm, orthopedic surgeon, at the age of forty-five, had achieved and acquired everything a man could hope for: faithful devoted wife, healthy kids going to the best schools, investment real estate and a fat stock portfolio, the standard finely-appointed house, and a mistress who would diddle him six ways to Sunday for just a taste of the Good Life. Sure, he was over-extended, and sure he spent more than he could immediately pay for, but didn't we all do that? Whether you made a hundred bucks a week, or a hundred thousand every month . . .

And it hadn't come easy. No way. The third son of a construction worker in East Lansing, Michigan, Frederick had worked his ass off to pay his way through college and medical school. Not like a lot of those shits he studied and interned with. The guys from the Northeastern prep schools and the family estates where they had stables as well as garages.

No way. Freddie Wilhelm had earned everything that had come his way. And nobody would ever take it away from him.

It was that kind of determination and willful attitude which had served Frederick so well. And it didn't mean he was ruthless or heartless or anything of the sort. If that were true, he would have never stopped when he'd seen the accident.

In the wet murk beyond his wiper blades, he saw the tangle of metal on the side of the Interstate. A 4x4 had sluiced off the road to mix it up with one of the stanchions which support the big green exit signs. It must have happened recently, because Frederick saw no other cars or movement of any kind.

Without hesitation, he braked down to the shoulder and slowly approached the twisted mess that had been an old Ford Bronco. He'd always kept an emergency kit in his trunk, and being a doctor, he'd kept it stocked with a sophisticated array of drugs, instruments, and supplies. Grabbing the leather case from the rear of his car, he moved quickly to the wreck.

The driver's side door had been pinched off and the cab had accordioned inward. The vehicle must have flipped on its side and slid into the upright support at high speed. The lone occupant, a flabby man in a red plaid shirt, had been thrown halfway through the shattered windshield.

Leaning into what was left of the cab, Frederick winced at the mixture of odors—coppery fresh blood and bad rye whiskey. Everything had been stained a black-red and he feared he was too late to help the driver. Anybody losing this much blood was severely injured. He had to act quickly. Being too cautious meant lost time, and then it would be too late.

As he struggled with the man's bulk, getting him the rest of the way out of the cab, the worst of his injuries became clear—his left arm was practically severed at the shoulder and the main brachial artery was pumping out blood like a ruptured hydrant. Frederick worked quickly, with the cold efficiency which came from twenty years' experience. Rather than just stanch the wound and lose the arm, he attempted miracle-surgery in the cold rain. Whether an act of hubris or heroism—motivation never crossed his mind. It simply occurred to him that his skills might save the man's arm as well as his life.

It wasn't the prettiest sight, but by the time the paramedics arrived and the victim was hurtling off to the nearest county hospital, the arm had been re-attached and throbbed with the pink glow of flesh not dying. Frederick gave his name and address to the highway police, drove to the nearest motel where he changed out of his ruined clothes, and resumed his trip home. As he cranked up the CD, he found himself smiling, feeling good about himself. He'd done one of those Good Things—he'd saved a man's life and perhaps his occupation when he preserved the severed limb.

Funny, he'd thought: he never even got the guy's name.

But he learned it about six months later when he was slapped with Donald Raczkowski's malpractice suit. The legal brief charged him with administering medical attention without the patient's permission, and causing Raczkowski to lose more than fifty percent of the utility in his left arm, further resulting in the loss of Raczkowski's employment in the local pickling plant. The only job the scumbag had ever been able to keep.

Sure, it was a bullshit case. But in a backward, bullshit state where they'd never got around to passing any "Good Samaritan" laws, it was also a case that would stick.

Frederick wouldn't have really cared if he'd kept up his malpractice insurance premiums, but Christ, with Anthony in his third year at Princeton, and Jennifer Louise accepted at Stanford, he'd been a little short, and he figured he had to rob

Peter to pay Paul for little while. When his insurance carrier claimed default, and Donald Raczkowski claimed victory, things went very badly for Frederick.

Very badly and post haste.

The settlement required the liquidation of almost every asset Frederick had ever acquired. The houses, the cars, the boat, and of course the entire stock portfolio. But it didn't stop there. When he tried to sell some of Tina's jewelry and furs, she decided she'd suffered enough indignity and took off for her parents's home in Shaker Heights—*with* her jewelry. Telling the kids they'd have to complete their educations at the local State diploma factory drove a stake through the heart of whatever had been left of their fibrillating relationships. In addition, his colleagues considered his malpractice conviction the equivalent of a kiss on the cheek after a Mafioso dinner. Not only did every doctor in the county stop referring patients to his office, but also stopped talking to him as well. When his country club refused to offer him a membership renewal, Frederick really wasn't all that surprised. But perhaps the final, and most telling blow, was the hasty departure of Shawna, his young, long-legged mistress, who really didn't need to tell him she'd loved Frederick's money a lot more than the man himself.

For a while, Frederick continued to believe in his own self-worth. He attempted to retain his dignity, rebuild his shattered practice, and remove the tarnish from his reputation. Living in a small suburban apartment complex colored with grim, blue-collar workers and legions of screaming, chocolate-mouthed kids on Big-Wheels, Frederick continued to plummet into the abyss of his private desperation. The growing reality that things would never be as they once had been began to crush him down like the great heel of a socialist government.

Every day became a monumental struggle. To pay the bills, to be civil and polite, and finally to even be a competent physician.

When not scrounging up local industrial accident cases, and the occasional neighborhood broken arm, Frederick spent his time alone. Assuredly, he would never see his wife again, unless it was over the shoulder of her divorce attorney; his children were both embarrassed and outraged at his failure to protect himself and properly educate them. Shawna of the long, tanned legs and high breasts had, by this time, wrapped her perfumed flesh around a new Sugar-Doc; and there were certainly no more Sunday afternoon ball games or golf-foursomes in his future.

Alone.

Either in his Spartanly appointed office, for which the rent seemed eternally due, or in his meager apartment populated by yard-sale furniture and a yeoman-class television. Alone, with thoughts which grew increasingly more torturous. He grew to realize it was probably bearable to live only the skeleton of a real life—if you've never known any better—but impossible if you've ever been on top. Campbell's tomato soup instead of a rich bouillabaisse? Montgomery Wards after Abercrombie and Fitch? A Ford Fiesta where a Mercedes once purred? And didn't you just know off-the- rack permanent press slacks didn't have the feel and fit of custom-tailored worsted wool? But it wasn't just the money, Frederick knew. It was the entire mindset, the ambiance, the way a man's trappings served to define him. The way a man perceived himself.

Frederick slipped gradually down the chute to madness. The worst part of the journey being his almost total awareness of what was happening to him. Reality became increasingly plastic and mutable, all according to the whims of his tortured psyche, and even though he knew it was happening, he couldn't do a Goddamned thing about it.

But then, there was something to be done, wasn't there?

Not a rectifying, restorative act, to be sure, but a sweet enough substitute for any man exceeding the posted limits on the Oblivion Expressway.

Frederick accepted his mission with a semi-stoical smile—if there can be such a thing. Revenge is that special chord played out in the mind which has worked through the whole sliding scale of emotional responses and found them wanting. And revenge, Frederick discovered, became his raison d'etre.

In several weeks he'd transformed himself. From ruined orthopedic specialist to a far more romantic amalgam: tactician, private investigator, commando, and most importantly, avenging angel. He watched his prey from close range, studied his habits, made his plans, and when the time was just right, reached for his Gladstone bag . . .

. . . and unleashed the instrument of his revenge. Even in the feeble light of the bedroom, the scalpel shone with a preternatural brightness. As Frederick bandied it gracefully, like a conductor with his baton, before Raczkowski's bugging eyes, it seemed to grow brighter and shinier still.

Such a tiny little blade, thought Frederick. Ever since medical school, he'd been amazed at how efficiently a cutting tool it was. Laying its flat surface on the flabby skin of Donald's shoulder, Frederick let his former patient feel the cold kiss of the steel. He let the moment linger, like a foul odor that won't go away, in Donald's mind. The anticipation of the first cut would be worse than the actuality, wouldn't it?

Yes, of course it would.

Then with a simple, confident turn of his wrist, a subtle downward pressure, and the little blade was plunging effortlessly through Raczkowski's doughy, mole-blighted flesh. Blood seeped at first, but as the capillaries gave way to heavier plumbing, things began to get a little messy. Raczkowski tried to scream, but the Xylothal wouldn't allow it.

Frederick smiled. A big, burly asshole like Raczkowski making these wimpy, gaspy little kitten mewlings was kind of funny. Pausing, Frederick peered down at his ex-patient with an expression most psychiatrists would describe as flat. Now what was he going to do about the major arteries and veins? Of course—just tie them off crudely, seepage be damned. That would hold things at least until he'd finished sawing through all those tough tendons and ligaments.

He smiled and went back to his work, moving the blade with renewed confidence, trying to retrace the scar-marks of his previous work. Raczkowski's pain levels were red-lining now. Even under the hammer-lock of the Xylothal, the man was managing to give the suggestion of writhing on the blood-soaked bed. If eyes could bulge voluntarily from a skull, his would have long-since left their sockets.

The pain must have been exquisite, thought Frederick.

At last, all remaining gristle had been separated, the final shreds of connective fascia flensed away, and Frederick's work was completed. Raczkowksi was beginning to hemorrhage badly, beginning the long slide into terminal shock. Frederick left him to leak away in the cruel moonlight.

He paused to wrap the arm in a Hefty bag, then wash up before slipping into the comfort of the darkness. Within minutes, Frederick was motoring down the Interstate. It had started to drizzle but he didn't care. When he was several miles along, he hurled the bagged arm out the window. It landed on the highway's shoulder and he chuckled at the ironic appropriateness. Oddly enough, though, the great sense of vindication he'd expected remained absent. Oh, of course he was pleased Raczkowksi had received suitable punishment for his gross ingratitude, but there was not the expected feeling of completion, of a mission finally ended.

Worse (or perhaps, better), Frederick discovered something new about himself. In a truly transcendent moment, while slicing through the last remnants of what had been a human arm, he'd realized he liked what he was doing. How odd his life had taken such turns until it now lay at the antipodes of all to which he'd ever aspired.

White Healer turned Dark Destroyer.

He smiled. There was a curious, but fulfilling symmetry to it all. Yes, he thought as he gripped the wheel and peered out into the murky pre-dawn, maybe somebody out there needs me? Maybe they need a Good Samaritan . . .

*There is a very sweet and wonderful couple living in a northern section of Baltimore known as Roland Park. The neighborhood is full of gigantic trees and large Victorian homes, and looks like it fell through a time-warp from an earlier era. Much like the couple themselves—John and Joyce Maclay, are as gentle and warmly intelligent as a husband and wife could be. John has been a writer for as long as I've known him, but he and Joyce are also publishers of fine small press books.[1] Maclay & Associates has published a variety of non-fiction books about the cultural side of Baltimore, and also an impressive array of horror and dark fantasy anthologies, edited by John and Joyce, and a handful of others in the field.*

*When John invited me to contribute to a limited edition anthology he was putting together, to be published by his own small press in Baltimore[2], I jumped at the chance to work with him again. Entitled* Voices from the Night, *it was not a theme anthology; in fact, John was not looking for any particular kind of story. He just wanted his contributors to write a story that was "dark," I think was his exact word to me.*

---

[1] *He and Joyce, in their incisive wisdom, were the publishers of the initial volume of our anthology series,* Borderlands.

[2] *A metropolis which, in addition to being the home of the Ravens and Orioles, could also claim the title as the Capital City of horror and dark fantasy small press publishing. Jack Chalker's Mirage Press, Maclay & Associates, Cemetery Dance Publications, and Borderlands Press all created a fabulous array of trade limited editions during the Nineties. Borderlands (that's Elizabeth's company) moved to New Hampshire in 1996.*

*When I sat down to do the following piece, I wasn't sure what I would come up with because I was in the middle of a novel (like, when am I not?), and it is sometimes hard to "switch gears" and downshift to the short fiction mode from all that lengthy exposition of the book-length manuscript. No, strike that from the record—it is* always *hard to change modes. But I always make the attempt because I love the short story form, and I love the endless challenge of writing them. So anyway, I start staring at my keyboard and I think Maclay, and I think of Baltimore, and I decide to set the story in that city, and my protagonist will write for the* Baltimore Sun, *and let's see . . . let's make him a real son-of-a-bitch-bastard of a guy . . .*

Jerry Leigh sat at his desk, oblivious to the idiot-thrum of the other reporters in the hive.

Carved up into half-assed little cubicles with partitions that looked like they'd been upholstered with carpet remnants, the Copy Room of the Baltimore Sun was a kid's giant maze, or an English squire's hedge labyrinth, filled with desks and computer terminals. In a far corner of this mess, near one of the rare windows overlooking Calvert Street, sat a stoop-shouldered man of about fifty, pounding out his story on a stained keyboard. Jerry's fingers moved nimbly over the letters, belying his overweight, out-of-shape appearance. This was writing by the numbers, he thought with a wry, lopsided grin. After almost thirty years as a journalist, he knew how to slap together familiar copy the way an old carpenter could make a doghouse with one hand behind his back.

Sucking on a Pall Mall (did anybody else still smoke the damned things?), Jerry nodded and smiled as he typed merrily along:

*. . . and a spokesman for the Baltimore City Fire Department stated that Towanda Jefferson did not have a smoke detector installed in her rented home on Baker Street.*

"No shit," said Jerry, shaking his head, chuckling to himself. "No way you're gonna spend any of those welfare bucks on something sensible, hey baybee?!"

"It must be nice to amuse yourself so easily," said a voice behind him, the voice of fellow-reporter Rick Schmidt.

Swiveling in his worn chair, Jerry faced a kid of perhaps thirty, handsome in an Ivy League, waspy kind of way. "Don't you wish, huh Ricky?"

"That's the Jefferson fire story you're doing?"

"Yeah, what's it to you?" Jerry tried his best sneer on him. He didn't really mind Schmidt—the kid had tried to be friends ever since he'd started working at the paper, but lately he'd been getting a little uppity. They all got that way after they'd been here a little while. After they figured there wasn't anything else to learn from the veterans, from the *real* reporters . . . Rick Schmidt shook his head slowly, trying to be dramatic. "I can't figure you out, Jerry. That woman lost three little kids in that fire. How can you be such . . . such an *assshole?"*

Jerry pushed away from his desk, faced the kid squarely. "You know, Ricky, if I didn't like you, I'd get up from this chair and bust your face. Matter of fact, there was a time, when I was about your age, when I would've done it anyway. Like you or not."

"Yeah, I'm sure."

"Ricky, you don't walk up to people you work with and call them assholes. Didn't they teach you that when you went to college to learn all that 'journalism'?" Jerry said the last word like it was something distasteful in his mouth.

"I heard you sitting here in your little warren, your little insulated cocoon, *laughing,"* said Schmidt. "That's pretty sick, man."

"Oh, bullshit! Why don't you wake up?"

"Wake up?! Me? What about *you?* You make your *living* writing about people *dying!* How can you get any humor out of that?"

Jerry shook his head, pulled a drag off his cigarette. "You ever go down to City Morgue, kid? You ever sit in on an autopsy?"

"No, I don't know if I could handle it . . ." Schmidt cleared his throat. "What's that got to do with—?"

"Only everything!" yelled Jerry. "How do you think the M.E. gets through his days, how do you think any of those pathology guys get through all the death business? They have to laugh about it once in a while or they go bugfuck! Don't you see that?"

"Paramedics and coroners, even the cops . . ." said Schmidt. "That's different. It's not the same thing at the Paper."

"No, Kid, it's *not,* and that's the whole point. You've totally missed the point of what the newspaper is all about, and that's death and dying! Where the hell's your head been since you been here, Kid? It's nothing *but* death and dying. The 'gooshy stuff!' *That's* why people buy the paper. If you're a newspaper man, you're dealing in death, you Bozo! The sooner you learn that, the better off you'll be."

Schmidt stood there for a minute, considering everything.

You could tell he didn't like what he was hearing, but he knew there was a lot of truth in it. "I've never heard it put like that," he said finally.

"Take my word for it, Ricky—a newspaper is nothing if it ain't about death. It *is* death."

"Well, maybe it is, but I still think you can have a better attitude . . ."

Jerry grinned as sardonically as he could. "Shaw wasn't kidding," he said.

"Who's Shaw?"

"George Bernard . . . didn't they teach you about him at your college?"

"Of course," said Schmidt, "and if you're planning on wheeling out that tired old bit about 'youth being wasted on the young', why don't you just stuff it, okay?"

"Now you're starting to sound like a newspaper man, Kid."

Rick Schmidt shook his head, turned to leave Jerry's cubicle, then paused, looked back at him. "You know, you're not supposed to be smoking in here anymore, Jerry."

"Is that why you *really* snuck out of your cage for? To hassle me about that crap?"

"It bothers other people," said Schmidt. "And it's bad for the computers, too."

Jerry chuckled. This kid was such a straight arrow. He still had so much to learn about *everything*. One of these days he'd realize that all mickey-mouse rules and regs were just more bullshit to keep your mind off the important stuff, the stuff they don't want any of us really thinking about.

Jerry took a long drag, exhaled slowly, making sure he sent plenty of exhaust in Schmidt's direction, then dunked the butt in his Styrofoam cup of cold coffee.

Jerry looked at his watch. "Jeez, it's getting late. I gotta get this thing in for the next edition. And you should start thinking about going home to the little wifey-poo."

"Jennifer works, too. We both get home around the same time."

Jerry scowled at him. Schmidt was starting to bug him now. "Yeah, like I give a shit. Look, I'm trying to be nice, but it's time for you to make some tracks. You know what I'm sayin' here: go away, kid, you're bothering me. You're outta here."

"You know what I think, Jerry . . . ?"

"I don't really care what you think." Jerry swiveled back to his keyboard, dismissing him.

" . . . I think you're a lonely, miserable man."

"Yeah, right . . . so leave me alone and let me be miserable, okay? I got work to do."

Jerry chuckled as he reached down and pulled a bottle of Old Granddad from the bottom drawer of his desk, and poured three fingers into what had originally been a Skippy peanut butter jar.

Schmidt frowned his disapproval, but said nothing as he left the work area.

Jerry smiled to himself, knocked back the bourbon with one healthy swallow, and forced himself to finish his story.

"And I'll tell you another thing," said Jerry, his words started to slur just enough to make him sound less than serious. "Lawyers are the worst of the lot! Did you know that 75% of all the lawyers in the world—in the goddamned *world!*—are practicing right here in the U. S. of A.?!!"

"Get outta here, you're kiddin' me," said Frankie. He'd been the bartender at Alonzo's for more than twenty years, and he'd heard all of Jerry Leigh's half-drunk rants enough times to recite them like sixth-grade poetry. But Frankie also knew how to treat regular customers, earning their trust and their tips. So he listened like all good barkeeps and responded at just the right times with just the right words.

In the background, the drone of an ESPN announcer described the action of an Orioles game; the basic weave upon which all the bar's other conversations would be tapestried tonight. Jerry Leigh liked his baseball, but he'd had more highballs in his glass than the Tigers pitcher had been able to get over the plate. The score was out of hand and so was Jerry.

After he finished with the lawyers, he started in on the dentists and their outrageous prices that they seemed to just pull out of their butt-cracks. Only problem was, he'd already diced up the DDS crowd, and people on both sides of his stool were starting to get weary of his bourbon-fueled tirades.

"Hey, buddy," said the long-haired guy next to him. He was wearing a leather jacket, and looked like a refugee from a Bugle Boy commercial. "You're starting to repeat yourself . . . how about listening to the ballgame for awhile, huh?"

Jerry looked at the guy—probably close to forty, but in good shape, and looking kind of ethnic, Italian, maybe. Odds were he wouldn't take much bullshit from a flabby coronary candidate.

But Jerry couldn't help himself.

"Fuck you and your ballgame, okay?" Old Granddad had a way of making him do things he later regretted.

Longhair kind of smiled. "Can I take that to mean you're not going to stop annoying everybody else around you?"

The guy was, Jerry realized, giving him one last chance to lurch back in the direction of civilization.

He chose barbarism.

"You can take it anyway you want it, pal, as long you break it off in your own ass."

The guy slowly reached in and grabbed Jerry's tie. Even more slowly, and with a certain style, actually, he pulled down on it. The effect was to move Jerry's face inexorably closer to the edge of the bar until his right jowl was polishing the mahogany.

"I don't usually bother people," said Longhair. "But, you, sir, are a menace—to yourself and to the rest of us."

"Lemmie go!" slurred Jerry. The guy's grip was like a vise. "Frankie! Tell this asshole to lemmie go!"

The bartender approached him. "Why don't you try to calm down, Mr. Leigh," said Frankie. "Tommy doesn't want any trouble . . ."

"He doesn't want any parts of me—that's what you mean!" Jerry tried to yell with his mouth pushed up hard against the wood.

"Can't you get him out of here?" asked a woman's voice.

"Frankie, call the cops, why don't ya?" said someone else.

"I think it's time you took a walk outside," said Longhair Tommy. In one quick, fluid series of movements, like a dance team, Jerry was whirled and spun and positioned off his stool, onto his feet, and facing the front door. He still felt like he was being vise-gripped, and the first suggestion of embarrassment began to rise above his reptilian thoughts.

"Let's go," said Longhair Tommy.

Just as they began to surge forward, the door to Alonzo's opened to reveal a beautiful young blonde woman. She was dressed fashionably, but not flashy. Style, grace, passion—she possessed all these things, and you knew it instantly. She was the kind whose entrance into a room compelled everyone to take notice, and it was happening now. Jerry Leigh's barroom passion play was a pale memory.

She stood there scanning the faces of her audience, obviously looking for someone, apparently distressed. When her gaze reached Jerry Leigh, it fractured like a delicate vase in the hand of a dolt.

"Daddy!" she half-whispered, half-cried out the word.

The collective empathy of the patrons filled the room with its immediacy. The inherent tragedy of this beautiful girl/woman being in any way related to the slug at the bar touched everyone.

She moved to the bar, glanced at Longhair Tommy and enacted a small smile. "It's okay, I can handle him. Thank you."

Elegant. Direct. Whatever, it worked.

Both men relaxed as Tommy retreated to his own stool and Jerry struggled up from the depths of his self-pity.

"Karen . . . Jesus, what're you doin' here?"

"I waited for you, Daddy. I looked for you. When you didn't come, I got worried."

"Huh?" Her words slipped past his ethanol sentries, making sense when he wished they wouldn't. "What's goin' on, baby?"

"Daddy, how *could* you . . . ?" She was shaking her head slowly, biting her lower lip. This man had embarrassed her, but far worse, he had failed her.

"How could—?"

The front door swung open again to reveal a young man in a tailored suit. He looked like he could have sculled for Princeton or Brown and he should have a name like Kyle or Coates.

"Chip!" Karen said to him. "I found him!"

Okay, so it was Chip—Jerry had been close . . . .

The young man moved quickly to their position at the bar. His expression belied his relief, sadness, and disgust. "I *told* you this is where he'd be," he said.

"What's goin' on, Baby?" slurred Jerry.

"He doesn't even know why we're here!" said Chip, anger contorting his features. "He forgot! I *told* you he forgot!"

Who the hell was this indignant snot? Jerry tried to stand up, face his accuser. "Forget *what*, buddy?"

Chip started to speak, but Karen beat him to the punchline. "Daddy, I graduated from law school tonight."

"Tonight? That was *tonight?!*"

A dim alarm sounded in some back room of his mind. Law school. Lawyers. Of course, that's why they'd been on his mind. Somewhere, amidst the clutter of his life and his thoughts, lay the discarded note to attend his daughter's commencement at the University of Baltimore Law School. Downtown. Right down the street from his desk at the *Sun*, right down the street from his favorite oasis where Karen had found him . . . .

"Jesus, baby, I'm sorry! I can't believe I forgot . . . It's like I was so busy at the paper, I guess everything caught up with me. But I'll make it up to ya, I promise, you'll see."

"Let's go, Karen," said Chip, who had sandy hair. Naturally.

Jerry reached back toward the bar. He needed a knock of bourbon. Bad.

"Oh, Daddy, I can't believe this . . ."

"C'mon, Karen, he's too drunk to even know what's going on."

"No! No, I'm not," Jerry said in a loud voice. "So how'd it go, huh, baby? You a lawyer now?"

"Daddy, I've got to go. Chip and I are driving up to Deep Creek Lake with some friends. They've got a great cabin up there. We're going to celebrate." She paused and looked at him with an expression of terrible sadness. "We've got to go."

"Now? Tonight? You're going up there *now?*"

"Yes. But I didn't want to leave without finding out what happened to you. Now I know." She almost bent forward to kiss him on the forehead, but stopped herself. Then she backed away and turned toward the door. "Goodbye, Daddy."

"Karen, wait a minute!"

But Ivy-League-Chip had her by the arm and they were already moving together away from the bar. Their exit through the front door a sharp punctuation to the encounter.

Shaking his head slowly, Jerry wheeled back to the bar.

"Freshen me up, Frankie," he said.

The bartender shook his head. "It's damned sad when a father don't think about his kid . . ."

Jerry grinned sloppily. "What you mean—*Karen?* Ah! She'll get over it. C'mon! Fill'er up!"

"I think you've about had it, Mr. Leigh," said Frankie. "I think you better be gettin' home."

"Home?" Jerry looked fatuously at Frankie. "I ain't got nothin' at home."

"Yeah, well, you ain't got nothin' here, either. Goodnight, Mr. Leigh."

It must have been one of those fucking blackouts . . .

The next thing he knew, he was sitting at his desk in the *Baltimore Sun* building on Calvert Street. Ambient light from the city leaked through the nearby window to cast long, dim shadows across the sea of workstations, desks, and partitions. Other parts of the building hummed with nightshift hive-life, but all the reporters in this department were long-gone. It was late; even the bars and the after-hours joints had folded their tents for the night.

But still carrying a healthy buzz around in his skull, Jerry reached for the bottom-right drawer. It was like a galvanic response, or more appropriately, a tropic reaction. Like an amoeba being drawn toward a light source, Jerry was attracted to his Granddad bottle. He ignored the formality of his peanut butter jar, and pulled off a shot or so straight from the neck. The bourbon scorched a sweet path down his throat and he tried to remember what he was trying to forget this time . . .

Something bad.

Something embarrassing, he knew that.

And gradually, the memories reached him, like the inevitable rising of the tide, and he lapsed into ever-greater self-pity. What an asshole . . . ! His own daughter. He was hopeless.

If he had any balls at all, he'd—

An odd sound interrupted his thought. Odd, but familiar too.

A rustling, crunching sound. Of newspapers being wadded up . . .

It was more than that. There was a rhythm, a cadence to the sound, as though someone was walking across a great plane of old, balled-up sheets of newsprint, and their footsteps were still crunching up everything pretty good.

Sitting there in the dark, Jerry held the bottle an inch from his lower lip, looking across the gray night of the newsroom. He was listening to the sound, as toasted as he might have been; his attention had been hooked.

Lurching forward, he tried to isolate the source of the noise.

Beyond the vast room, out in the corridor. It grew steadily louder. Whatever it was, it was coming down the main corridor, closer to him.

"Hey! Anybody out there?!" Jerry's voice lost its power as it echoed across the room and slinked out the door.

The crumpling-papers sound stopped, as though his voice had in some way signaled it to halt. Jerry listed forward in his chair, waiting against the silence like a man leaning against a cold, stone wall.

Several eternities glaciered past.

Nothing.

Fuck it. Make yourself a nightcap and get the hell home.

He pointed the bottle towards his face, and the sound of newspaper whispered across the shadows.

"All right, what's goin' on! Who's out there?"

Again, silence.

"Goddammit!" Jerry slammed the bottle on the desktop, lurched to his feet. He'd had enough of the goddamned games. He'd fix 'em, whoever it was . . .

Amidst the phalanx of desks and partitions, he worked his way to the open door. Some sonuvabitch thinks he's funny, tryin' to fuck with my head . . . Yeah, we'll see about that . . .

Jerry reached the door, stepped out into the hall—

—and stopped abruptly. Gasping for a stale breath, he felt his heart hammering. It was like opening your eyes and discovering you're standing on the edge of the Grand Canyon.

Something was wrong with the light, the corridor. The perspective was all wrong. Across had become down. Up had lost all meaning. Everything was . . . stretched. Distorted. Skewed. He grappled for the right word, then realized it didn't matter, didn't change the reality of what he was seeing. Jerry had been white-knuckling the doorjamb unconsciously. If he let go, he would go hurtling down the corridor like a body sailing down an open well. The sound had ceased again, but there was something moving far away, at the vertices of the corridor, where the lines of perspective converged. Beams of light spiked around the object, lancing the mist that accented the seemingly endless shaft.

Mist? Where the hell was he?

Jerry had heard of drunks that gave you these kinds of hallucinations, but he'd never had one till now. Time to change brands . . .

He tried to pull back from the edge of the gravity pit, but something held him there. Whatever it was at the far end of the hallway was moving, behind the light, breaking and re-fusing in its beams. The sound of the newspapers being crumpled up echoed up the hall. There was a rhythm to it, a cadence that commanded his attention. Gradually a shape resolved itself out of the distance. Something large was moving towards him and Jerry felt a *tightening* all over his body, as though his skin was no longer the right size.

The shape grew ever closer. Tall, thick, and bipedal. It lurched towards him. Mythic archetypes flooded him with images of menace. Minotaur, yeti, golem, whatever it was, he thought, it was bad news.

At that moment, he had no idea how terribly accurate his idiom might be.

The effects of a long night of alcohol and self-pity had been leached out of him in an instant. He was no longer stewed in his own foul juices, and his feelings of surly indifference had been replaced by a growing sense of unease, of true fear.

"All right, what the hell is this?!" His words fell limply down the shaft dripping gobbets of false bravado.

The shape lumbered closer. It was big, imposing, formidable.

The sound grew louder, more intense.

The sound of newspapers dying.

*"Jerry . . ."*

The thing spoke to him, and it was like somebody just tried to yank the bones out of him. Its voice, soft as a whisper, but serrated with dreaded familiarity, sawed through him.

He tried to back away, but there was no place to go. The door he'd passed through was gone, and he stood in the endless corridor, leaning forward, feeling like he'd drop through the center of the planet. Everything in him was drying up, and his nuts felt like a couple of dried peas rattling around in a gourd. A coldness entered him like smoke, and if he could have moved at all, he would have trembled. But even that was taken away.

The shape was close now. Close enough for Jerry to see it for what it was.

*"Jerry . . ."*

"Get away from me," he said mindlessly. The thing was reaching out to him, beckoning, as though it meant to curl him into its tendrilled arm. Massive in size and bulk, its thickness was masked by the suggestion of robes; its head cowled in what might be a hood or some hideous extension of its own shape. Like some scarecrow gone wrong, it appeared to be made of newspapers.

A paper man. A newspaper man.

As it moved, the print of its flesh swirled and flowed like ink, forming rivers and estuaries of words, columns. Like a tattooed man from the darkest carnival, the figure loomed over him.

*"Do you know who I am?"* it asked in a voice that was the whispery folding and crushing of old papers. It was a mesmerizing sound.

"No," Jerry forced a croak from his freeze-dried throat.

*"Yes, you do, Jerry . . . I am the Newspaper Man."*

"What do you want . . . ?"

*"You said that I am Death . . ."*

"What?" Jerry Leigh hung upon the words of the apparition, and as awash as he might be in the backwaters of alcoholic poisoning, he knew he faced an entity of cosmic proportion.

*"And you know what, Jerry . . . ? You're right."*

"Right about *what?* What is all this? What do you want with me?"

*"Look,"* said the Newspaper Man. He leaned forward displaying the length of his arm with stylish flourish.

Against his will, Jerry watched the maelstrom of type upon the papered skin. Headlines formed for an instant, then sank beneath the surface . . . **Hurricane Amy Claims 32 . . . Terrorist Bomb Kills 5 . . . Asian Flu Lethal For Elderly Couple . . . Suicide Rate Climbs For Troubled Teens . . .**

*"I am death. I am the 'gooshy stuff.'"*

Jerry twisted against the forces which toyed with him like a spider spindling its prey. A coldness had invaded him, a touch from the void of all that has lost life's spark.

*"Have you seen the news today?"* it whispered.

The Type again moved and sank and resurfaced. Jerry watched a new headline rise up like the head of an ancient beast: **Two Die in Fiery Crash near Deep Creek Lake**.

The cold that had been nesting within his soul collapsed like a dying star, it fell in upon itself, and sucked in all that was left of him.

Karen was gone.

The final connection, the last link to the fire and juice in life, had been severed. There was nothing left to keep him from plummeting into entropy's heart. Nothing left. Inside or out.

Jerry threw himself at the Newspaper Man, but fell short.

"Help me! You gotta do something!" he screamed.

*"I do nothing. I simply am."*

"Take me instead!"

*"This is no cheap melodrama, Jerry. I did not come here to strike a bargain."*

He was sobbing openly now, and the sting of Karen's loss had become the only heat-source in the dead-star coldness of his being. "Then what are you doing here? What's the point of it all?"

*"If you don't know by now, then you are far more wretched then even I can grasp."*

"Then . . . what now?"

The Newspaper Man bowed mockingly and began to recede from him. *"For you, more of the same. Unless you choose differently."*

"Wait!" cried Jerry. "It's not supposed to end like this! Isn't there something else?"

*"Only this . . ."* the Newspaper Man raised a hand and fanned his long fingers. In doing so a daily edition curled into being. Then with the smooth motion of a twelve-year-old boy, he launched the paper at Jerry. Like a Cruise missile, the rolled-up paper homed in on him, piercing his chest with a cleansing fire.

There was flash of golden heat, and then—

One of the cleaning ladies found him curled up in the third-floor hallway of the *Sun* building. Alarmed, she called 911 and the paramedics came to gather up Jerry Leigh.

As he rode in the back of the ambulance, the tortured visions of his ethanol nightmare refused to take their exit. Outside, the sun remained several hours away. What had happened to him? Had he been standing at the threshold to one of the universe's composing rooms? Or had he been ass-deep in the worst episode of delirium tremens this side of the boneyard?

He was afraid to find out if he'd been handed a tout sheet for tomorrow, or maybe just a friendly warning from his conscience to be a better man, a better father. And somewhere in the darkness, the presses banged and stamped and rolled, and another *Sun* waited to be born.

Jerry knew that he would dread the sound of its birth as it slapped upon the wood of his front porch.

*Have you seen the news today?*

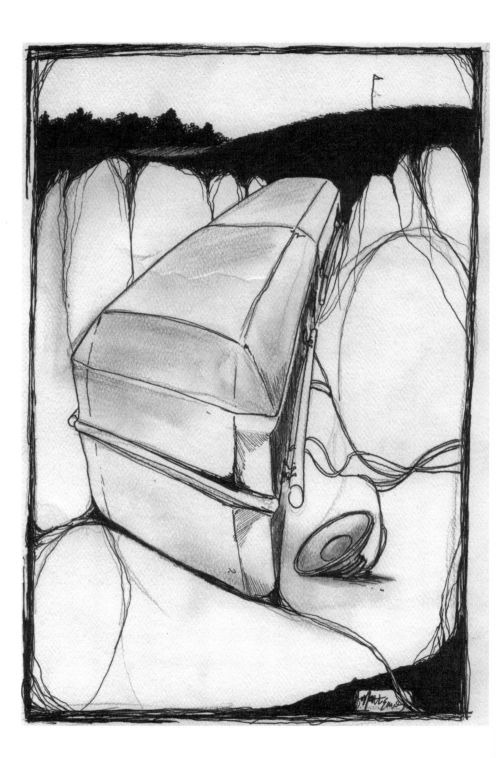

*'Round the time Elizabeth and I were think-
ing about moving to New England, I get a letter
from a writer in England who'd kind of burst onto
the publishing scene with a bunch of stories and
a few novels. His name was Peter Crowther, and
in addition to a story he'd sold to our* Borderlands *anthologies, he had also written several un-
forgettable pieces for* Cemetery Dance *magazine.
I was impressed with the guy's energy and his
clean, wonderfully readable style—mainly because (and I fully cop to being a reactionary na-
tionalist on this one) he writes more like an American than the average Englishman. I like Pete's
writing and I like him as a person.*

*But I digress.*

*He had come up with an idea for an anthol-
ogy called* Touch Wood, *stories which explored
some aspect of a superstition—its origin, its power,
it effectiveness, etc. I thought it was a challenging idea, and I promised him I would come up
with something. I sat down and made a list of
superstitions and waited for some sort of spark of
white-heat inspiration to synapse through me, and
. . . nothing was happening. Nada, Zerocity, Uh-
uh, and all that. So I shared this with Elizabeth
and she suggested taking the literal approach,
saying "okay, the book is called* Touch Wood . . .
*well, did you know that the real superstition about
knocking on wood says that it's good luck only as
long as the wood does not have legs."[1]*

*Well, I hadn't heard that one, and it still didn't
give me an idea for a story, but it got me thinking
about what kind of wooden objects had legs as
opposed to those that had none. And then I started*

---

*trying to free associate, and thought about Pete Crowther being British, and then I thought about Alfred Hitchcock being British, and maybe I would do an* homage *to the kind of story Hitchcock used to do on his absolutely brilliant television show from the Fifties and Sixties. That got me into motion, and it seemed to me that one of standard sub-genres of the TV show, and of the kinds of stories in the Hitchcock anthologies, were ones which used the staid, mannered setting of the Old World Gentleman's Club— replete with polished wainscoting, cigar humidors, and the obligatory oil paintings of The Hunt.*

*All I needed were a few contentious characters and a plot device, which are always laying about the workshop. So I grabbed up the required items and went to work on this next one . . .*

For an instant, Gordon Kingsley had forgotten where he was.

Had he drifted off to sleep? Impossible! After what he'd just experienced . . . no, it was plainly impossible.

And yet he'd felt himself blink, felt his entire body spasm, as though he'd been abruptly awakened, as though from a trance.

The darkness held him like a fist, and although he had not reached out to touch the walls of the coffin, he knew the prison of its wood loomed terribly close. He wished he had his watch with its luminous dial, just to check the time. But that would be against the rules.

The bastards, he thought with amusement. They're all probably jowl-deep in their Wall Street Journals by now, but Gordon knew at least one of them would be monitoring the simple control panel Huntington had designed for this particular little adventure.

That was one of the conditions—someone would always be monitoring both of them in case there was either (a) an emergency, or (b) capitulation.

Gordon Kingsley cleared his throat, wondering if the sound was loud enough to arouse whoever might be listening. No, that's right; they couldn't hear him unless he flicked on the mike. He thought about turning on the light, but that would enact one of the other conditions—for every minute you kept your light on, one was subtracted from your total time.

No, he thought. For now, I'll just lie here in the dark and think about why I'm here . . .

Murder is always murder. So is theft.

Gambling, however, is one of those fascinatingly odd pastimes that wears the clothes of its practitioner. If you're tuxedoed to the nines at Barclay's Casino in Soho, playing roulette and baccarat all night, you're the jaunty gentleman. But if you're throwing dice behind the YMCA or getting toasted at Aqueduct's two-dollar window, you're the biggest scumbag in Manhattan. There is something elegant about betting with bankers and industrialists, but altogether tatty when you do it with steamfitters

and housepainters. Gambling carries both its own social stig-
mata and imprimatur. It's not what you do; it's whom you do it
with.

And so it was with the members of The Colonial Club—the
oldest men's club in New York, dating back to the earliest days
of New York's inclusion into the original thirteen colonies. Gambling among its brethren was as natural as hand-rolled cigars or
imported sherry. To hear a wager being offered or taken in the
Club's drawing room was as acceptable as a market price being
quoted. Topics ranged from the most mundane of sporting events
to personal boasts of prowess to the outcomes of political and
financial futures. Amounts ranged from paltry dinner tabs to
portfolio items. In all, the Colonial Club found gambling to be
a delightful pastime.

But sometimes, a wager could take on a new level of meaning, of competition, and perhaps an even sinister nature.

This kind of bet was rare, and usually only witnessed between men who were sworn adversaries. There are certain types
of men who require a personal nemesis to give them the energy needed to live life most fully. Men such as these are reso-
lutely bored with the usual challenges in life; they have met
these impediments and have vanquished them. In other words,
they have made their fortunes, raised their children, divested
themselves of sour marriages, traveled the world, and proved
their manhood in all the other customary ways.

To truly enjoy their jaded lives, men such as these need a
personal demon, someone to hate, someone they can best at all
costs, someone whose misfortune will make them feel good.

The Colonial Club stabled men such as these—J. Gordon
Kingsley and Henry Pearce Huntington being the most notori-
ous.

Gordon had taken an instant disliking to Huntington the
moment he'd met him. The Huntington family had only come
into their wealth during the Thirties. Before that, they'd been a
loose circle of laborers and railroad louts. The worst part of this
history was that Huntington continually blared out his nouveau
riche status, as though he were proud of the fact that his grandfather swung from the back of a caboose. He may as well have
declared that his ancestors swung from trees. Gordon was certain that if he searched through the Huntington genealogical

record, he would find more than one Irishman in the wood-pile, and that would more than account for the lack of Henry Pearce's manners and general sense of decorum.

At fifty-five, Henry Pearce Huntington was in remarkably good shape, boasting at the amount of exercise in which he indulged. Despite his suspected mongrel status, Huntington sported the finely-chiseled features of true nobility. This too irritated Gordon Kingsley, who had allowed himself to grow soft and weak as time and gravity stepped up their assaults. Indeed, everything about Huntington grossly annoyed Gordon Kingsley. Gordon found himself actually studying the man, watching his every move and hanging on his every word, searching for ever more reasons to loathe this poseur to true American aristocracy.

And so, Gordon Kingsley never let an opportunity pass wherein he might embarrass, chide, or challenge Henry Huntington. Not that the former had any trouble carrying on his end of the unspoken agreement; it seemed that Huntington found Kingsley's neo-Tory arrogance and his corpulent presence an equally hated target. If these men had lived in the age of dueling, they would have both carried more slugs than an Uzi's magazine. Neither man could hurl enough insults at the other. They were the Ford and Chevy of their social set; the oil and water; the yin and the yang.

Tensions between them became the norm at the Colonial Club, and their tête-à-têtes became legendary sources of interest and amusement. A wager between the two men invariably meant bravado, guile, and a certain amount of spectacle.

The latest engagement, however, had no equal.

Huntington had been sitting in the lounge sipping, contemplating the onion in the depths of his martini, when Gordon had entered the room. Feeling flushed from the victory of their last showdown—a marathon poker game in which one or the other would clean out his opponent's $100,000 table stakes, Gordon had let loose on Huntington.

"So, Henry Pearce, how's it feel to be a hundred thousand lighter these days?"

Huntington forced a smile to his lips, enacted a shrug dripping with ennui. "A straight flush beats a full house every time, Gordon. I can live with that."

"What's that supposed to mean?"

"Only that any baboon can draw cards to his hairy belly," said Huntington, warming to the call to combat.

"I'm not sure I follow you, old man," said Gordon.

Huntington smiled. "Really? Well, follow this: don't start bragging about luck. Your winning hand had nothing to do with your skills or abilities—unless you've got a talent for leger de main?"

"Are you accusing me of cheating?" Gordon Kingsley's voice ascended the octave range.

One could almost hear the collective attention of everyone in the lounge shift to the molten core of their conversation.

"How declasse," said Huntington. "Of course not, enemy mine. What I mean is this: a reliance on luck cheapens the contest, don't you think?"

"Cheapens!?"

"Just so. However, I've been considering a wager that depends upon nothing but the sheer, tensile strength of our wills, Kingsley."

"How's that?"

"Have you ever read Poe's 'Premature Burial'?"

"It's been a long time—at Andover, but yes, of course. Why?"

"Ever think about what it must have been like for any of those poor bastards who woke up in their coffins, sunk six feet in black dirt?"

"What's the game, Huntington?"

"Ever think about what it would be like if you woke up in your coffin?"

Gordon paused, hesitant to say something, anything he might later regret. He didn't like the gist of their conversation. Something lurked beneath its polished surface. Something dark and slippery. Something dangerous. What the hell was his nemesis getting at?

"Earth to Kingsley . . . are you there, Gordy?"

"Yes," he said softly. "Yes, I've thought about it. Haven't we all?"

"I would think so," said Huntington. He sipped his martini with a measured precision, then stared at his adversary.

This made Gordon uncomfortable but he forced himself to look directly into Huntington's eyes. Something was going on behind them, dark and slick as Timkin bearings, and he had to fathom it out. He could let his sworn enemy think he might be getting the best of him.

"Is that it, then?" asked Gordon. "I mean, come on now, Henry—what's the point of all this? All this talk of the dead and their coffins . . . ?"

Huntington smiled. "Hold on! No one said anything about the dead . . ."

"No, I suppose you didn't. But what of it? What's the game, Huntington?"

Henry Pearce Huntington, that living monument to the nouveau riche, grinned like a Cheshire. "Simply this: do you think you could (1) stand to be buried in a coffin wide awake, and (2) stay down there longer than me?"

The silence that punctuated his question hung heavy in their midst. The eavesdroppers seemed to hold their breath as one. Could he be serious? Had he gone too far this time? What kind of a mind could even conceive of such a proposition?

Gordon scratched his nose, cleared his throat. A quick glance about the room confirmed the stolid gazes of his fellow Colonials—each one trying to seem less interested than the next, but attentive as hungry dogs nonetheless.

"What kind of a question is that?" he said, his words seeming to actually boom throughout the room.

"Just what it sounds like," said Huntington. "I've offered you the terms of a wager, Gordy. Are you man enough?"

"You're insane," said Gordon.

"Most likely. But I've got another hundred thousand that says I can stay down longer than you."

"What?!"

A soft murmur colored the room.

"If we both stay down for 30 days, we call it a draw." Huntington smiled. "What do you say?"

Again, the weighty silence enclosed as the room itself seemed to take anxious pause. They were all listening, all waiting to see what kind of a man he was. Kingsley had agreed to the skydiving and the bungy-jumping and even the William Tell re-enactment, but this latest escapade, this one danced upon the wall of true madness. Gordon had always believed he was a touch claustrophobic, and just the thought of being in that kind of tight space made him shudder.

"Well, what's your answer, old sport? Have I finally called your game, or what?"

"Can I assume that you've already worked out all the details? And that you've put together a set of conditions?"

Huntington grinned. "After all this time, all the wagering we've done, how could you even ask such a question? But yes, I thought I might call them ground rules, eh?" He laughed at his small pun.

Gordon nodded, swallowed hard. "All right then . . . let's hear them."

"Does this mean you're on?"

Gordon hesitated only for an instant. "I'm game. One hundred thousand."

Someone coughed; the tension in the room spidered and cracked like an old windshield. Exclamations of shock and encouragement, salted with the odd deprecation, filled in the empty spaces between his thoughts. What the hell had he just agreed to? What came next?

Huntington smiled broadly, bringing together his hands in a steeple. "All right, Gordy. Here's the way I envisioned it. If something offends you terribly or strikes you as unworkable, just raise your hand and stop me. We can talk about it, okay?"

"Go on . . ."

Huntington hunched closer across the bar, warming to the subject. His eyes grew brighter, the voltage of his imagination having been stepped up a few notches. "Okay, here's the way I see it. Two coffins, buried side by side, you in one, me the other. I have a game preserve in Hansford, Connecticut. Plenty of land, we can do what we want there without any interference or prying of the locals. Anyway, we outfit them with some special equipment and supply lines."

Gordon raised a hand, feeling foolish for acting so obediently. "What kind of special equipment?"

"I think we'd want an intercom, and maybe a lamp of some sort. Then there's air, food, water, getting rid of waste. A system of buried tubes and cables should do it just fine."

Gordon shuddered again. The thought of being down there long enough to want to eat, to have to take a piss . . . who could last that long?

"And you solved these problems?"

Huntington nodded. "I'd say so. Studies confirm we could live on nutrient-enriched liquids for months if necessary. And we don't have to worry past thirty days, right? A catheter and a simple pump will take care of liquid waste, and there wouldn't be any solids—a good nutritionist could see to that."

Again the image of actually being in the coffin slammed into his thoughts like a left jab to his jaw. It was madness! No one could go through with it, he thought. And perhaps that was the rub—this was an elaborate joke on Huntington's part. An attempt to show him up, make Gordon look silly.

"What's the matter, Kingsley? Having second thoughts? I know what you're thinking, and I had a hard time getting used to the idea myself. All that dark earth on top of you, all around you, and that little tight, dark space for a home. The Brits have a name for coffins, you know—narrow houses! I'd say they're right, eh?" Huntington laughed, tossing back his head dramatically like the villain in a bad Thirties film. Gordon watched him, thinking he looked more than a little mad. "No light, no sound. Just the hammerfall of your own pulse in your ears, and of course the faint burrowing of the worms, trying to get through to you!"

Again a murmur suffused the lounge. The Club members were getting their money's worth this day.

"Yes, I've thought about it," said Gordon, running his fingers through his pale, thinning hair, "and as bad as it sounds, I know I can outlast a loudmouthed showman like you."

"Well, we're going to see about that," said Huntington. "Any last questions?"

"Only one," said Gordon. "When do we start?"

. . . and so went the preamble to what now transpired.

Gordon stared upward in the darkness, noticing for the first time how he was already losing sense of spatial orientation. Were it not for the insistence of gravity, he wouldn't know which end was up. It made him think of a study he'd read somewhere—the Smithsonian or some other pop-science magazine—about subjects who underwent sensory deprivation tests. Seems that when you put someone in a special chamber that canceled all sense of smell, taste, hearing, feeling, or seeing, you were pretty well sure of pushing them off the edge of rational thought and experience. What usually happened, the researchers discovered, was that when a person cannot receive any sensory input from outside himself, he will create his own. Subjects reported seeing strange creatures, hearing bizarre music, etc.

Would that eventually happen to him?

And what of Huntington? If he went mad, how would he know Gordon had bested him?

Stop thinking about it. Just lay here and take it like a man. Right. Easy to say. Gordon had kept reminding himself that the best way to handle the situation was to try not to think about where you really were. Yes, of course, but that would be—

"I say, old sport, are you there?"

The voice was canned, electronically flavored, but achingly familiar. It poured from a speaker near Gordon's head. What was going on now?

"Kingsley, are you there? Don't tell me you've had your overdue coronary and we can just leave you down here?"

"Fuck you, Henry."

"Ah . . . ! There you are! Good to hear your usual self."

"Would you mind telling me what the hell's going on?!" Gordon tried to sound most outraged, but honest to tell, he welcomed the human contact, even from a fool like Huntington.

Laughter filtered into the narrow house. "Did I forget to tell you we'd be connected by the intercom system too?" Huntington paused for effect. "Yes, Gordy, just a little extra bonus I thought up at the last minute. And, it's on its own channel, so anybody on the monitoring equipment can't hear us. Just you and me, buddy."

"You never cease to amaze me with your boldness, Henry."

"Thank you."

"I mean, why? What's this for? To irritate me? To amuse yourself? Isn't it a violation of your own rules?"

"Of course not! No contact with the surface, remember? We're both down here. Nothing said or agreed that we can't talk amongst ourselves . . ."

"Henry, I've known you too long. What gives?" There was a bad smell to things already. Gordon felt himself tensing up, he fought the urge to push upward on the solid lid just inches from his face. At any moment everything could just collapse in on him.

Soft laughter.

Then silence.

Henry Pearce Huntington was obviously going to play psych-warrior. Well, fuck him. Gordon could play too. Don't give him the satisfaction of a reply.

Seconds ticked past him like gnats crawling on his arm.

Finally the speaker crackled: "You know, Gordy, I'd bet it's never occurred to you that you've been had . . ."

Don't answer him. Ignore the nonsense he was suggesting.

"I mean, how do you know, really know that I'm down there with you, old sport? Sure you saw me get sealed in, just like you. But did you see my coffin get lowered into the ground and the dirt piled on . . . ?"

How could that be? Impossible. The Colonials . . . there were witnesses . . .

"And don't think I'm not beyond paying off a member or two . . . or that there aren't larcenists in our little Club that are down on their heels enough to take a bribe or a little blood money . . ."

"Don't be ridiculous!" The words escaped him like air from a ruptured bellows. He hadn't wanted to sound so out of control.

Again soft laughter. "Is it, old sport? Well, you'd better hope so . . ."

Gordon waited for more, but there was only a deadly silence. The closeness of his prison suddenly gripped him, even in the absolute darkness. He thought about the PVC airshaft ever flushing the chamber with fresh oxygen, suddenly realizing what a totally fragile connection to the surface that tube represented. How easily it could be interrupted or sealed off with something as silly as a sock or as intentional as a cupped palm.

Huntington wasn't that crazy. Murder could not be explained away . . .

"We're an influential lot, we Colonials. A police inspector would be told to listen closely to whatever we said, Gordy. We—"

"Shut up, you moron!" Gordon stiffened, pushed against the sides of the enclosure. It was like the bastard was reading his mind, anticipating his every thought . . .

"Yes, Inspector, it was an unfortunate accident. We were engaged in a . . . a contest, if you will. Sort of an initiation into a secret order of the Colonials. Oh yessir, you know about such things. Yes, that's correct, they have them at places like Yale and Harvard, sir. And yessir, I do believe our current President is a member of a such a secret club. Well, at any rate, it was a terrible accident when the air compressor failed like it did . . . yessir, it was very tragic, and yes, we at the Colonial Club would certainly appreciate the lack of publicity concerning Mr. Kingsley's unfortunate demise . . ."

"I said shut up, Henry! You're just trying to shake me up." said Gordon, summoning up what strength remained to him. "What happened? You get down here and realize you're not going to be able to take it?"

A chuckle fell from the little speakers, clattered all about Gordon's head.

"You underestimate me, old sport. That's why you lose so many of these little wagers."

"What do you mean?" Gordon fought to keep the panic from his voice. "Don't you know that if I'd really intended to outlast you, I'd have trained for the event long before wising you to the game! Why, I'd have been sleeping in a casket, with the lid up, then down, then spending a few hours every evening in my little narrow house—building up my endurance, acclimating myself to the environment."

Gordon was stunned by the concept. Of course! That's exactly what Huntington would do!

Without thinking, Gordon had put his hand to his mouth. It was an odd uncharacteristic gesture, made more awkward by the cramped area in which he could move his arm. He reached down to the toggle switch on his left and clicked on a soft halogen lamp.

Almost instantly, he wished he hadn't.

The light only served to emphasize the horrible closeness of where he was. The satin lining of the casket, with its sickly pearlescent shine made his stomach lurch.

Is this what it's going to be like?

Forever . . . ?

He could see his stockinged feet seemingly so far away. What had it been like to actually bend and touch them?

So close.

Nowhere to move.

Nowhere to go.

Just stay right where you were. Just like this. Forever.

Thumbing the toggle switch, the darkness engulfed him and he welcomed it. The lamp, he realized now, had been another velvet trap set by Huntington. There was no comfort in its hard illumination, only a special kind of horror.

"Earth to Kingsley . . . come in . . ." the speaker crackled, followed by the softest hint of Huntington's sardonic laughter. "I know you're down there . . ."

The bastard! Gordon had no idea what to do, much less say. If what Huntington said was true, then no one knew they could converse like this. If his opponent was trying to psych him out and Gordon panicked, pushing the alarm button on the right side of the casket, then he would not only be scammed, but he would lose the wager.

But how could he even think about something so mundane? The primitive forebrain of his consciousness was screaming at him to preserve the life essence, to get out of this hellish prison at any cost. Fuck the wager! And fuck Huntington!

Surely he could prove that there had been tampering, collusion, or whatever you'd want to call it.

"Earth to Kingsley . . ." His nemesis paused as if savoring the phrase. "You know that's quite a pun isn't it, under the, shall we say, 'gritty' circumstances . . ."

"Dammit, Huntington," he said softly, trying to retain control. "This is a shabby stunt. Trying to trick me into quitting the game. You must be desperate."

"You mean you still really believe I'm down there with you? Do you actually think I'd be stupid enough to let myself be interred in a bloody fucking coffin!"

More laughter. This time a brutal cascade full of mocking disdain.

"Especially when you consider where you are . . ."

"Why, Huntington? Why all this? Because you're such a sore loser, you had to cheat your money back? By conning me into quitting? Because if you think—"

The remainder of his sentence stuck in his throat. Silence held their conversation in a timeless void. Licking his lips, he forced himself to speak.

" . . . Huntington, what did you just say . . . ? If I consider what where . . . ?"

"You really are a piece of work, Gordon." Then more of that idiotic chuckling.

"Get to the point, man! What're you talking about?"

"Just two interesting points of fact. One—that you didn't inquire as to why I selected the particular location for this wager, and two—that you're interred in land once owned by your family. Bought and sold several times before I purchased it, of course."

"I'm afraid I don't follow you . . ." Gordon's mind galloped ahead of his words, of Huntington's reply. There was something ominous, something sinister in the man's tone. Even in the tight space, Gordon felt the leathery pouch of his scrotum tighten, contract.

"Your family is from Connecticut, Kingsley. Originally from the town of Hansford, which is the name of my game preserve. Strange that you didn't comment or make any connection . . . I half-expected you might."

What in God's name was Huntington getting at? "Hansford," said Gordon. "Should that name mean something to me?"

"Come on, Gordy, didn't your father ever tell you about the Hansford Sanitarium?"

"Other than the fact that Grandfather had built it, or that we owned it . . . no, why?"

Huntington clucked his tongue, sighed. "Did you ever remember hearing or reading about the Great Influenza Epidemic of 1918?"

"Huntington, cut to the chase, would you!? You can damn well bet I don't know what you're talking about!"

"It was a terrible thing. More than 30% of the population of the cities on the East Coast died in a 12 month period. A half million dead. People were dying so fast, nobody knew what to do with them.

"Nobody except your Granddad, that is . . ."

There was an absence, a distinct void, as Huntington's voice trailed off. Gordon felt himself almost lurch forward in the oppressive darkness. He knew he didn't want to hear what Grandfather might have done. And yet, he must. When he spoke, he sounded hoarse, weak, even puny.

"What did he do . . . ?"

Huntington cleared his throat. "Well it seems your grandfather had a small army of Irish laborers working in his quarry near Wallingford. When the influenza ripped through their ranks like cavalry, the poor micks swelled the Hansford Sanitarium to bursting. When they started dying like blowflies, your grandfather didn't want to be bothered with the details and the expense of getting them all back to their Manhattan tenement families . . ."

"What're you talking about? What did he do?" Gordon shifted uneasily on the soft padding of the casket.

"A most ingenious solution, really. He had all those dumb Irishmen's bodies thrown into lorries and hauled off to a big quicklime pit he'd dug just beyond the trees on the Sanitarium grounds."

"Huntington, you're a lying bastard!"

There came a soft chuckle. "No, old sport, I'm afraid you're the one who's lying—right in the middle of that nasty old quicklime pit . . ."

Like a blade, something twisted in the core of his being. He could not keep a silly, melodramatic gasp from escaping him.

"Oh, I know it's been a while now, Gordy, but I'd say you're not very far from a big pile of those poor micks' bones."

The confines of the casket were suddenly smaller, the air staler. His entire world reduced to a six-foot wooden hull embarked upon a journey into madness. His skin felt dry, itchy. Places he couldn't reach had started tingling with histaminic urgency. Although clutched in darkness, Gordon's eyes remained tightly shut. He didn't want to think about what lay beyond the thin wood of his cell.

Just get out. Just open your mouth and start screaming and push the button and get yourself out of this fucking pit.

. . . No, wait, stay calm.

"As a matter of fact, being a betting man, I'd wager there's more than one angry Irish ghost twisted up in the dirt and the bones that're wrapped around you like a fist."

Stay calm. Talk it out. Get a grip.

"Is this what it's all about, Henry? All this business about the Irishmen—Let's see if I can figure this out. Let me tell you what happened: my grandfather threw yours in the quicklime, right?

I always thought that crap about railroads was just crap. You grandfather was nothing but a common laborer, and his son made his money bootlegging with Joe Kennedy's bunch!"

"Ah, Gordy, you make me proud, me boy! You're smarter than I ever gave you credit for. But did you ever imagine that all the years and all the wagering has been nothing but a setup?"

"What's that? What're you talking about?"

"Revenge, old sport. Someone said it's served best when served cold, and I have to agree with that."

"You're a madman! A fucking loony!"

Huntington chuckled. It was a lilting, almost musical sound. "But not as crazy as you're going to be before you ever get out of there. By the time they get to your fat ass, you won't even know it."

"I'm sounding the alarm," said Gordon, summoning up the most authoritative voice he could find. Fumbling for the switch at his right hip, he massaged the button, but didn't push it.

"Kiss your money good-bye, Gordy . . ."

Caressing the button, his fingers tapped it lightly, but not enough to actually depress it.

This was exactly what Huntington had wanted all along, had been manipulating everything to get things to this point. The slick son-of-a-bitch thought he was going to con him out of the money, but Gordon Kingsley would show—

The sound was so subtle, so soft, he almost missed it . . .

"So, where's the alarm, Kingsley? I'm sitting here waiting for you."

"Shut-up, you blathering idiot! Shut-up-shut-up-shut-up!"

Huntington chuckled softly, but Gordon was listening to another sound—the barely audible sound of something scrabbling through the dirt, pawing, scraping, clawing . . .

He was suddenly aware of grinding his teeth together. The muscles in his jaws felt like piano wire, stretched to its limits. He tried to open his mouth, but couldn't. Something was wrong here. Something not right, and—

A new sound.

Not a scrape as much as a tick! along the side of the casket.

Along the outside.

Holding his breath, Gordon listened. The sound repeated itself. A rhythmic, series of tappings, as though something were signaling him in Morse code.

He had no idea how long he listened to the sound.

In the darkness, it was everything. There was nothing but the tapping on the wood. Time lost its sense, its measure. Gordon lay in the thrall of the sound and nothing else. Inanely, the notion that knocking on wood brought good luck passed through him, the shock of conscious thought released him from the hypnogogia.

He pressed his hand against the left wall of the casket, felt the vibration of the impact. Something was out there.

But that was ridiculous.

Impossible.

Out there.

As he struggled to rein in his panic, he realized the tapping has ceased.

But only for an instant.

To be replaced by a scraping sound. A deliberate gouging of the wood as if by some sharp tool, like an engraver's awl, or maybe even a . . .

. . . fingernail, or a . . . finger-bone.

He must have cried out, but had no memory of doing so. His mind full of white noise static, the radio burst of pure terror. A muffled voice spoke to him that could have been Huntington, but he was beyond the comprehension that accompanies hearing. The measured pace of the gouging and scraping had increased, faster and faster until it sounded like the machine-like digging of a dog for his bone. Kingsley, in fact, had begun his own gouging and scraping, having torn away the satin ceiling of his narrow house, and his own fingernails as he clawed at the wood just inches from his face. Maple has a sturdy grain and he'd made little progress, but he was beyond notice.

The thing that so furiously worked the wood at his left shoulder had fared far better.

When Gordon toggled his lamp and sounded the alarm, the last thing he saw was the splintered wood collapsing in . . . towards him.

"Oh yes, Inspector, most tragic," said Henry Pearce Huntington. "How could any of us have known old Kingsley's ticker was bad."

He stood in the four-car garage of his Greenwich, Connecticut estate. In addition to the police lieutenant, there were two uniforms and the county Medical Examiner, who was inspecting a body in a casket. The casket rested on a large table, trailing several tendrils of electric wire and plastic tubing.

The Inspector shook his head gravely. "Of course not, Mr. Huntington. I mean, who could know?"

Huntington nodded gravely. "And of course, I'm sure you're in agreement that there should be no publicity. Some of our most respected institutions have secret societies and initiation rites . . ."

The Inspector grinned. "Hey, what're you kiddin'? I heard the President was in one of these secret clubs when he was at Yale!"

"That is correct, sir," said Huntington, as he followed the Lieutenant to the side of the casket.

The Medical Examiner looked up, away from the slack-jawed, sunken-eyed corpse of Gordon Kingsley. His hair a dead-white, Einsteinian nimbus.

"Something scared the shit outta this guy," said the M. E.

One of the uniforms chuckled. "Guy must've been a flake," he said. "I mean, if he'd been buried in the ground, hey that would be one thing . . . but this guy, I mean, he was just layin' here in his buddy's garage."

*If you've been paying attention, you must have noticed by now that the anthology market has been, for me, over the years, a great repository of my short stories. Hey, I can't help it, people get an idea for an anthology, and* bada-bing! *they call me . . . and like any good pizzeria, I deliver.*

*So here's another one. Jeff Gelb[1], who created a whole line of anthologies under the* Hot Blood *title, also came up with a clever idea to ask a bunch of horror writers what their own, personal phobia might be, and then write a story about it. The anthology was appropriately titled* Fear It-self. *Now, what's interesting is the reaction to this premise from some of the writers Gelb invited. A lot of them are my friends, and many admitted they had to think hard and long to figure out exactly what it was that actually scared them, or what in this life they truly feared.*

---

*[1] Jeff Gelb is one of the good guys for other reasons than just being an adept editor. I once did a column about one of the signal events in my past that sent me shambling down the twisted path of mutant-dom, or as Paul Wilson calls it: "Otherness." I told a story of how I found this beat-up, tire-treaded, comic on the side of the road when I was all of six or seven, and how it was just about the scariest, weirdest, freakiest thing I had ever seen in my sheltered, little Catholic-boy life. I can remember keeping it hidden under my mattress for months, taking it out at night to just stare with awe and wonder and fear at the cover. The wrap-up to the piece contained a lament that I could never remember the name of the comic that had Changed My Life Forever, but I described the cover which haunted me for a long, long time: a guy sitting in a barber's chair, looking in the mirror, while the barber is hunched over him with a hideous straight-razor. You can only see the barber from the back . . . but he is looking in the mirror, and his face is . . . well, it's not a face . . . it's . . . a . . . skull! —continued on next page*

*Me, I didn't have any problem.*

*If I dismissed the abject terror I used to experience when I saw trailers for early-Fifties, giant, radiation-mutated, stop-action monster movies, then I had a fear that I'm sure I share with hundreds of millions of other sensitive human beings. I'm not going to tell you what it is because I think it might undercut the moorings of the story which follows, but I am confident you will be hip to the personal fear which drove me to write this next one.[2]*

---

*[1] footnote—continued*

*Yeah, scared the bejesus out of me, and stayed with me all my life. And I asked my readers if anybody out there could remember this comic so I could at least know its name. Eventually, Harlan Ellison helped me find the title by using this compendia called* The Photo-Journal Guide to Comic Books *compiled by Ernst and Mary Gerber—an incredible book full of photos of just about every comic book ever published. The comic was Volume 15 of* The Unseen . . . *not exactly an EC classic, but for me, it was my personal Necronomicon. A little while after this discovery, I receive in the mail, in almost perfect condition, a copy of* The Unseen #15. *It was a gift from Jeff Gelb, and I was blown away by his thoughtfulness and generosity. I said it then and I say it again now: thank you, Jeff, for giving me back a piece of my childhood I'd always imagined was forever lost.*

*[2]But I can tell you this: when I started writing the story, I needed a little girl's name and decided to use my daughter's—Olivia. But when I was about half-finished, I realized I wasn't going to be able to use her name.*

*Your children are not your children.*
*For their souls dwell in the house of tomorrow,*
*which you cannot visit,*
*not even in your dreams.*
                    —Kahlil Gibran

I'm not sure how much longer I can hold the son-of-a-bitch off.

For the past few days, I've seen more signs of his arrival. Each time I enter Becky's room, I think I smell the faintest of scents—a grim, olfactory wake of his passage.

He's so bold, coming here flirting with my daughter, thinking I have no sense of it. And yet, it is the driving force in my life. There is nothing that will give me more strength than to have the chance to beat him. He knows now that I keep an old Little League aluminum baseball bat in the pantry, but he also knows I am not afraid to use it.

It began the day Rhonda and I brought her home from the hospital. There is nothing more fragile than a newborn child—something I had never realized till that moment. I admit, being a cost accountant for Proctor & Gamble all my adult life, had perhaps kept me somewhat removed from the mainstream of life. When I brought a new life into the world, it was like getting slapped in the face.

The very first night, Rhonda kept her in a bassinet in our bedroom. I questioned the need for it until darkness fell over everything and the house had shut down to the point of the occasional creak of an old foundation. I could hear my wife's breathing at my ear, a signature of her exhaustion and a final release of tension, anxiety, and fear.

Little did I realize that mine had just begun.

I never slept that first night. An endless stretch of black time wherein I lay listening to what seemed like breathing of the most labored sort. I had no idea a tiny, living human could make such scary noises and survive till morning. Wheezing, coughing, rattling, mucous throttled sucking were only a few of the horrible sounds through which I suffered that night. It was so intensely awful, I became quite certain we would lose Becky before dawn.

But we didn't.

The bassinet remained in our bedroom another three or four weeks before I allowed my wife to have the baby sleeping in a crib so far away from us—her own bedroom down the hall. I had grown accustomed to the travail of her breathing, and it measured out the nights as a metronome of life itself.

It was just about that time when I was watching the Game of the Week (the Orioles against the Blue Jays, I think), and I saw the commercial. Actually, it was probably one of those Public Service Announcements, and what it was doing shoe-horned among the endless array of beer and razor commercials I could not imagine.

(Of course, I now know the message was placed there by Divine Intercedence. It was important that I receive the message when I did.)

The message? Oh yes, it was important all right. Have you ever heard of SIDS?

Neither had I! Imagine my shock as I sat there in my La-Z-Boy to see that there is this hideous phenomenon know as Crib Death or Sudden Infant Death Syndrome. Newborns, up to the age of six months, are suddenly found dead in their cribs, and no one has the foggiest notion as to how or why.

How come I've never heard of this? I ask myself. How come I've never seen anything about this terrible syndrome until now, until the very moment I have my own little baby who may be victim to this horrible thing?

This was positively incredible to me. But stunned though I may have been, I remained lucid enough to realize I had been given a Sign, a celestial memorandum so to speak, to be ever vigilant.

As the months ticked past, I took it upon myself to nightly approach the crib and listen for Becky's sweet breath. When my wife discovered my habit, she chided me for being so overprotective, and for a moment, I became suspicious of her. Surely, she could not be in league with any forces that would harm my daughter. In short order, I banished such thoughts from my head.

Well, at least I tried to . . .

Time continued its work, and Becky not only escaped the critical period of SIDS frequency, but she weathered bouts of commons colds, influenzas, chicken pox, measles, and mumps. It seemed like I blinked my eyes and she was four years old. She had been such a healthy baby and toddler, that I think I became lulled into a false sense of security during those years. We rarely allowed her to leave the house, other than to roam about our fenced-in yard. Whenever other children came over to play with her, I always watched them with a careful eye. I saw this movie once about a six-year-old serial killer . . .

When it came to protecting your daughter, you couldn't be too careful.

It wasn't until Becky started pre-school that I began to realize how foolish, how lax I had actually been. There were so many ways she could be in danger, at first I had a hard time tracking everything—until I took a page from my accountant's training and logged everything in a wonderful ledger with cross-referencing column and rows. Once I inflicted some order on the situation, I began to feel better about everything.

I didn't allow her to ride the school bus until I'd completed a dossier on the driver and had the vehicle inspected. The dossier thing worked so well that I used the same P.I. to work up files on everyone at the pre-school, my neighbors, and even Louise Smeak, the Sunday School teacher at St. Albans Episcopal. I wanted to have total control over everyone who would have any contact with my daughter.

You could never be too careful . . .

I heard his radio talk show where this guy who called in had postulated that many fatal diseases were actually transmitted by those plastic "sporks" they give out at fast-food eateries. I had never thought much about this, but it certainly made sense if you stopped to consider everything.

And then somebody told me that peanut butter is a major killer of small children. People feed it to them on the end of a spoon and it gets lodged at the intersection of the esophagus and the bronchial tubes or something like that. It's so dangerous that even the Heimlich maneuver doesn't work and of course there is always the truth that a spoon is pretty damned close to a spork. But can you imagine, that Death hides even in a peanut butter jar?

Well, you can bet that my Becky didn't eat any more of *that* stuff.

The years slipped away from me; I had risen through the ranks at P&G until I was the Chief of the entire financial division. Sure, I had plenty of time on my hands, but still not enough to administer to Becky's needs as well as I would like. Retirement was still many years off and my wife did not seem to share my over-riding concern for my daughter's welfare.

In fact, I was beginning to realize that perhaps Rhonda was not the ally I'd always supposed.

Becky turned ten, and that meant a whole new ledger, a whole new set of variables that I would have to start tracking. She was a very pretty girl and despite my efforts to discourage contact with other people, lots of the kids in her class wanted to be her friends. More dossiers. More money. But what did I care? I was being a good parent.

It was also around this time that Rhonda actually turned against me. It started slowly and with much subtlety, but I recognized it early on because I'd sensed it coming. She told her sister I had too much pressure at my job, that I was not adjusting well to Becky's pre-teen years, and worst of all, that I needed a hobby. Can you imagine such foolishness? I could have gotten very angry, but I knew how outward displays of domestic unrest can be harmful to children. An article in the International Enquirer said depression and teen-suicides tended to be caused by bad parenting, so by remaining tranquil, I was being a wise and caring father.

I knew that I would eventually discover a solution to the problem Rhonda was becoming. If I remained patient and vigilant, I would be given a sign, an answer. And it came to me the day I realized that Mr. Death had changed his tactics. I mean, it was no secret he'd been after Becky since we'd brought her home from Cook Memorial Hospital. It was only through my stalwart efforts she'd remained as safe as she had.

But Mr. Death is slick and he took to impersonating regular people that might come in contact with Becky. That's why I had to cancel all her dental visits, and of course there would be no more examinations by Doc Wilson. The biggest problem were those unexpected situations that could not be planned. For example, when Becky answered the door one after-school day to admit the meter reader for the local gas and electric company, I almost lost my usual composure.

(Where was her mother? you might ask—as I certainly did. How could she allow the child to do something so dangerous as answer the door? The answer lay ahead, as you shall see.)

You can already imagine how horrible it could have been if the gas-man had actually been The Gas-Man—if you get my meaning . . .

Yes, I realized I must learn from this experience. And learn I did indeed. After pulling Becky from her school, I arranged to have her education continued at home under the care of a carefully checked-out tutor. The young boys who had already begun sniffing around the hems of my daughter's skirts received stern warnings from me to simply Stay Away. I reinforced my messages with letters to all the boys' parents.

That seemed to help matters very much until a man in a charcoal suit with a red tie knocked on the door. He said he was from the State Department of Health and Mental Hygiene, and that he wanted to ask me a few questions. He also said he had a warrant to inspect my premises. He showed me some ID that said his name was Silverstein and some papers with official seals and notary stamps on them. He didn't know I recognized his true identity, and therefore misinterpreted my smile as I led him into the kitchen. I directed him to a chair at the dinette where I offered him a cup of coffee. He said yes and I asked him what kind of questions he had for me. I was going to grab my aluminum baseball bat right away, but I was curious as to what Mr. Death would want to ask me. Didn't he already Know Everything? And so I poured two cups of Maxwell House and sat down to listen.

He said a few things right up front about Becky that made me very angry. I almost reached for the baseball bat twice, and both times, I thought maybe I should listen a little longer, even though it was making me very angry.

"After reading copies of the letters you sent the Wizniewski and Harrison boys, I decided to contact you directly," said Mr. Death. "Initially, I spoke to your wife, and she told me about your . . . tendency to . . . ah, go on at length about your daughter."

I asked him what exactly Rhonda had said.

"Exactly? Well, sir, she said that she is very much afraid of you. Did you know that?"

I told him no. Anything else, I asked.

"She said that she had decided a long time ago she would tolerate your behavior—"

Tolerate?

"Yes, as long as it remained within the family, she figured it was safer, better for everyone involved."

Safer . . . yes, I see, I told him. But then, why are you here, Mr. Silverstein? (I needed to allay any suspicions he might have that I knew his true identity.)

"Well, it's hard to explain, but we've received a petition to have your case examined by a state psychiatrist," he said. "We have statements by neighbors and relatives and parents at Holbrook Elementary, plus an interesting letter from a private investigator, Lucius Mallory. It was forwarded to us from Lieutenant Karsay at the 3rd Precinct."

I moved away from the table, close to the pantry door where my aluminum buddy awaited my touch. "And what do these statements and letters have to do with me?"

Mr. Death almost chuckled. Can you imagine his audacity? "I think you know what this is all about. Your daughter, Rebecca, is dead, sir. She died when she was three months old from SIDS. More than nine years ago."

I think that's when I lost it—when he mouthed such a cruel lie, a heinous blasphemy in my house. I screamed something about what a liar he was and how I knew his true identity and how I would stop him from taking my daughter away from me.

He went down like a clumsy palooka from the first impact to the base of his skull. As his life fluids seeped across the tiles of the kitchen floor, I realized I'd made a mistake. This man, Silverstein, was a mere mortal. Another of Death's clever tricks, no doubt. I checked my watch, and knew I had little time. Rhonda would be due home from her part-time job at the neighborhood library at any moment.

There was no need to clean up the mess, however. None at all.

It has been a long weekend. The scent of death I mentioned earlier is getting heavy in here. The crowds of neighbors and police cars that have surrounded my little bungalow have been a terrible distraction, and I fear that Mr. Death will get in while I am forced to deal with the foolish meddling of those outside. The television says there is a dangerous hostage situation here. I think it is a good thing they don't know about Silverstein and Rhonda. They probably think I might do harm to Rebecca, which reveals them to be the fools they are.

Don't they know I'm her father?

And a father can't ever be too careful . . .

*I know I've already said I try to avoid writing stories which travel paths worn smooth by uncounted years of literary traffic. And one of the most rutted passages must surely be the tale of the vampire, right? But for whatever reasons, vampire novels and stories have enjoyed an enduring popularity, and anthologies about them also seem to spring forth with regularity. I've been asked to contribute to them over the years and have always begged off, but when Poppy Brite asked me if I had any fresh takes on the topic for her* Love in Vein *project, I thought I might have something that would work—something I had begun writing years previous and had never sold in the short fiction format.*

*You see, having enjoyed a traditional education in which Latin, Greek, and the literary classics were all part of a rigorous high school curriculum, I was shot through with plenty of material from mythologies both familiar and esoteric. I had remembered reading of the strange beings called* lamiae, *and was surprised to see so very little about it surviving in contemporary fiction.[1]*

*I'm glad she finally provided me with the impetus I needed to pull the whole thing together as I had originally imagined it many years earlier. What about you?*

---

[1] *Oddly enough, while I was working on the pages that would become both a part of a novel and eventually the following story, I discovered a book by Whitley Strieber entitled* The Hunger, *which I suspected might be investigating similar territory. That being the case, I decided I shouldn't read it until I finished my own work along those lines. Later I found* another *book by Tristan Travis called simply* Lamia, *and I have yet to read it. It appeared that at least two other imaginations, possibly the equal in brilliance to my own, had settled on the same mythic icon as I.*

TRIPTYCH DI AMORE

*Whatever the textbook/blueprint specifications might be for a* lamia *were clearly not well-known or established, so I figured I could pretty much fly this one by the seat of my pants. I could write my own manual for a lamia and no one could make much of an argument because I was dealing with what I like best— original material.*

*So I started writing a novelette which encompassed some of my ideas that a lamia would not feed off anything so mundane as blood, but would require a more heady mixture of inspiration, imagination, obsession, and the purest essence of creativity. I knocked it around, on and off, and eventually used some of the scenes in a novel called* Lyrica, *but I never put all the pieces together for the intended novelette until Poppy asked me for a story.*

Vienna, 1791

One of his earliest memories was of his father, Papa Leopold, touching the keys of a harpsichord or a piano and demanding the instrument's pitch to within an eighth of a tone. Before he had learned to read German, he was reading music in his mind. Little Wolfgang's ears had been magically sensitive, his fingers lithe and almost supernaturally quick. Crystalline memories of being in the circle of astounded adults as he played, while his father beamed with pride.

But memories seemed to be all he had lately. If only he were not such a goddamnably bad businessman! If only his Konstanze were not so sickly all the time! If only there were ways to protect and warrant the music he'd created!

If only the world were fair . . . .

Mozart laughed at this crazy little wish as he sat on the outdoor table of his favorite *konditore*, a pastry shop on the Domgasse near his previous home. He had lived in the Figarohaus for three years, until it became too expensive for him and his fragile wife. How he had loved that woman, and now . . . how he sometimes despised her!

She was as devoted to him as a house pet, as helpless as a child, and less passionate than either. What with his home life being so miserable, his financial situation taking him to the edge of poverty itself, and a new emperor ascending to the throne, it was incredible, even to Mozart, that he could still continue to produce musical masterpieces with the precision and punctuality of a Swiss clock.

The war with the Turks had finally ended and the Viennese court was starting to pay more attention to frivolity and the arts again. The ten-year reign of Joseph II had just ended and Leopold II was now in the palace, but Wolfgang hated the man. He seemed to have no soul for music, and even less understanding of what it meant to *create* anything. Leopold II, despite being told by many esteemed men (even Haydn himself) that Mozart was a "national treasure," refused to issue him a royal stipend.

Even though *Don Giovanni* proved to be the most popular opera in the history of the city, Mozart remained estranged from any of its profits—such had been the nature of his original agreement with the theater owners.

Almost destitute, Wolfgang had appealed to the Vienna magistrates, asking that he might be appointed as "humble assistant" to Kapellmeister Hoffman at Saint Stephen's Church. It was a grand ploy, except that the magistrates were so overwhelmed with such a modest petition, that Mozart was appointed to the post as an honorary employee without a salary.

*Fuck them all!* he thought viciously as he finished his pastry and coffee. It did not seem to matter anymore what happened to him. He had just nursed Konstanze back to a fair simulation of good health, and perhaps she would have to take in sewing or laundry to pick up a few extra ducats.

And I will continue to give music lessons to the few in this city who can afford me, he thought as he downed the last of his linzertorte. Picking up his coffee cup, he drank down the final swallow, the rim almost touching his forehead, obscuring his vision.

He didn't see her until he put the cup down.

Then, he could not stop looking.

Shining blond hair enveloped her head like spun gold, and her long, aquiline face seemed like a piece of Greek sculpture, so perfect were its lines. She had eyes of the most penetrating green he had ever seen, and their gaze had him fixed like a butterfly under a pin. If she'd told him her name was Helen of Troy, he would have only smiled.

Suddenly she was sitting at his small table, having somehow slipped down in front of him, during the instant that he sipped the last of his coffee.

*Astonishing!*

He cleared his throat and tried to speak. "Yes?" The word fell off his lips hoarsely.

The woman smirked, her mouth glistening with the sensuous moisture of youth. "You are Wolfgang Amadeus Mozart?"

He nodded. "There is none other."

"Oh, I know . . . your music aspires to Olympus. Surely the gods themselves have never heard such strains." Her voice was even and refined, suggesting a maturity that was unexpected in one so young.

Mozart laughed nervously. "Well, I've never heard anyone express it quite like that, but, yes, I agree with you: my music *is* special."

The woman smiled openly this time, prompting him to continue.

"My father keeps telling me to write more simple stuff, so that more of the people can understand what I am doing. 'What is slight can still be great,' my father said, but that is not my style. I would first jump into the Danube before writing less than *my* music!"

"Good for you, my Amadeus. It is said that you are the world's foremost musical genius, and upon even first meeting you, I am already inclined to agree."

She stroked his ego so skillfully he did not even think to ask her name or her purpose in sitting at his table. By the cut of her clothes, it was apparent she was an extremely wealthy woman—the wife of a great land-owner, or perhaps a duchess, maybe even an emissary from the Court of Leopold II. It would be wise to not be too arrogant with this woman until he knew more about her.

"Uh, thank you, madame . . ." he said more cautiously, as he watched her breasts heave and swell above her bodice. It seemed as though they had a life of their own, that they were straining to break free of the constraining cloth. Finally, coming out of his trance, he addressed her once again. "As much as I enjoy the praise of strangers, I am compelled to ask if there is anything I might do for you . . ."

She reached out to touch his hands.

"These are the fingers which dance upon the piano keys with such magic, are they not?"

"So I've been told, yes."

She stroked his fingers lightly, stirring passion in him that he had not felt since his first times with Konstanze. "I would have you give me lessons, Mozart . . ."

He was stunned! Surely she did not mean what she said. He had never had a female student, and indeed, it was rare to hear of any women studying under one of the masters in the city.

"What?" he asked politely, but not hiding his surprise. "You wish to study the piano?"

"In a sense. More precisely, I wish to study you, Amadeus."

"Me? You mean my music?"

She tilted her head slightly as though considering her answer carefully.

"Well, your music will make a good beginning . . ."

And it did.

The woman introduced herself as the Countess Bellagio from the city of Como in northern Italy. She had a large house on Schullerstrasse complete with servants and maids on every floor. Although she was not Austrian by birth, she understood the Austrian concept of *gemdltliebkeit* very well: good living with charm and graciousness. On every visit to her home, Mozart was treated to the finest breads, cheeses, wines, and pastries.

And she took her music lessons very seriously for several weeks, until the roles of teacher and pupil became reversed.

Wolfgang had been seated with her at the piano when it happened. She had been practicing a little rondo he had written especially for her lessons, when he became aware of what could only be described as an overwhelming scent. It seemed to envelope him like the snakes of Laocoon tugging at his consciousness, squeezing off his powers of will and concentration.

It was a raw, pungent, animal smell. It was the aroma of rutting, the heat-musk of desire. It was the scent of mating and release. The music in his mind, in his ears, faded away like smoke. The only thing he could concentrate upon was the ripe body of the woman seated by him.

She stopped playing, turned to face him, and he could see an inferno boiling like a volcano beneath the Sargasso green sea of her eyes.

"Is there something wrong, maestro?" she asked with a coy upward turn of her lips.

"I, I don't know . . ." was all that he could say.

She laughed with a suggestion of cruelty and stood up from the bench they shared. The rustle of her skirts seemed loud and exaggerated, almost like a melody in itself. He sat transfixed, as though under the influence of a powerful drug, and watched her unfasten her gown. With a smooth, graceful motion, she peeled off the pieces of clothing, which seemed to fall away from her like the layered dried husk of a butterfly's cocoon.

Golden light of early afternoon entered the conservatory window, bathing her flesh with a warm, vibrant light. She seemed to surge with an inner energy, a sexual power that was unstoppable. Wolfgang became as rigid as a maypole, feeling as though he would burst from his britches, hurting himself from the wretched codpiece. He tore at his clothes with a feverish joy, laughing and smiling, on the edge of hysteria.

The countess joined him in his merriment as she climbed up on the bench, spreading her legs over him as she let the final piece of underwear slip away from her. He had never seen a woman so free in her nakedness, so bold and so proud. In the middle of the day, with no shame! It fired his passion to the point of confusing him as though made drunk. His fingers became clumsy imitations of themselves and he fumbled free of his clothes like an awkward child just learning the task.

Taking his head in her hands, she guided his face into the golden triangle of her pubic hair, which was fine and wispy and soft as the down on a newborn chick. Her lips seemed to part magically as he raised his tongue to her. When he touched her, a galvanized current passed through his body. She was like an electrolyte, the heedless fire of an animal in heat. Her body odor was sweet and heavy. He had never imagined a woman could be so *clean.*

Pulling her from the bench, he threw this madwoman, this sex-creature, across the top of the piano. She landed with such force that the strings and hammers gave forth a single discordant sound, but she responded with laughter that was most musical in itself.

And so she became the instrument of his pleasure, atop what had always been the instrument of his pleasure. It was a glorious, hedonistic coupling, the likes of which he had never known. Compared to this woman, his wife was a cold slab of stone.

When she was finally finished with him, there was a brief, silent rest, and suddenly they were at each other again. Wolfgang had never known himself to be so full of sexual energy but here he was, standing at attention, and ready to cavort once more . . .

. . . and it was after dark by the time he stumbled away from her house, feeling as though he had just run a race through the Alps. His head was surprisingly clear for such an experi-

303

ence, and upon introspection he found it odd that he had been able to draw upon such boundless sexual reservoirs. He never had known himself to be much of an animal when it came to lusty adventures, and yet this Countess Bellagio had totally enflamed him, torched his very soul.

If only he could write music that could have such an effect on people! Then his immortality would be guaranteed, he thought with a sad smile.

The lessons continued for the next month. And the things she taught him were wondrous and dark and full of magic. He often fancied that she might indeed be some kind of witch or sorceress, but in the final analysis, he didn't give a damn what she might be.

His life was in a curious state of flux, and he was not sure how to deal with the strange brew of emotions and ideas which filled his mind and his soul. The countess had made him feel more alive than ever with her bedroom spells, but his health in general seemed to be on the decline. He had contracted the ague, and now it threatened to overtake him completely. His breath whistled in his lungs and he coughed up great gobbets of catarrh each morning, sometimes mixed with blood.

On the economic side, his finances seemed like they might take a turn for the better. He was being paid a handsome fee from the countess for her "lessons," and of course there were the plans of Herr Schikaneder, the owner and manager of the Meisterhaus Theater.

Wolfgang did not care for Schikaneder as a person, even though he belonged to the order of the Freemasons. There was something oily about him, something which suggested a foulness, a despicable aspect. But the small, thin man had come to him with an offer that seemed attractive, an opportunity which would be hard to resist.

Herr Schikaneder had written the libretto to an opera called *The Magic Flute*, which showed surprising merit. Schickaneder wanted Wolfgang to compose the musical score for the opera, and they would share the profits. In spite of the man's horrible reputation, Wolfgang was attracted to the prospect of writing music for such a story: full of fairies and spirits and creatures of the night. It was a dark and magical tale that fitted his moods and his general outlook.

Even the countess encouraged him to embark upon *The Magic Flute*. She told him that it was a monumental project which would guarantee him a place in the pantheon of musical giants; she felt it would be a fitting use of his great mental energies.

Wolfgang was flattered by the words of Herr Schikaneder, but he was more inspired by the encouragement of Countess Bellagio. Before meeting her, he had been feeling so bereft of human feeling that he had been channeling all of his soul into his music. But now the woman was bringing him back to life! For the first time in many years, Mozart was beginning to feel happy again.

He began seeing her as often as time would permit, and gave her the nickname "Lyrica" because her presence in his life were the words to his music. Together, he felt, they captured the pure beauty of a *lieder*, a song.

He accepted Schikaneder's offer and began work on the musical score of *The Magic Flute*. The oleaginous theater owner was so overjoyed at this decision that he had a small pavilion built on the grounds, where Mozart could work without distraction or pause. At first Wolfgang thought this gesture was a magnificent demonstration of the esteem and regard of Herr Schikaneder, but he soon realized that the pavilion was more like a prison.

His meals were brought to him there and he was not allowed to leave the premises until his daily work had been inspected by the theater owner each evening. The pavilion was hastily constructed and was therefore full of drafts—on rain-filled afternoons, Wolfgang would sit in the small confines of his musical jail wracked by a terrible chill. His illness progressed unchecked, and the coughing spasms became worse. He complained to his wife and his employer that his strength seemed to be leaving him and he began to again revel in thoughts of death.

At one point he told Schikaneder that "death is the only worthwhile goal in life. It is our only real and devoted friend."

Schikaneder smiled and agreed with him, saying only that he should stay away from his friends until the opera had been completed.

Mozart managed to do this only because he had become obsessed with finishing the musical score. Lyrica would come to him in his tiny pavilion in early evening, and they would steal a few precious minutes of lovemaking from his work, and their encounters left him in a most curious state. During their bouts of love, he felt as vigorous and strong and full of life as he had ever in all his days . . . but when she had left him, he felt more drained and pale and weak than ever before.

The day finally arrived when the completion of the opera was in sight. Wolfgang had finished all but a few parts for a few instruments, and he could already hear the entire orchestra roaring in his mind. It was not good music, it was great music— even by his own high standards. He knew this in the depths of his soul, and he was pleased beyond measure.

He sat in the pavilion that evening, putting the finishing touches on the vellum sheets, when there was a soft knock on the door behind him. Turning and throwing up the latch, he watched a familiar figure enter. It was Lyrica wearing a black gown that made her seem thin and waspish.

Moving to him, she straddled his legs where he sat on the tiny stool, and lifted her skirts. He could smell the essence of her loins rise up and intoxicate him, and he was instantly ready for her. Lowering herself, she seemed to draw him up into her more deeply than ever before. and he felt as though he could not bear the sensation. But just as he was about to explode into her, she grabbed him with her secret muscles and shut him down, preserving the pleasure and the moment of final release. As she rode him wildly, he felt that she could play him like that indefinitely, and the pleasure crashed over him in ever-heightening waves, until the pleasure became a pain, a torturous thing from which he cried out for release.

Afterward, as she kissed him and prepared to leave, she paused and looked deeply into his eyes. "I have a surprise for you," she said in a soft whisper.

"Any more surprises from you, I don't think I can bear," he said only half in jest.

Reaching into her cloak, Lyrica produced a sealed envelope, which she handed to him. "Open it."

"What is it?"

"A commission."

His heart leaped wildly, and his hands began trembling. "What? From who?"

"Please, open it."

Breaking the wax seal, Wolfgang tore away the parchment paper and began to read the document. It was indeed a commission naming a handsome sum of money to write a *Requiem*, a mass for the dead.

But it was unsigned . . .

Mozart looked up from the parchment to Lyrica. "Is this a joke?"

"No, of course not."

"But there is no signature. It is invalid."

Lyrica tilted her head, and her lip curled up in a slight, impish grin. "No, it is valid. The person who commissioned this piece wishes to remain anonymous, that is all. The commission will be paid through me, as I have been named the executor of the transaction. Everything is perfectly legal, meistro."

"But . . . he wants to be anonymous? I've never heard of such nonsense! I thought the nobility wanted it to be known that they were patrons of the arts?"

Lyrica smiled. "Some of the true nobility do not need such gratification."

Wolfgang sighed and slipped the commission and the promissory note into his blouse. "Very well, I shall begin it directly. The music for *The Magic Flute* will be completed on this very day, and I am already thinking of the dominant themes I might employ in this new Requiem."

"That is wonderful news, my Wolfgang." Lyrica turned to leave the pavilion.

"One more thing . . ." said Wolfgang. "For *whom* is this *Requiem* being written? Do you not think I should know this?"

For an instant, she looked grim and serious, but she banished the expression with a sultry smile. "No. Your patron would like that to be also a secret . . . ."

Wolfgang grinned. "Oh, he does, does he? Well, you tell him that I shall most likely discover his secrets, despite his silly wishes!"

Again she appeared serious as she took her leave. "Perhaps you will, Wolfgang . . . perhaps you will."

*The Magic Flute* was an incredible success. The opera played to full houses for more than two hundred successive performances. It was a record unequaled in the history of Viennese theater. Unfortunately, because of the wording of their contract, Wolfgang received very little of the profits, and Herr Schikaneder became impossibly wealthy at his expense.

The oily bastard was having a statue of himself erected while Mozart struggled to pay the rent on his small dwelling!

But this injustice was slight compared to the other slaps of Fate he had received. Konstanze was again confined to her bed with the ague, and Wolfgang himself had been deteriorating badly, losing strength to the point that he could barely cut his meat at the table. His work on the great *Requiem* slowed because of his ebbing strength and spiritual energy. Despite his great musical achievements, he lived like a pauper, and he simply did not care any longer.

Even his noble wench, Lyrica, had been giving signs of deserting him.

Not that he could blame her. She was so young and full of flame and breath! And he already seemed like such an old man. Their lovemaking was a pale and hollow shell of what it had once been, and he now felt so weak, so sickly, that he feared it would be impossible for him to perform.

As he lay in bed with a raging fever, his thoughts ripped about in his mind like sails in a storm. He shifted his concentration between the unfinished *Requiem* and his sweet Lyrica. He could not remember at what point the realization struck him, but he suddenly knew he would never recover from the terrible fever which consumed him.

He knew at that moment he was going to die.

Goddamn it all! Fuck them all! Nothing matters now . . .

But he knew that was not true. There was much that mattered to him. He became angry and frustrated because his power and his life were slipping away.

He drifted off into a hazy dreamlike state, opening his eyes to discover that he was standing at the conductor's post in a large concert hall, which was filled to capacity. It was dark beyond the proscenium, but he could sense the presence of the audience—a large, tenebrous mass behind him. With a flourish, he guided the orchestra through the *finale* of his final composition, and listened to the building thunder of applause at his back. But there was something about the sound of their clapping that was wrong—it was too harsh, too sharp. It was a ratcheting sound like sticks of wood being struck together. Slowly, Wolfgang turned to face his audience and he saw the sea of bone-white faces, the eyeless sockets, and eternal grins. They called out to him with ghostly whispers of "Bravo!" and "Encore," and he finally understood for whom he had been composing his mighty *Requiem . . .*

*Arles, 1899*

There is a small antiquarian shop in the center of this French town of 20,000 people. Situated close to the Rhone River, and Port-St.-Louis on the Mediterranean, Arles caters to a fair share of international tourists and vacationers from the surrounding provinces. The antiquarian shop has become, therefore, something of a souvenir shop, as well as a repository of things old, and most times forgotten.

Its owner, an old man in his eighties, died two summers ago, and since there were no known heirs, the place and all its contents were put up for public auction. The shop seemed like the perfect diversion for a widow in her early forties, who had inherited her husband's vast wealth after a boating accident. The sums from the insurance policies alone would allow her to live out her days in comfort, but she wished to have an idler's profession, and the purchase of the curiosity shop was just the ticket.

It was a small shop, but its interior seemed to defy the laws of physics, seemingly holding more than its numerous shelves and nooks and alcoves than would seem possible. The shop was truly a gestalt experience: a case of the sum of the parts being far greater than the whole. It was so jammed with junk and memorabilia of earlier times, that no one could accurately detail all that was contained in it.

The prior owner had long-ago stopped keeping track of his inventory, and the acquisition of old junk had merely become a natural part of his life as natural as eating and sleeping. The junk would come in, and some of it would go out. It was the natural order of things.

The new owner, the youngish widow, was not altogether interested in what might be found in her shop. She simply needed a profession, a place to go each day where she might have the chance to meet interesting people, to talk, and to generally enjoy herself with little pressure or insistence.

And so it was that she did not know of the thick leather-bound journal that rested in a far corner of the shop, buried halfway down a stack of old photograph albums and bound ledgers.

The book had been stolen by a housekeeper, after its owner had committed suicide. In the confusion and shock which followed the man's death, no one missed the journal. The housekeeper had mistakenly thought it might be worth some money someday, but she died without making a franc. The journal was bound up with a stack of other old books, sold to a junk man, and it eventually reached the dusty confines of the shop.

If anyone might ever have it, they would be in possession of one of the great artifacts of the art world—an additional look into the disturbed mind of a man who signed his tormented paintings with only his first name: Vincent.

*December 12, 1888*—I have finally done it! I have left the drab cold landscapes of the north for the hot suns and bright days of the south of France. My friend, Paul Gauguin, has urged me to leave Paris and I have now believed him. He promises to meet me here and says we will share a studio together. That I will believe when it happens. Gauguin is such a bombastic, impulsive ass! And yet I admire him, as he admires me. We shall see if he is good to his word.

*January 4, 1889*—1 have just received another letter from Theo, wrapped about 150 francs. What a wonderful brother I have in Theo! No man could ever want a better sibling, that is for certain. His "allowance" to me keeps me alive. Is it not crazy to imagine that once I begged him to quit his lucrative position at Goupil's Gallerie to become an artist with me!

Then the family would have had two starving wretches to worry about! At least Theo makes my father proud . . . while I, at the age of thirty-five, am still a problem child, still a crazy dreamer.

Speaking of dreamers, I am still waiting for Paul, yet a letter says that he is on the way as I write these lines. Somehow, I must confess to believing him. He claims to have a great need to be in the south for the colder months. He claims it is good for the soul, and I believe him. Arles is truly a beautiful place, where even in the winter there are flower gardens of crocus and daffodil, and greenhouses where there are blooms and flowers all year through!

It is the color—the vibrant living color of this place—that will set me free, that will save me!

*January 17, 1889*—He is here at last! Paul arrived by coach with a brace of baggage the likes I have never seen. He claims that he sold a painting in Paris just before he left, and had to wait for payment—thus his delay in arriving. We will work well together, this I am sure. We will fight well together, of this I am also sure!

*January 29, 1889*—I have been in this village more than a month and I still have not had one of their women! The southern girls are easily more beautiful than any of the northern peasant stock. Their faces are so finely angled, their eyes so big! They sit on their porches and in their sunny parlors sipping absinthe, and smiling at all the men who pass by. And yet they avoid me like a disease, and I dream of finding the prostitutes of this town. Always the whores for Vincent! Why must it always be this way for me?

*February 18, 1889*—I had a terrible fight with Paul. We started drinking early in the day, and we ended up hurling insults, and finally our glasses, at each other. He is off at one of the cafes now, finding a woman, while I sit here with a pen in one hand, my prick in the other!

If I do not have a woman soon, I feel that I will explode like a cheap bomb. And yet I am painting like a madman already. To count up, I have painted ten gardens in ten days! It is nothing for me to spend fourteen hours a day at my easel. The colors are finally coming to life, and I can feel the energy of my body flood through my brush and alight the colors of my palette!

I feel that I am painting well, and the thought comes to me that perhaps fucking and painting are incompatible, that a man cannot do both well, and must make a choice.

For me, the choice is already made! The women won't have me . . . not yet anyway.

*February 22, 1889*—Paul is truly my friend. He has brought a young woman to meet me from the cafe where he drinks. She wanted to see my work, and she stayed to fuck me! What an experience! She was lean and young and full of energy. Such a rocking and a thumping—she, me, and my straw mattress! She has given me the inspiration and the element in my life which has been missing. Now I feel like I can paint forever. Just give me some tobacco, some drink, and an occasional woman, and I can be the artist of my dreams!

March 7, 1889—Spring comes early to this part of France! Already the gardens are blooming with color and my palette is aswirl with inspiration. I have been learning to express the passions of humanity by means of reds and greens! There is a relationship between my colors and life itself! I can feel it and I know it! I am painting sunflowers because there is a special essence in the sunshine that these plants have captured, and capturing the flowers on canvas, I will thus capture that special essence of the sun!

*March 9, 1889*—Paul and I share a studio where the light pours in like golden liquid. I am supremely happy here. I paint all day and spend my evenings in the cafes and brothels. The prostitutes are like sisters and friends to me. They do not reject me as an outcast because they are themselves outcasts. Yes, the whores give me my pleasure, but I long for a wife! I am filled with energy and the passion of all great art! Thank God for the wine which keeps me from becoming too crazy. When I take another drink, my concentration becomes more intense, my hand more sure, my colors more correct. Sometimes I believe that my painting can do nothing but improve because I have nothing left but my art. Sad? Yes. True? Unfortunately, yes.

*April 14, 1889*—Some days I am high as the birds which

wheel and keen in the skies above my easel, and then suddenly I feel as though I belong with the white, eyeless worms beneath the flat rocks of the garden paths. My life is a jagged run of great joy and great pain. Sometimes I grow so tired of the starving conditions, the wretched life I choose to lead while I wait for the world to recognize me.

Am I truly crazy, as some say I am? Some of the village children have taken to waiting outside my studio window, only so that they might scream "madman!" when I come to the sill for a breath of air.

But my thoughts are this: I don't care if I am crazy—as long as I become that 'artist of the future' which I spoke to Theo about.

*April 23, 1889*—Today is the most glorious day of my life! My painting, *The Red Vine*, has been sold! Instead of working today, 1 have begun drinking as soon as I received the news, and I will no doubt drink up the profits of the sale within the next sunrise. But I care not!

*May 3, 1889*—Today, Paul refused to eat at the same table as I because he claims I am a filthy pig and that he risks catching diseases by eating with me. Enraged, I threw my cup at his face and he struck me with his fist before storming off to the cafes. I fear we are incompatible, despite the wondrous atmosphere of this place, despite the stupendous number of canvases we have created here.

*May 17, 1889*—I have often felt that if I did not have a woman I might freeze and turn to stone. I may never need feel that way again—Her name is Lyrica Rousseau and she entered my studio as though coming from a dream. To say that she is the most beautiful woman I have ever seen is such a silly cliché I am embarrassed to think in such terms. And yet it is true.

She was dressed like a woman to the manor born, a woman of social standing, education, and exquisite breeding. She told me she had come from Paris in search of artists, having heard that the truly talented have left the city for simpler climes. I smiled and told her that I was perhaps the finest artist in all of France, but no one yet knew that fact. I showed her my work and I am convinced that she was impressed with its vitality and utter newness. She even told me that she had seen nothing like it in all her days.

Pressing my good fortune (after all, one does not have an angel walk through his door every day!), I asked her where she would be going, and how long she planned to stay in Arles. To my surprise, she said that she lived by no man's schedule, and that she traveled freely in search of what she wanted. She said that it was possible she might be staying in Arles for a good while. I told her that there was only one good hotel in the village, and recommended that she stay there. She smiled at this, excused herself, and returned to her waiting carriage.

I walked to the door of the studio, watching her, trying to imagine what kind of perfect body might be hidden beneath the folds of her dress. I told her to visit me at her convenience, and to my shock and delight, she said that she would be doing so!

*May 26, 1889*—Lyrica has come again! And again, she chose a time when she knew Gauguin would be out on one of his binges. She offered to pose for me, but the painting was never begun. As her clothes dropped away, I became overwhelmed with desire and a hardness in my prick I hadn't known since being fourteen years old!

To say that we fucked would be a blasphemy, a miscarriage to describe what truly took place. Locked together like a single organism, we aspired to the place of the gods. This woman, this Lyrica, is different, in an almost scary way. I had always thought that only men actually liked sex, and woman merely tolerated our affliction and our hunger for it. But here is a woman who seems to like the sport as much as I!

*June 24, 1889*—With Mademoiselle Rousseau as my inspiration, I am painting with a furious, soul-burning energy. When I paint I am not conscious of myself anymore, and the images come to me as if in a dream. When I am painting like that, I know that I am creating beautiful art. Until I met this woman, only when I was painting did I ever feel that totally unleashed, totally free feeling of wanton fulfillment. But now my fucking is like my painting and I soar to the heights of my soul with her. She is an angel, this woman, and she tells me that she knows in her heart that I am a gifted painter, a great artist, and that someday the world will recognize my potent talent, my "special vision." That is her phrase: *my special vision.* She says that I see the world differently, that I "feel" the world differently . . . and that is why she comes to see me.

*August 15, 1889*—My entries in this journal—what I have come to call my "secret" journal—have been more erratic lately. Still, I pour forth the letters to Theo as a way of resting and relaxing from the furious pace of my work, but there are things I do not tell him, that I can explain to no one, and those are the thoughts reserved for this separate ledger. Lyrica has been coming to see me less frequently, and when I ask her why, she only smiles. When I ask her where she goes when she is away from Arles, she only smiles. She is the most mysterious woman I have ever known, and she is easily the most self-assured, the most confident. I commented upon this once, and she laughed very musically, saying that she had learned how to act from the best teachers—men. For some reason, this threw me into a wildly depressive state, and I drank myself into a disgusting stupor after she had left my studio that day. I think that I had been entertaining crazy fantasies of marrying this independent woman! I think that I had become terribly possessive about her little "honey-pot," and the thought of other men dallying about with her drove me into a frenzied state of mind. How silly of me to think that I could possess a woman so magnificent. I should consider myself fortunate to merely use her on the off occasion!

*September 10, 1889*—Lyrica visited me today. She has begun the curious habit of inspecting my work, my output of canvasses, from one visit to the next. She seems overly concerned about the chronology of when they were completed, comparing the times to the times of her visits to me. She looked especially hard at a canvas of a row of green cypresses against a rose-colored sky and a crescent moon in pale lemon.

*October 2, 1889*—The energy to paint fourteen hours a day is no longer in me. I find that I grow tired so quickly and that the visions and dreamy images of my work are not as clear.

This bothers me and when I tell Paul he simply laughs. When I mention it to Lyrica, she only nods in silence, as though she understands perfectly.

*October 27, 1889*—I am alone more and more. Paul is so disgusted with me, so angry and passionate all the time, that we can no longer talk. This morning it occurred to me that he has never met my Lyrica . . . it is uncanny how she has timed her visits to avoid him . . . and he has accused me of fantasizing the whole affair with this mystery woman. He claims that no one in the village has ever seen her come here, that no one knows of her, and that she probably exists only in my "demented" mind. How bizarre all this is becoming! Could it be that I have imagined such a woman? Could I have imagined such fucking? No, it is not possible—she is as real as I am! And yet the laughing jeers of Paul has set me to thinking that perhaps I am as crazy as everyone says.

*November 23, 1889*—This is the worst day of my life, and I am very drunk as I try to pen these words. Lyrica has left me! A messenger delivered her note today: a terse, cold sentence which said that she must leave for Italy, and that she could see me no longer. I can't believe it! To neither see nor touch that incredible creature ever again! It is unthinkable, yet she states it so simply that there is a part of me which believes it totally. It is to laugh or cry. I don't know what to do. I know that I feel more sick and more troubled than I have ever felt. And if this is the pain of love then I have finally felt it!

*November 30, 1889*—She is truly gone. Of this I am certain. I have tried painting to soothe my pain and suffering, but there is something missing, and I know that I must struggle to regain it. I am tempted to tell Theo of this woman and her effect on me. I am tempted to hire men to investigate her past, to track her down. And perhaps I would do this if I had the funds to finance such a hunt. But alas, for me it is only a fantasy, a fairy tale in which I find her and bring her back to my studio forever. I find myself thinking of painting with very dark colors, with the bloodiest reds I have ever mixed, but I know not what to paint. And I am ill with a list of petty diseases. I cough up terrible gouts of mucous, and I shiver when there is bright sun on my skin. I have terrible fits at night when I lie in my bed in a sweat. I must start sleeping at longer stretches, must stop sitting up in my bed, staring at the moon while Paul grinds on through the night with nose-rattling snores.

*December 19, 1889*—A month has passed and I am truly mad for her touch and the lingering smell of her cunt in my beard. My health continues to slide as I do not eat regularly, and I do not take care of what Paul calls my "most basic needs." But worse, I know I am truly mad. None of the colors look right anymore! My palette is a place of confusion and the colors of the oleanders and the rose-colored twilights come no longer to me on canvas. I thought the absence of her would be good for my painting, but I have seen little to cheer me. It occurs to me again that painting and fucking are not compatible. This fucking weakens the brain. If we really want to be potent males in our work, we must sometimes resign ourselves to not fucking too much! There are times when my thinking seems to clear, when I do not hear the flies buzzing in my ears, when I can think clear thoughts and plan beautiful canvases. It is at those times that I know that she was bad for me, that her fucking was killing something in me. In ways that I can never explain. And then I think about this and I know that this also sounds crazy, and that I am probably so sick and so mad that it no longer matters what I think or what I feel.

*January 15, 1890*—I feel so embarrassed for what has happened, and yet there is no way to show these feelings. After the argument with the whore, I still do not recall cutting my ear, or the first days in the hospital. Only Theo's face bending over me do I really remember. Upon returning to the studio, I learned that Paul had left, heading for Brittany, says Theo. I am tempted to say that I am happy he is gone, but that would be untrue. More truthful is to tell how lonely it has become without him. Even his quarrelsome nature is preferred to the silence. I don't even want to think of how much I miss the woman.

*April 13, 1890*—The calendar says that it is April so I must believe it. I have lost track of the passing of the days and nights, and even the months. I have only recently broken my silence and written to Theo. I feel used up, like an old, ugly whore! I am mixing colors again, and I am seeing the colors of spring come back to this place with a wild and happy vengeance, but I am not painting good canvases.

*May 16, 1890*—The world seems more cheerful if, when we wake up in the morning, we find that we are no longer alone, and that there is another human being beside us in the half dark. That's more cheerful than shelves of edifying books and the whitewashed walls of a church, I'd swear! And that companionship is something that the Fates have denied me. Lyrica is less than memory, like a half-remembered dream. I cannot imagine ever being happy in my life. Even the village is against me now, having the inspector jail me for being an incompetent. I have been in and out of the hospital so many times that I fear I am becoming a nuisance to everyone. It is only too true that heaps of painters go mad. I shall always be cracked, but it's all the same to me. When I become a nuisance to me, I will simply kill myself.

*Scarpino, Sicily 1891*

"This is the village of my ancestors!" Mauro Callagnia said proudly to her.

He was a tall, handsome boy of nineteen, who literally bristled with energy and invention. Everything he touched or attempted became a natural ability under his hand. He was an expert horseman, a deadly archer and swordsman, an accomplished musician, poet, and painter. He had so much to give, he was like an unending fountain.

"It is so small and unimposing," she said as they drew their horses to a stop before the old wall and gate which marked the entrance into the small mountain village of Scarpino. Miles below them, huddled in the hazy cloak of twilight, lay the city of Palermo, the current home of Mauro's family.

Mauro smiled. "It is from such humble beginnings that many great things may come," he said.

318

She nodded, and looked carefully down the narrow streets ahead, then started to direct her mount toward the central avenue.

"Wait," said the boy who was already a man. "We should wait for the rest of the caravan, don't you think?"

She did not really wish to wait for Mauro's family, especially his father. She did not feel comfortable in the presence of the Duke. "Very well, Mauro. You are right."

She looked back down the trail, which snaked back and forth across the hills, to see the remainder of their party slowly negotiating a narrow path. The line of horses carried men and women in gaily colored dresses and suits. Even in the failing light, she could see the mark of breeding and royalty in their carriage. Her young Mauro was the product of admirable bloodlines, and it was certainly no accident that he was so talented and gifted.

A minute passed in silence as Mauro's father, a Duke whose family title originated before the formation of the now defunct Kingdom of Two Sicilies, appeared over the nearby ridge. She noted that he was a hale man with great stamina and strength for his age. The Duke's face was creased from the years, but a fierce intellect raged behind his bright eyes. There lay a hard casting of determination in his features. The Duke carried a reputation as a man to be respected, and to be dealt with fairly.

Lyrica was forced to admit that, although she feared few men, she could possibly fear the Duke of the House of Callagnia.

"What took you so long, father!" Mauro smiled after his greeting.

"A slower horse, and not my age, if that's what you imply, my son!" The Duke turned and signaled to the rest of the family party. "Follow me, it is not far now!"

Mauro assumed the lead, and led the procession down the central avenue of the village. It was a narrow street which leaned to the left, and ascended the hill toward the small village church, whose spire rose above the low-slung houses like an aspiring dream.

As they approached the rectory, a moderately large residence beyond the church, she felt a twinge of apprehension. She had come this far because she had always been cautious, always watchful of the fears and superstitions of the humans.

It was easy to become overconfident, and she had always tried to be vigilant against that failing. Of Mauro, she had no fear or distrust—he was so in love, so infatuated with the joys of the flesh that he could never be a problem.

But there were others who were not so intoxicated. It was as though certain men—admittedly few through the ages—were immune to her powers of entrancement, and while she had only seen the man several times, she suspected that the Duke might be such a man.

And so, she thought with a sense of adventure and daring, perhaps it was a reckless thing to accompany this brilliant boy to his parents' anniversary dinner.

She would know soon.

The procession wound its way toward the rectory, and as the line of horses passed, many of the villagers appeared at windows and doors to have a look at the last of the village's *nobilia* in a time when nobility was a dying art form. She looked down at the people in their ragged clothes and their ragged faces, returning their stern expressions with looks of patronizing kindness and false friendliness. It was the haughty carriage that the peasants expected, and she gave it to them with little effort.

Finally they reached the rectory where they were greeted by two small boys, presumably acolytes who worked for the pastor. Everyone dismounted as the boys tended to the steeds, and faced a tall, wizened old priest who walked forward with open arms to greet the party.

"Welcome, my children," said the priest. "Come into my home. Dinner is almost prepared."

They entered the foyer to the stone and stucco rectory, and she was introduced to Pastor Mazzetti.

"Lyrica," said the Duke's wife, Dulcima, "I would like you to meet my mother's brother, my uncle, the Pastor Francesco Mazzetti!"

The old priest reached out and took her smooth white hand in his. His palm felt like the bark of an olive tree. He smiled and his runneled face looked as though it might crack like old leather. She smiled back and curtsied, but she could not avoid the intensity of his gaze. This was a man of great confidence and faith . . . and, therefore, power.

"I am pleased to make your acquaintance, signorina," said Mazzetti. "You should feel privileged to attend what has become a grand family tradition . . ."

"She is my guest tonight, uncle!" said young Mauro with a burst of pride as he cut into the conversation. "Is she not beautiful!?"

The old priest smiled, nodding. "Yes, nephew . . . she is that, and more, I am certain."

An old woman appeared in the doorway, which led deeper into the house, and nodded silently, catching Father Mazzetti's attention. He looked about at the assembled guests and brought his hands together in a practiced gesture. "And now the dinner is served. This way, everyone . . ."

The anniversary dinner was indeed a wonderful affair. Seated at a long table headed up by Father Mazzetti were the Duke and his wife, her brother and his wife, their daughter Carmina, and of course Mauro and herself. Mazzetti had arranged the chair assignments so that Lyrica was seated at his right hand— presumably the place of honor, but she was beginning to wonder what might be the true motivations of the priest. He kept looking at her throughout the dinner with intense, probing eyes.

After having glossed over the usual family pleasantries and toasts to good health and long life, the conversation about the table had drifted, inevitably, into politics. Lyrica knew this topic was not unusual among the noblemen of Italy because there were finally signs that the unending upheaval and unrest of the country might be nearing surcease. She listened to the banter with a halfhearted interest, while running her long fingernails up and down Mauro's thigh beneath the table.

". . . and I think the best thing that ever happened to us as Sicilians, was getting rid of Premier Depretis," said the Duke as he reached for more wine from a crystal decanter.

"Of course, brother-in-law!" laughed his wife's sibling. "You belabor the obvious, don't you think? Since our new prime minister is a Sicilian, it is to be expected that he would look out for the interests of the Island!"

The Duke nodded. "Perhaps, but he must do it with some tact, with diplomacy, yes?"

"Francesco Crespi is no fool," said Father Mazzetti. "Let's not forget he fought with Garibaldi many years ago. He has made the ascent to power up the rear face of the mountain—he knows how difficult and delicate and lonely it can be at the top."

Lyrica watched the priest as he spoke. He seemed to be totally engaged in the conversation, and yet, she had the distinct impression that he was observing her, recording her every movement and reaction. Even though he appeared to be in his late sixties or early seventies, he appeared bright and strong. An interesting old man, she thought with a smile.

"Still," said the Duke. "I think Crespi's taking office is the most important thing to have happened to all of us since the beginning of the *Risorgimento!*"

The Duke's brother-in-law shook his head. "Some would say that Humbert the First's ascension to the throne is the real key to everything . . ."

The Duke seemed to flush with a moment of anger. "That fool! Do you really think that the crown prince of Germany should be the King of Italy! It's time we throw out the house of Savoy once and for all!"

Father Mazzetti smiled. "Ah, me . . . the Duke will always be a headstrong man, a man of impulse and raw emotion."

Everyone laughed softly except the Duke.

"And what of it, uncle? My personality has served me well, has it not?"

The priest shrugged. "Perhaps," he said, "but you're starting to sound like Antonio Labiola."

The Duke appeared perplexed. "And who is he?"

"A professor at the University of Rome who has been teaching Marxism to his students."

"Marxism!" The Duke exploded with laughter. "Do you actually think that a nobleman like myself could ever espouse the writing of such a crackpot as Marx?"

"Why not?" Father Mazzetti said *sotto voce.* "You seemed to have embraced the socialism of Mazzini well enough."

"Oh, please!" said Dulcima, the Duke's wife. "Must we talk of politics endlessly?"

"I'll talk about what I please!" said the Duke.

Dulcima turned to the Pastor. "Uncle, I fear you agitate him. You do this for your own amusement!"

The priest smiled. "I am an old man . . . I need something for my amusement!"

Everyone laughed as the priest used the opportunity to gaze sharply and quickly at Lyrica. She could not escape the hard, cold aspect of his glance.

The moment was interrupted by the appearance of the pastor's cook, who began clearing away the main-course plates and dishes with a clattering efficiency. The conversation at the table fragmented as though on cue into smaller one-on-one exchanges. The Duke seemed to be upset with his wife, while Dulcima's brother was making amusing small talk with his niece Carmina.

"My family is rather outspoken," said Mauro, leaning close and whispering in her ear.

"Don't sound so apologetic," she said absently, trying to cast unnoticed glances at the priest. She was feeling more and more uncomfortable, and she was thinking of ways she could handle it.

"I'm not being apologetic," said the boy.

"Oh, yes, you are!" She smiled and kissed his cheek.

Even that small gesture seemed to excite him and she could sense his desire pulsing from his body.

The cook reappeared with a tray of Sicilian pastries and a small urn of espresso. She placed it in the center of the table and everyone 'oohed' and 'ahed' appropriately.

"And now the dessert!" said Father Mazzetti clapping his hands. Everyone smiled as he began to pass about the tray and the cook began pouring out small cups of the dark, sweet coffee.

The tray was passed to her, and she selected a cream and almond pasticceria. As she placed it on her plate, the cook offered her a small gold-rimmed porcelain cup of espresso. It was a delicate, exquisite piece of work, and she marveled at the relative opulence in which the priest lived when one considered the humble surroundings of the village.

Such were her idle thoughts as she sipped the thick dark liquid from the demitasse cup.

Drawing the porcelain away from her lips, she felt a stabbing pain in her stomach, and an almost instantaneous numbing sensation spreading outward from her head down into her limbs. It was a paralyzing effect, turning her to stone. Even her breathing seemed to be affected and she had the sensation of suffocating.

*Poison!*

The single thought pierced her like an arrow, and she glanced about the table as she began to straighten out like a plank and slide from her chair. She tried to cry out, but no sound would come. The power of the potion was strong indeed, obviously imbued with the priest's blessing to have any effect at all. She would need all of her cunning and strength to overcome it.

Everyone was talking at once at the table, and as she slipped into a semi-comatose state, she was only vaguely aware of the torrent of voices that swirled and eddied over her.

"My God! What's happened to her?" cried Mauro. She could feel his soft, gentle hands on her as he helped lower her to the floor.

"Let her be!" cried the priest in a sepulchral voice. "Stand back!"

Mauro turned to his father, who had left his chair, and was rushing to her side. "It's true, then? Is it *true*, Father?"

"Father," said Mauro, "what is happening here? Of what do you speak?"

The priest advanced and huddled over her. She could see him through a filmy, gauzy aspect which had overtaken the light in the room. She was fighting off the effects of the poison, and her body was sending signals that she would be able to overcome it with time. She was thankful for that, but there was still a panic deep within the core of her being. A panic like a glowing coal that threatened to burst into flame in an instant.

"She failed the tests!" cried Father Mazzetti. "Stand back from the Demon! Stand back from the Possessed Creature that she is!"

"What!" cried Mauro. "Have you all gone mad?" He reached out and pushed at the old priest, who was leaning over, peering into Lyrica's glassine eyes.

Suddenly the Duke lashed out with his large hand and smacked Mauro in the face. The force of the blow knocked him back off his feet so that he went sprawling.

"Silence!" cried the Duke at his son. "You mewling pup! What do you know of this woman other than the fire of her loins!"

Mauro propped himself up on one elbow, stunned and confused. "Father, what you speak is madness! She is no demon!"

"No, she is far worse!" cried Mazzetti, who now held a gold crucifix over her face. "Her food was laced with ground bitter-root . . . enough to choke a man, and she noticed it not! It is as the tales have told—a monster tastes not of man's food!"

The Duke moved to his son and held him in his arms. "My son, I am sorry for what I must do, but it is for the best."

"Oh, father!" The young boy sounded very panicked. "What are you going to do with her?!"

"We have suspected for a time that the young woman is possessed," said the Duke, as the rest of the dinner party gathered about to peer down at her in a ragged circle of faces. "And so we have brought her to the finest exorcist in Sicily—our own Father Mazzetti!"

"Bring her into the church!" commanded the old priest. "I must prepare myself . . ."

Lyrica could feel the effects of the poisons coursing through her supple body. Soon the effects would be lessened enough for her to affect a change. Soon but not yet. And so she was powerless to stop them from lifting her up from the cold stone floor and out into the night. The sky above the foothills was a brilliant, midnight blue, laced with stars and frosted by the wind. They crossed a small courtyard, past a fountain, and into the sacristy entrance of the church.

Her vision was blurred, but she could still determine that the tough old priest had already assumed the mantle of his office, his silk raiments of the priesthood. He stood like a man posing for a sculptor or a painter, striking a posture of defiant strength.

"Take her out to the altar," he said as calmly as his voice would allow. Even in her distressed state of mind, Lyrica could detect the metallic scent of his fear. Fear was indeed the mind-killer, and if she could capitalize on Mazzetti's own fears and self-doubts, she still possessed a chance.

She was carried out of the sacristy and into the nave of the church, where the white marble altar lay surrounded by statues of the saints and several elaborate stained-glass windows. As she was placed before the altar, the priest moved down beside her and anointed her forehead with oil. Her muscles were beginning to contract involuntarily. Either the effects of the poison were wearing off, or they were getting worse.

Suddenly there was a stinging sensation in her face, and after being so totally numb and paralyzed, she was ecstatic to feel even the faintest pain in her cheeks. Mazzetti had sprinkled holy water on her, and the droplets burned like acid. It stung, but it was such a sweet stinging.

She could see Mazzetti standing over her, holding up a gold crucifix. In a booming, echoing voice, he began speaking in Latin: *"In the name of the Father and the Son and the Holy Spirit, and by the power and authority granted to me by the Holy Mother Church and Pope Leo the Thirteenth, I invoke the rite of exorcism over this woman . . ."*

Mazzetti continued droning on as Lyrica secretly smiled at him. His prayers were totally ineffectual; she wanted to cry out and laugh at him, and tell him what a fool he was. More feeling was returning to her cheeks, her limbs. Soon, she would show them that their silly poisons and potions had little real power over a being as great as she.

Yes, it was happening now . . .

She could feel the power returning to her once-numbed body. In an instant, the juices of the changes were produced and shot through her soft tissues. She could feel her flesh hardening, flaking, and sloughing off, as she began the transformation to the True Form.

The Duke was the first to notice and he cried out in an uncharacteristic voice of alarm. "Father! Look! What does she become?"

"Oh, my God in heaven!" yelled Mauro. "What are you doing to her! She's dying! Can't you see that she's dying?"

Father Mazzetti paused, placed the crucifix upon the altar.

"Silence!" he said quickly. "It is all right! Behold the power of the Lord!"

Suddenly, the priest turned and opened the small tabernacle atop the altar, bringing forth a small golden chalice. Slowly, and with great reverence, as he continued to mumble through the endless Latin prayers, Father Mazzetti reached into the chalice and produced a large, paper-thin wafer of unleavened bread—she knew it was the host, the Eucharist. Holding it carefully between thumb and forefingers, the priest placed the host inside a magnificent gold benediction mantle. It was a chalice-like object that held the Eucharist face-outward in a circular, glass locket surrounded by delicate, radiant spires of gold.

The cast beams were intended to suggest a great irradiation of light from the central figure of the host, but in this case, it was not necessary.

As soon as the old priest turned to face his adversary, the Eucharist began to glow with white heat and light, a miniature sun in his hands. The shadows in the small village church were banished by the brilliant explosion of light. The golden benediction mantle became a torch so bright that no one dare look directly upon it.

Lyrica had almost finished the transformation and it progressed rapidly now. In the short moments of the priest's preparations she had assumed the changeling shape of the magnificent green serpent. She reveled in the return to her natural form, and writhed in ecstasy as the Duke and Mauro reeled back from the horror they now perceived. She moved quickly, arching up in her spine and dislocating the hinge of her jaws, unfurling her great hollow fangs. Cobra-like, she reared up to face the foolish priest and his pyrotechnic show to impress the masses. Tightening her coils, she prepared to spring—

—and was stunned into immobility by the searing white wave of energy which hit her like the shock wave of a fiery explosion.

How foolish she had been! How wildly overconfident and arrogant! She had amused herself by walking proudly and defiantly into the lair of her natural enemy, and now he was proving to be her match . . . !

"Behold the beast!" cried Mazzetti. There was a collective, horrified gasp from the assembled dinner party, Carmina had swooned into the arms of her mother.

"My God!" cried out young Mauro, who fell to his knees, grasping the legs of his father in supplication for forgiveness and in thankfulness for seeing the true evil with which he had become involved.

Lyrica could see everything taking place with a deadly clarity, but at the same time she felt totally blinded, totally overwhelmed by the power and light emanating from the Eucharist. It was the first time in her very long life that she had ever encountered such a force, and she was truly shocked by its fury and total domination. Resisting with all her strength, she could do nothing, and as the priest approached her with the Eucharist, the blinding light felt as though it would sear the flesh from her bones. The pain became an intolerable wave, and she succumbed to its numbing paralysis, slipping into a terrible coma-like state in which she was stingingly aware of everything around her, but completely and irrevocably powerless to react.

The priest reached out and touched her dry, scaling flesh. She tottered for an instant, then fell to the stone floor. Her coils remained stiff and tight in the grip of a rigor mortis-like power.

Moving to the altar, Father Mazzetti spoke again. "Lift the altar stone! Quickly now!"

"Father, what are you doing?" asked the Duke, as he moved with his son to fulfill the priest's request.

"Just do as I ask!" said Mazzetti, almost delirious over the show of power at his command.

Quickly, silently, Mauro and his father grasped the corners of the marble altar and heaved upward and away from the massive base. Lyrica lay frozen in constricted coils by their feet, watching and suddenly understanding what the priest intended. A shudder of abject horror rushed through her, and she wanted to scream, but no sound could ever come.

The two men eased the marble slab to the floor and looked up to face the priest.

"Take the beast and commend it herewith!" cried Mazzetti. He had a wild-eyed, prophet-in-the-desert look to his features. Mauro and the Duke moved rapidly, automatically. She could feel them as they hunched over, reaching out to wrap their fingers around her girth. The touch of their warm, soft flesh against her scaled coolness repulsed her, and a shudder passed through. Unable to fight back against the blinding heart-of-the-sun light of the Eucharist, she felt herself being lifted from the floor.

Up, over the edge of the altar she was roughly carried. The droning Latin prayers of Mazzetti accompanied this, and despite her terror, she felt a spasm of utter hate wash through her. She vowed her vengeance against this old man who deceived her. She would punish him! He would regret his actions of this day!

Now she was being dropped into the hollow center of the

altar. Like a thick-walled casket vault, like a coffin, it accepted her with a dark, mute finality. She felt the cold stone against her flesh, colder even than the scales that protected her.

No! This could not be . . . ! She fought against the paralysis which gripped her, railed against the force of the Host, but her power was for nothing compared to the awesome magic of the priest.

Looking up from her crypt, framed by its rectangular walls, she could see the streaming light of the Host still lacing her like a lethal radiation. She heard the grunting effort of the men as they lifted the capstone, an immense slab of white marble, and heaved it up to the edge of the altar.

"Enclose the beast called *lamia*!" cried out Mazzetti. "And the Lord shall entomb his Adversary forever!"

The sound of heavy stone, grinding, grating, sliding against heavier stone echoed through the hollow crypt of the altar. She cried out to them for mercy, but the sounds were only in her mind. She could do nothing but watch the rectangular slab slowly creep across the altar's topmost edges, sealing her within like a moldering corpse.

Except that there would be no moldering.

There would be no mindless, black oblivion here. No, she realized with a rising panic, with a thick column of terror rising up in her mind. Instead, she would be alive in this total darkness, in this state of eternal paralysis. She would be conscious of the nothingness that entombed her.

Forever.

The thought shot through her being with a searing, exquisitely painful reality.

No! The single word reverberated through her mind as she watched the last edge of light being constricted and finally pinched off as the slab slid into place. Stone met stone with a final resonant thud, leaving her in a place of total darkness, of a silence so deep and so profound that she felt she might go immediately mad . . .

Coda: *Scarpino, Sicily 1944*

The plane was a B-17, a bomber called the Flying Fortress. It had been coruscated by flak over Anzio and the navigator's instruments had been knocked out. The pilot, a 26-year-old farmer's son from Kankakee, Illinois named William Stoudt, had lost his bearings and was trying to pick up some landmarks by heading vaguely south from his target. He'd dropped his eggs just as some shrapnel ripped through his plane's underbelly, half-closing one of his bomb-bay doors, and hanging up the last 500-pounder in his bomb-release rack.

As he struggled to get his crew home, they scurried about the tunnel-like fuselage of the plane in a desperate effort to free the final bomb. Making a landing with 500 pounds of H.E. in your gut would be suicide and Captain Wild Bill Stoudt knew they were all doomed unless they could kick free of that fat boy with its tail fin hung up on the hinges of the bay door.

Waist gunner Sammy Sharpe from Brooklyn, New York decided to be the hero. He unraveled his auxiliary parachute and tied his silks into the bulkhead. Always a daredevil, Sammy loved the challenge of dangling himself through the bomb bay 10,000 feet above the Sicilian mountainside. Inch by inch, he lowered himself down until his boot reached the jammed up bay door and the twisted hinge. A good kick and one of two things would happen: the thin white metal of the bomb's fin would collapse and the payload would drop free, or it wouldn't and the bomb would probably detonate against the bay door.

Either way, the problem would be over.

Leather touched metal and Sammy Sharpe from East 24th Street (just up from Avenue R) smiled as he watched the last half-ton egg fade away. The B-17 had just passed over Palermo, so the bomb should land harmlessly in the mountains. Nothing down there for miles but a little village, and what were the odds . . . ?

*When people ask what is the favorite story I've ever written; I usually tell them it's the one I'm writing at that moment. Mainly because it's true— I have to absolutely love what I'm writing, or it simply will not get written. But in some ways, I regard this next story as one of my favorites because it contains some deep, long ago autobiographical childhood stuff and also because I like what it says about the things that shape us. It also could be one of my silliest because the "bad guy" of the story might be nothing more than a few dumb pieces of wood. Of course, it might be something far more menacing, but that is for you to decide.*

*It was written for Peter Straub's HWA anthology called* Ghosts, *and again, I had no desire to write a story about something that has become such a shopworn staple of the genre as a ghost. Peter told me he wasn't getting very much good material, and I'd promised I'd try to get him something of substance—in length and quality. I had to stretch it; I had to give the standard ghost tale a good tweaking or I couldn't make myself do it. In my idea notebook, I spied a line which asked how a writer who'd run dry might recapture the magic that made him a writer in the first place? (In parentheses, I had added later:* is he looking for the ghost of his own childhood?*)*

*Perhaps he was. And perhaps I had found the kernel of a thought that could develop into my own personal vision of what a modern ghost story could be . . . .*

*I started writing and I let out all the chucks, both consciously and unconsciously. Even though this one is a long novelette, it almost wrote itself, and I think I had a first draft complete in about four days, which is damned fast for me. When I finished, I had a feeling I might have something pretty good, and Peter agreed with me. So did the HWA when they included it on the final Stoker*

LOOKING FOR MR. FLIP

*Awards ballot for Novella.[1] Some of you may recognize some of the source material for the story and the characters but I hope it will enhance, rather than detract from the reading experience.[2]*

---

[1] *It came in second to "Lunch at the Gotham Cafe" by Stephen King.*

[2] *The name of "Mr. Flip" comes from something Stephen King wrote in one of his earlier books. It was one of those things you read in other peoples' work that resonates totally with your own experience (like going to a drive-in with your parents to see* The Beast from 20,000 Fathoms*). Steve had this quasi-toy that was either incredibly similar or exactly the same as one I had as a very small boy, and when he described it, I was blown away as a rush of almost identical memories crashed over me. But King had taken me one step farther, because he actually remembered the toy's* name, *something I had refused to allow myself to do. As a little kid, I had wanted all reference to its existence banished forever from my mind. But here was Stephen King, dredging it up forty-plus years later, and I was amazed and gratified that we unwittingly shared an early trauma together. When Elizabeth read King's reference, she accused me of stealing it as my own, and I had a hard time convincing her that most of us writer-mutants have* many *shared experiences that left indelible marks. (Sometimes I think Paul Wilson and I led the same early lives . . . .) She remains, I fear, skeptical, preferring to believe we are all participating in a mass-psychosis.*
*Also: the meeting with Vonnegut on Third Avenue really did happen between him and me, and yeah, the conversation we had was pretty damned strange . . . .*

*A writer has nothing to say after the age of forty;*
*if he is clever he knows how to hide it.*
                                        —*Georges Simenon*


(It would be so easy to just unlock this sucker, slide it to the right, step out into space, and turn myself into a street pizza . . . )

Jack Trent stood at the window of his co-op overlooking the upper west side of Manhattan and the improbable swatch of Autumn they called Central Park. Fifty-five stories away from the land of yellow cabs and mid-eastern hacks, everything looked somehow unreal.

(How do people have the stones for it?)

Jack continued to stare downward, realizing that people who jumped out of windows were either a lot dumber or a lot crazier than he was. As bad as he was feeling right about now, (and for the past year and a half to be honest . . . ) there was no way in hell he could kill himself.

Another minute passed staring down at the micro-machine traffic in a kind of detached, fog-like state. So blanked-out. Not even aware of his thoughts. Then he stepped back and turned to face his office. It *was* a great looking room. Anybody who came to visit him always admired it openly. And who wouldn't? It was a tastefully decorated celebration of the achievements of Jack Trent—known to a book-buying public as R. Jackson Trent.

The bookcases covering the walls were bone white with blond oak trim. Four floor-to-ceiling cases were reserved for Jack's many appearances in print. Three and a half shelves of novels, story collections, and anthologies he'd edited. Another whole case for all the foreign editions of those. Then more than two entire cases of all the places his short stories, columns, articles, and interviews had appeared: hundreds of anthologies, magazines, journals, and newspapers.

Then there was the Henrendon *étagère* in the corner with all the awards. From every literary society, writers organization, and artsy cultural klatsch in Manhattan. The hall leading into the room was lined with photos of tuxedoed Poohbahs handing him statuettes, plaques, and sculptures.

Almost an entire *wall* of Jack Trent.

Sure, it was impressive, even to Jack himself. There were some mornings when he would shamble into this sacred space and the thought would just kind of smack him in the face.

(Jesus, did I really *write* all this stuff?)

Yes, he did. And therein, as Will Shakespeare once wrote, lies the rub.

You see, Jack Trent, whose agents at William Morris, just landed him a two-book deal for more than 11 million dollars, was totally burned out. Toasted. Crispy fried. Reamed, steamed, and dry-cleaned. Screwed, blewed, and tattooed. He'd been martinized, simonized, and sanitized—although not necessarily for his own protection.

Jack Trent couldn't write jackshit.

(For more than a year now . . . )

And this was from a guy who had literally *burned up* two IBM Selectrics, worn down countless type-ball elements, and kept the ribbon companies in the black. From a guy who, when word processing became the main heat back in the early Eighties, filled his 20 meg hard-drive with so many novels they had to be stacked up at his publisher like 737s waiting to land at JFK.

(Those were the days, my friend . . . )

He moved automatically to his desk, sank deep into the leather palm of his writing chair. Glaring at him like a modern gargoyle, a techno-demon of the White Space, was the paper-white screen of his Mac. The title of his next book, *Malefaction*, floated in the center of an empty page. The White Space that all writers must conquer was finally getting the best of him. As in *Poe's Narrative of A. Gordon Pym*, or Lovecraft's *At the Mountains of Madness*, the metaphor had finally come round to become horrifyingly real.

Picking up the keyboard, Jack placed it on his lap, stretched out in his chair and lightly laid his fingers on the keys. The letters had become alien symbols. Small runic scratches that held as much sense for him as stones written in Mycenean. His fingers felt cramped, unnaturally positioned over the home row. Myasthenia gravis or acute arthritis could not have crippled him more effectively than the sense of utter help-lessness, of . . . emptiness that encapsuled him.

To put it as simply as possible, the words would not come forth. For a half a thousand nights, Jack lay staring into the blackness of his ceiling, wondering if he was dealing with the symptoms or the disease. The questions rattled around in his head like seeds in a gourd. What was the sudden terror that welled up in him like a column of rancid vomit every time he even *thought* about trying to write? Could he have truly run out of things to say? How could he have ever grown weary of entertaining himself, of telling his stories to himself? Jack put the keyboard back on the desk, avoided looking at the book's title lying naked on the face of the monitor.

(Book title. Yeah right . . . )

It was *not* a book title. He chuckled to fight back the tears of frustration. It was merely a title—there was no book.

There was a sound from one of the other rooms in the apartment. Someone had entered the front door and the secu-rity monitoring system beep-beeped to let him know the door had been opened.

"Mr. Trent? It's just me." A female voice passed through the rooms to find him. Betsy, his office assistant, had reported to work.

(11:00 o'clock already? Christ, another day half shot.)

Time, Jack had realized for a number of years did not fly—it red-shifted away from us. Memories from childhood capered before him as though things from the night before. And they were as clean and crisp as the little Eton suits his mother used to make him wear. The memories were stacked up behind him like the pages of all his manuscripts.

(How many would it take to reach the moon?)

A presence filled the threshold behind him. Sensing it, he turned slowly and looked at Betsy Moranovic. She was what you would call plain. A late Seventies graduate of Smith or Barnard or one of those places—Jack could never remember. She preferred short brown hair cut in what they used to call a page boy style, tortoise shell glasses, and shapeless skirts and blouses that could not be called out of style because they lacked any style in the first place. Betsy was the perfect office assistant: soft-spoken, obsessively efficient, and almost totally invisible.

"How's the new book doing?" she said as she faced him with an armful of mail from the post office box.

"How many times are you going to ask me that?" said Jack, trying to control a sudden anger. "You know it's doing for shit!"

"I'm sorry, I really am," she said, sounding like an embarrassed child. Then she stood looking at her shoes, waiting for his next words.

(Just like my agent . . . and my readers . . . )

He looked at the huge stack of mail in her arms and was touched by a bittersweet reminiscence of how he used to *love* to get mail. How he'd drive to the post office like a kid waiting, expecting his cereal box toy. And every time he'd open the little box and see a manila envelope folded up in there, he'd feel a little piece of the dream wither up and die. But those rejection slips used to get him so juiced! So outraged that he couldn't wait to get back to his little apartment and write something so damned brilliant they *couldn't* turn it down.

But now his mail was just another pain in the ass in his life. More fan mail than any *ten* people could keep pace with; book galleys from friends and associates wanting blurbs; endless requests to write stories for anthologies, limited editions, special anniversary issues, charity-this and charity-that; and free stuff ranging from lots of book review copies to handmade quilts to tins of cookies which went instantly into the trash.

(Didn't people realize that only a true hydrocephalic would scarf up food sent through the mail, wolfing down little treats that could easily be suffused with enough toxins to drop a Tyrannosaur in mid-stride?)

"Mr. Trent, is everything all right?" Betsy's voice penetrated the thicket of his thoughts.

(Jeezis, have I started drooling yet?)

"Yes," said Jack. "I'm fine . . ."

"I was going to answer as much of this as I can get to," she said, waiting for confirmation.

"Yeah, that'll be fine. I'm going to go down and take a walk. Get a pack of cigarettes."

"Oh, okay." She stepped out of his path. "But you don't smoke . . ."

"I was thinking of starting again."

"Oh, okay."

"Cold out?"

"Cool. Low sixties." Betsy chanced a weak little smile.

Jack nodded. His *Baseball Forever* sweatshirt would be enough. And if it wasn't, well fuck it, he'd buy a jacket along the way. What good was the money if it couldn't take your mind off the trivial bullshit in your life?

Down the elevator to a lobby done up in gallery prints by Klimt and handmade carpets from Gaza. Ronnie, the overweight doorman, was waiting for him with his usual mongoloid smile.

"Hey, Mistuh Trent! Howzit hangin', huh? Howzat latest book doon'?"

Jack smiled and waved as he passed the caricature of a man dressed like a Latin American dictator. He always found it amazing that Ronnie would mention his books. The notion of actually reading a book had never, Jack was certain, sullied the doorman's forebrow.

He walked down Central Park West toward the 86th Street subway. The air had an edge to it. Football weather. No humidity, and none of the fetid summer-city smells that follow you around like an in-law cadging a loan. Everybody dressed in the latest fall designs, everybody walking fast, looking good. Jack moved under a lackadaisical gait, clearly a man with no place to go.

(You got that right . . . )

Down the gritty steps to the token booth, he sidestepped the obligatory bum and slipped a few dollars under the glass. He'd never really warmed up to politically correct posturing, and besides, *homeless person* just didn't roll off the tongue like *bum.*

Whenever he needed to take a break, he liked to go down to the village, drift through its shabby-chic neighborhoods and narrow streets, to absorb the life-scenes there. Maybe drop into McSorley's, catch a Guiness and a slab of cheddar.

(Yeah, that's the ticket . . . )

And so he was standing not really near the edge of the platform, waiting for the C-Train. Jack steeled himself at these times, ever watchful for some donut to sneak up behind him and throw him across the tracks to crisp up nicely against the third rail. He never could understand how people could stand right on the edge like they did. He tried to consciously think about *Malefaction* and how the plot would require several twists along the way. But he knew that was bullshit. His books never happened that way. It was like staring at something and not seeing it until you looked away. That's how his stories came to him. When he wasn't even trying, the whole narrative would just unfold like an intricate origami. It would just phenomenologically *be*, and he'd never questioned it and he knew he never should.

A low-register vibration passed through his Timberland hiking boots. Jack looked up to see the train exploding out of the tunnel, pushing a hot column of air ahead of it. In a burst of noise the train was upon him like a rough beast. Its doors sagged open and he entered into its belly.

As the train lurched forward, Jack found a seat among a familiar collection of New York faces—ethnic types from all the usual places, a few Suits, a few students, some women with their kids in tow. Everybody either buried in a *Daily News* or a paperback, or working on that numb-head stare Jack knew so well.

(Truly, we are a world of mooks.)

Jack grinned at his small philosophy. At least he could still amuse himself. When that left him, maybe it really was time to just step out that window.

The train pitched to the right as it came out of a dark turn and brawled its way into the Museum of Natural History station. Jack absently watched the exchange of passengers in and out, and found himself grinning again as he saw a young woman enter the car carrying his last novel, *Malignancy*, in its paperback edition. He always checked out whatever people were reading because their preference always gave you a major clue to who they really were. Being on the bestsellers list with every title had never jaded him to seeing his books being read in public. But within the last year or so, he'd begun wondering if he would ever see anyone reading a new R. Jackson Trent ever again.

The girl—(if they're younger than me, they're *girls*. Sorry, ladies . . . )—sat down on the seat across from him. She looked like a new bohemian: long purple-red hair trussed into a ponytail that shot straight up over head like a geyser, heavy eye shadow, esoteric far Eastern jewelry, a baggy peasant blouse and a Guarani scarf, long black skirt and knee-high boots.

She was not so much pretty or attractive as she was interesting. There was something wrong with the way her features combined to keep her from ever defining the ideal of Helenist, feminine beauty, but she broadcast a message that said she was intelligent, iconoclastic, artsy-fartsy, and maybe a little bit of a flake.

Looking up, she caught him staring at her. Normally, when caught like that, Jack would instantly beam his attention elsewhere, but the way he was feeling today, he didn't give a damn. So he held her gaze for a moment, then looked away with feigned languor. As he pretended to be reading the ads running across the tops of the windows, he could feel the heat of her stare.

But he did not look up until she spoke to him.

"Excuse me, but aren't you R. Jackson Trent?"

Believe it or not, this did not happen to him all that often. Even people who read a lot usually could not ID their favorite writers unless they were making commercials for American Express (Jack had turned them down). And so, it gave him a measure of satisfaction to get made like that in the subway. It was not the total invasion that rock stars and actors grew to loathe, but rather something nice.

Looking again directly into her eyes, he noticed they were also kind of purple.

(Contacts? Who gives a shit—they look great . . . )

"Yes, I am."

"Wow, that is very cool. I've read all your books. Most of them at least twice . . ."

Her accent was soft, educated, but still stretched out by the twangy locutions of the American South.

(Georgia? Alabama?)

He wanted to say something, but absolutely nothing occurred to him.

"I'll bet people say that to you all the time, Mr. Trent," she said.

Suddenly aware of others in the car looking at them, tuning into their contact, he stood up, stepped across the aisle and sat next to her. Their thighs brushed and she did not shy away from the touch.

"Actually, less than you'd think."

"Really?"

"Years ago," said Jack, "I ran into Vonnegut while I was walking up Third Avenue. He was leaning against a streetlamp, looking up at a mural on the side of an apartment building, smoking a cigarette."

"Did you talk to him?"

Jack smiled. "Yeah. I told him I thought 'Harrison Bergeron' was one of the finest short stories I'd ever read in my life. He nodded and asked if he knew me"

"Why?"

"Because I think he was trying to intimate that I was bugging the shit out of him."

"You're kidding . . ."

"No. I told him when I was about your age I'd just been elected Secretary of the Science Fiction Writers of America—just about when he wrote us a letter to say he was quitting the organization."

"Did he recognize you then?"

"Yeah, he did. But he also winced at even the *mention* of having been a member of the 'Space Faring Whores of Arcturus'." Jack chuckled. "Hey, I know how he felt now. I quit that thing a couple of years later myself."

She smiled, and it was a nice smile. "Then what happened?"

"What? Oh, he basically blew me off. I think I blurted out that after 16 books, I'd just had my newest novel, *The Apocalypse Man*, reviewed favorably in the *New York Times* and he gave me a bogus smile and said something like: 'That's nice, Mr. Trent . . . and I'm sure it's a nice book . . . and I'm sure *you're* very nice . . . and I hope you have a nice day . . . as a matter of fact, have a nice life.' And then he looked back up at the building mural, took a drag off his Pall Mall, and summarily ignored me."

"Jeez, I hope you're not going to do the same thing."

"No, not at all. And please, just call me Jack. *Mr. Trent* is what everybody used to call my father."

"All right, I can certainly do that."

She paused, obviously casting about for something to say, but not getting flustered or fan-girl silly. There was a confidence, a control, about her he admired already.

"This one is great," she said holding up *Malignancy*. "I really love the way you develop your characters. I feel like I've known Sam all my life. And D'Arcy! Wow, she is *so* deep."

"Thank you," said Jack.

"Someday, I'm going to do characters like you." This was offered up softly, but with determination.

The train grabbed them with the momentum of its stop at 79th Street. They'd jumped a local, and it would be an annoying ride south with all the stops.

"So you want to be a writer?" He looked at her just long enough to assess her age.

(Late twenties? Hard to tell. She could be twenty-two and just livin' hard . . . )

"I've already sold around 20 short stories, and I'm almost finished my first novel."

"Really, where'd you sell the stories?" He was expecting to hear the usual litany of we-pay-in contributor-copies-only "literary magazines" and poetry journals like *The Sewanee Review, The Pacific Quarterly, The Midwest Chronicle of Fiction*, etcetera . . .

"Well, let's see . . . a couple of anthologies—*Borderlands* and *Shadows*, and magazines like *Omni, Penthouse, New York, Harpers, F&SF, Pulphouse*. . . . And some smaller ones too."

"I'm impressed," said Jack. And he was.

"Well, that was after a couple years' worth of rejection slips," she said.

"Oh yeah," said Jack. "I know that whole drill. I've still got most of mine. Saved them in a file somewhere."

"So what're you working now?" she asked, not knowing how her words lanced him.

He paused, before answering. Then simply: "Can you have some lunch with me?"

They emerged from the tunnels at 4th Street, found an alfresco place that specialized in pastas and soups plus the usual gelatos and capuccino, and spent the afternoon unloading baggage.

She told him that she was from New Orleans, still lived there, in fact, but was visiting in the city to meet the literary agent she'd just landed, and also pose for some nude pictures for a pro photographer friend of hers who had his brownstone studio up on West 85th. She thought it would be innovative to appear on the jacket of her first novel wearing lace gloves and nothing else. She talked a lot about mystical bullshit and off-path mythic systems, esoteric religions like Zoroasterism, always making sure she explained the arcane significance of each piece of her many jewelry accessories. Despite her young age, she said she'd worked the expected catalog of Weird Writer Jobs: including, but not limited to, dog trainer, nude dancer, dynamite truck driver, gaffer, and a deckhand on a shrimpboat. She claimed her name was Nemmy—short for Nemorensis, the goddess of fertility. The name she used on her stories was Nemmy O. Brand.

"What's the O stand for?" Jack asked.

Nemmy shrugged, pushed a strand of purple hair from her cheek. "What's a big O usually mean to you?"

Jack grinned. He liked her. She seemed wise beyond her years, and showcased more confidence in herself than anybody her age had a right to. He listened to her talk about what she wanted to write about and he knew Nemmy had been to that secret place where the Pool of Ideas waited for young writers to come peer into its endless depths.

Jack had known that place well. Not only had he *been* there, he'd purchased a condo.

But sometime during the last year or so, he'd lost his map.

When it was his turn to explain a few things, he started off with the worst of it. He was on the wrong side of forty-five, and the total number of words written on his new book in the last eighteen months: *zero.*

(That's the *real* big O, sister. May you never know the terror it brings . . . )

He told her how suicide broke the surface of his thoughts like predatory fins every now and then, even though he knew he was much too much of a chicken to ever act on that kind of craziness.

Then he unloaded some of the more usual stuff: his unending love for baseball; a disastrous marriage now twenty-five years buried; his sibling-free childhood; the long hours alone while his parents both worked; his mother running off when he was sixteen with some guy who sold Timken bearings; his college days at Pitt; the first story he sold; places he'd been; people he'd met. He even told her that the R stood for Randolph and that everybody called him "Randy" in high school and college. Then his agent strongly suggested that an on-the-rise writer should have a strong American handle. He shortened the family name of Jackson, and after all this time, he couldn't imagine thinking of himself as anyone but Jack.

"So let me get this straight," said Nemmy. "You've got more money than you can count, three houses, traveled all over the world, a wall full of books you've written . . . and you're still miserable?"

"Don't talk in non-sequiturs." Jack sipped on his fifth cup of capuccino.

"Huh?"

"No Latin in your education?"

Nemmy rolled her violet eyes. "Not even much English. My Dad was a fundamentalist preacher. He said all books of fiction were works of the Devil and fit only for the idlest of minds. But I was just being funny."

"Funny?"

"Come on, Jack, I'm a writer—of course I'm hip to non-sequiturs. But seriously, you've got a lot to be happy for."

"You're all full of juice, Nemmy. You don't know what it's like to be sweating through a cold night, wondering if you've vented all the steam in that pressure cooker we call the subconscious. Believe me, *that's* a fucking problem!"

She looked away for a minute, as though watching the endless parade of Village natives and cleverly disguised tourists pass their table. The afternoon was dying off, and the evening grew ever cooler. People in their leather jackets and military greatcoats were starting to look pretty damned warm.

"You know what your problem really is?" she asked.

(That I don't get laid enough . . . )

"No, what? Tell me?"

She kind of smirked at him. "If this were a bad movie, this is where I'd say you're not getting enough leg. And I'd instruct you to come immediately to my loft over Washington Square where I would fuck you stupid."

(Maybe I should be a screenwriter . . . )

"You're so insensitive," he said. "How do you know that wasn't exactly what I was thinking?"

Nemmy's eyes narrowed. All humor leaving them in that instant. "Au contraire, Jack. I *know* it was."

(Great, make me feel like more an asshole than I already do.)

"Okay, okay, I give up. What's my real problem?"

"Actually, you're kind of cute, even if you *are* an old guy . . ." She downed the rest of her cup. "But I can't."

"Really?"

"I abstain from sex every other month—it keeps my ancient energies focused."

"And this is the wrong month, right? Just my luck."

She looked at him intently. "You're problem is simple, Jack. You don't believe in the ghosts of your childhood any more."

"What the hell does that mean?" He was prepared to listen to her, but Jesus, he was getting a little tired of the neo-hippie routine.

"It means you've lost touch with the things that shaped you, that not only pointed you in the direction you took, but *drove* you there. Forced you to take the path most people never even notice."

"Okay, I'm listening. Go on."

"You know what I mean, Jack. We're mutants, you and I, and all the people like us. All the poor fucks who *have* to write, or dance, or paint, or sing, or whatever . . ."

Jack nodded. "Okay, so far. A little romanticized, but basically true. What else?"

"You tell me, Jack." She leaned closer to him as though ready to share a government secret. "Take me down the hall, take me back to the times when you were getting *shaped*."

Jack drew a deep breath, exhaled. The air was getting downright brisk, almost cold. When Nemmy leaned forward, the edge of the table tightened her blouse against her breasts, and for an instant he could see her hard nipples.

(Knock it off. This is important.)

And it was. He sensed she was onto something that he'd been avoiding. This strange, petite, purple-haired woman-child had thrown the latch on one of the trapdoors to his past, and there was no turning back now. Either he grabbed the lantern she was handing him and headed on down the rickety steps of memory, or whatever he'd been keeping locked up below was going to come up and get him anyway. The catch was thrown, and it was too rusty and too warped to wedge back into place.

"It's funny, but I've always told people my imagination got jumpstarted when I was about seven years old, after I'd found this horror comic called *The Unseen* on the side of road. Scared the hell out me, but it fascinated me too. From there it was on to dinosaurs and monsters and aliens and bad movies and telling stories and all the other stuff we all did."

"That's not it, Jack. You *know* it's not."

(She's right. Wish she wasn't, but . . . )

"Okay, okay. Lemme see if I can get this out . . ."


And he started talking about the time in all of our lives when we lack the vocabulary to codify our experiences in terms of real words. Because before the words, there are the images and the primal sense impressions. Mommy smells Good. Daddy smells funny, but he's still Good. The blanket is Warm. The Sun is Bright. Mr. Flip is Bad.

(Mr. Flip. Yeah, he's the one, all right . . . )

Nemmy sat back and allowed a small smile of satisfaction to curl her magenta lips. Before leaning forward again, she signaled for yet another cappuccino.

(Where was she pouring those things? She must have a bladder the size of a casaba melon . . . )

Jack felt a sudden urge for a cigarette, as strong and vicious as if he'd just stubbed one out after a long night of drinking. He shrugged it off, trading it for the mantle of his unburdening.

Mr. Flip came to his house when he was a very small boy. Little Randolph had his own room in the bungalow on Crescent Street in Bethel Park, Pennsylvania. Situated on the second floor at the end of the hall, the room was warmed by late afternoon sunlight that streamed in through gauzy yellow curtains.

Always warm.

Till Mr. Flip made the scene.

He came one day with Randolph's Godparents—Aunt Helen and Uncle Eddie. They brought him as a birthday gift when Randolph turned four years old. He remembered the dark maroon wrapping paper from Kaufmann's department store, and his Dad peeling it off from the box, and the cardboard flaps barn-dooring back to reveal Mr. Flip for the first time.

Little Randolph stared at the thing called Mr. Flip for a long time. Jack could still remember what it looked like, as if he'd just torn his gaze away from it. It was a squat, homuncular little creature, wearing a clown face and stubby little arms sticking straight out. This likeness was painted on a panel of wood that hinged upward from the long end of a piece of furniture resembling a small shoemaker's bench.

Little Randolph didn't know it at the time, but Mr. Flip was a child's dressing stool-combination-clothes valet. You could *flip* (hence the oh-so-clever name) the panel down to make a seat, then up to hang little shirts and pants on its foreshortened, and therefore grotesque, arms.

Whoever had painted the image of the Mr. Flip's clown face was either a bad artist, a tortured soul, or plainly mean-spirited. Because the visage on that clothes valet was easily the most hideous, nightmarish face he'd ever seen in his life. The eyes had an almost three-dimensional quality, as they seemed to bulge off the wood like the two halves of a hard-boiled egg. But it was the mouth that captured Randolph's attention so completely. Rimmed by a thin, white ring, warped into what passed for a smile, was actually a leering rictus. A gaping space that spoke of bad things . . . Randolph always found himself staring into Mr. Flip's mouth—into that void between the parted lips where the suggestion of teeth, little pointed ones, glinted at him. The open mouth bothered him. Randolph knew even back then, that mouths opened to either speak or bite, and Mr. Flip just didn't look the talkative kind of guy.

But somehow, his parents and the other grown-ups didn't see it that way. They all clapped their hands and made happy noises, and talked about how "cute" Mr. Flip was, and don't-you-just-love-him-Randolph?-go-give-Aunt-Helen-and-Uncle-Eddie-a-kiss-and-say-thank-you.

Why couldn't they see him for the horror that he was? How

could they let such an ugly little thing into their house? Randolph was terrified, but he had been raised even at this early age to be a little gentleman, and he knew he could *never* tell them how much he loathed this intruder.

But that was not the worst of it.

No. His mother had decided that Mr. Flip would receive a place of honor in Randolph's room, *at the foot of his bed* near his door leading down the hall.

And so began the transformation of his thoughts, of the way the little boy perceived the world. Every night, when his Dad would sit on the edge of his bed, reading him a story from the Golden Books collection, Randolph would listen half-heartedly, watching the pictures in the book with one eye, while casting a cautious glance at Mr. Flip. Admittedly, Randolph had evolved a partial solution to sharing a room with such a malformation by actually *using* the valet as much as possible—shrouding it with every shirt and pair of pants he could get his hands on. His mother would boast to her friends what a nice and neat boy he had become since Mr. Flip arrived.

While not a solution, his tactic kept Mr. Flip under wraps except for Laundry Day. And on those days and nights, Dad's stories were never long enough. When he would close the Golden Book and tuck Randolph in with a kiss and a sweet-dreams-champ-see-you-in-the-morning, the little boy would feel all his insides kind of seizing up like an old Chevy that suddenly lost its oilpan.

Because, on those nights, Mr. Flip was free to cavort naked and revealed.

After his Dad switched off the light with a resounding *click!*, he would leave the door half-open, walk down the hall and switch on the bathroom light. The thinking here was to allow a little ambient light to flow down the passage and softly lap against Randolph's bedroom threshold. Thereby giving him some comfort against the darkness.

(But it didn't work that way, did it?)

The cast of light, the positioning of the clothes valet, the angle of sight from the boy's bed, and a certain slant of imagination all conspired to imbue Mr. Flip with a dark and living essence. Transfixed, Randolph would lie propped against his headboard like a prisoner chained to his cell wall, looking into the predatory gaze of Mr. Flip. The longer he watched, the lolling egg-yellow eyes would begin to track about the room as though searching for him . . . and the arms. More like flippers, really. Sticking straight out with over-sized, flat hands, Mr. Flip became the vile thalidomide mutation iconized. But the worst had been the rows of shark-teeth, folded away during the daylight, that would rise up from the impossible dimensions beneath the surface of the wood. The boy could almost hear its words falling from that mouth in a hideous whisper: *Flip-time! Gonna flip you, Randy. That's what I'm gonna do. Gonna flip you out . . .* one night, when left naked, Randolph knew, he would shake free of his guise and gambol about the room before scaling the heights of the bed.

An immeasurable gulf of time passed over the little boy as the Laundry Days piled up like dirty clothes, stretching into months. The terrors dispensed by Mr. Flip ran rampant through his dreams until they began to leak through, contaminating his daytime thoughts. He began seeing other images in terms of Mr. Flip. Ordinary everyday objects became as yellow or round as his eyes, as red as his nose, as flat as his hands, as dark as the vacancy of his mouth.

*Gonna flip you out . . .*

And it continued like that until Mr. Flip finally *Went Away.*

Well, actually, he was *taken away.* It happened after he'd finally broken free of the wood that held him, shambling out of the hallway light and into the nourishing shadows of Randolph's room. He danced obscenely in the moonglow, and whispered to the boy as he approached the bed. *Flip time! Yes it is! Gonna flip you out! Mr. Flip's gonna flip you out!*

Closer and closer it dragged itself, but before he could clamber up the bedclothes, the little boy had unleashed a shattered-crystal scream. A scream that yanked Daddy from his dreams of late mortgage payments and vindictive supervisors to come running down the hall.

A *click!* and the room filled with light. Randolph gibbered uncontrollably, able only to point at the clothes valet which now stood rigid and idiotic by the door. The pantomime of tears and heaving, sobbing relief continued until Daddy got the message. Hey-c'mon-Champ-is-this-thing-what's-bothering-you-well-don't-worry-about-that-Daddy'll-fix-that-right-now.

Randolph could remember the hard, warm power in his Daddy's hand as he grabbed him up from the bed, carried him up against his pajamaed chest, while in the other, he gathered up Mr. Flip and headed downstairs, through the kitchen, and out into the backyard. Moonlight through Elm branches crosshatched their path to a flagstone pit barbecue his father had built the previous summer. The little boy watched as his Daddy carefully stood him up and said okay-watch-it-son as he swung Mr. Flip like Willie Mays going after a high, hard one. In one incredibly rapid motion the clothes valet struck the chimney of the barbecue and simply . . . *exploded*. The pale yellow cast of the Indian Summer night captured the spectacular splintering of Mr. Flip and etched the image across time itself. Recorded in majestic slow-motion, the end of Mr. Flip would remain with Randolph forever.

There were other recollections since faded—till now—the cool, wet grass under his feet; the warm rush of joy that surged through him; Mommy yelling at Daddy to get-back-in-the-house-it-was-the-middle-of-the-night-you-maniac . . .

But the good stuff remained. Somewhere in the dredged up muck of that early terror was the tarnished crucible in which a child's terror had been transformed from base metal into gold. The place where Jack's headspring had been wound up tight—full of the chimeras and hydras that would for a lifetime chase him through invention's maze.

(Well, *almost* a lifetime.)

He had never imagined the spring would run so slack, that the tension would be lost. And there was no longer a Mr. Flip around to twist the key.

"Pretty cool, Jack," said Nemmy. She tilted back the rest of her cup. "I like it. Told from the heart . . . or the gut . . . or whatever. I believe you."

"Believe me? I didn't know I was under oath."

She grinned. "Only to yourself."

The sun had westered into Jersey and beyond, and their waiter hovered nearby. If Jack didn't order some dinner, they would be expected to make room for some paying customers.

"What's that supposed to mean?"

"Isn't it obvious? You have to go back and get Mr. Flip—wherever he is."

A little jolt tensed through him. Some sort of somatic response to the idea of what she was suggesting.

"What?"

The waiter was looking at him, and Jack numbly signaled for the check. Nemmy was leaning forward, her eyes bulleting him.

"You can't be this dense, Jack. You *need* Mr. Flip. Now go find him."

The waiter passed the table, pausing only long enough to drop his check on a little tray. Jack covered it with a stray fifty from his pocket, and nodded slowly. Nemmy had whanged him with a psychic tuning fork and he was still resonating from the tone so struck. The very *notion* of needing Mr. Flip, even symbolically, withered him. He must have been turning this idea over for an extended time, not speaking, not even seeing anything, until he was aware of a touch at his sleeve.

" . . . earth to Jack . . . you still with us, man?"

"What am I supposed to do?" he said with a half-hearted chuckle. "Go back to Bethel Park?"

Nemmy looked at him with an expression of amused tolerance. "Of course, Jack! That's *exactly* what you must do."

"But why?"

Nemmy was clearly disappointed in him. "What do I have to do?—connect all the dots for you? Jack, you're displaying all the signs of a severely atrophied imagination. And that's the problem. Even if only unconsciously, you gotta realize Mr. Flip was the boss moment, the big-deal catalyst in your life. He taught you how to be *scared*, he taught you that this is a fucking scary place. And once you discovered that, there was no turning back. Monsters from the id, Jack. That's what it's all about. You know it, and I know it."

She paused for dramatic effect. Her eyes lasered violet light into him.

"You've got your money and your automatic rave reviews and your guaranteed million sales, so what do you need with motivation, with any galvanic fear response from the time that shaped you? That's the problem, Jack—you don't think you need it anymore and the fact is you need it more than ever. So yeah, go back to Bethel Park and get whatever you left there. Go get that little shit."

He thought about that for an unspoken moment while he looked at this wacky-looking young woman, who in the space of a few hours had discovered more about him than the last ten years' worth of girlfriends. He knew already their relationship had somehow transcended, or at least stumbled past, the physical, and oddly enough, that was fine with him. He was not, in the final encoding of this encounter, attracted to her; but he still felt he needed her in his life. Of all the ways he'd tried to find a solution to his personal terrors, only Nemmy O. Brand had offered up any counsel of possible worth.

Again the urge for a big old nasty Marlboro laced through him. He exhaled, watched his breath defined by the now cold air.

"Okay," said Jack. "You're right. I only have one more question."

"What's that?"

"Will you come with me?"

✧

*(Not on your fucking life.)*

Jack recalled Nemmy's reply as he guided his gun-metal blue Lexus across the winding treachery called the Pennsylvania Turnpike.

That's what she'd said to him.

And pretty soon after that, he'd put her in a cab and had never seen her again. No phone calls, no keep-those-cards-and-letters-coming-folks. Nothing.

(No, that wasn't completely true.)

About a week after she'd faded into the Soho evening traffic, Jack found a little package mixed in with the day's bag-o-mail. It was wrapped in brown paper, had a New Orleans postmark, and no return address. Inside, Jack found a charm or amulet attached to a small silver necklace chain. He was not familiar with the design although it resembled any number of mandala-like designs he'd seen. A handwritten note said:

*This is the talisman of my namesake. Wear it during your quest and you will succeed, but only if you believe in its power.*

*N.*

Jack smiled as he remembered his reaction the first time he'd read her words.

(Yeah, and don't forget to click your heels three times. And a pair a red shoes wouldn't hurt . . . )

Funny thing was, Jack realized, until he'd received that little charm, he hadn't decided he would actually go back to Bethel Park.

A green and white sign slipped past him. *Pittsburgh 15 miles.* He would be getting off at the Monroeville exit, which was coming up fast. Another half hour or so and he'd be home.

And yeah, he knew all about Thomas Wolfe and the going home shtick. But that guy wrote standing up using the top of his refrigerator as his desktop . . . so what the hell could he know about anything? Besides, Jack was pretty damned sure that *Look Homeward Angel* wasn't the result of a close encounter with a clothes valet.

(I'm going home, all right. You bet your ass, Tom.)

Jack tried not to anticipate anything. Not having been back to his hometown for almost twenty years, he had no idea what to expect other than lots of changes. Experience had taught him a few things, including the folly of trying to figure out ahead of time how a particular scenario might run down and how to deal with it. His up-and-down life as a writer had schooled him well: take everything as it comes; don't try to plan *anything*; and don't lose sleep over things beyond your control.

Half an hour since leaving the Turnpike, he realized he was probably lost. After a stint on the Parkway and more turns and stops than he'd remembered, he realized he was closing in on the old neighborhood. It was incredible how little had changed in all these years. There was a part of him that hadn't wanted his return to be so easy, and he was just discovering this.

(Weird how the mind works . . . *my* mind, anyway.)

He turned a corner and there was something about the configuration of the tall trees, that barn-red clapboard house on the corner, the curving tracks of the trolley. Tapping the accelerator, Jack surged forward two more blocks.

Crescent Street.

As he slowly guided the Lexus into its turn, entering the long shady block, he felt everything hitching up—his breathing, the fluids in his throat, his fingers gripping the wheel, tears in his eyes. For the first time since that morning, he remembered Nemmy's talisman hanging about his neck beneath his L. L. Bean shirt. Fumbling around his button-down collar, he felt the thin silver touch his fingertips.

(Why am I doing this? Just get on with it.)

Crescent Street lay in wait for him, enshrouded by gigantic chestnuts and oaks. Over the encampment of two-stories, they formed an impenetrable canopy of Fall color. Jack stopped the car, escaped its leather womb, and stood looking up the street. The houses had remained unchanged and without thinking about it, he found himself ticking off the names of the families who'd lived in each of them during the chrome and Formica Fifties: the Edmonds and the Ottenheimers, the Geatings, the Paseks, and of course the big victorian on the corner where old lady Howard passed her days behind drawn windowshades.

Jack walked slowly up the block. Still no sidewalks and still no need. Crescent was off the beaten track; the only traffic had always been its residents and the occasional delivery van. There were a few yardheads out raking and and pruning and trimming, a kid on his bike; otherwise the street was very quiet. His target lay hunched among the shadows of two immense trees, its white aluminum siding accented by black shutters and awning over the front steps. Jack remembered the day he helped his Dad install that awning; it was an Autumn Saturday very much like this one when he wanted to be off to his high school's football game. But not until he finished his detail as no.1 tool-handler and garage-gofer. Dad was forever showing him how to use another esoteric tool; and even now Jack knew his coping saws from his calipers.

The awning still protected the steps—a testament to Dad's skill. As he reached the front walk, Jack felt a sudden attack of disequilibrium, as if he'd jumped up from a chair too soon. Only dimly sensed, forces swirled around him.

(You're just getting emotional. Go on. Get going . . . )

Advancing up the walk, Jack shook off the impression of passing through a long tunnel. When he stood under the awning, he could almost hear Dad calling the self-tapping metal screw *a little whore* for not turning properly. He smiled at the memory and knocked on the door.

355

It opened after a moment to reveal a plain-looking woman in her early thirties. She wore a sweatshirt and jeans; carried a box of Frosted Flakes in her hand. Ambient noise of a cartoon show and kids arguing behind her. TV was probably on the kitchen counter.

"Yes?" No smile. Wary, despite Jack's purposely well-groomed appearance.

"I hope you'll excuse me, ma'am, but my name is Jack Trent—I used to live here. In your house."

He paused to get a read on her. While he spoke she'd been once-overing his topcoat from Barney's and his Italian leather loafers with those little tassels on the tops.

"Yes . . ."

Still non-committal. But that was fine. At least she hadn't slammed the door in his face or informed him she didn't want to interrupt her husband while he was cleaning his guns.

"Well, I have a kind of unusual request. You see, I grew up in this house, and when I moved out—almost thirty years ago, well, I never came back. My parents sold the place, moved to an apartment."

She leaned against the doorframe, definitely more relaxed now.

"I don't think I understand, Mr . . . ?"

"Trent. Jack Trent. Just call me Jack."

"Mr. Trent, okay, Jack. What exactly do you want."

Jack smiled the smile his girlfriend invariably said made him look like a little lost boy.

(only this time, they might be right . . . )

"Well," he said, pausing a little drama and feigned reluctance. "I wanted to rent your house for a little while."

She half-smiled. "Rent *my* house? We *live* here, Mr. Trent! What're you talking about?"

He pushed on. "I won't need it for very long. Maybe a week, maybe only a few days. You could spend a few days on mini-vacation, maybe. Stay at a nice hotel, whatever . . ."

"Listen, I don't want to sound rude, but I'm a single parent, I work two jobs, and I don't have any time or money for any 'mini-vacations'."

Jack smiled. As they said in the sales seminars, it was time to make his close. "I'm sorry, ma'am, I don't have your name . . ."

"Sudbrook. Dorothy Sudbrook."

"Well, Dorothy, how about this—you see, I've made some money in my time. And time *is* money, so what would you say to, ah, me renting your house for, oh, say, whatever it would cost you to pay off the mortgage on this place?"

She actually laughed, albeit sardonically. "Look . . . Jack, or whatever your name is, I don't have time for this. Are you crazy?"

"Yeah, I guess I am." Jack pulled a paperback edition of *Malignancy* out of his topcoat pocket. The cover hyped the usual *#1 New York Times Bestseller* across the top in gold foil. He flipped it over to expose his full-color photo on the back. "But I'm also rich," he said.

Two days later, Jack was sitting alone in the kitchen where his mother once served him up eggs in every cookable mode on an almost daily basis. He smiled as he considered those precholesterol-conscious days, and realized for the first time how *small* the room actually was. Yet it had been the nexus for his little family. Resonating with the after-images of 20,000 shared meals, 5,000 homework assignments, and at least several hundred lethal domestic battles, Jack let the ghost-memories of the house pass through him like radiation.

The Sudbrook house wrapped itself around him in a quiet blanket. Dorothy and her two pre-schoolers had packed up and headed for DisneyWorld so fast you'd have thought they'd hit the lottery.

(And in a way, they *had*.)

After their station wagon cleared the driveway, Jack had gone immediately to work by walking through each room of the house, (well, almost each one . . . ) just absorbing whatever might still remain there of his childhood. He'd noticed two things almost instantly: the first was the inability of Dorothy Sudbrook's furniture and general *stuff* to disguise the house's true identity. In every room, Jack saw everything the way it had been, the way it was *supposed* to be. The second thing was less obvious, but no less true: the house literally *hemorrhaged* with memories, impressions, vibes, whatever you wanted to call them. They flowed out of the walls and into Jack with such force it was actually a physical sensation.

Nemmy had been so right on. Everything he'd ever become could trace its roots back to this house. If there was any hope to recapture what had been leached from him, it would be found here. A knock at the door stopped his woolgathering; he stood up to stare at it in stark panic until he remembered phoning in a pizza.

Hungrier than he'd figured, Jack wolfed down four slices without hardly taking a breath. Nervous energy required a lot of fuel, and he was a lot more scared than he'd figured he'd be. Outside, sunlight faltered, then finally retreated from the windowpanes, leaving a dull smear of twilight on the glass. It would be dark any minute.

(Time to find you, old buddy . . . )

Jack helped himself to the paper towels over the little sink and cleaned himself up. Then he passed through the living room where the old Emerson television had squatted for years, dispensing the magic of Winky-Dink and Howdy-Doody and Film Funnies. Shadows followed him as evening surrendered and Jack stood at the foot of the stairs. A brief memory gammaed through him: a 4-year-old Randolph at the top of these same stairs, naked and dripping wet after he'd run from the bath so excited to hear Daddy walk in the front door. An extra step and he'd tumbled ass-over-end to the spot where Jack now stood. Somehow, he'd been unhurt; Daddy said it was a miracle as he carried him back up.

But now there was nobody to carry him, nobody to help, if anything were to send Jack rolling.

(Anything? No, it's not *any*thing . . . I'd say it was a very specific thing . . . )

Jack grabbed the polished banister, worn smooth by years of human traffic, and began the ascent into his past. The passage seemed to narrow as he drew closer to the top. The landing ended in a blank wall, with a brief left onto the main hallway. To the left lay a master bedroom full of scattered women's clothing, a little girl's room straight across and to the right a bathroom and a third and final bedroom.

Turning right, Jack fumbled for the hallway lightswitch, then decided against it. Memories leaked out of the walls, battering him like bad poetry. It was better this way, he knew. He stepped forward, down the hall, past the bathroom, toward a door half-closed.

Since entering the house, Jack had avoided this final room. He knew the time was not yet right. But now, as he neared the last threshold, the final barrier between his origins and his present sorry-assed state, he could feel it playing out like a well-written script. Something surged and lurched within the frame of the house, something massive, yet amorphous. A *presence*, yes, but more like a substantial abstraction than merely a physical thing. Jack had no words to describe whatever seethed within the very fabric of the house, but he could feel it just fine, thank you.

*Flip-time!*

That's okay with me, you little fucker . . . Let's get on with it . . .

*Gonna flip you out, Jack.*

Just as his hand closed in upon the doorknob, Jack snapped back as though tire-ironed. Had he actually *heard* that? Had it called him by name?

(Go on. Time to find out . . . )

He touched the knob, half-expecting some kind of blue flame to dance across the gap to spark his flesh. But the brass was cold and dead, ignoring him. The door swung inward and the secret place, the sanctum sanctorum of the only child, the boy of dreams, the fantasy chamber, gave up its mysteries.

There was no light and yet there was all the detail he'd ever need. The shadows spoke to him, and he knew the fixtures of Dorothy Sudbrook's child did not inhabit this place. Scents assaulted him with their ancient powers of memory: airplane glue, crayon wax, and neetsfoot oil.

Jack stepped into the room, and touched the talisman at his neck. The ancient metal burned him with its purity—a cool, clean, non-polluting energy-source. He looked into the space before him.

And like an old, brown-gray photograph, the room reflected the hazy continuum of a small boy named Randolph Trent. It was more spare than he remembered it: a dresser, a low set of shelves full of toys and comic books, and a desk. A few Crayola drawings on the walls, chintz curtains at the window.

And right in front of him, so close its wood almost brushed his leg, sat Mr. Flip.

Incredibly, Jack hadn't seen it when he first entered the space. But his old buddy, although translucent and gauzy, was undeniably there as Jack eased past its traditional resting place. Slowly, it gathered more reality to itself. Form and configuration. Substance.

Moving quickly, Jack strode to the corner of the room where his old single bed waited like an old friend. He could feel the eyes of Mr. Flip lazily tracking him as he sat down to confront the ancient nemesis.

*Flip-time, Jack!*

Ever since deciding to return to Crescent Street, part of Jack had always figured that any contact with his old enemy would reveal Mr. Flip to be nothing more than a silly boojum from childhood, a lifeless icon.

But the thing that waited for him, that had waited for more than two generations, remained as repellent and loathsome as ever. Jack felt a dark aura issuing from it like a poisonous vapor. Whatever it had been, whatever of it still remained, this grotesque piece of furniture was much more than that. It possessed an animus, an essence that held him.

Without thinking, Jack reached up to touch Nemmy's talisman. The cool silver contact felt mildly galvanic.

*Gonna flip you! Gonna flip-flip-flip you out, Jackie boy!*

(What *are* you?)

The thought slipped out of him so effortlessly. He hadn't planned a dialogue with this monster taking shape before him. If anything, it was uglier than even he had remembered it.

I *am a part of you, Jack-bo. I am a piece of the the rock—the original chaos. I am the stuff of time and matter. The stuff that's always trying to return to the primal center of things. I am the Reducer. I see order and I abhor it. Reductio ad absurdum.*

(But why me? What did you want with me?) Jack felt another one of those sudden, molten *needs* for a cigarette or a pull off the bourbon bottle.

*Don't flatter yourself. I'm just here for you. Don't you see it yet?*

Jack had seen enough, had felt enough. He understood now that his old nemesis was nothing more than an energy source, as were all the passionate events of our lives. And that the most wondrous paradox of it all was this: Mr. Flip didn't want him, didn't need him; it was the other way around.

Standing up, Jack's body seemed to fill the little bedroom. The whole house appeared to be getting smaller, as if he'd Alice-like drank from a magic phial.

As though it sensed the essential, yet unexpected truth, Mr. Flip began folding into itself, collapsing into that null-space where nightmare and trauma reside. But before it could warp back to that place, Jack made his move.

(Sorry, but I need you, old buddy . . . )

Jack reached down and grabbed for the apparition, only half-shocked to feel his hands touch something rough, hewn, something *real.* How could it be back after all this time? Jack saw it destroyed forty years ago, and yet he knew that his need had made it real again.

The wood, or whatever it was, grew hot as the skin of his fingers sang out with pain. He wanted to break loose from the thing, but it was too late. The smell of his own seared flesh was only as real as he would allow it. He knew that now. The furnace-room of his imagination, cold and slaked by success, had been fired up again. Mr. Flip was his dilithium crystal, Scotty, and he knew he was going nowhere without him.

(We're going to play this out . . . no stopping it now.)

And then he was half-running down the hall, passing through the rooms of memory, bursting free of the place and into the cool, blue arms of night. Mr. Flip along for the ride, following the fiery path of a father's cometary mission to deliver his son from terror. Jack felt an atavistic burst from the core of his . . . (soul?) *being,* a surge of true power, trunk-lined to one of nature's primal generators. As he covered the back yard in long strides, he felt more vital and full of purpose than he could ever re-member.

And Mr. Flip had stopped talking to him.

No more whiny sing-song voice carving up the darkness with its vile rhythms. No, no, no. As Jack covered the distance in the backyard with long strides, the thing writing under his grip could only manage a pitiable and plaintive moan. This monster he freighted across the plains of his childhood, what-ever it truly was, sensed its destiny, and if it was capable of fear, it was feeling it now. Jack knew now for the first time that the piece of furniture, long-gone, had only been the host to this psychic parasite, this mindworm of the soul.

Jack knew this.

(And knowledge was indeed power, wasn't it, you little piece of shit?)

He touched the talisman again.

The corner of the yard loomed in the gray half-light. Dad's old barbecue chimney had crumbled away years before, but something still waited in its place. Like a lighthouse, a beacon, the ghostly shape of the chimney remained, gaining mass and reality as Jack bore down upon it like a ship emerging from the front of a storm.

Mr. Flip began to scream. It *knew*.

It knew that this time there would be no escape from the splintering it would receive. It knew all along what Jack had only discovered—that it thrived only when Jack had finally let it back into the world. After forty years in the magic lamp of Jack's id, success and ennui had eroded the seal. The monster was out of jail. Jack listened to its scream and threw back his head to join with it—a scream of unholy harmony.

Because that's what it was, wasn't it? All those years, Jack had been singing his song and not knowing it had been a duet. When his father obliterated Mr. Flip so long ago, the little boy who stood witness had done more than merely watch. Like the warriors of Borneo, he had absorbed his enemy totally.

Jack smiled as everything fell into place.

He ran with the abandon of a ten-year-old fueled by the elation of a childhood past unstoppered and pouring down the funnel of time. Nemmy had been so right; he realized it now, as he reached up to grab her charm in his fist, to hold it tightly through this final circuit of his journey. Bounding through the yard, cutting through the night, his hand burst upward to his throat in a miscalculated motion. The thin chain ruptured, sending the silver symbol into the darkness.

For an instant, Jack felt everything locking up like a bad clutch. His hesitation leaked a message to the thing bunched under his arm and he felt it swell and pulsate like some diseased organ.

*What's-a-matter, Jack-boy? No more magic twanger, eh?*

He almost stopped right before the image of the barbecue pit, to wonder if it could really be there, to question his own beliefs and needs. Nemmy . . . that silver trinket . . .

The ediolon of his childhood twisted and blistered under his grip. It sensed that it could, after all, still be free of him. Free to mock him in his helplessness. Jack struggled to keep his psychic balance. He couldn't let it get this far just to fall on his face, to let this thing crush him. He didn't need any magic charms.

(No. Fuck all that. I've got this little bastard right where I want him.)

He could almost hear Nemmy's voice in his head, Obi Wan to his Luke: *use the Force, Jack.*

He threw back his head and laughed at the moon. (Talismans? We don't need no stinking talismans!)

He could feel the entity shrinking again under his grip. It was attuned to him, there was no doubt. It knew him and could read him with an expert rating. Jack was no longer surprised by this affirmation of his spirit. This thing had been encysted within his psyche

Running now, he swung the thing that had called itself Mr. Flip up over his head in a terrible arc, gaining speed and power as it curved down toward the ancient flagstone.

*Gonna get you, ja—*

A final, high-register wail dopplered from the thing as Jack drove it into the face of the magic chimney, the stones fashioned from his father's hands. There was an explosion of light and heat. Then everything stopped and reversed itself; the scream swallowed up in a larger implosion. The thing was yanked from this world, rattling down the rails of entropy, and the air itself snapped shut with a loud *pop!* to mark its exit, its transfiguration.

Suddenly Jack was standing alone in the corner of his old backyard.

Alone. Hands empty. No trace of the flagstone pit barbecue.

No Mr. Flip.

Not where you could see him, anyway.

Drawing a breath, he became aware of himself once again. It was as if he'd blinked his eyes to find he'd sleepwalked to the edge of an abyss and awakened just in time. A calm held him like the doldrums, but there was no panic, no desperation in it. Rather, Jack felt a new purpose that coursed through him with the fire of sour mash whiskey, lighting him up like a ballpark scoreboard.

Turning he looked up the length of the yard, traced in moonlight, to the house where everything had begun. Jack knew he could now leave its old comforts and far older fears. A cycle had been completed, a mythic transference achieved. A new beginning sparked amidst the ashes of an ending.

R. Jackson Trent rediscovered the oldest secret of all our lives; the one most of us forget. He'd invaded the sanctity of childhood's tomb, escaped with the treasures we always leave buried there.

. . . and lived to tell about it.

*The next story was written for yet another HWA anthology, entitled* Psychos *to be edited by Robert Bloch (the associational appropriateness should be obvious to all but the most numbheaded among you . . . ), but two things happened between the time I started writing it and the time I sent it in for consideration.*

*One was the internecine war that flared up within the ranks of HWA in the early Nineties. I'm not sure how it even happened, but the earliest sparks of the eventual conflagration seemed to have started on a now defunct quasi-internet/ bulletin board/chat room system on GENIE, which was an early attempt at getting Us All Connected. As I recall it, HWA had this members-only area where everybody logged on and aired out opinions, ideas, suggestions, reviews, etc. It soon became sadly apparent that a lot of the participants, who would normally (i.e. in person, face-to-face) be polite, mannered, and respectful had suddenly become arrogant, aggressive, and in some cases libelous in the things they said about other members of the organization. It was weird to see the outrageous, inflammatory words of people you* knew *were sad sacks, wimps, and chess-club geeks jittering across your screen. They had assumed they were somehow invulnerable because they launched their verbal assaults behind barricades made from the cyber-ether and keyboards.[1] The basic theme of it all was simple enough: the Old*

---

[1] *Several of them had said things about me or to me that were either untrue, rude, belligerent, or sometimes downright vicious. And when I finally caught up with them at the Stoker Awards banquet in Las Vegas and the World Fantasy Convention in Minneapolis, they suddenly reverted to type—ball-less wonders, who made fools of themselves by being* overly *friendly and attentive and polite. If I had been younger and crazier, I would have given each and every one of them a few knuckles of remonstrance. But as it was, I looked each one in the eye and told them if they had any problems with me, I was willing to listen right* now. *Nobody did.*

BETWEEN FLOORS

*Guard of writers, the ones who were present at, and participated in, the creation of the HWA had made a fine mess of things, and deserved to be excoriated, humiliated, and if possible, decimated. The assault on the seasoned veterans went on for a few months, escalating to the point of getting libelous when attacking various candidates for office.*

*Cutting to the chase, the civil war between the older writers and the young Turks became so heated that almost* all *of the professionals in HWA who actually made their livings as writers did the only rational thing remaining to them—they quit* en masse. *Practically overnight, the organization was gutted of all its "name" or even "semi-name" writers, and the inmates were running the asylum.[2] And so, yeah, I quit with them. I hadn't even thought about the story I'd submitted to Robert Bloch's* Psychos . . .

*Which brings us to the second happenstance referred to at the beginning of this introduction—Bob Bloch became terminally ill before he could actually do much of the editing on the HWA project. It was a sad chapter in the history of modern horror/suspense writing when Bloch could no longer participate in the genre he had helped create. When he died, the editing of the project fell into the hands of an individual of whom I'd never heard of, and this guy summarily rejected my story for the HWA anthology* with a form letter.

*Yeah, it pissed me off, but don't forget, I* was *one of the rats scurrying down the hawsers away from a listing, sinking scow, so it didn't piss me off all* that *much . . .*

*But all of this is a bit of a digression (don't you just love a good digression?), but a necessary one to explain where the story came from in the first place. And it eventually found a nice home as a signed, limited chapbook from Bill Schafer's Subterranean Press with a great illustration by Roger Gerberding.*

---

[2] *In the guise of people who were doing most of their writing for TV and film and video game novel-knockoffs or selling short stories to all the low-pay/ no-pay "magazines" that solicit material in a small press newsletter with the unlikely, but fairly apt, title of* Scavengers.

**"I** can't believe you're doing this," said Charles Jameson.

He stood before the massive desk of Alan Markley, CEO of MegaCorp International, feeling like a doomed gladiator facing the Emperor's dais.

"All things come to their natural ends," said Markley.

"I always tried to do a good job . . ." Jameson listened to his own voice; it was weak, ineffectual.

Alan Markley's gaze continued to be fixed on Jameson, but the CEO said nothing—his usual style. Behind his chair loomed an executive's perspective of the Manhattan skyline—always impressive from ninety stories up.

Finally: "Goodbye, Jameson. I'm sure something will turn up."

And that was it. Total dismissal. Jameson stood for a moment, perplexed, but realized he had no choice other than to exit the double-doored office. As he walked past Ms. Bremen, Markley's secretary, she didn't even look up from her make-work.

Like I wasn't even there, you bitch. That's how they treat you after you've been given the old corporate ax. Maybe someday you'll find out for yourself . . .

His thoughts jangled like loose change. Fired. Shit-canned. Bounced. It didn't matter how you phrased it. Jameson was gone. But he still couldn't believe Markley'd called him in there to get "terminated." Twenty-two years with the Corporation and now he was like a piece of fax-paper in Ms. Bremen's wastebasket.

Charles smoothed his silvering hair and adjusted his money-green power-tie as he entered the hall that bisected a series of glass-walled offices. He looked boldly from cubicle to cubicle where his former colleagues hunched at desks and consulted PC monitors.

The bastards. Everybody was giving him the leper treatment now. Can't get too close, can't even look the pariah in the eye, or you might catch the same disease.

He didn't bother to perform the ritual cleaning out of his desk. Where he was going, he wouldn't be needing any appointment books or matching pen and pencil sets. These days, when you're fifty years old and carrying a fat salary around your neck like a dead-meat rotting albatross, you're about as attractive to companies as a mugger in an alley. Jameson passed his former cubicle without a backward glance. He'd be lucky if he could get a job at Dunkin' Donuts punching holes out of their dough . . .

As he passed the bullpen area where the phone-and-copier grunts pursued their specialized routines, he almost envied them in their faceless, going-nowhere servitude. Nobody really cared enough about them to place any value on their work, and so their jobs were secure. It was only when you aspired to greatness that the Corporate Gods stuck a lightning bolt up your ass.

Ambition? Hubris? Yeah, sure, Jameson. Why don't you just bend over while we take aim here . . .

He glided past the receptionist with the wild, I-just-rolled out-of-your-bed nimbus of red hair, and she smiled at him as he approached the polished chrome doors of the elevators. She obviously hasn't been told, or there would have been no smile.

Studying himself in the reflective metal after pushing the down-arrow, Charles Jameson tried thinking about how much his life was going to change. Losing the house and the cars and the time-sharing condos in Aspen and Barcelona would crush him out, sure, but kissing off such an exotic piece of woman-flesh as Alaina would be the worst of it. A mental conjuring of her long, tanned legs and silky flanks sparked and fluttered as he thought of his wife. Naturally, Anne would remain steadfastly by his side. She was such a pathetic, sycophantic bitch . . .

No, that wasn't being fair. She certainly was no bitch—she didn't have the juice, the passion, to be that memorable or distinctive. Actually, Jameson felt sorry for her. The poor woman had bought the whole Fifties ramadoola: let your husband bust his ass, forsake any career or identity for yourself, and build your life around a gaggle of kids who are only going to desert you as soon as they stand up on their hind legs. She did, and they did; and now all that remained of Anne Jameson was a bittersweet female ravaged by menopause and the realization that she had no skills, interests, or anything to which she might personally aspire other than twenty years of solitude after widowing a corporate coronary victim.

That's if you believed the Insurance Companies actuary tables . . .

But none of it really mattered any longer. Jameson's life effectively ended back there in Alan Markley's wainscoted office.

A soft electronic *ping* interrupted his meandering thoughts and a red light indicated which of the bay doors would open next. He approached it and watched the chrome panels recede to reveal two passengers doing their best not to look at him. Entering the small chamber, he checked them out almost automatically. A messenger boy, wearing his obligatory Walkman and headphones, boogied and head-bobbed to secret tunes; and a female ladder-climber who wore the required costume of an ugly, tailored suit, foppish blouse and bogus-cravat. Looking like somebody had just crammed something cold up her narrow rear, she stood there stiffly. A real prunesicle, this one.

The doors closed and the three of them descended ten floors until Ms. Corporate Posture departed. Three floors later, in walked a skinny guy wearing a suit that looked like its hanger was still in the shoulders. He promptly turned, tilted his neck upward, and began the required watching of the illuminated floor indicator. Two more floors, and the rhythmic messenger slipped free and the doors entombed Jameson and the tall, lean guy in great need of a tailor. Jameson kept trying to retreat into the snarled web of his dark thoughts and self-pity, but there was something about his fellow traveler that kept distracting him. Even though the guy kept watching the blink of each passing floor like you're supposed to do, he seemed to be twitching and moving beneath his clothes like there were bugs crawling over him.

Weird.

After descending into the mid-sixties, there came a *thunk!* and a heavy, ratcheting sound. The floor slipped away from their feet for an instant before a keening sound pierced the space above their heads. The elevator car was screaming like a seagull trapped in the shaft, squawking to be set free. Jameson's stomach pressed up against the bottom of his ribcage as the car plummeted downward.

Jesus, we're in free-fall!

Jameson reached up and grabbed the light-fixture over their heads, hanging in mid-air as the other guy collapsed in a heap.

369

Down they rocketed through the core of the building, picking up speed. The entire car started vibrating, keening, almost singing like a tuning fork. Jameson's eardrums felt like they might pop inwards. The sound became impossibly loud, insanely loud. His fingers curled over the edge of the overhead light, felt like they were being crushed against an egg-slicer. His stomach worked its way up his throat. Much more of this and it would be in his mouth.

Then, suddenly, it was yanked back downward like it might be pulled out the other end of him. A hideous *screeching* sound filled the car. A million fingernails across a million chalkboards.

Gravity returned like a fist grabbing them, tugging them earthward with a single final surge. It had all happened in the space of a few seconds. Jameson's grip on the over-head fixture was pulled free, almost slicing off the top digits and he fell to the carpet. He steadied himself, attempting to stand only when he was certain the car had stopped moving downward. Silence covered them like an oil-soaked rag, heavy, thick.

Almost instantly, a sensation of being sealed in, trapped, slapped him like an angry woman. Charles used his Dale Carnegie training to push the fear off the edge of his senses. No place for panic now.

"My God," said Baggy Suit as he jittered to his feet. "What was *that?*"

"I don't know," said Jameson. "Sounds like the emergency brakes locked in. We might have lost our cable."

"You're kidding! . . . where are we!?"

Several numbers on the indicator strip blinked. "If you want to figure from that, it looks like we're between the 39th and the 40th floors . . ."

"I don't know if I can handle this," said the tall, thin man. His hair was matted to his skull with some sort of gel. It shined like a cheap plastic helmet. He wore thick glasses which magnified his eyes when he looked straight on.

Jameson grinned sardonically. "I don't think you've got a hell of a lot of choice." Speaking of panic, this guy looked like he'd been first in line when they were handing it out.

"You don't understand," said the man. "I've *got* to get out of here!"

Jameson could hear the tension rising in the man's voice. Great. Just what he needed—spend a couple hours with a claustrophobic yahoo . . .

"Calm down, I'll call Security and see what's going on." Jameson smiled as he opened the glass door to a phone. He keyed in the security code and waited for moment.

"Security . . . this is Williams . . ."

Jameson quickly recounted his and his companion's situation.

*"We already got you covered, Mr. Jameson. The big computer board's got you lit up and we've sent an emergency crew on the way to get you out of there."*

"And how long might that be?" asked Charles.

*"Oh, an hour tops, they told us . . ."*

Only an hour, thought Charles. Apparently Security had not yet been told of the falling ax either.

"It sounded like we lost our cable . . . is that right?"

*"I think so . . . but don't worry, sir. The Building Engineer sez them emergency brakes'll hold you up there forever. Sez they work on gravity or somethin'."*

"All right, then . . . thank you, Williams."

Charles hung up the red phone, looked at Baggy Suit, who was staring at him anxiously.

"Well, what'd they say!? What's going on? They gettin' us outta here . . . or *what*?!"

Charles explained the situation as succinctly as possible.

"An hour!" The man grabbed at his lapels, pressed his hands against his chest. It was an odd nervous gesture. "Goddamn better not be that long!" The man's eyes were round and bug-like behind his lenses.

"I'm afraid we don't have much to say about it," said Charles. Again he felt the dank feeling of utter confinement pass over him. He shrugged it away.

The man allowed himself to slide down the wall of the car, settling on the rug in an ungainly position in the corner. "Looks like we may as well get comfortable," he said.

Suddenly, standing seemed inappropriate, and Charles felt the urge to join his companion on the carpeted floor. He tugged at his Armani suit trousers so the knees wouldn't bag, and eased himself down, edging into the corner opposite the stranger.

They sat staring at one another for a minute or so. Charles studied the guy more intently. He appeared to be maybe forty-five, but he could have been a harried, stressed-out thirty-five. He never stopped fidgeting with his hands, and was always wriggling in his clothes like he was wearing a hair-shirt. The man's gaze turreted from the floor number display to the red phone to Charles Jameson. A timed cycle of movements: numbers, phone, Jameson; numbers, phone, Jameson . . .

The guy probably wasn't wrapped real tight. His jittery demeanor gave him a distinctly paranoid aspect. Charles decided he didn't like the fellow even a little bit.

The silence between them grew more prolonged, hanging in the air like a foul odor. The guy continued his metronomic gaze-shifting. It had become unnerving, and was starting to piss Charles off. But then, maybe that wasn't such a good idea— getting angry with an odd duck like Mr. Baggy Suit here. It occurred to him for the first time that maybe, just *maybe* being trapped with a character who *might* be a little unhinged wasn't such a great idea. If Charles hadn't been so pre-occupied with his own personal tragedy, he might have been thinking more clearly about any potential problems of a more immediate nature.

The guy in the opposite corner was getting more animated by the minute. Sweat had popped out all over him like dew. He looked like a pressure cooker waiting to blow. Charles cleared his throat and spoke to him, "If we're going to be here for awhile, I guess we should get to know each other . . . My name's Jameson. Charles Jameson. What's yours?"

In truth, Charles had no desire to know the creep in the corner, but felt any distraction from the man's current state of high anxiety was safer.

The man looked at him, swallowed with great effort. His eyes grew wide and glassy. "Hello, Mr. Charles Jameson. My name is Doctor Doom."

Great. I'm trapped in an elevator with some donut who calls himself 'Doctor Doom' . . . Yes, Charles, you're having a special day, all right.

"Doom?" asked Charles as nonchalantly as possible. "Is that with two o's?"

"Yes, I suppose it is." The good doctor looked at him with an expression that could only be described as suspicious. "Nobody's ever asked me how to spell it before."

"Well, it's an unusual name, you must admit."

"It's getting hot in here," Doom said, as though to himself.

"I hadn't noticed," said Charles.

"You wouldn't by any chance be employed by MegaCorp, would you, Mr. Jameson?"

Charles managed a thin, ironic smile. "No, not any longer . . ."

The donut's gaze became more focused, a tic in the corner of his mouth intensified. "But you *were* part of that international gang of pirates!?"

"That's an interesting description of the company . . . but yes, that's correct, I was a 'part'."

The man opened his mouth to say something but was interrupted by a strange sound—a clanging concussion that reverberated through the elevator shaft.

"What was that!" he almost screamed.

"Probably the rescue crew," said Charles.

"How much longer!?" The man was actually screaming now.

"Hey, take it easy . . . they said everything would be fine."

The man laughed, half-rolling his eyes. He looked like Jack Nicholson chewing the scenery in Kubrick's *The Shining*. "Of course they think it's going to be fine! They don't know they're dealing with Doctor Doom!"

Suddenly the space between Charles and the stranger seemed far too small, too confining. For the first time, a sense of claustrophobia raged over him. Could he *fear* this thin weasel of a man?

Yes, he could.

Standing up, Charles, pretended to smooth out his clothing. He figured he was better prepared for any problems if he wasn't balled up in a corner. He noticed the man watching him intently.

"How do I know you're not one of them?" said Doom.

"One of *who?*"

"The MegaCorp agents. They're everywhere, you know."

"Trust me. I'm not. I just got fired."

"That's right! I was asking you what part you played in MegaCorp's Grand Scheme . . ." Doom's expression was so pinched, so perfectly aimed at Charles, he answered reflexively.

"I was a vice-president . . . in charge of Environmental Affairs."

"Did you say *'environment'!*"

"Well, almost . . ." Charles tensed, knowing he'd pushed one of this walnut's hot-buttons. He watched as the man scrambled to his feet, his hands fisting and unfisting nervously.

"That's why I'm here!" the man cried.

Above them, there was more clanging and banging, but this time, it was ignored.

"How serendipitous," said Charles. He watched the word cause momentary confusion in the man called Doom.

"I am here to save the world from the ravages of men like you!" said Doom. Placing his hands to his white shirt, he ripped it open to reveal what first appeared to be a flak vest under his clothing. No wonder his suit had been such a bad fit . . .

"What the hell are you doing?" Charles tried to back away, but there was no place to go. There were more loud noises above their car. The muffled voices of rescue workers echoed through the metallic ceiling.

"Did you think you could go on raping the Earth forever!" Doom laughed, even adding a little melodrama by throwing back his head. "No! Not after today!"

"What did you have in mind, Doctor?" Charles knew it would be best to keep the guy talking. The more he looked at the vest and the spidery network of wires and circuit boards, he knew he was looking at some kind of explosive device.

"I have enough C-4 on me to take off the top of this building . . ." Doom grinned. His teeth were tiny, perfectly even, and seemingly all the same size. " . . . and that's exactly what I'm going to do IF I EVER GET OUT OF HERE!"

"Calm down!" said Charles sharply as an idea slowly came to him.

Doctor Doom looked startled, caught up short by Charles' sudden show of authority. "What?"

"Why do you think I was fired, you fool?" said Charles. "I wanted to stop the de-forestation of the Amazon rainforest; I wanted to stop the Colorado strip-mining and the nuclear waste dumps . . ."

Doom considered this. Then: "How do I know you're not lying?"

Footsteps clumped on the roof above their heads. The red phone rang explosively and both men jumped back from it.

"There's no *time!*" cried Charles. "You've got to trust me . . ."

Without waiting for a response, Charles answered the emergency line.

*"This is Williams, Mr. Jameson. Engineering just ten-foured us . . . they say they'll have you outta there in another minute, okay?"*

"I'm afraid there's a problem," said Charles. "I'm being held hostage . . ." He looked at Doctor Doom, who appeared genuinely surprised.

*"What's that, Mr. Jameson?"*

"You heard me right, now listen closely . . ."

When the rescue team got a look at Doom's wardrobe by Dow Chemical, they became *very* cooperative, escorting the good doctor and Charles Jameson up the fire stairwell all the way up to the Executive Penthouse where Alan Markley, CEO, has agreed to meet with the mad environmentalist to "discuss the issues." The obligatory SWAT teams, fire fighters, and support personnel had all taken up their positions on station below the Penthouse level on the top floor of the MegaCorp Tower.

*That's it, Mr. Markley,* squawked the speakerphone on the CEO's desk. *Everybody's been evacuated from the floor.*

"Very well," said Alan Markley. "I will call you as soon as my negotiations with Doctor Doom have progressed."

The corporate demagogue keyed out the phone with a diffident air. Charles had to hand it to the old man—he was handling things very well. Even the way he referred to the mad bomber sitting in his leather desk chair as though he were a visiting dignitary. Markley adjusted his tie, and looked coolly into the eyes of his adversary behind the desk. Beyond them, corded drapes framed a glass walled view of the Mid-Town sprawl ninety stories below. Charles stood off to the side, watching the proceedings, waiting for . . . for exactly *what* he was not yet certain.

"How do we know you're not bluffing, sir?" said Markley.

"I left a small piece of plastique in the elevator car for the good old 'authorities' to analyze," said Doom. "Why else do you think everybody's being so nice to me."

Markley nodded, but said nothing.

"So, let's talk about a few things, Mr. Markley, shall we?"

Doom looked more calm, more in control now, but his resemblance to a weasel or a ferret was stronger than ever. The vest-bomb with its wire-harness accents looked decidedly real, and the only way Charles was dealing with the idea that he could be vaporized in an instant was to utilize his Executive Awareness Acuity Training. He was finally grateful for those company-sponsored rah-rah retreats in the Adirondacks with motivational gurus.

"Go on," said Markley.

"For starters," said Doom as he pulled a handgrip from his pocket attached to a thick wire. It looked as if it had been fashioned from the handle of a joystick on a computer game. "I want you to get on the phone and stop the Brazilian operations immediately."

"What!? That's impossible!!" Markley's voice jumped up the decibel range. "I . . . can't! I won't!"

Holding up the handgrip, Doom displayed a little red button. "You don't want me to push this . . ."

Markley sneered. "You don't have the *balls* . . ."

Doom jumped up from the huge, throne-like chair, rushed at Markley and thrust the detonator to within inches of the CEO's face.

"No!" screamed Charles. "Not yet!"

Both Doom and Markley looked at him sharply.

"You haven't gotten what you want," said Charles. "You won't solve anything by doing it now."

"You're right," said Doom, lowering the detonator, but keeping it firmly in his grasp. "But don't worry—even when I push this in, we've still got sixty seconds before it goes off. No way to reverse it after that. More dramatic that way, don't you think?"

"Definitely a nice touch," said Charles. He paused to breathe deeply, then to his former boss: "Go on, Alan, make that call. This guy's serious as cancer . . ."

An hour later, after several exchanges with the SWAT Commander and the FBI goons, plus phone calls throughout the global satellite net, Doctor Doom had managed to halt the Amazonian deforestation, shut down MegaCorp's worldwide plutonium plants, stop all their strip-mining, save the whales, dolphins, and baby seals, and, just as an added treat, ensured free healthcare for the homeless. Doom acknowledged this last item was not really an environmental issue, but it was a deserving liberal cause nonetheless.

Pleased with himself, Doom had returned to the warmth and comfort of Markley's throne. He looked at Charles and smiled his tiny-toothed smile. "Well, Charles, I think we've done it."

Markley looked at his former VP with loathing. "You piece of shit!" he screamed. "You're really in on this, aren't you, Charles?!"

Jameson laughed. "You give me more credit than I deserve, Alan. But I have to tell you—it couldn't have happened to a nicer company and a nicer bunch of corporate assholes."

"You'll pay for this, Jameson!"

Charles laughed. "I have no connection with the Good Doctor here. Any good attorney would have no problem establishing an airtight defense. What are they going to convict me of?—disagreeing with my boss?"

Markley's face had become florid and his composure was falling away in great talus-laden chunks. A large vein in his forehead pulsed like an invertebrate beneath his flesh. The man's blood pressure red-lined as his hands shook in frustration and rage.

Doom chuckled. "This is good. I hadn't expected entertainment along with my adventure. You know, I'd really like to stay, but as they say, I've got a plane to catch—a helicopter, actually . . ."

"Shut up, you little . . . you little do-gooding *nerd!* Do you really think they're going to let you just fly out of here?!"

"What do you mean?" It was obvious Doom had never considered any alternative.

"They'll blow you out of the sky!" bellowed Markley.

"Not if you take him with you," said Charles.

Doctor Doom's confused expression brightened into one of instant gratification. "Yes! Yes, of course!"

"You *bastard!*" shouted Markley. The CEO stood opposite the desk literally convulsing like an amok wind-up toy, about to shake itself to pieces

"Call the hotline," said Doom. "Tell them to bring that chopper to the roof now."

Charles keyed in the number to the SWAT commander while Markley unleashed a hot jet of profanity on both of them.

"Are they coming?" asked Doom.

Charles nodded, hung up the receiver.

"I'll *never* go with you sons-of-bitches! You can't make me! They'll pick you off like a bird on a wire as soon as you set foot on the roof!"

Doom seemed to consider this—again it was something he'd not thought about too deeply. He looked at Charles as a bumbling monarch might seek out a crafty advisor.

"Not if you tie him to *you* . . ."

"Jameson! You fucking . . . you fucking *turncoat*! What're you doing!?"

"Brilliant, Charles!" said Doom. "But how can we manage it?" Muffled by the glass wall, the subsonic *thoomp-thump* of the approaching helicopter punctuated their words.

Charles moved quickly to the floor-to-ceiling glass wall. In a single motion he grabbed the draperies and pulled everything down. Pulling the heavy brocaded tie-back cord from the mess, he held it up triumphantly.

Doom applauded and smiled. "Excellent, Mr. Jameson. You have a fine mind for this sort of thing."

The bomber stood up and approached Charles. "Attach one end around my waist, if you would."

Charles nodded, carefully affixed the cord in a double half-hitch of which any yachtsman would be proud. He turned to regard Alan Markley who was so flushed with anger, he looked like he'd fallen from a lobster pot. "Sir, if you would please step forward . . ." Charles said with his most deferential smile.

Markley was fairly well *seething* now. He tried to speak but he'd lost that ability as it was subsumed into the atavistic magma of his rage. He sputtered and gagged on his words as he lunged over the edge of the desk, his clawed hands reaching for Jameson's face.

But despite the years of racquetball and Nautilus, Alan Markley missed his target. Charles had spun away in a move learned long-ago on the football fields of Princeton, and watched his former boss impact with Doctor Doom in the high-backed executive throne.

Everything happened so quickly, it would be difficult to reconstruct the sequence of events for the police, but it went something like this: Markley's momentum propelled himself, Doom, and the huge chair backward on its well-oiled casters; like a runaway boxcar, the rolling mass shattered the glass curtainwall and slipped off the leading edge of the skyscraper; the cord in Charles' hands snapped like a bowstring suddenly taut, almost pulling him out into space, but his grip hadn't been strong enough. He stood for an instant, stunned, trying to assess what had happened, what was still going on. One end of the thick cord remained tangled in the mess of fabric still attached to the metal frame and motorized drapery track; the other held fast around Doom's waist.

Walking cautiously near the wind-swept maw of the shattered curtainwall, Charles looked over the edge to see Doctor Doom dangling like a broken pendulum ten feet below. And hanging onto the twisting rope like a wharf rat was Alan Markley, an expression of exquisite terror etched into his face. Beneath them the side of the building sloped away to a vanishing point. Vertigo reached for him, and Charles leaned back, steadying himself.

"Jameson!" cried the CEO. "Pull us up for God's sake!"

"No!"screamed Doom, trying to hold the detonator high to be seen. "Let him go, or I'll blow us all to hell!"

Charles grinned as he watched the two men struggle at the end of the wind-whipped tether. Markley had wrapped his arms around the cord and his legs around one of Doom's. The bomber had extended his detonator arm as far from the CEO as possible while using his free hand to stiff-arm Markley in the face. Time slowed and stretched as the two men twisted in the air-currents that criss-crossed the building.

As if viewing the action through a long lens, Charles focused on Doom's thumb as it depressed the detonator.

"Sorry, Jameson!" yelled the  madman. "No choice, really!"

"Christ almighty, Charles!" Markley's voice sound puny and small in the wind. "Do something!"

"Oh, I will, Mr. Markley," Charles said loudly as he stepped back from the edge. Making sure he was free of the debris, Charles pulled downward on the bowstring cord still anchored to the drapery track. His effort, combined with the weight of the two struggling men, was enough to break it loose.

It sagged downward with a sickening lurch, and he heard Markley scream. Then the cord snagged for an instant, jerking the dangling men like bungee-jumpers.

How much time? thought Charles. How long is a fucking minute?

"Jameson, no!" Markley wailed above the wind like a banshee.

Charles grabbed the cord, gave it the final tug it needed, then stepped back as the drapery rig rattled off the wall and over the edge.

If either of the men screamed, he could not hear them in the vortices of wind corkscrewing around the building. Tracking their descent, he estimated they'd plummeted more than halfway down before the plastique turned them into a miniature nova. Not enough to blow off the top of the building, as Doctor Doom had hoped, but more than adequate to light up the ennui of even the most jaded New York rubber-necks.

There is a company called Tekno-Books that is what you would call a publishing juggernaut. It rolls and clanks across the landscape like one of Wells "land leviathans" and it blows away all the competition when it comes to producing that great patron and benefactor of the short story— the anthology. Tekno-Books is headed up by a dynamic, hard-working guy, Marty Greenberg, who has discovered the secret of talking publishers into doing anthologies on just about anything you can think of. I have no idea how many anthologies Marty has created, but I am sure the number could be several hundred by this time. Many of his anthologies have been critically acclaimed and produced tons of award-nominated material.

As Darth Vader once said: "Impressive . . ."

But the best part is that Marty is a very nice guy. I met him more than twenty-five years ago at a Nebula Banquet when we were both rookies, and we've been friends ever since. Every once in a while he, or one of his minions, will send me a letter wanting to reprint one of my stories or ask me to contribute something new for one of his projects. No matter how busy I am, I always try to come up with something because Marty Greenberg is truly one of the good guys.

Now, concerning the story which follows, it was written for an anthology called The Conspiracy Files (an obvious ploy to capitalize on the at-the-time fascination with TV's X-Files) edited by Scott Urban. Now, I have to admit this one had special appeal to me because I am one of those guys who wants to believe Oswald probably wasn't even the shooter, that FDR was the architect behind Pearl Harbor, and well . . . you can dig it.

I like conspiracy theories, and I liked the challenge of coming up with a story for this project.

A MIND IS A TERRIBLE THING

*The format of the story is again one I have used on occasion because it forces me to play an extra level in the writing game— create a series of inter-related pieces, and let the reader assemble them so a larger story gradually becomes clear. I also wanted to come up with a conspiracy that wasn't a riff on any of the obvious or topical ones, so that forced me to stretch as well. I figure: if I'm going to dial up the energy to create a short story in the first place, I'm going to challenge myself and try to be as original as possible.*

*And so, the story that follows is part investigation, part indictment, part revelation as to why we have people running around with diplomas in their paws who cannot tell you what a decimal might be, locate Pakistan on a map, or identify the combatants of the Spanish-American War.*

*What do you think?*

**The Baltimore Sun (AP)** It was reported by Lieutenant Detective Patrick Monaghan of the Homicide Division of the BCPD yesterday that the bomb blast at Saint Andrews High School in East Baltimore is now believed to be the work of what Monaghan termed "professional assassins." He said this after a preliminary investigation into the explosion which killed Brother Ignatius Sanborn, the principal of the non-sectarian independent school. "There are additional facts and some extenuating circumstances surrounding his death that are, at the very least, kind of strange," said Monaghan. "We aren't ready to divulge all the details yet, but I can tell you this—something stinks."

From the PDX transcripts, 32nd Precinct, BCPD:
Call initiated 5:42:03 p.m.

MONAGHAN: This is Monaghan . . .

CALLER: Lieutenant, this is Special Agent Fred O'Brien, FBI . . . I was wondering if I could have a few words with you . . .

MONAGHAN: Sure, Fred . . . what can I do for you?

CALLER: The Sanborn case you're working on . . . my office is going to be taking it over.

MONAGHAN: You're kidding! You mean I was right?

CALLER: About what?

MONAGHAN: Professional job. That's what I figured . . . especially after I saw the bomb-squad reports. So the Feds are going to be working with us from here on out, eh? Sounds like—

CALLER: Not exactly. I said we'll be taking it over. *Alone*. You local boys are off.
MONAGHAN: . . . hey, wait a minute! That's not how it usually works around here. What happened to the team-concept?
CALLER: Not on this one. Sorry. Can't tell you anything else. Classified up to its ass.
MONAGHAN: Yeah, well it might be just that, but I'm going to need more authorization than a phone call from some guy I've never met. Why aren't we going through channels here, Fred? Does my Captain know about this yet?
CALLER: Just you. I thought I would pay you the courtesy of telling you first . . . instead of getting all bent out of shape after you see the inter-office memo.
MONAGHAN: Yeah, I see. Pretty damned thoughtful of you, Fred. And you know what—? Just to show you how much I appreciate you being such a right guy, I wanna buy you some lunch when you stop by the Precinct House. How's that sound?
CALLER: I wasn't planning on being there.
MONAGHAN: Well, let me tell you something, Special Agent Fred O'Brien—you'd better plan on it. Tomorrow morning.
CALLER: I think I should tell you, Detective . . . you've got the wrong attitude on this one. I'm trying to tell you as discreetly as possible: leave this one alone.
MONAGHAN: You know, you federal guys make me wanna puke, you know that? You think a fucking phone call just when I'm ready to pack it in for the night is going to make me back off my investigation? Just because you say so? Because it's got federal jurisdiction?
CALLER: Detective . . .
MONAGHAN: —well, that's bullshit, Mr. O'Brien, or whoever you are! You can come into the precinct and we can talk about this face-to-face or we don't talk about it at all.
Call terminated 5:44:16 p.m.

─────────────────────────

Claudius Cheever
Private Investigations Unlimited
1209 University Parkway
Baltimore MD 21210

Dear Mr. Cheever:

    I am writing to you because I don't trust the telephones anymore—at least when I'm talking about my brother, Ignatius

Sanborn. You probably remember what happened to him from the news stories and the TV stuff. The bomb that blew up Saint Andrews killed my brother and now I was just told by the cops that they've been ordered to drop the case because the FBI said it has something to do with National Security.

Mr. Cheever, this is ridiculous. I have discovered that people saying they are "government agents" have been talking to my friends and family, and anybody else that ever knew Ignatius. From all I can tell, they haven't been asking questions about him to help him in anyway. Instead, it looks to me like they were trying to dig up some kind of awful dirt on him. They even tracked down people who'd been his first students when he was teaching Catholic grade school, right out of the seminary more than 25 years ago. And they asked them point blank if Ignatius had ever molested them sexually. Can you imagine?!

Thank God, my brother was like a saint, Mr. Cheever. He never did anything to ever hurt anybody. He was a good man, a god-fearing and god-loving man. All he ever wanted to do was help people. The job he did at Saint Andrews certainly proved that. And those government people didn't ever find a thing they could use to make Ignatius look bad—and that's exactly what I think they were trying to do.

Anyway, when I complained to my congressman, I didn't hear anything more on it, and when I tried to call the City Police Officer who was originally working on my brother's murder (I've enclosed a newspaper clipping), they told me Lieutenant Monaghan was killed last week in a shoot-out "by an unknown assailant." Nobody seems to want to tell me much of anything. But I want some answers.

Anyway, I have a little money from my brother's life insurance policy and I think I'd feel best spending it on a way to find out who killed him and why.

If you are willing to take this case, please write me as soon as possible at the address on the top of this page. I will come into the city to meet with you and get you all settled up. Thank you in advance.

Sincerely,
Cecilia Sanborn Mattheson

THE ARCHDIOCESE OF BALTIMORE
MEMORANDUM

To: Brother Ignatius Sanborn
From: Joseph Cardinal Sheehy

It is my sad duty to inform you that the Archdiocese can no longer subsidize the operating expenses at Saint Andrews. Diminishing funds and rising costs are a familiar refrain, and we can only afford to operate secondary schools that have sufficient enrollments to ensure a stable tuition-base. The neighborhood surrounding Saint Andrews High School has been on the slippery slope for quite a few years now, and the time we all feared when it might take the school with it has finally arrived.

I would, however, like to take this opportunity to commend you on your excellent record of academic achievement in the face of continuing adversity. As Principal of Saint Andrews, you should feel very proud of all you have accomplished.

You will eventually be receiving a new assignment from the Xaverian Office, but I trust you will require some time to tie up any loose ends at "Saint A's."

<u>Good luck and may God bless</u> you.


From *The Catholic Review*

**Parochial High School Now Independent**
Despite a joint-decision by the Archdiocese and the Order of Saint Francis Xavier to close Saint Andrews High School at the end of last year's Spring Semester, the 128 year-old secondary school continues to operate as a non-sectarian "independent" school. Spurred on by a valiant fund-raising effort by Principal Brother Ignatius, and a task-force of con-

cerned parents, Saint Andrews High will remain open, serving as a beacon of stability and enlightenment to an embattled community trying to fight back against the onslaught of drug-traffic, violent street crime, and unrelenting poverty. Saint Andrews will keep its venerable name, despite having no religious affiliation. Current plans do not include any possibility of subsuming the school into the city's public school system, although one should not rule out Federal funding.

*from the scrap book of Ignatius Sanborn:*

National Education Association Mid-Atlantic Regional Stat Sheet, page 16

|  | Saint Andrews High School (Ind.) | Nat. Avg. (Public) |
| --- | --- | --- |
| % Sr. Graduates from Fr. Year | 91% | 69% |
| % Graduates Attending College | 86% | 46% |
| % of SAT scores above 1000 | 81% | 52% |

*You have reached the Principal's Office of Saint Andrews High School. I'm sorry I cannot take your call at the moment, but if you leave your name, number, and a brief message after the beep, I will call you back as soon as possible . . . BEEP!*

Hello, Brother Ignatius, my name is Alec Cristopolis and I'm with the U. S. Department of Education. I would like to set up an appointment to stop by and talk to you about an exciting new Federal Program that your school might be eligible for. Please call me at 202-555-0989, extension 086.

Ms. Cecilia Sanborn Matheson
8310 Winter Walk Lane
Pittsfield MA 01203

Cecilia:

In keeping with your request to not use telephones, I'm sending you this short note to keep you up on what I have discovered so far.

Which is not much, I'm afraid. However, I think you'll agree that what I am NOT finding is telling us maybe as much as anything I could find. Let me explain:

1. All BCPD records of the Saint Andrews bombing have been "removed" from their files. No one seems to know how or why this could have happened.

2. The shooting death of Lieutenant Patrick Monaghan has not been investigated by any metropolitan homicide or internal affairs divisions. It was turned over to Federal authorities, on the Feds' request, but there was no evidence to indicate Federal jurisdiction.

3. Your brother's apartment on Cross Street had been completely "sanitized" within several hours of his death. That means someone had thoroughly and methodically searched and seized anything and everything your brother owned that might be informative. From what I can learn, there was not a single scrap of paper, computer disk, or record of any kind in his living quarters. This is almost impossible. People always keep things—receipts, notebooks, calendars, etc.

4. I am convinced that your brother was indeed killed for reasons we cannot yet fathom. It most likely involves local or Federal authorities.

It is possible he was a criminal, but highly unlikely. Impossible, actually. And you know, the more I investigate this case, and the more I learn about Ignatius, the more I realize it's my loss for never knowing him. People like your brother are rare and special and I wish he'd been a friend of mine.

Anyway, my guess is he stumbled into something he wasn't supposed to . . . and somebody didn't like it much.

Cecilia, this is very important. Do you have anything that belonged to Ignatius? Any correspondence, keepsakes, safe deposit keys, or anything you can think of that he may have given you that would lead us in the direction of additional information?

Please spend a little time thinking about this, because it may be the only lead we will have left to follow. Because I have to be honest with you—I am running into brick walls everywhere I turn.

I await your next letter with great interest. In the meantime, I will make every attempt to find out what really happened to your brother.

Sincerely,
Claud Cheever

---

*In a stack of things to be shredded:*

Inter-Office Memo
Department of Education
Washington, DC

From: E. D. Frost
To: A. Cristopolis

Just saw your report on the I. Sanborn case.

Imperative that he get with the Program. You're authorized to do whatever it takes.

---

Dear Claud:

After reading your last letter, I must confess to spending a little time being all teary-eyed. Despair is like a disease and you have to fight it off. I could not shake the feeling that we are stopped good and final, but I tried to be strong. I prayed to God and the Saints and I tried to put everything distressing out of my mind.

My trust in the divine was just what I needed because I began to think more clearly and looking into my memory was like looking through new glass.  One of the things that could be important was a man named Thaddeus Bowen. My brother mentioned this man several times over the last three years or so, saying that Mr. Bowen had told him things nobody would ever believe, but that someday, the whole country would understand. I confess I never asked Ignatius what he was talking about, and I never met Mr. Bowen myself, but I just recalled his name and thought you might want to talk to him yourself.

Another thing I had either forgotten about or maybe just never thought was important till now is something my brother told me last Christmas. He was sitting at the dinner table after the family had finished clearing it. And it was just me and him sitting there with our coffee. He said: "If you ever have any questions you can't get answered, you can always go to Theresa for the key."

It was one of those funny things people say that you really don't understand, but you're afraid to say so . . . do you know what I mean? I can remember Ignatius looking at me with a very solemn expression, and I was embarrassed to tell him I had no idea what he was talking about. So I nodded my head slowly, and with great seriousness. The moment passed and we were distracted by this or that, and it never came up again.

Theresa was the name of our sister. She died when we were both teenagers and she was just eleven years-old. Ignatius had loved her so much, and he'd been very affected by her passing. He never forgot Theresa and I guess I imagined he meant that no matter what kind of trouble we ever found ourselves in, that maybe Theresa would be there to watch over us, to help us.

But thinking about it now, what with the confusion and how we do have questions we can't get answered, maybe there was some other meaning?

Do you have any suggestions how we might be able to make sense of this?  Or do you think it doesn't mean anything at all?

Please get in touch as soon as you can. I will be happy to do anything I can.

Sincerely,
Cecilia

*from the notebook of Claudius Cheever:*

Thaddeus Bowen.
black male. divorced.
employed by National Teachers Union for 21 years
killed by a hit-and-run driver

To: IClaudius@USOL.com
From: TSkunk@UVMChamplain.edu
Subject: USEPGP
cc: not a damn soul

Hey old buddy:

If you're reading this, you remembered your own key-code and that's the way it's gotta be. Anyway, the hackwork you wanted was a piece of cake. Ignatius Sanborn was a BIG internet user. Found his cookie crumbs on the Archdiocese of Baltimore servers, and was able to follow the trail all the way to his mailbox and a digital safe-deposit box.
That's the good news.
Bad news: somebody had been there before me. They cleaned out his mailbox. Whatever was in there's been scarfed up.
More good news: The SDBox was a different story. Ignatius used PGP and as you know there's no way in hell anybody cracks that w/o the key-code.
If you have the key, access to the ISP is 410-555-1330 and Sanborn's password was XAVIER.
Good luck. Next time in the Big B. You owe me dinner at Tio Pepe's for this one.

yr buddy,
The Skunk

Dear Cecilia:

Enclosed you will find print-outs of some of the documents written by your brother. I cannot tell you how I found them, but you should rest easy knowing I couldn't have done it without you, your excellent memory, and your sister, Theresa. After you read them, I would suggest hiding them in the safest place you can imagine, or maybe even just burning them. I don't know anymore what is wise and what is foolish—after getting even an inkling of the kind of forces we are all up against.

Although I cannot verify anything, I must concur with your belief that Ignatius was murdered. His involvement with Thaddeus Bowen appears to have been one of the factors which led to his death. Mr. Bowen, as you will see from the documents, was something of a hero in my eyes, and as such, was the kind of person your brother would champion.

Ironically, it seems as if Ignatius's relationship with Bowen would have been a safe one if not for an accidental meeting with Alec Cristopolis. But you will see what I mean by that after you've looked over your brother's notes. It's pretty much all there.

There really isn't much more I can do for you in any official capacity. You have been more than generous in my compensation, and to be honest, no more is necessary. There is only one final matter to be considered and dealt with—what to do about what we have learned.

Going public with any of this may be very injurious to our health, but I don't see much choice (at least for myself). Getting to know your brother, even in the displaced manner forced upon me, has frankly inspired me to be a better person. Me, I'm all by myself. No family and few real friends. I don't have all that much to lose. You have kids to raise and lots of responsibilities, so if you want to just throw all this stuff in the woodstove, I will more than understand.

I look forward to your next note. Stay well and try to feel good about what was going on in your brother's life when he died. After you read the batch of papers behind this letter, you will at least know he believed he was doing the right thing.

Take care of yourself and your children.

It's the children that we should all be concerned about.

Sincerely,
Claud

*excerpted from the notes of Ignatius Sanborn:*

. . . but none of what Bowen tells me is all that surprising when I consider the historical record. The information is all there. In the libraries, the databases, the annual reports. So boldly placed before our eyes, and no one bothers to read what it is really saying. Not even a question of reading *between* the lines—no one is even reading the lines themselves.

. . . From what I can see in the enclosed documents, it appears to have begun in 1913 when two other significant events took place: the creation of the Federal Reserve Corporation and what has become known as the Income Tax on individuals.

Something happened in America that year that has been eroding the very foundation of what had been the most creative, inventive, industrious dynamo in the history of civilization. A place where the common man was not only allowed to dream, but also *achieve.*

No constraints. Not one.

And that scared some people.

Some very important, very influential, and very wealthy people.

. . . and it was clear that something had to be done before there were no such things as *privilege, breeding, or aristocracy.*

Bowen said something that stays with me, haunting my thoughts endlessly. "The ideas upon which this country had been established were clearly working *too well.*" Even without civil rights for blacks and women, the country was still becoming a juggernaut of outrageous *freedom of thinking* that would eventually destroy even the *idea* of a ruling class.

. . . and that was, ultimately, unthinkable in itself.

And so, as the banks and the bureaucrats began the quiet and seemingly benign assault on the privacy of the "common" man, so did the super-elite band of academics begin to employ their new methodologies in the classrooms of America.

. . . it *is* somewhat unclear how things changed so deliriously and so quickly, but there is no doubt that they did. What had been the model of public education for the entire civilized world has been gradually dismantled and replaced by a system riddled with disinformation, distraction, politicized claptrap, and endless new and deadly theories.

The goal of self-esteem has replaced that of knowledge, and it has been accomplished with a purpose so grim and relentless that its phosphorescent slimy trail can be traced back four generations.

I knew we were in the grip of a deadly malaise when a President could proudly proclaim to an audience of a quarter billion people that our country needs millions of "volunteers" to teach our children to read by the *third grade* . . . and elicited thundering applause at such a pitiful notion.

No shame. No conscience.

. . . The educational establishment seems proud of its failures . . . because it has been allowed to do so. And yet I was so hard in accepting it, not believing such a great piece of machinery could ever be set in motion and kept so, grinding ever more exceedingly small, the hopes and dreams of those not privileged. But people like Bowen have traveled deep into the bowels of the Great Machine, and they have come back white with terror.

. . . until we cannot recognize ourselves. The supreme irony is the subtle manner in which all the perversity has been engineered and presented to us. The corruption and the evil that has lurked behind the mask of humanitarianism and the lofty ideals of the political left have never been glimpsed by any of us. And who could ever suspect something so pernicious, so conceived in darkness.

"Operation DumbDown."

That's what the super-elite call the century-long program that is fast-taking us into a new dark age . . . where our graduates cannot point out continents on a globe, cannot read their own names, cannot make change from a dollar bill. The mysteries of the world await, ready to devour them like mindless plankton in the sea.

Of all the evil in the world, this is the worst I can imagine.

A plot so vile that it thinks to poison our future to protect the greed of its present.

Unthinkable.

. . . but isn't that the point?

> **The  Baltimore Sun (AP)** Police are baffled by the violent nature of the attack in the Roland Park home of Private Investigator Claudius Cheever. "It's possible it was a gangland 'hit'," said a spokesperson from the Baltimore City Medical Examiner's Office. Information was later disclosed confirming the death of Mr. Cheever by electrocution, but only after sustaining many hours of torture normally associated with very intense interrogation. "When you consider the victim's business, there's no way to tell what he may have been involved in," said an officer who wished to remain nameless. "I have a feeling we're being kept in the dark on this one . . ."

*The first time I saw the art of Alan Clark, I knew I was looking at the work of a very special imagination. I can't remember at which convention I met Alan, but hey, it's been more than ten years, I know that; and I liked him as much as his paintings immediately. His work is distinctive because of his use of color, his incredibly precise control of the brush, and most importantly, his personal, paranoid, and surreal view of the world. Elizabeth and I own many of his signed prints, and would have at least one of his originals (but his wife, Melanie, reminded him he'd already sold the one we "purchased" to someone else.)[1]*

*Alan favorably impressed editors and publishers as well and has gone on to create a wonderful career for himself doing covers and interiors for hundreds of books and magazines. When he asked me if I would be interested in participating in a book project with him, I jumped at the chance. It was called* Imagination, Fully Dilated, *and it was an anthology project which paid homage to the grand old pulpzine tradition of editors handing out drawings and paintings[2] to their stable of regular contributors to "come up with a story to go with this!" The book would contain color plates of Alan Clark paintings to accompany each story inspired by them. A great concept. I couldn't wait to get started—especially since I had many "favorite" pieces for which by Alan I would* love *to do stories. All I had to do was pick one.*

---

[1] *The painting was called "Towing Jehovah"*

[2] *by such artists as Virgil Finlay, Hannes Bok, Frank R. Paul, Fredrick Blakeslee and Margaret Brundage.*

*Only Alan had us all do it with a Nineties verve—all the writers had to go to his website and select a painting from a huge display of maybe 40 or 50. In a classic bit of miscommunication, Alan and I had gotten the dates wrong for when the website would be up and running, and consequently when writers could begin picking the paintings. Upshot of the whole thing was I was very late, and every one of the Clark pieces that had intrigued me were* gone.

*Not that the remaining pieces were bad, or anything close to that end of the esthetic spectrum; it was just that, I wasn't as jazzed about any of them the way I'd been for some of the other stuff. You know the feeling—you drive ten miles to your favorite ice cream place to get the Pistachio or the Triple Fudge Chocolate Explosion . . . and they're sold out of both of them.*

*I can't lie; I was disappointed. But I would make the best of it, and selected a painting, which I will try to reproduce here, but if that doesn't work, I'll give you the description as well. A brick or masonry wall of some sort that suggests a castle, a crypt, or a gothic construction of some sort. The wall has been breached, blown open, penetrated—there is a ragged hole in the stone work, and peering through the whole is an eye. A big, red eye, surrounded by scales, which suggested something reptilian, saurian, and of course malevolent. It is an effective painting which stirred up images from my childhood when I spent hours every Saturday cringing in my movie seat as Double Features of giant, radiation-mutated monsters capered and gibbered across the black and white screen. I was certain I'd be able to come up with a cool story to go with it.*

*But I didn't.*

*Try as I might, false start after false start, the story just wasn't happening. I'd tossed several concepts on the scrap heap and was running hard against the deadline. I was starting to worry and the assignment was becoming a monkey on my back[3], and I was wondering if the Old Master was losing his touch. I guess it was bothering me more than I realized because one night, I suddenly woke up from a deep sleep, and the first thought in mind*

---

[3]*Actually, it was more like a giant, blue-assed, mandrill.*

was the painting and the story I needed to write. The second thought was I had a solution to the whole thing, that the story had worked itself out, down in the engine room of our minds they call the Subconscious. Easing out of bed to not wake up Elizabeth, I went to the kitchen, found a pencil and wrote a few lines on an envelope waiting for me on the counter-top.

The next morning, I had trouble reading my handwriting (what else is new?), but I decrypted enough of it to see where the story could go. As it turned out, I kind of cheated on the assignment, but the story was one of those that told itself as it went along, and I had no idea how everything would fit together until I reached the last line.

*The more minimal the art, the more maximum is the explanation.*

—Hilton Kramer

"What is it?" said Theresa.

She stood cautiously next to the trap-door stairs leading down from the attic. She was always the cautious one.

"Just an old painting," said her sister, Frannie, as she pulled an unframed canvas from beneath a dropcloth of oddments. "My God, there's a lot of junk in here."

"Be careful back there," said Theresa, pushing a strand of blonde hair from her cheek. It was hot up here, especially for early Fall, she thought. It was like all the heat of the summer had been kept prisoner up in the attic—just like all the junk Frannie had insisted on checking out.

"It's just a lot of old stuff, Tess. Come on, there might be something worth some real money up here." Frannie chuckled to herself and kept sorting through the stuff. "Don't you remember that guy in Massachusetts? He found an original draft of the Declaration of Independence—in his attic! Probably an attic just like this one."

Theresa nodded but said nothing. She watched as her sister continued to explore the contents of the room. Sunlight beamed in through a semi-circular window up near the roof's peak, sculpting Frannie in soft, amber light, accented by swirling storms of fool's gold motes of dust. Frannie's dark brown hair shimmered in the warm window-glow, and for an instant, Theresa thought the entire scene looked too perfect—like one of those sappy photo-greeting cards you can get at the mall stores.

But the tableau did fill her with a wonderful sense of security and love. All because of Frannie. She was the strong one, the smart one. Frannie could always be relied upon to make things okay. After all, wasn't it Frannie who'd decided they should use the money they'd inherited from Aunt Vanessa to buy this fabulous old house? And then invest the rest?

And they'd done just that; and just the interest was providing them with a good monthly income, plus enough left over to help with the start-up costs for their bakery business. Smart. That was Frannie, all right.

Theresa drew a long, calming breath, then exhaled even more slowly. There was a kind of luxuriant, almost sensual feeling whenever she did that. It was one of those things she did whenever she felt herself getting too . . . concerned. That was her own word for excited.

"Oh, wow . . . this is weird!" said Frannie, her words cutting through Theresa's thoughts like a cold blade.

"What?" Panic stirred in her. "What is it?"

Pulling the canvas out from between two small end tables, Frannie held it up in the afternoon light. "Look!"

And Theresa did indeed look—at one of the strangest paintings she'd ever seen.

"See what I mean? Is that ever weird or what?"

Taking a step closer, away from the comfort of the steps leading back down to the regular, normal part of the house, Theresa tilted her head as she felt herself being drawn into the center of the picture. It was like staring into the ever-deepening center of a whirlpool, a dark maelstrom of color and light.

At first, the image refused to resolve itself, then finally assumed its true form—the eye of some creature peering through a cracked and ruptured membrane.

"Oh God, Fran, that's awful! What is it?"

"I don't know . . ." her sister's voice was hardly a whisper. "It's really strange, isn't it?"

"What's it supposed to be?" said Theresa. "It looks like a monster."

"Yeah, doesn't it?" Frannie stared at the painting for a long time before speaking again. Time seemed to go on hold up in the attic, and Theresa felt everything slowing down, as if she were losing her sometimes tenuous hold on the way things should be.

"But, you know what . . . ? I kind of like it, Tess. You see how it almost makes you want to look at it? That's pretty neat."

"I don't like," said Theresa, grasping onto the sound of her sister's voice like an anchor, using their conversation to pull herself back to the real world.

"You don't have to like it," said Frannie, pulling the canvas all the way free of the other stuff which held it edgewise in the pile of unused stuff. "I'll hang it in my bedroom."

"All right, Frannie . . ." said Theresa, backing away from the now fully exposed painting. She didn't really want to look at it, but she could feel it—almost a compulsion to steal one last look into the depths of that strange and terrible eye. And she hated herself for agreeing with her sister so much! She didn't really like the idea of that picture being in her bedroom, for more than one reason, but she went on and acquiesced, as usual.

"Okay, let's go," said Frannie, obviously unaware of the tension within her sister. "I want to go clean this up and find a nice frame for it."

Obediently, Theresa eased herself down the narrow staircase.

Later on that evening, after dinner, wherein they'd followed the usual ritual of Frannie cooking one of her gourmet specials, and Theresa washing up the mess, the two of them drifted off to their own parts of the house. It was part of the unspoken, unplanned evolution of their relationship that neither ever questioned. Although, sometimes Theresa took pause enough to step back and actually look at what they were doing and how they were measuring out their lives to the metronome of routine.

They'd been together almost always, even though they were almost two years apart. Theresa's earliest memories were of playing with Frannie, who had always assumed the role of her protector and mentor, and who'd always liked doing it. Theresa had no memory of their parents, who'd been killed by a carjacker's bullets in Boston when the sisters were only two and four years old. For all practical purposes, their Aunt Vanessa had been their mother; a situation that worked out well for everyone. Aunt Vanessa's wealthy banker husband had been unable to father children, and so they'd readily adopted the two little girls. Auntie Van had provided them with culture and education, but she and Uncle Edwin had been short on affection and compassion. Their spacious townhome in Cambridge operated with all the rigidity and punctiliousness of Edwin's State Street bank.

But Tess and Frannie had learned to compensate by taking care of each other's emotional needs. Other than the hours in separate grades of schools, they were inseparable, always at the other's side for the love and support otherwise missing from their lives. They flourished in the proper Bostonian atmosphere of learning and etiquette, and grew up to be educated, attractive young women.

As they eased out of their early twenties, so too did Aunt Vanessa slip out of their lives with a quiet illness that took her with grace and dignity. Nothing like the heart attack which had hammered Uncle Edwin to the pavement in Harvard Square while they were both in college. It had been a shock, but the effects were nowhere near as profound as that of their Aunt's serene, bedside passing.

In the months that followed, both Theresa and Frannie discovered they couldn't continue to live in the staid and stately townhouse, with its baronial clutter and old-world insensibility. Too many memories, Frannie had said. Too many ghosts.

And she'd been right, Theresa knew that now. For almost a year after their Aunt had died, they found themselves both walking about the old house like strangers. As if they'd never belonged there, and most certainly no longer did. The atmosphere of the place and their situation had served to seal them off from the rest of the world. Neither of them had men in their lives, and since neither worked in the city, neither had a circle of fellow employees from which to cull any friends.

But they did continue to have each other.

The thought had given Theresa great comfort, and if pressed, she would gladly admit that Frannie was all the companionship she would ever need.

And so on the evening after she'd found the painting, they tried to continue on as usual. Frannie had gone off to the study, where she worked at her computer, doing whatever she did to keep the business side of their little bakery on Main Street reconciled. Every evening, the same thing. Do the accounting, the purchasing, the bill paying, then a few hours reading one of her history books before bed. During those hours, Theresa felt a bit aimless, like a sailing ship in the doldrums, but she'd learned to fill the solitary hours with cable-TV and the occasional video. Not that she preferred it, but it was a passive activity requiring little of her, and seemed to fit the parameters of her personality well enough.

This night was no different than all the rest. At least, that's what she imagined as she sat in the den, only half-listening to the news from the Manchester channel. Someone had been murdered in Nashua. The weather was going to be warmer tomorrow, a typical New Hampshire early Autumn. Indian Summer, the granite-staters called it. Theresa remoted off the TV, and went upstairs to her room. Frannie was still downstairs, which was part of the routine. She wouldn't be up for another half-hour or so. Passing the open door to her sister's bedroom, Theresa paused to peer inside.

She couldn't help it; she'd noticed that awful picture.

Incredibly, Frannie had already found a frame and the time to hang the painting. Over her dresser. And even from the distance, standing out in the hall, if you looked into the room, you could not avoid staring into the center of that malevolent red eye. And you could not avoid the eye looking back at you.

As Theresa stood there, transfixed, she knew that last notion wasn't quite right. The eye wasn't really looking back at you. More like looking into you . . .

With conscious effort, she turned away from the threshold, continued down the hall to her own room. Shedding her cotton blouse and long skirt, she moved to the mirror to look at herself. Having always avoided the sun, her complexion remained clear and pale, complimenting her blue eyes and cornsilk hair. She looked every bit the New England girl, that's what Frannie always said, and she liked being thought like that. But the warm and pleasant thought would not stay with her. Replaced instead by the recurring image of the painting, the eye that seemed to look at you with a lasciviousness, a leering penetration.

She could not stop thinking about it. And the sensation of disequilibrium, of disorientation when she'd first seen it, returned. No. I won't let it happen, she told herself, and forced herself to take a step towards her dressing table, to push the feelings away.

She pulled on a long T-shirt depicting the gardens at Saint-Gauden, stepped out of her panties, and climbed into bed.

Lying on her back, under the soft glow of a small night-table lamp, Theresa waited for her sister to come to bed.

The next day unfolded like a late summer flower, everything Theresa expected. She and Frannie had an early breakfast before going into Warner to open the bakery. After the lunchtime crowd of dessert and coffee seekers had dissipated, Frannie looked up from the cash register, and spoke to her.

"I need to know more about it."

And Theresa knew exactly to what the "it" referred.

"I don't like it," she told Frannie.

"I know, I know. You've told me a thousand times."

"It's ugly. It bothers me . . . I think there's something wrong with it." Theresa told her about standing outside the bedroom and feeling like that painting was watching her. And she admitted not being able to stop thinking about the image, the eye.

"I know what you mean," said Frannie. "I've felt it too."

"You have?!"

"Sure," said Frannie with a casual shrug. "Why else would I want to know more about it?"

Theresa stared at her sister for a moment, deeply surprised by her lack of anxiety or fear. But she understood Frannie's growing compulsion with the painting. She felt it herself, but was expressing it differently, as usual. Frannie—always forthright, direct, facing every challenge life tossed her way. Theresa had always been the retiring type; shy and reactive, some would even say passive; unable to assume control of who she was or what she should do.

And every time she'd passed by the open door to her sister's room, she couldn't resist pausing to peer inside, to gaze upon the painting. There was something about the colors, the pigments that seemed to almost glow, as if powered by some unknown source of power.

That evening, after dinner and their usual routine, Frannie came to her room. Theresa brightened, putting down the book she'd been reading.

"I found a name!" Frannie said in an excited whisper.

"What?" Theresa was openly confused. "What're you talking about?"

"The painting!" said Frannie, her dark eyes sparkling in the solitary glow of the bedstand reading lamp. "Down in the corner. It was so small and dark I didn't notice it at first."

Theresa felt her body knotting up, not with the familiar tension of anticipation, but revulsion, and perhaps even fear. The painting again. That's what her sister had come to her about.

"Frannie, I don't want to—"

"Just a single name. J-A-M-E-S."

"James?" said Theresa, interested despite her apprehensions. "Is it a first name or last?"

Frannie shrugged. "That's what we're going to find out. Oh, and I also found some writing on the back—looks like a marking pen or a Sharpie. It said Under Your Skin. Probably the title of the picture, don't you think?"

"Makes sense," said Theresa. She was angry with herself for being so intrigued with Frannie's revelations, but she couldn't help it.

"Anyway, it's something," said Frannie, as she gave her sister a pat on her leg and stood up from the edge of the bed. "Now I have a good place to start."

She was right.

As the days passed, the painting in Frannie's room continued to assume a more central role in their lives. Days were still consumed with the bakery, but the evening routine became altered as Frannie spent more time in the study, tracking down the identity of the artist known only as James.

Theresa tried to pretend she had only slight interest in her sister's detective work, but they both knew it was just a pose. Frannie came to her with every new development and Theresa listened intently. Several calls to the McLaughry Realtors failed to reveal much because the agents there were reluctant to put Frannie in contact with the previous owner of their house, a Mrs. Virginia Keat, who had moved to Massachusetts to live with her son and his wife.

But Frannie persisted, and finally reached Mrs. Keat, who provided vital information. The house had been rented for three years to a James Czernak, who was indeed a painter, and his girlfriend, Laura Childress, a sculptress. The couple moved to Boston about six months before Mrs. Keat sold the house to Theresa and her sister, and that's all Mrs. Keat could tell them.

But it was enough. Using that information as a springboard, Frannie launched herself into an exhaustive survey of all the art galleries and bohemian organizations to see if there was any record of James Czernak or Laura Childress. Contacting the right people and cajoling the information from them proved to be slow and frustrating, but Frannie seemed driven to know as much as possible about the painting and the man who created it.

Each night, Theresa found herself drawn to stare at the picture, sensing there was more to it than mere pigments smeared on cloth. There was something else, something strange and intoxicatingly dangerous about it that she could not articulate. Staring into the ebon center of the scarlet eye was like leaning forward, looking into the mesmeric vortex of a whirlpool. What did it mean? What was it doing to them?

Theresa knew its mere presence among them had, in some way, changed them, but again, she lacked the means to express it clearly. In Frannie, she'd detected a new . . . intensity in everything she did, a characteristic most obvious when she took her sister to her bed.

Several evenings later, Frannie received a return-call from one of the galleries she'd contacted in Cambridge. "We're really onto him now," she said as she walked into the den where Theresa had been watching a bad movie on the cable.

"Really?"

Frannie consulted a notebook where she'd scribbled pages of facts and information. "This lady just talked to me from the Charles River Artists Boutique—she remembers James Czernak. He appeared in Boston about three years ago with crates of paintings and a dark-eyed, brooding girlfriend."

"Laura Childress."

"Right," said Frannie, grinning triumphantly as she continued. "Anyway, James pushed his way into the inner circles of the arts community in Boston. The Boutique lady remembers him making several scenes at openings and shows."

"What kind of scenes?" Theresa leaned forward, her curiosity piqued.

"Oh you know—the usual eccentric artist stuff. Lots of screaming and boasting, plus the required public argument with the girlfriend. Anything to make people take notice . . . and of course remember him."

Theresa shook her head. "He sounds like a nut. Or an asshole."

Frannie chuckled. "Yeah, probably, but listen. Whatever he did must have worked because pretty soon, he was getting shows and exhibitions for his paintings. He claimed he'd started a new 'school' of painting."

"A what?"

Frannie checked her notepad. "He called it 'Genre Organicism.' and at first nobody paid much attention, which is usually the case with these kinds of things."

Theresa nodded. "But let me guess—pretty soon he was the talk of the Boston art-set, right?"

Frannie's grin faded. "Well, I don't know that yet."

"What do you mean?"

"The Boutique lady said he was too crazy and that I should just forget about him. She wouldn't tell me anything else."

"You're kidding. Then why'd she call in the first place?"

Frannie frowned. "Basically . . . to tell me to leave this guy alone, that he was pretty much bad news."

Theresa weighed the information and deemed it pretty sound advice, but she could tell from the expression on her sister's face, and the burning fire behind her dark eyes that the matter was far from dismissed. Still, she needed her suspicions confirmed. "But you're not going to do that, are you?"

"Do what?" asked Frannie.

"Forget about him."

"Of course not! I just got started."

The days shortened, and the New Hampshire winter began to tap upon their windowpanes with the season's first snowflakes. Frannie learned more about James Czernak in bits and pieces, slowly assembling the jig-saw shards of his career and identity.

He'd stayed in Cambridge for several years, trumpeting his talent until galleries began exhibiting his work, which seemed to be an unending series of pastiches of commercial genre art—

the kind seen in advertising and publishing in which the style communicates not only mood, but message, and familiarity. At least that's what Frannie said she'd been told. And since neither she nor Theresa were steeped heavily in the argot or parlance of the critical art-world, they would have to take their betters' word for certain parts of the story.

Frannie told her that most of James Czernak's critics and customers found his work intriguing despite a sometimes prosaic array of subjects depicted and explored.

"He was bought and collected, not so much for his paintings as much as what he was saying about them—about the way he created them," said Frannie one night over dinner.

By this time, Theresa had given in to the obsession over the creator of Under Your Skin. The painting had plainly become a central icon in their lives, and she had accepted that. If a simple two-dimensional object could exert influence over peoples' psyches, then it was surely this aptly named picture. She looked across the table at her sister and urged her to continue.

"What made James' method of painting unique and of interest to the collectors was how he made his colors, his pigments," said Frannie. "He created his paints by combining elements of objects from the real world that would become his subjects on canvas."

Theresa wasn't sure she was following that.

Frannie, now more comfortable with the deconstructionist language of the art-set, continued: "He was trying to absorb the essence of his subject matter, to . . . ah, capture it not only visually, but metaphysically as well."

"Frannie, that sounds like such pretentious crap." Theresa giggled at her own forthrightness.

Her sister grinned, but shook her head. "Not at all. It's pretty simple, really, what he was trying to do. Look—if he were painting, say, a butterfly, he would grind up the colors of the bug's wings into his paints. He would use the natural substances to make the colors. Makes sense, doesn't it?"

Theresa paused, nodded. "Sure, I've got that. Why did you have to make it sound so complicated?"

Frannie looked a bit disdainful. "Because, actually, it is. James started trying to capture the essence of things not commonly seen or palpably realized—things like fear or empathy or sorrow."

"Or . . . desire," said Theresa.

And Frannie just looked at her as if struck in the face. It was one of those moments of revelation accompanied by profound, surprised silence.

"That's right," said Frannie. "Wow . . . like that's what's going on in our picture.

"I don't know why I even said that," said Theresa, feeling embarrassed, confused. "I just . . ."

"You sensed it," said Frannie, unconsciously. "You just knew it—just like I did."

"Okay, so if that's going on, well, then, how did he do it. What's really happening here? What did he make those paints from?" For some reason, Theresa felt herself recoiling from her own question, as if she didn't really want to know the answer.

And none was supplied for another several weeks . . . until Frannie found James Czernak's notes.

Her enthusiasm, curiosity and obsession all rejuvenated, Frannie had embarked on a cellar-to-attic mission to find any other traces of James' presence in their house. She believed the painting could not have been the only piece of the artist left behind. (And that started Theresa wondering—why had only that one canvas remained? Had there been some purpose in its presence in their attic? Some method to what seemed at first to be nothing more than carelessness?)

The envelope had been taped to the top surface of a set of built-in cabinets in one of the upstairs bedrooms. It contained lined pages torn from a cheap spiral-bound school notebook, and Frannie came bursting into the den on the night she discovered them holding aloft like the felled trophy of a long-endured safari.

Theresa felt her pulse jump when she saw the pages, folded errantly as though in haste or lack of concern for precision. "Have you read them yet?"

Frannie shook her head. "No, I was too excited. And I didn't have my glasses. Come on, we'll read it together."

Theresa made room on the couch and the two of them sat thigh-to-thigh, leaned over the crinkled pieces of paper. The handwriting was a curious blend of both cursive and printed letters, and was at times barely legible. Theresa could see no reason or system for the abrupt slippages of printed writing into cursive, and then back again. It was the writing of someone in a hurry, or perhaps someone who seldom handwrote anything.

Slowly, Theresa read aloud the deciphered notes:

*It's time to move on. Each stage of evolution brings its own problems and joys. But there is true power in what I am doing. I have tapped into something, I am sure of it. I have imbued my paintings with a force, an energy, and strangely, once I've accomplished that, I have derived a form of sustenance from the work. It is a symbiotic relationship in the truest, most incestuous sense.*

*Each piece I infuse with elements organic becomes an artistic rune, a monolithic marker along the path of the dragon. The path I walk every day. Just as the Old Age priests believed, so do I—that we leave our spoor everywhere, and it is a true tragedy that few of us ever attempt to retrace our steps.*

*But I have vowed to not make such a mistake. I will create and never forget the legacy of my beginnings. I can never go forward unless I can also go back.*

*The marker combines some of the most atavistic and primal elements I could imagine. In celebration of the lizard, I have extracted the gray magic from the bulb of its hind-brain. The ancient unchanging messages of the R-complex live eternally in the crude wiring of creatures like this one. Elegant in its simplicity. Fierce in its energy. To create and destroy. The unending dichotomy trapped in the reptilian maze of another time.*

*And when combined with the wine of the brood-mothers, as I have combined it, there forms not mere pigment, but an alchemical potion. A means of transferal and transfiguration. My pieces thus become the talismans we all seek. The result is a beacon, sending out its terrible heat and light—both a warning and a beckoning.*

Laying down the pages, Frannie looked at her sister. "What does that mean?"

Theresa shook her head slowly. "I'm not sure. I think we should both read it over a few times and study it."

"It sounds like a lot of crazy ranting, doesn't it?" Frannie handed the papers to her sister.

"I don't know," said Theresa. "James is obviously bright and well-read. Just because we don't understand some of the language or the references are obscure doesn't mean that it's 'crazy,' you know."

Frannie seemed to consider this. "You're right, Tess. If we were trying to read a physics textbook, we'd have just as much trouble understanding it."

Theresa stood up, still holding the pages in her hand. The note admittedly fascinated her, challenged her. Frannie was right to think it was the ravings of a madman, but maybe not. They'd both sensed something . . . different about that painting. If not a real power in and of itself, then it was at least capable of producing a psychological or emotional response that was formidable.

And wasn't that the desired effect of all great art?

Theresa felt confused, but suffused with a desire to unravel the mystery. Finally she understood what had been driving her sister so incessantly. Their study was actually a very large library. Uncle Edwin had been a great lover of books as well as an antiquarian collector of rare tomes, palimpsests, and other incunabula; she and her sister had therefore inherited a vast storehouse of knowledge both secular and arcane.

For the next few days, every spare minute found Theresa in the library, where she accessed and examined countless volumes on art, creativity, psychology, physiology, ancient religions, archeology, semantics, philosophy, mythology, cosmology. She searched for references, parallels, analogs, etiologies, allegories . . . anything that might provide a key to understanding the complexity who was James Czernak.

It was also at this time that Theresa spent as much time in the presence of the painting's watchful, malevolent eye. It remained in Frannie's room, across from her bed; and so did Theresa. Never, in all the years, had they felt so intimately entwined as now. They agreed something decidedly different was taking place, and if it served convenience to attribute it to the painting, then so be it. Sometimes, in the middle of the night, as the house huddled and held its woodstove warmth, Theresa could feel the slick gaze of that solitary red eye upon her nakedness.

"I think I've figured it out—as best I can, anyway," she told Frannie, who was sitting in one of the old leather chairs opposite an eighteenth century writing desk.

"Well, I hope you've done better than me," said Frannie, whose efforts to locate James Czernak had hit a dead-blank wall. She'd traced the artist and his girlfriend into Manhattan to a fashionable loft in Soho, but soon afterward, Laura Childress was no longer seen with him. As his fame and status grew, James Czernak grew more distant from the subculture who had created him. One day, he simply disappeared, leaving a single painting in his studio/loft apartment.

Theresa held her hand parallel to the blotter, tilted it back and forth as if to say mezzo-mezzo. "We'll see, sister dearest," she said, picking up her notes. "But I should tell you right now . . . it isn't pretty."

Frannie chuckled darkly. "Somehow I had a feeling it wouldn't be. Go on . . . I'm ready for it."

Clearing her throat, Theresa arose from the desk and walked slowly towards the nearest wall of bookcases. It was as much a dramatic gesture as anything necessary, and she enjoyed Frannie's full attention. She also liked the heavy textures and aromas of the room, ever reminding her of the weight and substance of true knowledge.

"Okay, listen: I think James Czernak believes he isn't human."

Frannie giggled. "Tess, puh-leeeze . . ."

"No, listen. I mean he believed he was evolving into something else—some sort of god, maybe. That's what that reference to evolving or evolution means, I think. He obviously took his role as a creator very seriously and needed to objectify with the . . . uh, 'organic' pigments. Remember that stuff about making his colors and all?"

"Yeah," said Frannie. "Kind of creepy, really."

"As intended, I think. And that 'path of the dragon' refers to these lines of force that surround the earth like magnetic lines, only they're something different, something like ley lines or feng shui, the oriental equivalent."

"You're losing me," said Frannie.

"James was into the earth as the prime energy giver."

"You mean like Gaeia—Earth Mother with Chronos and all that?"

Theresa nodded. Frannie knew her ancient history and mythology, so this should all make sense to her. "You got it. He believed he'd become a conduit for the earth's natural organic forces. Nature as the only true artist, and that sort of thing."

Frannie assumed a more somber cast. "You got all that from those ragged pages? I'm impressed."

"Well, it's more interpretive than anything," Theresa said softly. She brushed her blonde hair back off her face, continued. "But in all the research I did, I would occasionally find phrases or references or cosmological models that fit what he was saying."

"Okay, I'll take your word for it. What else?"

"He leaves his paintings everywhere he's been."

"Yeah, that much I kind of figured," said Frannie.

"But he does it the way you would mark your trail in a forest or a maze," said Theresa. "For a reason."

"You mean he's planning to come back?"

"I think so. He calls them markers and beacons. Seems obvious. I think he wants to see the effects of his . . . talismans."

"But he could mean he travels backwards metaphorically or symbolically . . . through his work." Theresa paused, touched a slender index finger to her lower lip. "And he's not coming back in any real sense to any of the places he's left his . . . his artistic 'spoor,' as he put it."

Frannie shook her head. "This is too weird . . ."

"Blood," said Theresa, after a short pause.

"What?"

"He called it the 'wine of the brood mothers'. Didn't you want to know what the hell he was talking about there?"

"Yes, but are you sure—?"

"It's a term from the Druids," said Theresa. "It means menstrual blood."

"Oh God, that's sick!" Frannie continued to shake her head slowly. She didn't particularly like what she was hearing.

"And he combined it with the primitive reptile brain," said Theresa. "He pretty much spelled that out. Do you see what he was trying to do?"

"No," said Frannie. "I don't."

"The R-complex is supposedly the primitive part of our own brain, the part that controls our base instincts for survival and procreation. Sex, Frannie. Naked, debased fucking."

"Tess, you never talk like that."

Theresa smiled. "No, but I act like that sometimes, don't I? And so do you. That's what the picture means, Sis. It's that instinct and that heat that drives us. Oh, it's under our skin, all right. It's the part of us we're always told we have to keep in check, to keep bridled and caged. It's our monster from the id, Frannie. It's in every one of us, and I think James Czernak was trying to learn how to peel back all the counterfeit layers . . . and let it out."

Frannie stood up, began pacing back and forth across the room. "This is all a little too whacked for me."

"I told you it wasn't pretty."

"Menstrual blood, my God . . ."

Theresa nodded. "I know. You were wondering whose blood he used, weren't you?"

"Yes, but I figured it has to be Laura's, right?"

"A good guess," said Theresa.

Frannie stopped pacing, stood by the window, which looked out upon the swale of the back lawn, now layered in white like a delicately frosted cake and glowing the palest of blues in the moonlight.

She stood silently like that for what seemed like a long time, and Theresa watched her, waiting, as if she knew her sister needed to speak.

"There's something I haven't told you yet," she said in half-whisper. "Something . . . not good."

Theresa felt the bottom of her stomach begin to fall away. She felt an ice-pick touch of fear deep inside. "What is it?"

"All the checking I've been doing on our mysterious James . . . ? I told you he's vanished. And Laura Childress had disappeared too?"

Theresa nodded, knowing what was coming.

"Well, they found her—dead."

"I knew you were going to say that. From all the reading I've been doing, and figuring what's happening to James . . . if he believes he is walking the path of the dragon, then he would be drawn to that power, that power of death."

"Tess, he killed that woman,"

"I know. Once I learned what he was doing, I knew he would have to, eventually." Theresa felt a strange calmness settling over her even as her sister grew more distraught.

"What's happening to us?" said Frannie, her voice fragile, making her sound so vulnerable.

"I'm not sure," said Theresa. "We could be participants or observers . . . or both."

"I was more worried about becoming victims." Frannie, giggled nervously, tragically.

Theresa stood, moved to her sister's side as they looked out the high window. She placed her arm around Frannie's waist and drew her close, feeling a spike of excitement at the sensation of her astonishing body-warmth, her softness. The winterscape beyond the glass stretched away from the house like an endless, ghostly-pale plateau.

He was out there, somewhere, they both knew, walking the ancient path in solitary silence.

Frannie and Theresa stood listening to the silence as one listens to some terrifying but brilliant atonal symphony, as one listens to an approaching storm at sea.

They would listen; and they would wait.

*I have always loved* The Twilight Zone. *It was one of those things that came along in my life at exactly the right time. In fact, Rod Serling was one of my heroes. He was doing exactly what I would have wanted to do with my life. It's funny because most guys I grew up with had their idols and heroes they wanted to grow up and be like— Mickey Mantle, Davey Crockett, Zorro, Batman, G. I. Joe. And I may have fantasized about that bunch as well, but I threw them all overboard when I encountered this intense guy who would always be standing just to the right or the left of the set when the camera would PAN LEFT for a MEDIUM CU.*

*There was a lot to like about the TV series— the wonderful texture and crisp contrasts of the black-and-white film; the endless parade of talented actors; and of course, the stories full of stark morality and high irony. I liked both Serling's original stories and his adaptation of well-known SF and Fantasy tales; plus the scripts by Richard Matheson and George Clayton Johnson. Wonderful stuff, all of it, and as I passed through my teens, I knew I would like to write stories like those on TZ.*

*And I do, on occasion, although I can see, after looking back over the body of work in this collection, my stuff tends to be a little nastier and vengeful than the gentle fantasies Serling proffered to us all. But once in a while, I do hit a lot of the same chords, and that makes me feel like I nodded gracefully to my influences (always a good thing).*

*The story that follows comes from one of those true life anecdotes I remember hearing from a guy on a train. I was sitting there working on my laptop, and this Suit is sitting next to me, and he starts talking and we talk about writing and all that stuff, and he tells me a story about his best friend who goes back to his hometown (Philly)*

*neighborhood after twenty years and finds that the house he grew up in has been turned into a strip-club or something like that.* Isn't that a weird story? *the Suit asks me. And I'm thinking: not weird, just dumb.*

*But oddly enough (and I told you before— you always have to be on the lookout for sources of good stories), it does get me thinking and with my superior abilities, I* am *able to take this guy's mundane recounting and spin it into something wonderfully original and something Mr. Serling might have liked very much. I sent it to a good writer and fellow* pasian, *Al Sarrantonio, who was editing this mega-anthology called* 999, *and he said in his intro to the story that it was "pure* Twilight Zone," *so much so, Al could almost swear he'd seen it on the show.*

*Well, he* might *see it on TV someday. I sold it to a show called* Night Visions, *which is a one-hour weekly series that was supposed to air on the Fox Network, but has yet to appear as I'm writing this. My agent tells me the producers have thirteen episodes "in the can" already, but no word on when (if ever) the series will be broadcast—TV is weird like that. So, if Fox buries its stillborn, it may show up as a filler-piece on the SciFi Channel someday . . . or, it may* never *be seen.*

*But for us literate beings, that is of little consequence. The story exists here, in its purest form for our pleasure and wonderment. So, let's turn the page . . .*

**D**ominic Kazan walked through the darkness, convinced he was not alone.

The idea cut through him like a razor as he fumbled for the light switch. Where was the damned thing? A sense of panic rising in him like a hot column of vomit in his throat, but he fought it down as his fingers tripped across the switch.

Abruptly, the lobby took shape in the dim light.

It, like the rest of the Barclay Theatre, was deserted. Crowds, actors, stagehands—everyone except for Dominic— had left hours ago. And he knew he should be alone. He was the janitor/nightwatchman for the Barclay, accustomed to, and actually comfortable with, the solitude. But for the last few nights, he could not escape the sensation there was something else lurking in the darkness of the big building.

Something that seemed to be waiting for him.

He enjoyed working alone; he had been alone most of his life. He did not mind working in almost total darkness; he had lived in a different kind of darkness most of his life.

But this feeling that he was not alone was beginning to bother him, actually frighten him. And he didn't want to have any bad feelings about the Barclay. It was his only true home, and he loved his job there. There was something special about being intimate with the magic of the theatre—the props and costumes, the make-believe world of sets and flats. Sometimes he would come to work early, just to watch the hive-like activity of the stage-hands and actors, feeling the magic-world come to life.

All his life, there seemed to be something stalking him. A mindless kind of thing, a thing of failure and despair. Somehow, it always caught up with him, and threw his life into chaos. He wondered if it was on his trail again.

Tonight. Trying to make him run away again.

And he was so tired, tired of running away . . .

. . . Away from the fragile dreams of his childhood, the traumas of adolescence, and the failures of manhood. His father used to tell him there were only two kind of people in the world: Winners and Losers—and his son was definitely in the second group.

Thirty-two years old, and it looked like the old man had been right. His life already a worn-out patchquilt of pain and defeat. After pulling a stint in the Army, he had drifted all over the country taking any unskilled job he could find.

Seasonal, mindless work in Lubbock oil-fields, Biloxi docks, Birmingham factories. Ten years of nomad-living and nomad-losing.

When he had been much younger, he had tried to figure out why things never worked out for him. Physically, Dominic was almost handsome with his thick dark hair and bright blue eyes.

And mentally, he could always hold his own. He used to read lots of comics and books and never missed a Saturday afternoon double-feature. He even watched a play now and then, back when they used to run them on live television.

But after he left home and never looked back, things seemed to just get worse. After ten years, he started getting the idea that maybe he should go home and try to start over. The letter telling him that his father had died was now five years old, and he had not gone back then. He had not even contacted his mother about it, and that always bothered him.

Something gnawed at his memories and his guilt, and he had finally quit his rigging job and started hitching East through the South—Louisiana, Mississippi, Alabama, Georgia.

One night, he was sitting in a roadhouse outside of Atlanta, drinking Bud on tap, watching a well-dressed guy next to him trying to drown himself in dry martinis. They had started talking, as lonely drinkers often will. The guy was obviously successful, middle-aged, and out-of-place in the roadside bar.

At one point, Dominic had mentioned that he was going home, back to the city of his birth. The stylish man laughed and slurred something about Thomas Wolfe. When Dominic questioned the response, the man said, "Don't you remember him? He's the guy who said 'you can't go home again,' and then he wrote a long, god-awful boring book to prove it."

Dominic never understood what the man was talking about until he reached his hometown. It was a large East coast city, and it had changed drastically in his absence. Lots of remembered landmarks had vanished; the streets seemed cold, alien.

For several days, he gathered the courage to return to his old neighborhood, to face his mother after so many years.

When he was finally ready, arriving at the correct street, the correct address, he found his house was *gone.*

The entire street, which had once been a cramped, stifling heap of tenements, row houses, and basement shops, had been wiped out of existence. Urban renewal had invaded the neighborhood, grinding into dust all the bricks and mortar, all the memories.

In its place stood a monstrous building—a monolith of glass and steel and shaped concrete called the Barclay Theatre. At first he saw it as an intruder, a silent, hulking thing which had utterly destroyed his past, occupying the space where his little house had once stood. Perhaps Thomas Wolfe knew what he was talking about.

But after thinking about it, he thought it was ironic that it was, of all things, a theatre that wiped out his memories.

Ironic indeed.

In the days that followed, he tried to relocate his mother, but with no success. She had vanished, and a part of him was glad. It would have been difficult to face her as a man with no future, and now, not even a past. For no good reason, he decided to stay on in the city, taking day-labor jobs and a room at the YMCA.

As Dominic drifted into summer, he had made no friends, had not found a steady job, and had given up finding his mother. He read books from the library, went to matinee movies, and lived alone with his broken dreams. Occasionally he would walk back to his old neighborhood, as though hoping to see his house one final time. And on each visit, he would stand in the light-pool of a street lamp to stare at the elegant presence of the Barclay.

He seemed to feel an attraction to the place, old dreams stirring in a locked room of his mind. One day, when he saw an ad in the paper for a janitor/nightwatchman at the theatre, he ran all the way to apply.

They hired him on a probational basis, but Dominic didn't mind the qualification. He made a point of being on time and very meticulous in his work. As the weeks passed, he felt a growing warmth in his heart for the Barclay; it became a haven of safety and security—a place where he could live with the old dreams.

When his diligence was rewarded with a permanent position and a raise in salary, he was very happy. He began coming early to watch current productions, and he learned the theatre jargon of the stagehands, actors, and directors. The dreamscapes of the theatre became real to him, and he absorbed the great tragedies, laughed at clever comedies.

But late at night, when the crowds had dispersed, was the time he loved the best. He would go into the main auditorium and listen to the lights cooling and crackling behind their gels, and think about that night's performance—comparing to past nights, to what he figured were the playwright's intentions. For the first time in his life, he was happy.

But then something changed. The feelings of not being alone started to grow out of the shadows, growing more intense . . .

. . . until tonight, and he felt that he could bear it no longer. There was a small voice in his mind telling him to run from the place and never return.

No, he thought calmly. No more running. Not ever again.

Above his head, the cantilevered balcony hung like a giant hammer ready to fall. He stepped into the main auditorium and listened to the darkness. The aisle swept down towards the stage where the grand drape and act curtain pulled back to reveal the set of the current play. Pushing a carpet sweeper slowly over the thick pile, Dominic noticed how truly dark the theatre was. The exit light seemed dim and distant. Row upon row of seats surrounded him, like a herd of round-shouldered creatures huddled in deep shadows.

The entire theatre seemed to be enclosing him like an immense vault, a dark hollow tomb. He knew there was something there with him. Acid boiled in his stomach, his throat caked with chalk.

Looking away from the empty seats back to the stage, he noticed that something had changed. Something was wrong.

The set for the currently running production was Nick's Place—a San Francisco saloon described in Saroyan's "The

Time of Your Life." But that set was gone. Somehow, it had been struck, and changed overnight. An impossibility, Dominic knew, yet he stared into the darkness and could make out the configurations of a totally different set.

Walking closer, his eyes adjusting to the dim illumination of the Exit signs, Dominic picked up the details of the set—a shabby, gray-walled living-room with a kitchenette to the right.

Dumpy green chairs with doilies on the arms, a couch with maroon and silver stripes, end-tables with glass tops and a mahogany liquor cabinet with a tiny-screened Emerson television on top.

It was a spare, simple room.

A familiar room.

For an instant, Dominic recoiled at the thought. It couldn't *be*. It wasn't possible. But he recognized the room, down to its smallest details. As if the set designer had invaded a private memory, the set was a perfect replica of his parents' house. The house which had been located where the theatre now stood. As Dominic stared in awe and disbelief, he could see that there was nothing dreamy and out-of-focus about the set. He stood before something with hard edges and substance, something real, and not distorted by the lens of memory.

Without thinking, he stepped closer and suddenly the stage-lights heated up. The fixtures on the set cast off their grayish hues and burst into full color. An odd swelling sensation filled Dominic's chest, almost becoming a distinct pain. The pain of many years and many emotions. The thought occurred to him that someone might be playing a very cruel joke on him and he turned to check the light booth up above and beyond the balcony. But it was dark and empty.

The sound of a door opening jarred him.

Turning back to the stage he saw a woman wearing a turquoise housedress and beige slippers enter the room from stage left.

She had a roundish face going towards plump and her eyes were flat and lackluster. There was an essential weariness about her.

Dominic felt tears growing in his eyes, a tightness in his throat, as he looked, stunned, at his *mother*.

"Mom! Mom, what're you doing here? Hey, Mom!"

But she did not hear him. Mechanically, his mother began setting a simple table with paper napkins, Melmac plates, and plain utensils. Dominic ran up to the edge of the stage and yelled at her but she ignored him. It became clear that she could neither see nor hear him—as though they were dimensions apart, as though he saw everything through a one-way mirror.

What the hell was going on?

Dominic grappled with the sheer insanity of it all, trying to make sense out of the hallucinated moment, when it continued.

The door at stage center flew open and his father entered the set.

At the sight of the man, something tightened around Dominic's heart like a fist, staggering him. His father was dead. And yet, there he was, standing in the doorway full of sweat and shine and dirt. There was a defiance in the old man's posture, in the way he slammed the door shut behind him. He wore greasy chino pants and a plaid flannel shirt. One hand carried a beat-up lunch pail with the word "Kazan" stenciled on the side; the other the evening paper.

Dropping the lunch bucket on the kitchen table, his father moved quickly to his favorite chair and unflapped the paper. If he had acknowledged the presence of his wife, Dominic had missed it. There was a somehow surreal quality to the scene—suggesting more than was actually taking place. He sensed this moment could have been taking place at any point in their lives over perhaps a twenty-year span.

Dominic fought off the emotional waves which crashed over him, trying to concentrate on the images on the stage. He was surprised to see how plain his mother actually was— not the pretty woman of his memories—and how much smaller and less imposing his father seemed. Again the convex glass of memory had worked its distorted magic.

The door at stage left abruptly opened and a small, frightfully thin boy of perhaps nine years entered the room. The boy had large ears, bright blue eyes, and Brylcream-slicked dark hair. Dominic felt stunned as he recognized the boy as *himself*.

He had never realized how frail and odd he had looked as a child; he winced as he heard the young boy speak in a high-pitched voice.

BOY
Hi, Daddy!

The boy advanced to his father's chair, carrying a sheaf of papers.

BOY (cont'd)
Look what me and Beezie are goin' to do . . . !

The greeting was met with silence. His father's face remained hidden behind the newspaper.

MOTHER
Joseph, the boy is talkin' to you.

FATHER
Eh! What does he want?!

The paper dropped to the working man's lap, and the father stared at his son with a slack, almost hostile expression.

BOY
Daddy, look! Beezie and me are goin' to direct a play! And we're goin' to charge ten cents apiece for all the kids to come and see it.
(hands some papers to his father)
Here's some drawings I made . . . See, this is Snow White's house, and—

FATHER
Play? Snow White . . . ? That's a fairy tale, ain't it?

BOY
Yeah, it's like the Walt Disney movie, and—
(The father laughs roughly.)

FATHER

A fairy tale is for a buncha fairies!
(he sweeps out his hand, scattering
the drawings across the floor)
That's nothin' for a boy to be up to! Plays
are for fairies . . . you want to be a
*fairy*, boy?

BOY

But, Daddy, it's a good show, and—

FATHER

Listen, pick up this crap and get it outta
here. And don't let me hear no more about
it. You oughta be out playin' ball . . . not
foolin' with this pansy crap!

Dominic stood in the aisle, his mind reeling from the impact of the scene. How he remembered that night! His father had so thoroughly crushed him that evening that he had given up the play with his friend. He had let a little piece of himself die that night.

A sudden anger surged through him as he forced his mind back to the rest of the memory, and he remembered what happened when he'd started picking up his drawings.

Up on the stage, his younger self was bending down, reaching out for the scattered papers.

Stepping closer to the stage, Dominic cried out. *"Watch it! Don't let him get to them first . . . he's going to tear them up!"*

The skinny, dark-haired boy paused, looked out into the darkness of the audience, as though listening. His mother and father had clearly heard nothing, and for a moment, seemed to be arrested in time.

BOY
(looking down towards Dominic)
What did you say?

"Dad's going to tear up your drawings . . . if you let him," said Dominic. "So pick them up now, fast. Then tell him what you're thinking, what you're *feeling*."

BOY

Who *are* you?

Dominic swallowed hard, forced himself to speak in a clear, calm voice. "You know who I am . . ."

BOY
(smiling)
Yeah, I guess I do . . .

The boy turned back to the stage and quickly grabbed all his drawings as his father reached down a large hand and tried to snatch them away.

BOY
No!  You leave them alone! You leave *me* alone!

FATHER
(a bit shocked by the boy's words)
What're ya gonna do?  Grow up and be
a fruitcake?  Whatsamatter with baseball?  Too tough on ya?

The boy held the papers to his chest, paused to look out into the darkness at Dominic, then back to his father.  The boy was breathing hard, obviously scared, but there was a new strength in the way he stood, staring at his father.  He was almost sobbing, but he forced the words to come out clearly.

BOY
Yeah, I like baseball just fine. But I like
this stuff, too.  And . . . and, I don't care
if you don't like it. Cause I do!  And
that's what's important!

The boy ran from the room, carrying his drawings.  His father stared after him for a moment, then returned to his newspaper, trying to act unaffected by the small exchange.

His mother stood by the table with a beaten, joyless expression on her face.

The stage lights dimmed quickly, fading everything into darkness. Dominic blinked his eyes as the figures of his parents became phantoms in the shadows, growing faint, insubstantial.

Another blink of his eyes and they were gone. Slowly the set began to metamorphose back into the barroom of Nick's Place.

Dominic's heart cried out silently, but it was too late. The vision, or whatever it had been, had vanished.

He took an aisle seat, let out a long breath. Rubbing his eyes, he felt the fine patina of sweat on his face. His heartbeats were loud and heavy. What the hell had been going on?

He had been awake, yet he felt as though he had just snapped out of a trance. He felt crazy, but he knew that he was not dreaming, not unless his whole life had been a nightmare.

It had seemed so real. How obvious the dynamics of his family seemed to him now. He wondered why he had never seen what things were really like when he was a kid. But then, maybe he did know back then . . .

Children picked up things on a different level than adults.

They hadn't spent much time building up defense mechanisms and rationalizations for all the shitty things that happen in the world. Kids take everything straight, no chaser. It's later on we all start bullshitting ourselves.

Dominic stood up and looked about the auditorium as an eerie sensation washed over him. It was as though he was the only person left in the whole world. He felt so totally alone. And he knew that it was time to get away from this place. Try to forget all the pain—isn't that what life is all about?—not wallow in it.

He walked back to the lobby, slipped through a side door, and then down a long corridor to his office. After turning out the lights, he locked up, headed for the employee's exit. Just as he reached the fire door, he heard footsteps in the shadows behind him. He whirled quickly and saw a small, hunched-over black man carrying a broom.

"Evenin', Mr. Kazan . . ." said the voice.

"Oh hi, Sam," said Dominic. "Take it easy now. Goodnight."

He pushed out the door to the parking lot, leaving the old janitor/nightwatchman alone in the building.

The next day when Dominic Kazan awoke, he felt somehow *changed*, but there was nothing he could think of which would explain the feeling. He had no memory of the previous night's experience, other than a nagging question in his mind. It was a crazy idea he must have been dreaming about, but there was something he wanted to know.

That afternoon, before going down to the Barclay, Dominic stopped at the City Office Building to speak to some people in the records division of the Department of Urban Planning. They were as cooperative as bureaucrats can be, and after more than two hours of hassling around, Dominic chanced upon a few intriguing facts.

In the theatre that evening after the performance, Dominic went about his duties. As stage manager, he had to make certain that all the props were back in place for the next show, that the set was restored to pre-curtain readiness, and that all the light and sound cues were in the proper order in the technician's booth. He went through his tasks slowly, waiting for the rest of the Barclay personnel to depart the large building. Entering the main auditorium, Dominic walked down the aisle and sat in the first row of the orchestra seats. A silence pervaded the place as he closed his eyes, letting his thoughts run free. His discovery at the Department of Urban Planning kept replaying in his mind—the proscenium stage of the Barclay occupied the very same space that was once filled by his parents' house in the middle of the old neighborhood block.

Dominic opened his eyes slowly, focusing on the stage. As though on cue, the lights heated up, gradually filling the set with hard illumination. But this time, he didn't feel fear as much as anticipation. He felt like he was about to embark upon a long-awaited trip.

Dominic looked up to see his familiar living room warming under the stage lights . . .

The door opened and his father entered the room. He wore his usual work clothes, carried an evening paper and his lunch pail. Normally a quick-moving, broadly-shouldered man who seemed to radiate force and raw power, Joseph Kazan appeared stooped and oddly defeated.

> FATHER
> Louisa! Louisa, where are you?!

There was no immediate reply and he shrugged as he moved to his favorite chair. He began to open his folded newspaper, then threw it to the floor in disgust. A door opened at stage left and Dominic's mother appeared carrying a dish towel.

> MOTHER
> Joseph? What are you doing home so
> early?

Joseph looked at her with anger in his eyes, his lips curled back slightly. Suddenly the anger drained away from him. Looking away from his wife, he spoke with great effort.

> FATHER
> We got laid off again today . . . Got mad
> at my foreman. I left after he told us all
> not to come in tomorrow morning.

There was a pained expression in his mother's face.

> MOTHER
> Why do they always do this right be-
> fore Christmas? It's not fair.

> FATHER
> I'll have to find somethin' quick. We got
> bills to keep up. Nobody's hirin' now,
> though . . . the bastards!

His mother moved to his father's chair, put a hand on his shoulder.

MOTHER
Well, we've gotten by before . . . we'll
do it again.

Joseph shook his head, slapped his leg absently.

FATHER
Some husband I been! A man's s'pozed
to take care of things! Take care of his
family better'n this!

The door at stage center opened and an adolescent version of Dominic entered the room. He was carrying a stack of
books under his arm, his parka under the other.

BOY
Hi Mom. . . hey Dad, what're you doing
home early?

FATHER
(ignoring the question)
Where you been?

BOY
We had a rehearsal after school. Just
got finished.
(to his mother)
Can I have an apple or something, Mom?

FATHER
Rehearsal-*what?* Another one of them
plays?

BOY
C'mon Dad, you know I'm doing a play
for the one-act contest at school. I wrote
it myself, remember?

His father shook his head slowly, wiped his mouth with
obvious irritation, then looked at his mother.

433

> FATHER
> I'm worryin' about takin' care of this family, he's out writin' stuff for faggots!

His mother touched her husband's shoulder again.

> MOTHER
> Joseph, please don't take it out on him . . .

> BOY
> Yeah, Dad. We've been through this stuff before, haven't we?

Dominic's father did not speak as he exploded from his chair and backhanded the teenager across the face with one quick, furious motion. The force of the blow slammed the boy's head against the wall and he staggered away, dazed and glassy-eyed.

> FATHER
> More! You want more! You smart-assed kid! You don't speak to your father like that . . . not *never!*

His mother moved to help her wounded son.

> MOTHER
> You didn't have to hit him like that.

> FATHER
> You stay away from him, Goddammit! I oughta give it to him twice as hard! He don't respect his father. At his age he oughta be out workin'—like a *man*. He oughta be helpin' his family!

The teenaged boy looked at his father with terror in his eyes. He appeared helpless, but he forced himself to speak.

BOY
What do you want from me? What have
I ever done to hurt you?

FATHER
(in mocking effeminate voice)
What have I ever done to hurt you!

His father grinned at his little joke, then raised his hand
towards the boy, just to watch him shy away.

FATHER (cont'd)
I'll tell you what you done . . . you ain't
acted like a man! And that hurts more'n
anything. But that's gonna stop. As of
today you're gonna be a man.

BOY
What do you mean?

FATHER
You're goin' to work.

BOY
But I already have a job . . .

FATHER
Ha! You call that paper route a job? I'm
talkin' about a *real* job. Make some *real*
money! It's about time you started helpin'
your mother and me.

BOY
But what about school?

His father laughed, then stared at him defiantly.

FATHER
What about it? You're old enough to
quit . . . so now you'll quit! I hadda

leave school in the fifth grade! You
think you're any better'n me?

BOY

But Dad, I don't want to quit school. I
can't quit *now*.

FATHER

Don't tell me what you "can't" or what
you "want" 'cause that don't mean shit
to me! I'm tellin' you what you gotta do
cause I'm your father! That school's just
fillin' your head with a bunch of crazy
shit anyway. . .

BOY

Dad, I can't believe this . . .

FATHER

Shut-up and listen to me or I'll bust you
again!

Dominic had been watching the scene with a morbid fascination and a growing anger. Things seemed so much clearer
now—how things worked in his family. He could not allow
his younger self to succumb to the ravings of a beaten, humiliated man.

Without thinking further, he stood up and called out to the
younger version of himself: "Hey! You tell him to keep his
hands off you! And that if he tries anything again . . . you're
going to stop him!"

As before, neither his father nor mother seemed to have
heard Dominic's voice. But the adolescent boy reacted immediately. He turned to the edge of the stage and peered into
the darkness.

BOY

What did you say? Is it you again?

"Yes," said Dominic, his voice almost catching in his throat.

"It's *me* . . . now tell him what I told you. Tell him what you're thinking. What you're *really* thinking."

Dominic watched the boy nod and turn back towards his father. There was a sensation of great tension in the air, like an electrical storm gathering on a humid day.

> BOY
> You can't hit me like that anymore.

The boy stood there, seeming to radiate a new strength.

> FATHER
> What?

> BOY
> You can't hit me—just because you feel
> like doing it. I haven't done anything
> wrong and I'm tired of you making me
> feel like I have.

> FATHER
> I'll bust you any Goddamned time I—

> BOY
> No! No you won't! I won't let you!

His father smiled and shifted his weight from one foot to the other, his arms hanging loose as though ready for a fight.

> FATHER
> Well, what's this? A little *manliness* af-
> ter all this time, huh? How about that?

> BOY
> I'm not quitting school. And you can't
> make me do it. There're things I want
> to do with my life that I can't do if I quit
> school.

His father looked at him silently, a confused expression on his face.

> BOY (cont'd)
> There're things I want to do . . . things
> that you could *never* do.

> FATHER
> What the hell's that s'pozed to mean?

> BOY
> You have to understand something, Dad.
> I'm not going to be made responsible
> for anybody's life . . . except my own.
> Especially not yours. I can't live your
> life, but I *have* to live mine.

> FATHER
> (looking confused, off-balance)
> Listen, you little shit . . .

> BOY
> No, Dad, I think it's time *you* listened.
> Maybe for the first time in your life.

The boy turned and walked to the door stage center, opening it.

> BOY
> I'm going out for awhile.

He exited the stage, leaving his father standing mute and stripped of his power.

Dominic fell back in the theatre seat as the stage quickly darkened and the figures and props dissolved into the shadows.

In an instant the set was gone. He felt rigid and tense and there was a soft roaring in his ears like the sound of a seashell. He felt as though he had just awakened from a dream. But he knew it had been no dream.

A memory?

Perhaps. But as he sat there in the darkness, he had the feeling he had no memories. That the scene he had just witnessed was a solitary moment, a free-floating, always existing piece of the timestream. A moment out of time.

What is *happening* to me? The thought ate through him like a furious acid, leaving him with a vague sense of panic. Standing up, he knew that he must leave the place. Dominic walked up the aisle to the lobby, refusing to look back at the dark stage.

The light in the lobby comforted him and he felt better immediately. Already, the fears and crazy thoughts were fading away. It's all right now. Better get on home. As he moved towards the exit, he heard a sound and stopped. A door slipping its latch.

"Mr. Kazan!" said a familiar voice. "What're you still doing here?"

Turning, Dominic saw Bob Yeager, the Barclay's stage manager, standing in the doorway of his office.

"Oh hi, Bob. I was . . . I was just going over a few things. Just getting ready to leave."

Yeager rubbed his beard, grinned. "Just getting over those first-night jitters, huh? I can understand that, yes sir."

Dominic smiled uneasily. "Yeah, the first night's always the worst . . ."

"Hey, you did a great job, Mr. Kazan. Just fine."

"I did?"

Yeager nodded, smiled.

"I suppose I'll have to take your word for it," said Dominic. "Well, I guess I'd better be heading home. Good night."

When he arrived at his townhouse, he found that he couldn't sleep. He had the nagging sensation that something was wrong, that something in his life was out of whack, out of synch, but he couldn't pin it down. After making a cup of instant coffee, he wandered into his den where a typewriter and a pile of manuscript pages awaited him on a large messy desk.

Sitting down, he decided to go back to that play he had been trying to write. Every actor thinks he can be a playwright, right? Some ideas started flowing as Dominic began to type, and it was very late before he went to bed.

The next evening's performance had gone better than opening night, but it was still rough. Dominic was playing the part of Alan in Wilson's "Lemon Sky," and although the director was pleased with his characterization, Dominic was not. He had learned long ago that you cannot merely please your audience; you must also please yourself.

He remained in the dressing room, dawdling and taking his time, waiting for everyone else to leave. The rest of the cast planned to meet at their favorite bistro for drinks and food, and he had declined politely. There would be time for such things later. Tonight, Dominic felt compelled to go back into the theatre itself, back into the empty darkness where careers were made or destroyed. He was not really certain why he felt the need to stay behind. But he had feelings, or rather, memories. Or perhaps they were dreams . . . or memories of dreams. Or . . .

He was not certain what they were, but he felt convinced that the answers lay in the dark shadows of the auditorium.

Finally, everyone had cleared out and he left the dressing room for the theatre itself. As he entered through the lobby doors, he saw no one, not even Sam. There were no lights, other than the green, glowing letters of the exit lights, and as he moved down the aisle, he had the sensation of entering an abandoned cathedral. The darkness seemed to crowd about him like a thick fog, and he began to feel strangely light-headed. As he drew himself deeper into the vast sea of empty seats, he could see the dim outlines of the set beyond the open act-curtain—a modern suburban home in El Cajon, California.

Then slowly, the stage lights crackled as they gathered heat, and bathed the stage in light and life. The shapes which took form and color were again the props of a tortured childhood.

The shabby living room, the kitchenette, worn carpets and dingy curtains.

The door at stage center opened and his mother entered, wearing a simple, tailored suit. Her hair was silvering and had been puffed by a beauty shop. She appeared elegant in a simply stated manner. He had never remembered his mother looking like that. She looked about the room as though expecting someone to be home.

MOTHER
Dominic, where are you?  Dominic?

She appeared perplexed as she closed the door, calling his name again. Then turning towards the footlights, she looked beyond them to where he stood transfixed.

MOTHER (cont'd)
Oh *there* you are.  Dominic, come up
here!  Come to me . . .

The recognition startled him, but he felt himself responding as though wrapped in the web of a dream. There was an unreality about the moment, a sensation which prompted him to question nothing, to merely react.
And he did.
Climbing up and onto the stage as the heat of the lights warmed him, he felt as though he were passing through a barrier.
It was that magic which every actor feels when the curtain rises and he steps forth, but it was also very different this time . .
.

DOMINIC
Where's Dad?  He wasn't there, was he?

MOTHER
(looking away)
No, Dominic . . . I'm sorry. I don't know
where he is.  He never came home from
work.

She paused to straighten a doily on the arm of the sofa, then turned back to him.

MOTHER (cont'd)
But Dominic, it was *wonderful!* So beautiful a play, I never seen!  And *you* were
wonderful!  I am so proud of you, my
son!

Dominic smiled and walked over to her and hugged her. It was the first time he could remember doing such a thing in a long, long time. Overt affection in his home had been a rarity, something shunned and almost feared.

> DOMINIC
>
> Thanks, Mom.

> MOTHER
>
> I always knew you were a good boy. I always knew you would make me proud some day.

> DOMINIC
>
> Did you?

He pulled away from her, looked at her intently.

> DOMINIC (cont'd)
>
> Then why didn't you ever tell me when I was a kid? Back when I really needed it.

His mother turned away, stared into the sink.

> MOTHER
>
> You wouldn't understand, Dominic. You don't know how many times I wanted to say something, but . . .

> DOMINIC
>
> But it was him, wasn't it? Christ, Mom, were you that much afraid of him that you could just stand by and watch him destroy your only son?

> MOTHER
>
> Don't talk like that, Dominic. I prayed for you Dominic . . . I prayed into the

night that you would be stronger than
me, that you would stand up to him. I
did what I *could* Dominic . . .

DOMINIC
I think I needed more than prayers, Mom
. . . but that's okay. I understand. I'm
sorry I jumped on you like that.

Then came the sound of a key fumbling in a lock. The
click of the doorknob sounded loud and ominous. The door
swung open slowly to reveal his father, obviously drunk, leaning against the threshold. Joseph Kazan shambled onto the
set, seemingly unaware of anyone else's presence. He collapsed in his usual chair and stared out into empty space.

DOMINIC
Where have you been?

His father looked at him with a hardness, unaffected by
the glaze in his eyes.

FATHER
What the fuck you care?

DOMINIC
You're my father. I care. Sons are supposed to care about their fathers . . . or
haven't you heard?

FATHER
(coughing)
Don't get wise with me! I can still
get out of this chair and whomp you
one!

DOMINIC
(smiling sadly)
Is that the only form of communication
you know?—"Whomping" people?

FATHER
(laughing)
Ah, it's not even worth it! You and your
fancy words . . . What do you know
about bein' a man?

DOMINIC
Dad, I wanted you to be there tonight.
You *knew* I wanted you there . . . didn't
you?

His father looked at him and the hardness in his eyes
seemed to soften a bit. Looking away, Joseph Kazan spoke in
a low voice.

FATHER
Yeah . . . yeah, I knew.

DOMINIC
So why weren't you there? Did it really
feel better to crawl into one of those
sewers you call a bar and get filthy
drunk? Did you think that getting juiced
would make it all go away?! What do—

FATHER
Shut up! Shut up before I whomp ya!

His father had put his hands over his ears, trying to shut
out the offending words.

DOMINIC
No, I don't think so. I don't think you'll
be "whomping" anybody. Ever again.

FATHER
That's brave words from a wimp like you.

DOMINIC
Don't talk to me about "brave." Why
didn't you come to the play tonight? *My*
play! Your *son's* play!

FATHER
What're you talkin' about?

DOMINIC
What were you afraid of, Dad? That maybe some of your buddies might see you? Might catch you going to see a bunch of "faggots?"

FATHER
Hah! See, you even admit it yourself!

Dominic's mother moved in between the two men.

MOTHER
Oh God, look at you two! So much anger . . . so much hate. Please, stop it . . . !

DOMINIC
Hate? No, Mom, that's not right. A lack of love, maybe . . . but not really hate. There's a difference.

FATHER
(looking at his son)
What the hell do you know?

DOMINIC
I think that's the heart of the problem around here—not enough love in this house. There isn't any love here. No warmth . . . no love.

FATHER
Shit, I'll tell y'about love! I worked for yer Mom for thirty-five years. Worked hard! Did she ever have to go out'n take a job like other guys' wives? Shit, no!

His father was trembling as he spoke, his florid face puffy and shining with sweat.

DOMINIC

There's more to love than that, Dad. Like
the love between you and me . . . When
I was a kid, did you ever just sit down
and play with me?  Did you ever tell me
stories, or try to make me laugh?  How
about going fishing together, or flying a
kite?  Did we ever do any things like that?

FATHER

A man has to work!

DOMINIC

Did you really love your work *that* much?

FATHER

What do y'mean?

DOMINIC

Did you love your work more than me?

FATHER
(confused, angry)
Don't talk no bullshit to me!

DOMINIC

It's not bullshit, Dad.  Listen, when I
was little—no brothers or sisters—I spent
a lot of time alone. Sometimes I needed
someone to guide me, to teach me.

FATHER

I never ran out and never came home
late at night . . . ask your mother! I was
always there, every night!

DOMINIC
(smiling sadly)
Oh yeah, you were there physically. But
never emotionally, can't you see that?  I

can remember seeing other kids out doing things with their fathers, and I can
remember really *hating* them—because
they had something I never did. That
kind of stuff hurt me a lot more than
your belt ever did.

His father did not respond, but looked down at his lap
where he had unconsciously knotted his hands together.

MOTHER
Dominic, leave him alone now. Let's
all have some coffee, and we can—

DOMINIC
No, Mom. Let's finish it. Let's get it all
out. It's been a long time coming.
(to his father)
Hey, Dad . . . do you know I have *no*
memories of you ever encouraging me
to do *anything?* Except all that macho
shit.

FATHER
*What* kind of shit?

DOMINIC
Remember when I saved my paper
route money and bought that cheap guitar?

FATHER
Yeah, so . . . ?

DOMINIC
But I guess you've forgotten how you
screamed and yelled that you couldn't
afford music lessons, and music was only
for "fairies" anyhow?

FATHER

I ain't sure . . .

DOMINIC

Well, *I'm* sure. And when I told you I'd
teach myself how to play it, you laughed,
remember?

FATHER

Did I?

DOMINIC

Yes, and I don't have to strain to recall
how that felt. It's carved right into my
heart. The whole goddamned scene.

FATHER

So who ever heard of anybody teachin'
themselves to play music? It's crazy!

DOMINIC

Yeah, maybe . . . but I *did* teach myself,
didn't I? And I played in a band until
that night I came home late from a dance
and you were waiting for me behind
the door—Remember that, Dad? The
night you smashed my guitar over the
sink?

His father looked away from him. He seemed truly embarrassed now.

DOMINIC (cont'd)

That's what my life's been like, Dad;
me doing interesting things *despite* what
I got from you. Or maybe I should say
what I *didn't* get from you!

FATHER

That's horseshit.

DOMINIC
(shaking his head)
I wish it was. I really do. But it's all
true, Dad. All true.

FATHER
Why don't you just shut up!

DOMINIC
Because I'm not finished yet. What's the
matter, am I threatening you? I think that's
what the problem has always been—
you never liked the way your wide-
eyed kid had some natural curiosity about
the world, did you?

FATHER
(sounding tired now)
You're not making any sense.

DOMINIC
Well try this one: you weren't only threatened by your son, but just about *everybody*. Anybody you thought was more
intelligent than you, or more educated,
or had more money . . . you always had
something shitty to say about all of them,
didn't you?

FATHER
Now, it ain't like that!

DOMINIC
Wait! Let me finish. So then you wake
up one morning and you realize that
your own weirdo kid was not going to
grow up to be a beer-drinking macho
man, you just gave up, didn't you?

FATHER

What do you mean?

DOMINIC

I mean that when you saw that your own
kid was turning out to be a hell of a lot
different from you—but very much like
all those kinds of people you feared and
therefore despised—then you stopped
being a father to that strange son.

FATHER

I what?

DOMINIC

Didn't you know that all I wanted was a
little approval?   A little love?

FATHER

You talk like you got it all figured out . . .
what do you think you are—a doctor or
something?

DOMINIC

(grinning)

No. No "doctor". . . just a son. And if I
haven't "figured it all out," at least I'm
trying.   You never even tried!

His father stared at him and tried to speak, but no words
would come.   His lower lip trembled slightly from the effort.

DOMINIC

Don't you understand why I'm telling
you all this?  Don't you understand what
I've been trying to say?

His father shook his head quickly, uttered a single word.

FATHER

No . . .

> DOMINIC
>
> I can't think of anything else to say. No other way to make you understand . . . except to just tell you, Dad. I don't know why, but after all the years, and after all the pain, I know that I still love you, that I have to love you.

He walked closer to his father and stared into his eyes, searching for some glimmer of understanding.

> DOMINIC (cont'd)
>
> I love you, Dad.
> (pause)
> And I need to hear the same thing from you.

There was a long silence as father and son regarded each other. Dominic could feel the presence of some great force gathering over the stage. Then he saw the tears forming in his father's eyes.

> FATHER
> (stepping forward)
> Oh, Dominic . . .

His father grabbed him up in his arms and pulled him close. For an instant, Dominic resisted, but then relaxed, falling into the embrace with his father.

> FATHER
> My son . . . what happened to us?
> (pause)
> I . . . *love* you! I *do* love you!

Dominic felt the barrel-chest of his father close against his own and he was very conscious of how strange a sensation it was. Suddenly there was a great roaring in his ears and he was instantly terrified, disoriented. His father had relaxed his emotional embrace and Dominic pulled back and looked into the man's face.

451

He was only vaguely aware of the stage lights quickly fading to black, but in the last instant of illumination he saw that his father no longer stood before him.  He now stared into the face of a stranger.

An actor.

The roaring sound had coalesced into something recognizable, and Dominic turned to look out into the brimming audience—a sea of people who were on their feet, clamoring, applauding wildly.

Then the curtain closed, sealing him off from them, from the torrent of appreciation.

He was only half aware of his two fellow actors—the ones who had portrayed his father and mother—as they moved to each side of him, joining their hands in his.

The lights came up as the curtain reopened.  The audience renewed its furious applause, and suddenly he understood.

Feeling a flood of warmth and a special sense of gratitude, Dominic Kazan stepped forward to take his bow.

*finale*

*When I was about fourteen or so, I was about two years into that great series of Ballantine Books paperback reprints of all kinds of classic science fiction, fantasy, and horror.[1] It got to the point that I knew each month when the new titles would be delivered to my local bookstore, and Mike Keating, Bobby Schaller, and I would go down there to scoop up whatever was new that month. On one occasion, I can remember Mike picking up this book with a strange looking cover and saying something like: "Hey, this one looks pretty cool . . . ." It was called* The Survivor and Others *by H. P. Lovecraft—and it proved to be cool, indeed.*

*I remember reading this tale about a guy who discovered this underground passage beneath an old house in a New England town. And although I've actually forgotten the details of the piece, I recall the protagonist dealing with dank chambers that had a strange odor as if some hideous*

---

[1] *Published in the early Sixties, the line of books proved to be a seminal influence on me and my writing. Many of them featured the surrealistic artwork of Richard Gid Powers—swirling landscapes of color and motion, populated occasionally by spindle-like mannequins—that were as captivating as the fiction therein. The Ballantine imprint introduced me to other magicians such as Ray Bradbury, Henry Kuttner, Theodore Sturgeon, Robert Bloch, Richard Matheson, Robert Sheckley, Joseph Payne Brennan, Frederik Pohl, Anthony Boucher, C. M. Kornbluth, William Tenn, John Wyndham, Harlan Ellison . . . and eventually some guy named H. P. Lovecraft.*

YOG SOTHOTH, SUPERSTAR

*creature had recently slithered along the path. I discovered a whole new lexicon of strange words like "Silurian" and "batrachian" and "obsidian," plus a bunch of strange references to places and things I never heard of—Arkham, Innsmouth, The Miskatonic University, and of course, the NECRONOMICON. And I haven't even mentioned the dark litany of names of the Old Ones . . . .[2]*

*Yeah, I was hooked on this H. P. character. I was fascinated by all the esoteric references to what appeared to be a large body of work about a race of beings that inhabited the earth hundreds of thousands of years, perhaps even millions, before human civilization had chipped out its first flint arrowhead.[3] I didn't know it at the time, but I would gradually piece together a much larger tapestry, a protohistory of sorts, which has been called the Cthulhu Mythos—a body of fictional references to beings, places, events, discoveries, and stories of encounters with an earlier age of the Earth.*

*I had also recently discovered Poe, so Lovecraft's outrageously florid prose didn't bother me that much. In fact, it probably infected me, and caused my own early writing to be heavily freighted with too many adverbs and adjectives. Years went by as I tracked down books and stories by Lovecraft, and the picture of his metaphysical arcana (see—he would love that phrase!) became gradually clear. The larger body of the Mythos has become a kind of canon to which many, many writers have contributed their own stories over the decades.*

---

[2] *The names I can't spell without looking them up; and since I'm sitting here comfortably, and nowhere near a book where I can check them, I'm just going to assume you're familiar with them to some degree. If not, then your development as a reader and mutant has been severely retarded; and you need to go out and get books with titles such as* The Outsider, At the Mountains of Madness, Dagon, *and* The Dunwich Horror.

[3] *Oddly enough, some very current thinking by scientist-thinkers like Graham Hancock and writers like Art Bell and Whitley Strieber have been discussing the possibilities that the Earth, through violent, cataclysmic changes of climate and topography, scrubs itself clean every several hundred thousand years (or less). And in the process, removes all traces of the detritus of any civilizations or beings which may have evolved and flourished on its thin crust.*

*If these guys are on the right track, wouldn't it be weird if Lovecraft was in some way, kind of half-assed correct? Can you spell irony? I thought that you could.*

*I still read a Lovecraft story once in a while, more in appreciation for the groundwork he put into place in the literature of dark fantasy, then to discover something new. His work remains popular with certain small presses devoted entirely to doing work about him and his fiction. One of them, Chaosium, planned a book entitled* Songs of Cthulhu, *which wanted stories in the Mythos, which employed a musical theme in the tradition of Lovecraft's classic tale, "The Music of Erich Zann." After accepting the invitation, I decided I might re-read "Zann" to see what the editor, Mark Rainey, was looking for. It was not a good idea, I discovered. Lovecraft's story pretty much "said it all" on the theme, and I was more bummed than inspired. I had no desire to re-invent the wheel, and had a tough time coming up with a tale that would be distinctively mine and yet nod in all the right directions.*

*Then one night, while I was still casting around for just the right idea, Elizabeth was doing her nightly channel-zap with the remote and she settled on the film version of one her favorite (she loves* musicals*) Andrew Lloyd Webber productions. I watched it for about ten seconds before I knew what I was going to be writing about. All I had was the title, but that was all I would need. The story, I was confident, would write itself, and as usual, it did.*

# F~AX~

DATE: March 3
TO:     Garrett Fairfax
FROM: Shirley Zuckerman, The Actors Advocates Agency

Great news, Garrett! I just got off the phone with Michael
Morrison (yes, *that* Michael Morrison). He wants you to audition for the lead in a new musical/rock opera he's going to be
directing.

10:00 a.m. This coming Tuesday. The Helen Hayes. It's
called *Lovecraft, I love you!* and I have no idea what it's about.
Morrison saw you in Soho. That dreadful little comedy about
Saddam Hussein, and thought you'd be perfect for the lead!

Call me as soon as you get this. Congratulations, and give
my regards to Broadway!

Shirley

---

(. . . *so leave your message after the beep . . . beeeeeep!*)
Shirley, this is Garrett. Just got your fax and Jesus Christ, I
can't believe it! Tell Mr. Morrison I'll be there, and he won't
be disappointed. Thanks, kiddo, for believing in me all this
time! This is the break I've been waiting for. Jesus, I can't
believe it . . . ! Call me and let's catch lunch at Marv's Deli. The
reubens are on *me* this time. See ya and thanks again.
(*click*)

---

April 14

Dear Analia:

So's how's my favorite sister doing back in Cincinnati? Are John and the boys doing okay? Last time I heard from you he was taking that new job at American Express. Hope it worked out.

Anyway, you won't believe what happened at the last casting call I went to—I got picked! Not only that, but I got the female romantic lead! That's the best part! I'm playing the part of Sonia, the girlfriend of the hero, a guy named Howard. I haven't gotten my script and songs yet, so I don't know too much about the story. It's a rock opera called Lovecraft, I Love You! and I heard it's about some guy who was a writer in Rhode Island. Sounds kind of boring, but who cares! Your sister is on Broadway! Can you believe it? I'm not sure I do yet.

Don't tell Mom yet. I want to write her a surprise note, okay?

We'll talk soon.

Love,

Estela

───────────────────────────────

MEMO

TO:  Michael Morrison, Director
FROM:  Isabel Cortez, Assistant to the Chairman

The Arkham Foundation Board of Directors would like to formally congratulate you on your commencement of rehearsals for Lovecraft, I Love You!

Please do not hesitate to contact me for anything you may need during this exciting phase of our production. The Board anxiously awaits opening night.

───────────────────────────────

(excerpt from *Lovecraft, I Love You!* songbook)

I don't know why you write those
Sill-lee stuh-uh-orrrr-eeees!
And I don't really care . . . .
The only thing I know is that
I luh-uh-uvvvvv you!
So you know that ease-a-lee I don't scare!

---

June 2nd

Dear Analia:

It's me, your sister. I know I could just call you and just tell you all this stuff, but believe me, the letter writing is very therapeutic. It slows me down. Makes me take my time. That way, I compose my thoughts and I keep things under control. Everything in this city is so . . . high-energy, so frenetic. I need some time when I simply can't be so UP—know what I mean?

Anyway, it's been more than a month since we started rehearsals on the musical and I don't know what to think. I've learned all my songs and my dance numbers, and sister-dear, I have to tell you—this thing is a squawking turkey. If we get through opening night with our reputations intact, we'll all be very lucky. If this show lasts more than a week, we should start dancing in the streets.

Analia, you know me—I would never bite the hands that feed me, and you know I would have probably killed to get this job (or any job, really), but I have to confide in you . . . this is the worst show I have ever seen. The songs are stupid and half of them aren't even written in English, I don't think. The story (what I can make of it, that is) is unbelievably dumb. And the main character is this racist recluse named Howard who writes scary stories in Providence. He discovered the remains of this ancient civilization and the names of some of the places and the people are like . . . unpronounceable! I'm telling you—it's the dumbest thing I have ever seen. Even our

459

director (a really famous guy who did <u>Dogs!</u> and <u>Goodbye, Molly!</u>) is embarrassed by this show.

I don't know why I'm telling you all this, except that I guess I never thought it could be like this. I always thought that getting a part in a Broadway show was like the best thing that could ever happen to you. I never imagined it could be so . . . so bad.

But that doesn't mean I'm not going to stick this one out. Some of the other people in the show who've become my friends, we all say that even if this one's a "bomb," we'll all have a "leg up" on the next audition, the next show. (That's a little theater-talk, for you)

So hang in there, sister. Tell John I said "Hi!" and give the little boys some hugs and kisses for me. If by some miracle my show lasts more than a week, I'll send you some comps. Not that you'll like it, but you should see it just to see how awful it is. You won't believe it. (The worst part is that it will kind of prove to John that he's right—that all musicals are dumb). Oh well.

We still have six weeks of rehearsal before Opening (and probably Closing) Night. I guess I should wrap this up and get some sleep.

Love,

Estela

---

( . . . *and I'll call you back as soon as possible . . . beeeeep!*)

Okay, Harvey, this is Michael! Now where the fuck *are* you, man!? Everytime I call you about this show you got me hooked into, you are *NEV-VER* fuck-king there! Harvey, if you're screening your calls, *pick up the phone goddammit!*

(pause)

Damn! I *have* to talk to you about this nutty show . . . Harvey, it's *terrible!* It's career self-immolation! I know I have a contract but I'm telling you—I *can't* stay on this . . . this theatrical *abortion!* So Harvey, I'm telling you—if I don't hear from you tonight, I'm quitting in the morning. I'm calling that Cortez harpie at that bogus Foundation . . . and telling her to find herself another Director. I'm telling her to get somebody who never wants to work on Broadway again.

Because I can tell you—that somebody ain't me!

---

From: R'lyeh@necronomi.con
Date: Sat, 18 June 23:34:53 -0500 (EST)
To: mmorrison@nymailex.com
Subject: Your Resignation

Mr. Morrison:

Your agent, Harvey Goldstone, has just informed me of your wishes to disenfranchise yourself from the project. I am very sad to receive such news. I must take this opportunity to inform you personally the same thing I said to Mr. Goldstone, *viz.*, you are under contract to the Arkham Foundation and are therefore an indentured employee of the Foundation. You have no choice but to fulfill your obligations. If you read the terms of your employment closely, as I have also requested of Mr. Goldstone, you might notice that you risk dire consequences if you attempt to disregard your contractual agreement.

Thank you for your understanding and expected compliance.

In sincerity, I remain,

Albert Hazred, Chairman of the Board

P.S. I am sending this message in duplicate by means of fax, phone, FedEx, messenger, and United States Postal Service as well because it is very important that you receive this warning.

---

**The New York Times (AP)**—It was reported by Lieutenant Detective Thomas Brancuso of the NYPD's homicide division that Michael Morrison, the well-known Broadway Director, was found murdered in his Park Avenue South co-

op early this morning. "The circumstances surrounding his death are very
strange," said Brancuso. "We aren't ready
to divulge all the details, but I can tell
you this—I've been on the force nineteen years, and I've never seen anything like it." Mr. Morrison was working
on a new rock-opera entitled *Lovecraft,
I Love You!* He was a native of
Painesvillle, Ohio, and was thirty-nine
years old.

---

*( . . . . so leave your message after the beep . . . beeep!)*

Hey Shirley, this is Garrett . . . aren't you *ever* home? Anyway, I guess you heard about Morrison—waking up this morning and finding himself dead. Know what I mean? The rumors
are flying around here like feathers in a pillow fight, and I was
wondering if you've heard anything or if you might know what's
really going on. The one that's flying through the cast and crew
is he quit the show yesterday. Not surprised 'cause it was no
secret he *hated* it. Got so bad he was starting to hate all of us,
too. Know what I mean? Bad scene all around. I mean, I gotta
tell ya, (but *please*, don't tell anybody I said anything . . .) the
show's a stinker. If we don't tank the first week or so, I'll be
shocked, stunned, and all the rest of that surprised stuff. But a
job's a job—especially if it's on Broadway. Know what I mean?
So look, give me a call as soon as you can, as soon as you
know something, okay? Somebody in the show told me they
have a friend at the 84th Precinct and he told her Morrison was
like . . . like torn into lots of pieces. Only some of the pieces
were missing . . . . So anyway, I'll be waiting to hear from you.
Ms. Cortez came by this afternoon and said we'll have a new
Director tomorrow. I'll tell you who it is when I find out. The
show must go on, right? C-ya!

*(click!)*

---

(excerpt from WVXN-FM's *Eye On Broadway* Weekly Feature:)

**EOB**: There's been a lot of speculation surrounding the new rock opera, *Lovecraft, I Love You!*, which is scheduled to open next week at the Helen Hayes. I'm speaking with one of the show's leads, Estela Duarte . . . How're you doing, Estela?

**Duarte:** Great, Margot, just great!

**EOB:** Your show has been pretty much of a secret from the beginning, but ever since the tragic death of your Director, the legendary Michael Morrison, the producers of *Lovecraft, I Love You!* have *really* put the clamps on, wouldn't you say?

**Duarte:** Well, yeah, I guess that's true. But I know they've always wanted to keep the whole show under wraps until we actually opened.

**EOB:** Do you have any idea why they've wanted it like that?

**Duarte:** Well gee, I don't know. Nobody ever explained it to us. I just know that it's in everybody's contract that we're forbidden to reveal anything about the show until after Opening Night.

**EOB:** Wow, then I guess my next question isn't going to get answered—I was going to ask you what could be so exciting in the show's plot that would make it more top secret than the Manhattan Project?

**Duarte:** (giggling) You know, I'm not sure. Why don't you ask me that question next week, after we've opened?

**EOB:** I certainly will . . . But in the meantime, what can you tell us about the rumors that several other people involved with the show have either died in horrible accidents or have been maimed terribly . . .

**Duarte:** I'm . . . I'm afraid I can't comment on that. I don't know anything about that.

**EOB:** Now, come on, Estela—which one is it?

**Duarte:** (shrugging, giggling) Well, I guess a little of both!

**EOB:** We've also heard there's some huge production expenses connected to this project. Care to comment?

**Duarte:** Well . . .

**EOB:** Our spies tell us that there's a scene where an ancient city, buried beneath the deepest part of the ocean, suddenly rises up in a breath-taking display of lightning and volcanoes, and lots of steam and boiling sea foam.

**Duarte:** (giggling yet again) Well if that's what your spies have told you, I guess you better decide whether or not to believe them.

**EOB:** Okay, well thanks, Estela! You've got us all curious, to say the least. This is Margot Vanderkelen for WVXN-FM and I'll see you next week with another *Eye On Broadway*!

---

*( . . . after the beep, do your thing . . . beeep!)*
Garrett, this is Shirley, calling you back. It's phone-tag again, and you're it! Anyway, sugar, tomorrow's the big night, huh? Just calling to wish you luck, and tell you I'll be there, but I'm going to be a little late. But I'll be there before Intermission, I promise. Despite what you think, the buzz is you've got a hit on your hands. With all that hush-hush stuff and all, you've got the whole theater gang pretty excited. I think you're just being too hard on yourself. Oh, and wasn't that awful about Margot Vanderkelen? Anyway, see you tomorrow night! Break a leg!
*(click!)*

---

July 20th

Dear Analia:

Okay, this is it. By the time you get this letter, Lovecraft, I Love You! will be a part of Broadway history.

Well, at least, your sister will be over her Opening Night Jitters. Everybody is nervous and some of the people are actually scared, or superstitious at least.

I mean, you probably didn't hear about it out there in Cincinnati, but this lady who does a radio show about all the Broadway shows fell in front of a subway a couple of nights back—right after the interview she did with me (I know, I forgot to tell you about it . . .) was on the air. There was a witness, a homeless guy, who said she didn't fall at all, that she was pulled out onto the tracks by something in the shadows, something that looked kind of like a big octopus.

Pretty silly, I know, but some of the people in the show

are a little freaked by the story. Especially after one of the crew got caught in the gears of the hydraulic lift at tech rehearsal last night. I'll have to tell you all the gooshy parts when I see you next week. (You are still flying in with John, aren't you?)

So give all the kids a big hug and kiss (each) from their Favorite Aunt. I can't wait to see you guys!

Love,

Estela

---

*(From the Sunday Times ENTERTAINMENT Section)*

Probably the most anticipated opening of the young season has to have been the Arkham Foundation's production of *Lovecraft, I Love You!* I know this critic had been hearing conflicting reports about the show on the jungle telegraph, and when you combine that with a few mysterious, albeit accidental, deaths of people connected with the show, well, I'd say you have something intriguing in the very least.

*Lovecraft, I Love You!* stars promising new talents in the persons of Garrett Fairfax and Estela Duarte, who portray the lead characters of Providence writer, Howard Lovecraft and his enigmatic ladyfriend, Sonia Greene. But before going on, I'd better make a small confession: despite the above actors' earnest efforts, I initially found them in a futile struggle to be believable. The show's opening songs and choreographies seemed so . . . *lame* (the only word that springs to mind) . . . that I was about to dismiss the production as a dismal and insulting assault on good taste. Indeed, I sensed a similar displeasure in the audience.

However, something odd and wonderful happened as the show picked up steam. The leaden cadence of the songs began to create a disposition not unlike that created by a selection of Gregorian Chants. The overblown lighting and special effects gradually passed from merely tolerable to palatable and finally engrossing. I experienced a transformation not only of mood, but of spirit. To feel my predisposed negative feelings be consummately dispelled was almost a religious, if not transcendental experience. Another oddly wonderful aspect of *Lovecraft, I Love You!* is its subtle, yet inexorable, revelation of an arcane mythology, which is far too complex to explore in this limited space. Be it enough for this critic to simply say the portrayal of the mythic system is fascinating, engrossing, and almost hypnotic. For an entirely original and exciting night of theatre, don't miss this one.

(blurbs from the billboards at Times Square . . .)

"Enthralling!" *The New York Post*
"Mesmerizing!" *The New Yorker*
"A religious experience." *The New York Times*
"Subversive and captivating!" *The Village Voice*
"Watch out for this one!" *The East Village Other*

(from a *Newsday* music review . . .)

For the third week in a row the chart-topper CD in the Showtunes category is *Lovecraft, I Love you!* Industry neophyte Necro Records must have been using a crystal ball on this one. By releasing an original cast CD of the hit rock-opera only two days after the Broadway opening, they've enjoyed the marketing coup of the year. This is the hottest disc in New York these days. No matter where you go, you cannot help but hear people humming the odd tunes, singing those songs with their weird and practically unpronouncable lyrics. Subways, buses, elevators, the streets, and even store clerks as they work. No doubt about it: the city's pulse can be found in the beat of this music.

**The New York Times (AP)**—Dr. F. X. Paulson, of Columbia University confirmed the reports of unusual seismic activity beneath the deep underwater canyons of the Hudson River and its confluence with the Atlantic Ocean. "It's very odd," said Professor Paulson. "It is as if there was something down there, trying to push its way to the surface. The pressure point is extremely precise and focused. I've never seen anything like it." When asked what the disturbance could be, the renowned geologist was at a quandary. "It's easier to say what it *cannot* be, which is an undersea volcano or a heretofore undiscovered faultline. Rather, these recent quakes seem to be caused by a solid object being forced

467

upwards through the earth's crust. Impossible, I know, but that's what it *looks* like nonetheless." When asked how big this "object" appeared to be, Paulson replied with a smile: "Oh, my . . . much bigger than Manhattan. That is why it's impossible, you see?"

---

(from the police report of NYPD Detective Sergeant Rick Sjoerdsma:)

After meeting with Officers Charles and Grant of NY Transit Police, plus compiling the accounts of numerous eyewitnesses (see attached) I have been able to piece together the events of the previous two weeks at the Times Square subway station and the connecting tunnels. The picture that emerges is not pretty and it frankly makes no sense. I've talked to people from some of the colleges, and also guys from the Health Department, and nobody can explain why all the rats and even all the bugs, have been clearing out. Sewer workers have been reporting the same kinds of things. People who've seen the rats say it's like watching cattle getting herded along the tracks and up the stairwells. Weird, but that's what they've told me.

The Transit employees I've talked with all agree that the bums have all disappeared, too. Right after the rats started leaving. Only the homeless people didn't pack up and vacate. They just disappeared, like I first said. My men found their cardboard boxes and blankets, their hordes of food and booze. But no bums.

Lots of people have reported seeing a green-glowing fog in the tunnels.

One trainman I talked to (who pleaded with me not to use his name and agreed to talk only when I put that promise in writing) says he saw some kind of monsters in the tunnels, also in the green fog. He said they were big, but didn't look like any animals he'd ever seen, more like weird vegetables or plants with long waving stems or tendrils, really. He said they moved quickly out of the way of his high-speed train, almost melting into the darkness of the tunnel walls. The guy doesn't sound crazy, but what would you think? No wonder he doesn't want his boss to find out what kind of trash he's talking . . . .

The thing that bugs me the most about the commuters who've been turning up missing is that we haven't been able to find a trace of evidence, not a thing. It's like these people never existed.

---

MEMO

TO: Isabel Cortez
FROM: Albert Hazred, Chairman of the Board

The Arkham Foundation would like to personally thank you for overseeing the production of Lovecraft, I Love You! Your diligence and attention to detail has been as much responsible for the show's outrageous success as its obviously seductive and powerful content.

Please accept as a bonus, a week's vacation aboard the Foundation's yacht, *The Innsmouth,* which will be sailing this week for a cruise to selected archeological sites. It will be an experience that would give me great displeasure were you to miss out.

---

*(from a CNN tape of an-on-the-scene broadcast)*

. . . thank you, Bernard! This is Mark Ashton in New York City coming to you live from the roof of the World Trade Center. Behind and below me lies the historic tableau of the city's harbor and Statue of Liberty, whose waters are dotted with the hulls of hundreds of ships. The boats you see are a collection of scientific and military craft, as well as those of onlookers who have been repeatedly warned to keep their distance. The underwater disturbances of the previous weeks in the waters off

469

Manhattan have been closely monitored after it was ascertained that an immense object is rising up from the ocean floor. Just exactly what this object might be has been beyond speculation and the authorities are not talking. The evacuation of the city has been as orderly as could be hoped for. Looting and violence have been sporadic and kept under control in most precincts. As I look towards the west, I see—uh, can you hold on one moment, please . . . ? We have an open channel to the NYPD's Special Task Force Command Center . . . I'm getting something from their spokesperson . . .

*(the camera-view shakes violently, the microphone captures a terrible, rolling rumble, like thunder but much longer and louder . . . )*

Something is definitely happening . . . What? I can't get all of that! Bernard, our signal's breaking up with the Command Center, but I can see from our vantage point that something is happening out there on the water. Another series of temblors have rolled beneath the city and the Twin Tower itself is swaying in reaction! I can see something out in the harbor breaking the surface! It's glistening white and—Jesus, it's fucking *huge!*

*(another quake rocks the camera-view, this time violently, and the image is tilted severely, then rezzed out, but the audio continues . . . )*

Oh-my-God! What *is* that thing?! The ships! The Statue of Liberty—! Everything's going down! We're getting outta here as soon as possible. The building is swaying wildly now! Christ, Gary, get that chopper in here! Jesus, it's big! It's impossi—

*Finally, we come to the last story.*

*It is, as I write this, the most recent short fiction I have written, although it will soon be eclipsed by something newer because, as you must realize by now, there are always new editors, new anthologies, and of course there are always new stories to be told.*

*This one was also inspired by the good folks at Tekno Books, who had sold a book of stories to a regional publisher up here in New England about one of the seacoast's most recognizable landmarks—its lighthouses. Of course, this anthology had a twist—haunted lighthouses.*

*Friends, I gotta tell you, when I read the letter of invitation from editor John Helfers, I audibly* groaned. *I couldn't imagine too many more themes showing* more *tread-wear than this one. The deadline was months away, and I figured, hey, you never know. Maybe something would hit me, but all I knew was there was no way I was doing some tired old business about a lighthouse keeper going stir-crazy and killing somebody or himself, or some sea-captain who haunts a lighthouse because the keeper forgot to turn it on and . . . whoops!-sorry-about-your-shipwreck-sir!*

*Yeah, this one would be tough. I called my buddy Rick Hautala, who, being one of the most suspicious of Suspects, to see if he had been invited to contribute to this worthy tome. Of course he had . . .*

*I asked him if he'd come up with anything yet, and he said he was working on a tale but it wasn't finished yet. I told him I was striking out, but wouldn't be giving up on it. I figured I would follow the advice I talked about in the beginning of this book, and I started to* ask the next question . . .

*Where do you find lighthouses?* By water.

*Okay, What do they do?* Show boats a safe passage.

*Right, well then, what kind of boats?*

*What kind of boats indeed . . .*

*Something got me thinking about the variety of vessels that might need some sort of illumination, and I came up with the perfect craft for my tale.[1]*

*But as I told the story and reached the ending, I realized I didn't have one. There was only one thing to do—check in with my personal Muse, Elizabeth, who agreed with me in so many words by saying: "The ending is terrible. You need to do it like this . . . "*

*I agreed, worked it out on the page, and now, the tale wraps up, no pun intended, brilliantly.*

*And so, with that final revelation out of the way, I'll leave you in the hope you've enjoyed your journey through the "forests of the night."[2]*

---

[1] *The title, by the way, for all you non-Latin scholars (and I suspect you are legion), means "light and truth."*

[2] *If you've been inspired, enriched, entertained, or angered, then I've probably done my job.*

"You want me to do *what?*" said Carlo Duarte.

He was sitting in a booth in a bar'n'grill called The Coach's Place in White River Junction, Vermont. Two different televisions displayed different college basketball games. Across from him was a woman dressed in black, and everything about her could be described by the word *indeterminate*.

Her age for starters, thought Carlo. She didn't look old, per se, but her smooth, elliptical face was somehow endowed with a *depth* of wisdom, experience, and that sort of thing. And going right along with that ambiguous leit-motif, Carlo was not certain whether or not this woman was attractive or plain. Sometimes, when the light and shadows played their parts, and she turned her head a certain way, her features combined to be intriguing and interesting in ways that only the face of a woman can be. At others, she looked odd, homely, or downright scary.

Her style of dress was also hard to pin down, so to speak. Kind of a decadent *chic*-ness. Loose and flowing blouse and long skirt, all black, evocative of the pen-and-inks of Aubrey Beardsley. Add a scarf here, some rings and bracelets, and she had a "look," that got your attention, but for reasons that were . . . well, indeterminate.

Same for her name. He was sure she'd given it to him when he'd called her for the job interview, and she'd said it again when they met for lunch, but damned if he could remember it. Ms. Stephanie . . . ? Something like that. Well, it didn't matter, really. Either he'd remember it, or she'd tell him again.

"Sir," she said in soft tones that still managed to convey her lack of patience with fools. "I made it quite clear. We're looking for a lighthouse keeper . . . on the White River. Are you interested, or not?"

Carlo held up his hands in mock surrender. "Whoa, yeah, of course I am. It would be perfect for me . . . but I never knew there was ever a lighthouse around here. Especially on the White River."

She gave him a patronizing and brief smile. "There has been none, till now. My . . . colleagues are building it as we speak."

"Oh, okay," said Carlo. "I understand. That's cool—when will it be ready?"

"Any time now . . ." The woman reached out and took both his hands in her own, and her touch was neither warm nor cold. "Tell me a little more about yourself. You said you're thirty-eight years old. Any relatives nearby? Wives? Ex-wives? Girlfriends, boyfriends? Any big commitments looming?"

Carlo withdrew his hands as he leaned back in the booth, placed them casually behind his head. "Well, like I said on the phone, I'm an artist. I do freelance illustration for some of the companies around here, but it's not steady income. I'm trying to get enough paintings finished to get a gallery interested, but that takes time."

"And you think being a light-keeper would afford you that time?"

"Yes, I do." He paused. "Why, am I wrong?"

"No, not at all. You'll have all the time in the world. Your duties will allow you to paint. But never be distracted from your one primary duty—to keep the light burning."

"No problem," said Carlo.

"No distractions. Hence the questions about the other people in your life."

Carlo smiled, feeling a little self-conscious. "Never married. No girlfriends. It's not that I have trouble meeting them or anything like that, but most women don't have much patience for my lifestyle. I need to spend a lot of time alone . . . because of my work."

"Perfectly understandable," said the woman, standing up and reaching across the booth's table to shake his hand. "I think you'll do just fine."

The lighthouse was located on the White River about 20 miles northwest of the Junction, where it joined the Connecticut River on its journey south. Architecturally, it was similar to most New England lighthouses of the present and past centuries. New Hampshire granite and lots of brick masonry gave it classic substance and silhouette against the evening sky. The only thing that made it any different from any other lighthouse was its location—about 150 miles from the seacoast.

Carlo Duarte thought about that anomaly and had attempted to ask his interviewer about it, but she had said everything would be explained to him in the "fullness of time." There were other oddities about his employment arrangement, but they were all things he didn't even *want* to question—he would be paid each month in *cash;* it was a *lot* of cash; they didn't ask for a Social Security Number, which meant no federal taxes or FICA deductions, and therefore no IRS; and absolutely *no* paperwork to fill out. That was copacetic with him; he believed paying and filing income taxes was voluntary under the law anyway.

Weird, yes. But a good deal as far as he was concerned.

So, in the meantime, after accepting the offer, he packed up all his painting gear into the old Chevy Blazer, plus enough clothes and supplies to last at least a few weeks, and he drove up Route 4 past Royalton until he found the dirt road leading off towards the lighthouse. With his painterly eye, Carlo had to pause to absorb the scene as evening began to leach the colors off into twilight. Despite the incongruity of the lighthouse on the White River—especially at a point where the distance from bank-to-bank was less than 200 yards, and the depth of the channel couldn't be more than 30 feet—there was a feeling of *rightness* about it. Carlo couldn't articulate what he was feeling, but he just kind of *knew* everything was cool.

The inside of the lighthouse proved to be far more than he'd expected. The furnishings were warm and comfortable, the fixtures and appliances all state-of-the-art. Windows penetrated the spaces in so many places, that every room was flooded with light. The effect was initially unsettling, because it seemed to *expand* the interior, woofing and warping the three-dimensional space of the tapered cylinder into a structure that was far larger on the inside than the outside.

A kind of architectural *gestalt,* thought Carlo.

Again he was forced to pause to realize how quintessentially weird the whole set-up was . . .

It was like those scenes in the cheesy horror movies where you want to stand up and scream at the protagonist: *Don't go in there . . . ! Don't you hear the scary music!?*

He smiled to himself. Indeed, he did hear the discordant violins, but he felt no sense of accompanying dread, no gut-level gnawing of fear. He knew he *should* be wary as hell of all the strangeness, but he rationalized it by telling himself he would keep bugging his employers to give him all the answers.

Entering the top floor of the structure, he found a space that resembled the deck of an air traffic control center—laminated, built-in consoles, the obligatory computer, phone, and a couple of self-explanatory control panels, which he presumed linked up with the huge glass lamp dominating the center of the space. It was all medium-hi tech, and more than enough for what seemed like a job anybody could do in their sleep. Lying next to the keyboard was a thick, richly-bound folio entitled *Procedures and Policies*, which ignited in him a brief moment when he expected all to be made clear to him.

Of course, he was wrong.

But he did learn how to turn the powerful lamp on and off, and how to synch up its rotation with the ever-changing celestial clock that marked off each new sunrise and sunset. The book was written in clear, precise language, and organized to such a Teutonic degree, that it made him uncomfortable. Nobody, he thought, should be thinking in so orderly a fashion. Although he had to admit—after a single reading, and a dry-run at the controls, he understood every nuance of responsibility and duty of the job. Technology and the whole tool-thing had largely eluded his interest, but after reading *Procedures and Policies*, he believed he could even field-strip the giant lamp into its components like a soldier with his weapon, fix, and gang-bang it back together again.

Not bad for somebody who spent most of his time worrying about running out of cadmium yellow or burnt sienna . . .

Several hours later, once he'd gotten everything stashed away in his living quarters, he was standing in front of a fresh canvas. He had chosen the room just below the top floor for his studio because he liked the placements of the windows in terms of the kind of light they admitted, and the views afforded (both banks of the White River and the nearby peak of Mount Ascutney). He kind of liked the idea of seeing that familiar peak—the same one Maxfield Parrish always included in his electrically lush paintings. Then, just as he was about to make his first brush stroke, he heard a sound that lay somewhere between a *buzz* and a *crackle* (the huge bulb of the beacon bursting into heat and light), followed by the whine of the motors that would turn the lamp on its endless axis. Outside the tower, evening had surrendered to nightfall.

Smiling, Carlo felt a flood of job-satisfaction wash his self-esteem centers. He'd set the timers, punched all the stacked commands into the systems, and waited for the semi-automation to take over. When it did it right, he felt good. The score was Carlo *one*, technology *zero*. Game over. Simple as that. The sensitive artist would no longer be intimidated and humbled by rampant science.

Again, he checked his palette, and prepared the initial dab of pigment, when it occurred to him, should he take the wrought iron circular staircase up to the lamp . . . just to see it how things looked. As he lay down his tools, Carlo realized the day would soon come when he would probably cringe at the sound of the lamp firing up and the motors sliding into motion, but for the moment, he was curious.

It was the artist in him, he thought. He needed to see what it *looked like.* That powerful beam sweeping out across the glassy surface and cutting through the blue aisle of night like a white-hot sword. He had to see it from the unique perspective of its *source . . .*

And he did.

Not surprisingly, it was a spectacular vantage point, and he never missed the hours that slipped past him as he sat first behind the thick glass, then later leaning on the railing outside, on the narrow gangway that encircled the beacon. Like a laser's lance stretched to the moon, the lamp's focused beam slowly turreted the Vermont river valley. Its sweep was cantered down at an angle that scoured the woods and the wide, languid bends in the river.

Beautiful beyond imagining, but something else . . .

There was *power* here. At the apex of this solitary tower, he stood like a general looking down from the soaring prow of his war machine. So striking the sensation, it made Carlo giddy. For the first time in his life he began to understand how it could happen . . . *why* it happened.

Power.

Hypnotic and utterly compelling.

479

Carlo liked it.

In fact, he liked the lighthouse-keeper gig in its entirety. He found himself anticipating the crackling ignition of the great filaments when the lamp would fire-up. And when it did, he'd run up the staircase and watch the servo-motors crank up the carousel of light and heat like a kid sneaking into a carnival tent. He'd never felt happier in his life. The job had become an intoxicating elixir. As the weeks passed, he began spending more and more of the night-hours just sitting up there, under the beacon's sweeping thrall, then doing more of his sleeping during the day.

Until then he was doing his sleeping while the sun was up.

Which meant he'd essentially *stopped* painting. Oddly enough, a month had slipped passed him before he even realized it. And when he was sitting at the lamp control console one evening contemplating how long it had been since he attempted to create an image, he surprised himself with the absolute calm with which he accepted it.

*Not* painting had always been simply unthinkable to him. It was something he had done every day of his adult life, and had become an organic part of his essence, his *Carlo-ness*. He'd always known nothing could stop him from painting. He'd been born to do it, and like the driven fools before him, the Monets and Renoirs and Van Goghs, he'd lived with the stink of turpentine under his nails.

Keeping his light kept him content. The passion to paint, in order to feel *good*, had been replaced, and it was okay with him.

And so it was at this point—when Carlo accepted his loss of his driving desire to paint—that he first saw the boat on its nightly crossing.

At first he was confused; because, either it had been there all along and he'd been too obtuse to notice it, or it had just started a new nocturnal schedule, or else he was slipping off into the world of weird happenings.

The boat was not large, nor was it small. Appearing on the lighthouse shoreline at the deepest hour of the night, there was no telling its color, its name or registration. Hard enough to even discern its "lines" (as the sailors used to say . . .). The craft's silhouette against the lamplight that boiled off the water's surface appeared simple, uncluttered. A low, sweeping gunwale and no masts made it seem like it could be the hull of a submarine up for a look-see.

Hard to tell, thought Carlo.

He shook his head, smiled only a little bit. Like his employer, the boat's major characteristics were largely indeterminate.

Although each night (and he was seeing the boat every night now), he began to notice more details. Not that it was difficult to study the target—its passage to the antipodal, dark shore proved glacially slow. Mainly because of the boatman, who pushed the shallow barque along with a long, willowy pole. He could have been in the Louisiana bayou, or a Venetian gondolier. Either way, his spindly, mechanical movements were unmistakable.

Then, one night, he noticed the boatman was not alone. Carlo could not imagine just not noticing such a detail; it must have been somehow kept from him till now. As he watched the boat pass through the sweep of lamp's beam, he saw its open deck *teeming* with passengers. Hunched and huddled together, they formed a countless horde of silent souls.

Carlo suddenly understood more than he wanted to, more than he would ever want to *believe*.

Not that any of it made any sense . . . none at all.

He tried to kill time until the next payday, the next time he would have any contact with his employers, the next time he would have a chance to ask a few questions. Hours slipped away with tarpit-slowness as he stood motionless in his studio, brush in hand, helpless to make it move. The elation and sense of completeness he'd previously experienced had left him, replaced by unquiet bewilderment. He could not create; nor could he make sense of the world of which he'd become a part.

"Remember what you said about 'the fullness' of time?" he said to her as she entered the lighthouse in her flowing skirts and blouse, her large, black shoulder-bag.

Looking at him with a smile that looked like an after-thought. "Actually, I do . . ."

481

Carlo motioned her to a small table in the kitchen, sat down opposite and folded his hands. He felt haggard and dazed. He'd been spending so much time alone, with his thoughts, he was finding it difficult to conduct an interchange with another person.

"I think I understand what's going on here . . . but it—"

"—doesn't seem possible?"

"It's crazy!" he said, suddenly finding an anchor for his thoughts. "What the hell's going on out here? No pun intended!"

She smiled. "I understand your confusion. We knew you would catch on eventually."

Gesturing through the window towards the White River, he said: "Last time I checked, that's not the Cocytus . . . or is it the Styx?"

"Well, it is . . . and it isn't." She reached into her bag and placed a large parcel wrapped in brown paper on the table. "Here's your stipend."

Carlo tried to look directly into her eyes, found it difficult. "Please, don't distract me," he said. "It's bad for the job, I'm told."

"We are very happy with your work."

"I'll bet you are," said Carlo, forcing out a bark of mock-laughter. "But I think I need some answers."

"All right, you deserve them. I like you, Mr. Duarte."

"And your name, by the way, I kept thinking it was Stephanie or something like that, but . . ." Carlo paused to arrange his thoughts into a coherent sentence. "But . . . I either disremembered it or you made me think it was something else . . . something other than what it is."

The woman with the ageless face nodded. "All right, that's close enough."

"Ms. Persephone, I presume."

She smiled.

"So *why?* How? What do you need me for?"

"Have you ever heard any of those theories, that talk about polar shifts, and the earth's crust slipping and sliding over the mantle? Any of that arcane geology?"

Carlo shrugged. "I guess I have. Never paid that much attention to it though. Why, are you telling me that things get moved around, like pieces on a chess board?"

Persephone raised an eyebrow impishly. "The gods are

capricious at times, especially Gaea. The process is more complicated than how you're putting it—although I am impressed with your perspicuity. There are cycles through which the world passes. All thing pass; everything changes. Right now. At this time and place, we need things to be *here.*"

"Okay, if I accept that as enough, what's with the light?"

She shrugged. "Obviously it is more than a light. It is like a key. It lights the path to the gates of Tantalus."

"So I'm a gatekeeper."

"After a fashion, yes. More like a 24-hour repairman."

Carlo stood, walked to the window which overlooked the banks of the White River. Evening was climbing the foothills of the Green Mountains. Everything looked so different, so benign, but it would change with the advancing darkness.

"Okay," he said. "So like I asked you before—why me? Why now? I keep asking myself—what happened to the other guy? The guy before me?"

Persephone chuckled facetiously. "Don't ask. He had some grand ideas that he could be the new Prometheus . . ."

Carlo nodded. "So now he's got what?—a bad liver?"

She shook her head and grimaced. "You could say that, yes."

"There's something else," said Carlo, returning to the table so he could sit facing her, as if this would somehow intensify the seriousness of what he wanted to say. "I'm not sure how to explain this, so I guess I'll just put it as plainly as possible: I haven't painted a thing since I've been here."

"I see . . ." she said, her gaze taking him like a maelstrom.

"Something's been happening to me. Something's been . . . I don't know . . . *changing* me."

"You are so perceptive," she said with a sad little grin. "But you haven't caught on completely, have you?"

Carlo didn't like the sound of that. He gripped the edges of the table, reminding himself to keep control. "What're you talking about. What's happening to me?"

"You're becoming a demigod."

He looked at her and felt a furious tightening in his gut. "A *what?* What does that mean?"

Persephone leaned forward, reached for his hands, taking them into her own. It was, however, a touch with something missing. He imagined she'd done it to make him feel better, but it left him cold and wary. "I will assume you have noticed how . . . how *good* you feel since you've been working here . . . ? How healthy?"

"Yes, I have noticed . . . go on . . ."

"That's because you've become *immortal* . . . well, sort of . . ."

Carlo pulled his hands away from hers, ran his fingers through his hair. Her words didn't surprise him, not really. For the first time, he admitted to himself that maybe he'd actually suspected such a thing on some deeper, unconscious level. And yet, he couldn't actually accept what she said at face value, either. The idea of living forever, while greatly appealing, also sounded silly—especially when you considered the little coda she added to the end.

"Ah . . . could we possibly get a little more explanation of the phrase 'well, sort of . . .'?"

"As long as you are here," said Persephone. "As long as you stay in the lighthouse . . . you cannot die. Nothing can harm you."

"Okay, so what does that actually mean?" said Carlo, wondering if he already knew the answer to his next question, and needing only to hear her confirmation. "What does that have to do with me and my painting?"

Persephone half-lidded her eyes, shook her head so subtly he almost missed it. "Carlo, you are very intelligent . . . I think you know."

Standing up, he backed away from the table and walked to one of the windows. The vista of the river valley was now draped in gray and purple mantles of twilight as he pondered her words. He *did* know, goddammit, and he'd kept thinking that if, somehow, he never spoke about it, never let his words make it real . . . then it wouldn't *be* real.

But it was.

The unspoken, but implied second part of the corollary proffered by Persephone was elegant in its simplicity—as he'd become more godlike, then, he must, by definition become *less* human.

And that meant . . . what? Just about everything, when you took the time to think about it. It was no accident he'd lost his passion, his turbine-intensity to create, because that kind of energy came from the dark well of the soul. From a place where the essence of what it means to be mortal is heated and forged and tempered in that weird crucible of human experience.

Oh yeah, he knew, all right . . .

There'd probably been some piece of him, some micro-fragments of the collective unconscious that shot through him like gamma rays at the moment of his conception, that had *always* known on the intuitive level what was going on. Always known a weird transaction had been completed here. And Carlo felt so ashamed of himself. He'd always lived his life knowing there's no such thing as a free lunch, but this time, he bellied up to this particular trough, self-deluding himself he was going to make it happen.

No way, baby . . . he thought as he turned back and looked at Pluto's main squeeze, sitting there like she was posing for Praxiteles.

"I want out," he said softly.

"Excuse me?"

"Don't act so surprised. Don't tell me there's no way out— I didn't sign any contract! No drop of blood, none of that Faustian crap here!"

Persephone stood and moved to him, her long skirt imparting for an instant the illusion she glided rather than walked. "No, none of that . . . you are correct."

Carlo exhaled, relieved at a very basic level. "So . . . what's next? Is this where you tell me that when I walk out of here . . . I'll die?"

She smiled. "You are an unusual man," she said. "I could grow to like you very much. I think I already have."

Backing away, he shook his head. "Uh-uh, we're not going there."

"No, I mean I admire you—in the classical sense. And you *will* die when you leave here . . . but not right away . . . but in the right and due course of your life. You will be mortal again."

He exhaled again. More relief. She had this way of keeping the tension-levels torqued way up there. Carlo was walking a metaphysical high-wire, and the subject of safety nets had never come up.

"Thanks," he said. "You've made me realize a few things about myself."

"You are most welcome." Persephone smiled, and for the time, allowed herself to look quite attractive.

"I guess I'd better gather up my things. I have this very strong hope I'll be needing them."

"You will," she said.

"Thanks. Thanks for everything. I hope you don't think I'm ungrateful, or anything like that . . . and I hope you understand why I have to go . . ."

"I do," she said. "Probably more than you. Good-bye, Carlo Duarte."

Carlo nodded, began walking towards the stairs to his studio, then paused, turned to look back at her. "What about this . . . job? Do you think you'll have any trouble getting somebody else?"

Persephone considered the question for only an instant, her gold-green eyes flashing a look first to the window which had become an oblong of shiny obsidian, then back to him. "No, I will be a little more careful with the questions I ask."

Carlo paused. "Meaning . . . ?"

"I will ask them if they are chasing any dreams."

Despite the swirled-palette of emotions he currently felt, Carlo couldn't keep from smiling. "Most of them won't know what you're talking about . . . you'll have plenty of unimaginative pinheads to choose from."

Persephone chuckled. "I'll take that as both a curse and a blessing."

As Carlo put some miles between himself and the lighthouse, he could feel his mortality seeping back into him, invading the molecular structures of his cells like the metaphysical disease that it was. And it felt good. He slipped his *Disraeli Gears* CD into the deck; and sang along with Clapton, Bruce, and Baker as they rattled through "Tales of Brave Ulysses"—a fittingly Hellenistic reference to the latest chapter in his own life-saga. By the time the song had ended, he noted the farther he drove, the less real the whole experience was becoming. In fact, the more he tried to concentrate on specifics, the more foggy and less distinct his mind-images became.

Weird. Very weird.

His thoughts kept him paying close attention to his driving;

and more than a couple of times he'd kind of *snap* back to attention with his hands gripping the wheel on autopilot. He felt like an idiot, looking down the shafts of his headlights as they tried to find the tortured two-lane "tar-road." It made him wonder how the hell he'd gotten to this point without realizing it. Had he passed that quaint bastion of socialism they called the Vermont Law School yet?

Where was he?

State Route 4 through this rural part of Vermont twisted through endless curves as it struggled to follow the course of the White River. It was a bad road in daylight, and downright treacherous at night. Everything tended to look the same until you were right on top of it.

It was just after he'd seen the signs for the town of Sharon and the Interstate, that it started to rain.

Drops as big and heavy as bullfrogs. They spattered on the window like little bodies exploding with the suddenness of a mortar attack. Carlo kicked in the wipers, but not quick enough. As he leaned close to the steering wheel, trying to see what lay beyond the smeared glass, he felt the Blazer's big tires lose purchase on an upcoming curve. Power-sliding towards the riverbank to his right, Carlo yanked the gearshift downward into second and buried the gas-pedal.

It was a brilliant maneuver, which saved him from a launch into the dark water, but Carlo couldn't stop the lurching SUV from crossing the center-line at the blindest point of the next curve. That's why the driver of the Peterbilt truck and trailer didn't see him until the dark hull of the Blazer literally *exploded* over the grill and hood of the giant tractor.

Carlo vaguely remembered the shockwave of the impact, but could recall no sound. Nor did he have any memory of being thrown clear of the wreckage . . . but he must have been, because he was now picking himself up, pulling himself out of the soft cloying mud of the riverbank. A cold nightwind laced through him as he turned away from it . . .

. . . to see the stark tower looming up before him. Its silhouette against the darker tapestry of the sky was hideously familiar, and its recognition vibrated deep into his soul like the idiot-hum of oblivion.

The sweeping beam of light passed over him, and as he acceded to Charon's gesture to come aboard, Carlo paused to look up for a last glance at the lighthouse lamp. He wondered who might be the "unimaginative pinhead" staring down at him from beyond the fortress of its glass.